White Picket Lies

A TONI PORTER MYSTERY

LILLY MIRREN

black lab press

Epub ISBN: 978-1-922650-10-8

Paperback ISBN: 978-1-922650-11-5

Version 1.0

Published by Black Lab Press 2022

First published worldwide by Black Lab Press in 2022.

Brisbane, Australia.

www.blacklabpress.com

For truth carriers and boundary warriors.

Chapter One

MONDAY

17TH OCTOBER

It wasn't the goals he'd never accomplish or the things he wished he'd done that flashed through the man's thoughts as he lay prone on the damp ground, the lifeblood seeping from his body. It wasn't like people said it would be. He wasn't scared or anxious, didn't scramble or fumble for a rescue that wouldn't come. He lay still and quiet, knowing what he faced and realising with a sudden clarity of thought, through the resounding throbbing at the back of his skull, that his time was now.

He tried to reach out for something to hold onto, but his empty hand fell back to the soil with a gentle thud. A sharp object pricked his wrist—a stone, perhaps, or a thorn. He couldn't say which. Waves shushed quietly in the darkness, curling to shore in the distance in a soothing rhythm.

No, the thoughts that launched themselves across his

mind's eye as he lay dying were his deepest regrets. The things he'd done that'd caused so much pain to the ones he loved most. The parts of himself he'd held back, the vulnerability he'd avoided because it was all too hard.

It didn't seem hard now, but his perspective was different.

His assailant was gone. Had left him minutes earlier with a rapid thudding of footsteps, pulling the gate mostly shut. He'd owned a dog once, years earlier. That crack in the gate would've been just enough for her to squeeze through. She'd always been an escape artist. She'd have shimmied her way through that gap and gone rogue for hours, panting her way around the neighbourhood until she'd terrorised every cat she could find. She'd come home covered head to toe in mud. He missed that dog. Saturn, he'd called her. He couldn't remember the reason. It'd meant something to him at the time.

He didn't know why he was thinking of that old dog now as he lay dying in his own garden bed. In the end, it was the things that mattered most that sprang to mind. Or perhaps it was simply the gap through the gate had prodded the memory. It irked him, but there was nothing he could do about it since he couldn't seem to gather the strength to stand.

What would his wife think? Would she manage without him? He supposed the answer to that question didn't matter, really—she'd simply *have* to manage, one way or the other. He should've taken out more insurance. It'd been on his honey-do list for at least three years.

Something about facing his own mortality kept him pushing it down the list. Meanwhile, he'd painted the fence, fixed the leaking roof, had the carpets cleaned, and built a garden shed from a flat pack. But the one thing he hadn't done was update the insurance. And, he realised with some alacrity, it was clearly one of the things he should've.

His head didn't hurt now, but his thoughts were muddy.

His mind wandered round and round as his subconscious thoughts drifted again to Saturn, then long hikes through mountains and over glaciers with friends he'd left behind aeons ago. Finally, he recalled all of the family ties and friendships he'd thought would never falter that had ended abruptly at various points in his life, and even now, looking back, he didn't understand why. Perhaps he should've asked, although he'd never been one to dwell on the past. If they ghosted him, he'd ghost them right back. Would any of them come to his funeral?

Chapter Two

THURSDAY

20TH OCTOBER

It was too early to get out of bed. The birds had sung for a full two hours and the sun was high in the sky, but still Detective Sergeant Antonia Kauffman had no intention of rising yet. She'd been up late the previous night, working the evening shift that would never end. Too many drunks, too few officers on duty to deal with it all, and so it was left to her, as one of the more junior detectives of the Tweed Heads Police Department, to deal with the kerfuffle going on at the desk.

It didn't matter that none of the male detectives had to deal with drunks at the front desk. None of them batted an eye over it. She couldn't say anything, either, because she'd never hear the end of it. They hated it when she complained about unequal treatment, as though she wasn't one of them after all, despite her protestations to the opposite. But if she didn't speak up, nothing would change. And so, she found herself at an impasse. She had to say something if she wanted to be taken seriously in her role, but if she did, they wouldn't take her seriously. It was a quandary she hadn't found an answer to, and one she wasn't sure she ever would.

She rolled over in bed and groaned when the snooze alarm sounded.

"You getting up?" Rodger's voice sailed in from the bathroom. Steam issued through the open door.

"Yep," she grunted. He was home at least. He'd been out late the night before. In fact, she couldn't recall when he'd come home. It happened more and more lately.

She rolled over and slung her feet to the floor with a yawn. Then stretching her arms above her head, she let the tension from the previous night work its way out of her shoulders as she leaned to the left, then to the right. At forty-six years of age, she was beginning to notice a shift in her body the way she hadn't when she started on the force eight years earlier. Everything was harder. Every muscle ached more and for longer after she exerted herself. But at least she was walking, which was more than she'd thought she'd be doing when she was shot five years earlier, on the streets of Sydney. The bullet missed her spinal column by mere millimetres.

With a grunt, she was on her feet and reaching for her toes. No matter what, she always did her stretches. It helped stave off possible injuries. She never used to worry about growing old because it seemed like some far-off distant thing that would happen to a kind, grey-haired, wizened version of herself. Not something that would happen now. She'd only graduated from high school a minute ago, and now she was forty-six years old.

Forty-six.

Where had those years gone? They'd disappeared in a haze of study, drunken parties, then sleepless nights with a baby and years of pounding along the streets of Sydney chasing crack addicts and criminals. So much of it was a blur.

She hadn't stopped to smell the roses often enough—that was the problem, according to her mother. She'd had to point out that there weren't many roses in crack dens, and if you stopped, you'd be shot or stabbed. Better to keep moving. But Mum had never liked the fact that she'd signed up to be a police officer in the first place. It wasn't ladylike, not something women should do. She'd have to work with hard men every day, they'd never treat her as an equal, she'd see too much of the underworld, and it would scar her. That was what Mum had said the first day when Toni had been heady with the glow of enrolling.

It'd angered her at first. Mum was being a downer and old-fashioned, and she didn't know what she was talking about. Eight years later, she didn't want to admit to her mother that perhaps she'd had a decent point or two. She was too proud for that. But she wasn't as harsh with her mother these days. She listened to her rants without rolling her eyes and tried to take her advice. That was about the best she could manage for now.

"You going to the station?" Rodger asked, walking into the bedroom still flossing. "Because I could do with a lift."

"Sorry, I'm heading in later than usual. Exhausted after last night."

"I bet you are. You shouldn't work so late. It isn't right—they're taking advantage of you." He stood in his boxer shorts, plucking the string from between his teeth and reinserting it over and over as he spoke.

She'd gotten home late, and he hadn't been there. She wouldn't ask him where he was last night. They'd only end up fighting.

"You should do that in the bathroom," she said.

He shrugged. "Always telling me what to do."

"I'm not trying to be bossy. But I swear I saw a piece of toast fly across the room and land on the doona."

He grunted. "Hardly likely."

Toni hated it when he flossed or brushed in the bedroom. It was one of her many pet peeves. In fact, there was very little that Rodger did these days that didn't raise her ire. She did her best to hide it, but it was harder some days than others.

He disappeared into the bathroom, returning with a scowl. "I guess I'll ride the bike to work, then. But it looks like rain."

"You can take the car if you like. I'll take the bike."

"Really?" He perked up. "Okay, thanks."

He tugged on a pair of chinos and a button-down blue-and-white striped shirt. "I've got parent-teacher interviews this afternoon, so I'll be home late."

"No worries," she said, undressing for the shower. "I'll pick up some takeaway if you like. How about Chinese?"

"Sounds good," he said. "Although, I'm kind of sick of takeaway. Do you think you could make that chicken pie I love?"

She pasted a smile to her face. "Sure, of course I can." He knew how tired she was, and she still had a full shift of work to do that day. They'd fought so much over domestic chores in recent years that they'd put together a chore chart even though the two of them didn't have any children living at home. It was like stepping back in time to when Ryker was at primary school. It made things easier—that's what she told her girlfriends whenever they asked about it. But the truth was, he rarely stuck to it. He usually found some excuse not to contribute to the upkeep of their small two-bedroom unit.

Chapter Three

Zoey Winton loved the quiet stillness of the early morning hours before the house awoke. Her husband, Dave, still snored softly in the master suite at the end of the hall. Her fifteen-year-old daughter, Isla, lay with arms and legs askew across the bed, her nose pressed directly into her pillow and her hair a dark brown mess that obscured most of her face.

But this particular morning was different from other mornings because today was her twentieth wedding anniversary, and although she'd never admit it, she found that an utterly depressing thought. It shouldn't be depressing, since she loved her husband and they had a wonderful life together with their daughter and frou-frou designer dog in their double-story house in the quiet seaside town of Kingscliff.

Actually, she still quite liked Dave even after all these years. If they ever had the chance to spend time together, just the two of them, they got along surprisingly well. Her friends often told her how jealous they were of her relationship. But the fact that her anniversary shouldn't depress her, and yet she *was* depressed, depressed her further still.

No, this was silly. She wasn't depressed. She couldn't be. She assured herself of that fact with a stern inner voice. No, depression was for people who were sad. And she wasn't sad. She was feeling a little low—that's all it was. And who wouldn't? Twenty years! Twenty years of living with the same man, washing his dirty underwear, cooking his meals, and listening to his snoring. It was enough to depress a saint.

When she thought about it, as she folded items of clothing that were strewn around the floor of Isla's bedroom and laid them in a neat pile on the corner of her desk, by every objective measurement, she had a very good life. Only it was a little dull. That was her one complaint. Well, perhaps that and the housework. No one told her how much of her life would involve standing over a kitchen sink or folding laundry. So much time spent alone. So many hours doing mundane tasks.

She did it because she loved them, of course. It was all for love and it'd been her choice, and faced with the decision again, she probably wouldn't make a different one. So why was she depressed...no, not depressed. Why was she down?

She'd have to analyse the feeling later because it was time to wake Isla and get her moving for school. The child was like a great big boulder that Zoey had to push up an enormous hill every single morning. Why did it take so long for her to find a pair of socks and pull them onto her feet? How many times did she really have to check her phone for messages in a five-minute period? These were the questions that Zoey asked herself each morning in the rush to get out of the house.

She leaned down to stroke Isla's arm, using her singsong voice to chant, "Time to rise and shine."

Isla had grown taller and lankier recently. The chubby cheeks had hollowed out years earlier, but now she was as tall as Zoey, and when she got ready for school, her legs were like two strands of uncooked spaghetti beneath the tartan skirt of her uniform.

She rolled over and yawned, her brown eyes blinking open. "Morning, Mum."

Zoey sat on the edge of the bed and tickled Isla's forearm. "Good morning, sweetheart. You've got PE today, so don't forget your swimmers, okay?"

Isla nodded with another yawn, then Zoey bounded to her feet. The next chore on her list was to let the dog out. The puppy was eight months old, definitely mature enough to be potty trained, and yet she still managed to crap in the house at least once per week.

Isla padded past her to the bathroom and frowned. "What are you doing, Mum?"

"Looking for the dog. Where is she? We've got to take her out."

Isla shrugged and ducked into the bathroom, shutting the door behind her with a bang.

"Don't take too long in there. I'm serious, Isla. I don't want to be late again. The school will freak out if we keep getting late notes every day. We've run out of reasonable excuses. You're in high school—you can't use the new puppy as a reason to be late anymore. They won't believe you."

Isla groaned. "Why do I have to go to school? There are a hundred better things I could do with my day."

"Too bad. We all have to do things we don't want to do. I have to do the laundry. You have to go to school. We've all got a cross to bear."

"I feel sick."

"You're fine."

Her voice rose, wavered. "You don't care about me!"

Zoey rolled her eyes. "Of course I care about you. I don't *believe* you. That's a very important distinction. Anyway, I can't be late to work today. I've got an urgent meeting. You need to get moving. Now! Willow!" she called, then whistled.

The dog never came when she was called. The only way to

get her to appear on command was to rustle around in the deli drawer of the refrigerator. She'd leap out of her hiding place in less than five seconds if she heard the cheese container pop open.

Zoey hurried down the hallway, whistling for the dog. There was still no sign of Willow. So she opened the fridge to crinkle a packet of beef jerky. Within moments, Willow was there. She didn't wag her tail but stood at a distance staring at Zoey, eyes gleaming beneath a swathe of curling, chocolate-coloured hair.

"There you are. Come on, girl. Let's go potty."

Zoey swept Willow up and carried her outside, then set her down to do her business. The day was already hot, with waves sighing to shore at the nearby beach. The air was filled with the scent of salt and dew. Overhead, a flock of seagulls circled. One landed on the fence and eyed Willow, head tilted to the side.

Zoey cinched the belt on her robe. She should really have dressed before she brought the dog outside. The neighbours on both sides could see directly into her backyard from their second-storey windows. Who knew what they would think of her dumpy, middle-aged figure in a too-short bathrobe. Although, Mark and Allegra were away on holiday, so at least she didn't have to worry about them peering down through their plantation blinds.

The dog did her business while Zoey attempted to find the poop bags. They were nowhere to be found, so Zoey called her to come. Willow stared at her, head down. Zoey set her hands on her hips and used a stern voice. She didn't have time for this. When they'd decided to get a dog, it was because Isla had begged so hard for so long. They'd given in, but only after she committed to being the one to take the dog out, walk her, and feed her. Zoey couldn't remember the last time Isla had done any of those things.

"Come here!" she commanded, but Willow didn't move.

She strode towards the small dog, irritation burning up her spine. "Come on. We've got to go inside."

As soon as she was close, Willow's tail came up, her head sunk to the ground and she jumped out of reach with a bark. Every time Zoey lunged for her, the dog ran until she was speeding around and around her in circles, barking.

"Willow!" Zoey shouted, her frustration mounting.

"What's going on?" Dave poked his head out the back door. He was still in his pyjamas.

"I can't get the dog to come inside, and I've got to get in the shower or I'll be late."

He grinned. "Here, Willow, inside you go."

Willow stopped circling Zoey and bounded indoors, tail wagging.

"That's not fair. She favours you, but I do all the work."

"Sorry, honey. Come on—we're having breakfast."

Zoey took a step towards the back door and directly into a pile of day-old dog doo. She screamed with frustration.

Dave returned to the door, his eyes wide. "What the hell, honey? People will think you're being murdered."

"I've asked you a hundred times to clean up the dog poop in this yard."

His eyes narrowed. "Well, you're already out there, so why don't you do it?" And he shut the door with a bang. She flipped the bird at his retreating back, then shuffled to the tap attached to the side of the house. As she washed the dog poop off her foot, she muttered beneath her breath.

"'Why don't you just do it?' I'll tell you why—because I do everything else around here. I asked you to do this one thing! Is that so much? And I'll bet you haven't even remembered it's our anniversary today..." Her tirade trailed off when she caught a whiff of air from the neighbour's house through the fence.

What was that? Something disgusting. It smelled even worse than what she'd washed off her foot. Perhaps they'd poisoned a rat, although it seemed like an irresponsible way to get rid of a pest, if you asked her. A poisoned rat could travel before it died and might be eaten by birds of prey or, heaven forbid, someone's beloved pet. Mark and Allegra certainly weren't reliable enough to hide the poison in a hard-to-reach place. They were young and childless and probably hadn't given safety a moment's thought.

With a shake of her head, she tiptoed through the still-wet grass to the fence and reached as high as she could, attempting to peer over it. It was no use, though. She wasn't tall enough at five feet two inches to manage anything like a six-foot fence. So she tugged a garden stool over and climbed up.

When she saw the man lying in the garden bed on the other side of the fence, at first she thought it was a joke. Then a moment later, she considered that perhaps Mark had fallen while gardening. But when he didn't move, she opened her mouth and screamed. This time with gusto.

Chapter Four

The shower was hot and soothed away some of the tension in Toni's shoulders and neck. By the time she'd emerged from the bathroom and dressed for work, Rodger had already left. He hadn't said goodbye.

She'd noticed lately that the little things they'd done to show each other they cared had begun to fall by the wayside. She wasn't sure if it was a normal part of being married, or if something was wrong. It felt wrong to her, but he'd probably say she was being dramatic if she brought it up.

The irony of that was he was by far the more emotional of the two. She was generally stoic and found it difficult to connect with her own emotions. It was something he complained about early in their marriage, and she'd done her best to work on it.

She grabbed a piece of toast with Vegemite between her teeth and headed for the underground garage beneath their small complex of units. Her car was already gone, but they each kept a bike chained up in a small storage compartment beside their single empty car space. She unlocked hers and tugged the bike free of a pair of water skis and a stack of gardening buckets.

Strange—his bike seemed to be missing. It had a distinctive purple seat with the word *Giant* printed across the back of it underneath where his rear end perched. Something she'd teased him mercilessly about when he'd purchased it. Perhaps he'd attached it to the bike rack on her car so he could go mountain biking after school. He often did that, although why he couldn't ride it to school and leave her the car, she'd never understand. She climbed onto the bike seat as she finished the last bite of toast and pedalled in the direction of the station.

The ridiculousness of her situation didn't escape her. Here she was, dressed in silk slacks, a bright red buttoned shirt, and with her hair and makeup neatly applied, riding a bicycle to her job as a detective sergeant at the Tweed Heads Police Station. And all because her husband had insisted he didn't need to rent a car while his sports car was at the garage getting upgrades to the engine and stereo, as well as a custom paint job. They could share, he'd said, since he loved to ride to the school where he worked, a ten-minute jaunt down a well-maintained bike path. Yet, here she was, riding her bike to work while he drove the car.

She chuckled beneath her breath at the absurdity but was determined to start the day with a positive outlook. Lately she'd felt a bit low and didn't want to sink back into the familiar spiral of despair that'd knocked her down after her first marriage ended in divorce and with Ryker going to live with his father while she only got him on weekends and holidays.

She didn't blame Malcolm for suing for full custody. She'd been in bad shape, and he'd stepped in. She was grateful he was a good father, even if he hadn't been the right man for her. Terrible husband, good father. Or maybe he wasn't a terrible husband at all. His new wife certainly didn't seem to think so. Maybe it was her. Regardless of who bore the fault, they'd been awful together. The two of them did nothing but clash over the few years of their marriage.

She'd wondered at the time how they could've possibly gotten together in the first place. But it seemed to her that he'd changed, and maybe she had as well. It was on the last day of her job as a secretary at an accounting firm. He was one of the accountants there, and he'd kissed her in the lunchroom. Like a romantic moment out of one of those movies that everyone else in the world seemed to love so much but that she couldn't stand. But it *had* been romantic, and so was he. Such a quiet, diffident man who blushed whenever he spoke to her and held her hand in a fumbling kind of way that made it seem as though he thought she was doing him the biggest favour in the world by letting him.

At the end of their marriage, Malcolm bore no resemblance at all to the bumbling, sweet, shy man she'd fallen in love with. He was angry, loud, and crass, and had no patience for her. It seemed by then that he was no longer grateful for her affection but impatient with it, as though it was an inconvenience he couldn't bear. And so their shouting matches escalated until one day, he left, and that was the end of things. Her mother was sick by then, her father had never been a part of her life, and she found herself with a young boy to raise all alone in the world. It'd been overwhelming.

They'd rushed into it, should never have attempted marriage. But Ryker came along, and they thought they were in love. So, when she fell apart, he raised Ryker himself, and even though it'd felt as though her heart was ripped from her chest when Ryker walked off hand in hand with her ex-husband, she'd grown to appreciate their arrangement over the years.

She hadn't been grateful at first. She'd howled and railed

against the injustice of it all. He left her and got to build himself a brand-new family, when she had no one. She'd done nothing wrong, yet she was the one abandoned. But as the years passed, she saw a counsellor, started a new career, and restarted her life from the ground up.

Now Ryker was seventeen years old, and the last thing any of them needed was for her to fall back under the weight of depression and lose everything all over again. So, she pushed away negative thoughts and did what her psychologist had taught her—she was thankful for the sunshine overhead and for the birds, she was grateful she had strong legs to push the pedals, and she marvelled at the way the rain clouds stayed at a distance even as they threatened to soak her.

She pedalled harder to outrun them and managed to padlock her bike and sprint to the overhang outside the station in time to arrive mostly dry apart from a few wet patches on her shirt. She shook off the helmet, raindrops pattering to the ground around her, and watched as the downpour intensified.

"You only just made it," said a voice behind her. "Another minute and you'd have been soaked."

She spun around to see her partner, Senior Constable Callum Fitch, standing in the doorway, a smirk on his chiselled face. "Lucky. Training for a triathlon or something, are you? Come on, boss, we've got things to do. While you're out here mucking around on your trike, I've been working."

She shook her head slowly. Positive thoughts. She had to keep those positive thoughts coming. "Shut up, Callum."

He chuckled. "Very nice."

They walked inside together. As she set her bike helmet on her desk and switched on her computer, the phone in her backpack purse buzzed. She shrugged off the backpack and set it on the desk, fishing around for a good minute before her hand finally clenched around the phone.

"Good morning," she said in a cheerful voice.

Zoey's was frantic. "Toni, you've got to get over here. Mark Cowderoy is dead. At least, I think it's him—I didn't get very close. And the smell...probably the heat. We've had a few *very* humid days. I mean, it's all a bit too much."

"Zoey, what are you talking about?" Toni asked as she held the phone to her ear with one shoulder, unlocked a drawer, and wrapped her gun holster about her waist.

"My neighbour, Mark. I found his body in the garden."

"Don't touch anything, and stay away from the body. I'll be right there."

Chapter Five

When Zoey and Dave first moved to the gated community of Pelican Grove in the small seaside town of Kingscliff, she'd been sceptical they could make it work. Dave's position as an engineer in his Sydney firm was everything he'd worked towards his whole life, but he was ready for something new. Something quieter after years of commuting on the city train, packed in with his fellow commuters like wieners in a can. So, when they visited Kingscliff for a family holiday, they'd both felt the appeal. What if they came here more often? Could they manage that? That's when Dave had suggested they relocate to live there.

At first, she'd dismissed the idea. Both their families lived in Sydney. She and Dave had spent their entire lives in the city. It was enjoyable to visit the tiny beachside hamlet and lay on the beach, to stroll to the shops for gelato and to ride bikes along the shoreline. But to live there? She couldn't imagine it. What about her friendships, her career, the life she'd planned?

But he'd been adamant. They only got one life, he'd said. They should seize the opportunity to live it the way they wanted. She wasn't entirely sure it *was* what she wanted, but he seemed determined, and so she gave in. After all, if it didn't work out, which she was certain it wouldn't, they could move right back home. She convinced him not to sell their place in Sydney—otherwise, there'd be no way they could get back into the market. And instead of buying, they'd rented in the Pelican Grove neighbourhood for the first two years. But then Dave had said she was living with one foot in Sydney and one in Kingscliff, that it was time for them to put down roots. They were staying.

She'd given in again, as she always seemed to do when coming up against her hard-headed husband, and they'd bought a place in the same gated community where they'd rented. It was home to them now. Dave loved it, Isla could hardly remember living anywhere else after ten years, and even Zoey had begun to embrace the small, tight-knit community as her own. Although she never quite felt like a local, at least she'd made some good friends in the last couple of years.

And now, as she waited in the front yard for the police to arrive, her mobile phone in her hand, she couldn't help wishing she'd had the strength to insist on remaining in Sydney. It was at times of stress that she missed her family—her mother and sisters were as close as any family could be. They'd gradually lost that connection over the years and saw each other only on the occasional holiday.

Poor Mark. Perhaps he'd had a heart attack. His cold body lay only a few feet away on the other side of the fence. It made her shudder to think about it. How long had he been there? He and Allegra were supposed to be on a family holiday up north.

Dave stepped outside and cleared his throat. "Listen, do you think it'd be okay if me and Isla leave? I mean, I didn't find the body, so I don't think I can help the police. And I've got a big project to deal with, the client is melting down over the added costs of excavation, and I've got to hand-hold them through the whole thing. It's a calamity. Plus, Isla says she has a biology exam this morning."

"You can't go anywhere. They might have questions."

"Surely not for me."

She didn't have the strength for another confrontation. "Fine. Go to work."

He kissed her cheek with a smile. "Great. Thanks, honey. See you later."

She couldn't believe he was leaving her with a dead body. She squinted into the rising sun as she watched his car pull out of the driveway. Isla waved goodbye, and Zoey blew her a kiss which her daughter studiously ignored. Never mind that Zoey had a big meeting to attend that day at the bank.

She and her assistant, Stella, were asking for money. Money they desperately needed if she wanted her design business to succeed. If she didn't get the money from the bank, she couldn't keep the business operating. And now she was stuck here alone waiting to talk to her best friend about her dead neighbour.

She'd rather have her fingernails surgically removed than deal with the fact that Mark was dead, lying only a few metres away from her. She'd prefer to think about anything else other than what she'd seen. She couldn't get the image out of her mind. Every time she blinked, his body was outlined against the back of her eyelids in sharp relief. She hoped this wouldn't take long. Then she could get back to saving her business from bankruptcy and forget all about the body in the garden.

* * *

When Toni pulled up in front of Zoey Winton's house in the police cruiser, she found her friend lingering on the front porch of her sprawling three-story home, her arms wrapped around her curvy frame, hair pulled into an effortless ponytail.

She parked at the curb and climbed out of the car, striding alongside Callum to the front door.

"Hi, Zoey," she said. "You okay?"

"I'm fine." She embraced Toni.

Zoey looked decidedly more rattled than Toni had ever seen her. Usually she was the height of sophistication and didn't get flustered easily. She was the kind of woman Toni generally regarded with awe and more than a little distrust. But Zoey had won her over with her earnest interest in Toni's life and her ability to disarm Toni when she was at her most guarded with a well-timed joke.

"Hello, Mrs Winton," Callum said. "You reported seeing a body. Can you tell us what happened?"

Zoey talked them through her morning, emphasising the moment she found the body, while she led them to the neighbours' front yard.

"The body's in the back garden, along the left-hand side of the fence," she said.

"I'll knock," Callum said, jogging up the front steps.

Toni donned a pair of gloves and put some booties over her shoes, then unlatched the side gate and glanced around the yard. It was still and quiet. From where she was standing, nothing seemed out of place.

"Through there," Zoey said, bending at the waist to point along the fence line.

Callum joined her, tugging on his own gloves. "No one answering the door."

"Do you know where the neighbours are?" Toni asked.

Zoey swallowed. "Well, Mark seems to be facedown in the garden..."

Toni shot her a derisive look. "I mean, where they're supposed to be."

"They told me they were going on a trip. Cairns, I believe, to see Allegra's parents. I was supposed to water their lawn, but it's been raining every day, so I didn't bother." Zoey's words faded into a sob. "I should've checked before now." She covered her mouth, eyes filling with tears.

Toni patted Zoey gently on the back. "There, there. It might not even be Mark—you said you didn't see his face. Let's not get worked up until we know more. And it's certainly not your fault. As you said, we've had rain every afternoon this week."

Just then the wind changed, and Toni got a whiff of something that singed the hairs in her nostrils. She shrank back, her nose wrinkling.

"Get a load of that," Callum said with a grimace. "Something's definitely carked it."

"Maybe it's a possum," Toni said.

Zoey sniffled. "It's not a possum. I think I can tell the difference between a man and a possum."

"Still, you never know."

Toni and Callum walked carefully through the yard. Toni took the lead, and Callum walked in her footsteps. They'd done some recent training on maintaining a crime scene. It wasn't often they got called out to a murder, and this was her first as lead detective, so Toni ran through the steps over and over in her mind. She was determined to get it right. Do it by the book. The boss would be furious if they endangered a verdict with sloppy police work.

The smell intensified as they progressed through the yard. When they found Mark Cowderoy's prone body in the garden bed, Toni hesitated. No matter how many times she'd done this, she'd never get used to seeing a dead body. She crouched to examine it, felt his neck, and found him cold.

"Deceased appears to be Mark Cowderoy," she said.

Callum took notes on his iPad. "You know him?"

She offered a brief nod. "He's cold to the touch, and there's a smell of decay."

"You can say that again." Callum jotted it down in his report.

Toni looked the body over. "No visible sign of struggle other than a bump on his head. Initial assessment suggests blunt force trauma. There appears to be some dried blood here beside the body, suggesting suspicious circumstances. This is now a crime scene."

While Callum called for the coroner and backup, Toni looked around the outside of the house. A clay flowerpot was missing from its saucer on the back deck. She found a smashed flowerpot near the edge of the house. There were also a few footprints in the mud that looked as though someone had run through there, possibly two people or more. She placed small flags next to each visible footprint as well as the flowerpot.

Callum took photographs of everything she flagged, and the two of them completed their analysis outside the house by the time backup arrived. She met them in the yard and updated the team on everything, then stepped aside to talk to Zoey.

"So, it's him?"

"Sorry, honey."

Zoey's eyes misted over. "He was a nice man. I mean, I found him irritating at times, but still, he was nice."

"Irritating?"

"They weren't the most considerate neighbours, but they were always friendly. I liked them."

"You wouldn't happen to have Allegra's number, would you? I'd like to give her a call."

"Of course. It's in my phone. I'll send it to you."

"Do you mind if I record you?" Toni asked. "I need to ask a couple of questions."

"That's fine. I don't know anything useful, but ask away."

Toni checked that she'd received Allegra's number, then pressed record. "We won't be able to give a time of death until the coroner does the autopsy, but by the smell, I'd say it was about three days ago. Do you recall hearing or seeing anything unusual three days ago?"

Zoey's brow furrowed. "Um... I don't know. I'll have to think about it and look in my diary to see what I did that day. I believe I went to work as usual at around eight a.m., dropped Isla at school on the way, and then had a hairdresser's appointment in the afternoon. I always try to get home about the same time as Isla, around four o'clock. I don't like leaving her to her own devices for too long. And that night, we had a quiet one and went to bed, I think. I don't remember anything unusual about that day."

"And what is the nature of your relationship with Mark and Allegra Cowderoy?"

"Um... They're my neighbours. And we've always gotten along well. Is that what you mean?"

"That's great. Thank you, Mrs Winton." She stopped her recording. "Sorry, have to make it official for the record. You understand."

"Of course. Do you have any idea what happened?"

"It'll take us some time to process everything, but we'll get to the bottom of it," Toni said.

"It's just that... I have to get to work. Is it okay if I go now?" Zoey fidgeted with the zipper on the front of her athletic top.

"Sure, that's fine. I can call you if I have any other questions. I'll need you to come to the station to make a formal statement as soon as you can, though. Okay?"

"Of course I'll be happy to do that." Zoey was already headed for her front door. "Thanks, sweetie!" she called over her shoulder, then with cheeks pinking, she clamped a hand over her mouth. "Sorry," she mouthed. Then loudly, "Thank you so much for your help, Detective Kauffman."

Toni shook her head.

"You ready to head off, sweetie?" Callum asked, his eyes dancing with laughter.

"Don't start with me."

"Why not? I think it's nice. We should have all the witnesses call us cutesy names. It might make the job a little easier. Better than most of the names we're called."

She laughed as they walked together back to the cruiser. "You're not wrong about that."

"What's your instinct on this one?" he asked as he climbed into the driver's seat.

She closed the passenger door and leaned her head against the headrest, eyes shut for a moment. Then she looked at him. "Someone's hit him over the head. No one's reported him missing for days. Other than that, I have no idea."

"It's a start."

"I'll call his wife while you drive. Maybe she can shed some light on what her husband is doing home alone while she's away on holiday."

He started the car. "Sounds good. Coffee?"

She nodded. "I need a vat of it."

"Maybe I should set up an IV..."

"Don't joke. I could go for that." She grinned as she dialled. "And a caramel slice."

"You got it," he said, pulling out just as the coroner's vehicle arrived.

Chapter Six

"Disaster," Stella said, tapping her short pink fingernails on the small round table at Singles. The café's name confused Zoey. Was it a café for single people, or was it named after their single origin coffee? She wasn't enough of a coffee snob to understand why single origin was better, but she'd heard coffee people talking about it as though it was somehow meaningful, and so she often wove it into conversation because it made her seem more informed than she was. In reality, she knew nothing about coffee other than that it tasted nicer at Singles than it did at home, but perhaps that was because it'd been made by someone other than her. And that was a universal truth rarely acknowledged.

The café was a small hole-in-the-wall place with blue-speckled paint on the walls and chintzy beach-themed decor. But the coffee was delicious, and the baked goods were to die for. Besides that, one of her favourite people in the whole world, Asher Lee, worked there. He was quiet, sincere, and good-looking in a beach magazine kind of way. Of course, he wasn't her type and she was completely and totally married, but they were like a couple of old friends even though she hadn't known him long.

She'd showered and dressed in record time and made it to work before the meeting. But none of their preparation made any difference at the bank.

"They're not giving us the money. Are they?" Stella scanned the menu.

"They might. We have to stay positive."

"What will we do if they don't?"

Zoey shrugged. "I've always wondered if I should take up yodelling. I'm pretty good at it. I think people would pay to hear me yodel."

"No one is going to pay to hear you yodel," Stella said with an eye roll. "And you're not taking this seriously. I'm a single mother. I can't afford to be unemployed. My daughter is small, but she has a big appetite. It's okay for you—you've got a husband who makes a fortune building stuff."

"Designing bridges and dams."

"What?"

"Dave doesn't build things—he designs them. And don't worry so much. We're not going under, and Katie won't starve. This is my dream. Our dream. I'll think of something. Let's order coffee and something sweet. I always think better on coffee and a hit of sugar."

"I don't drink coffee or eat carbs."

"Tea, then. You can get tea and a stick of celery, and we'll strategise."

"Okay, but we need a plan."

"Thankfully, I'm the queen of planning."

"You should get a crown and maybe a sash you could wear around town."

"Stop being smart."

"No, really. A sash would suit you. You could wave your hand—you know, like royalty does. Walk around in your suit, the one with the pinstripes, and wear your sash, and have people bow to you as you go by. I'm sure it would be a big hit with the tourists. They'd call you *endearing local colour.*"

"That suit's far too tight for me these days. I'd bulge right out of it," Zoey huffed as she perused the menu.

"Great. You'd get even more adulation."

"It's fine for you to mock since you have the perfect figure."

Stella's nose wrinkled. "This isn't about my figure."

"Still, we should talk about it. It isn't right that you had a child five years ago and you still don't have an ounce of fat on your body. No stretch marks, no sagging, nothing to show for nine months of pregnancy and the horrors of labour."

"I had a caesarean."

"Even better, where's your scar? I've seen you in that tiny little bathing suit you wear. I don't believe Katie's yours."

Asher interrupted them to take their order.

"What can I get you two lovely ladies?" he asked, a hint of a smile playing around his full lips.

"Asher, how is it you know exactly what to say?" Zoey batted her eyelashes.

He laughed. "It's my job."

"Oh, that's right. I'll have a cappuccino and a gigantic muffin, please."

"One of those days?" he asked.

She sighed deeply. "Definitely, one of those days."

He took Stella's order.

"What was that?" Stella hissed once he'd left.

"What do you mean?" Zoey donned her most innocent expression.

"The flirting! You're married. Why are you flirting with Asher?"

Zoey didn't see why it bothered Stella who she did or didn't flirt with. "He's cute, that's why. And I've been married for twenty years. Tweeennnty yeeearrrrs." She drew out each of the syllables in her words for emphasis. "Do you even know how that feels? Besides, it's my wedding anniversary, and not only did my husband forget, but my neighbour died and I had to stand on my front porch and wait for the police while I smelled his decaying body. I'm scarred for life and I need a distraction."

"Wow, that's horrible. Finding him like that must've been scary." Stella's eyes were wide. "Do they know what happened?"

"I'm not sure. Maybe he had a heart attack or something. It's possible I'm in denial over the whole thing. I've hardly thought about it since the police pulled out of my driveway, but when I do, it makes me shudder. I feel so bad for his wife. I doubt you know them, since you're new to the area, but it's going to be a big shock for the community."

Stella rested a hand on Zoey's arm. "I'm so sorry. You're going through a lot today. Flirt away. Only, are you and Dave okay?"

"I don't know. Today isn't probably the best day to ask me. Ask again tomorrow and I might have a different answer for you. Today, I'm a little frustrated with him and feeling kind of depressed. Did I mention it's been twenty years?"

"You did mention it once or twice. I think that's a fantastic achievement. You should be proud, and you should definitely celebrate."

Asher returned with their coffees and a large raspberry muffin with cream cheese icing for Zoey. She offered a piece to Stella, who looked at it for a moment before waving it away.

"Don't say I didn't offer," Zoey said, taking a large bite out of the side.

Zoey wanted to celebrate. Really, she did. But ever since they'd had Isla, they seemed to celebrate everything in life exactly the same way—dinner at their favourite Nepalese restaurant, followed by an early bedtime. When had they become such a boring old couple? "I'm sure we'll celebrate our anniversary, but for now, let me wallow with my muffin in peace. If I'm going to eat my entire day's worth of calories in one snack, I should at least be allowed to enjoy it."

"Fine, I'll be quiet, and you can enjoy your highly processed sugary treat."

Zoey's eyes narrowed. "You never did answer *my* question."

"What's that?"

"How do you stay so perfect? You're a mother, I'm a mother. I know the havoc it wreaks on a woman's figure—I've been through it. Come on, cough it up. It's not fair to keep those kinds of secrets to yourself."

"Shut up, please. I'm busy coming up with a plan for how to avoid bankruptcy." Stella waved one hand before she picked up her phone and flicked through emails.

"You don't have an answer, do you? She's adopted. I knew it. Perhaps it was your sister's child, and she wasn't ready to take care of her."

"I don't have a sister, and you know it." Stella continued scrolling, ignoring Zoey's tirade. "I was adopted. My parents couldn't have children of their own."

"Then tell me your secret because I've developed some kind of muffin top that I've never had before, and no amount of Pilates does anything to help." Zoey leaned forwards on the table and grabbed Stella's hands, knocking her phone onto the table.

"Maybe it's from all the muffins."

Zoey rolled her eyes. "You're hilarious."

"You're needy today." Stella's eyes narrowed.

Zoey released her hands. "Come on. I'm not even a little bit funny?"

"Not even. And you're not going to like my answer—

that's why I've ignored your question. But here goes. I don't eat carbs—that's the answer. Also, I run five kilometres every morning after I drop Katie at school and before I come to work."

Zoey shook her head. "You're an inspiration. I don't know how you have the energy. It's hard enough taking care of a kid *with* help, but you do it all on your own, without carbohydrates. Plus you somehow have the energy to go running. You're amazing, you really are. But I think I'll keep my carbs. Thank you very much."

"I sometimes wonder if it isn't easier without a husband," Stella teased.

Zoey laughed out loud. "Um, you might be on to something."

"So, what are we going to do about the business? We're out of money, and we still have that big job to complete up at Surfer's Paradise," Stella said as she poured tea from the pot into her cup.

"I've considered asking Dave for a loan." The truth was, Zoey had only come up with the idea that morning while she was waiting for the police on her front porch. But the idea had stuck in her mind ever since, and the more she thought about it, the better it felt.

Dave could invest in her business. A quick influx of cash would keep them going until they got on top of things for themselves. And he wouldn't mind. After all, he was her husband. It was a good idea, and she wasn't sure why she didn't think of it earlier.

* * *

On the way home from work, Zoey ran over their discussion in her mind. Did it make sense to get Dave involved in her business? She'd built it from the ground up and was proud of what she'd done. But the clients they served had gotten larger, the projects were bigger and required more upfront purchasing. She was struggling to meet demand. That was a good thing, as she'd explained to the bank. But it could sink them as well.

As she pulled into her driveway, she couldn't help thinking about her neighbour. Where was Mark now? Probably lying on some cold metal table—at least that's what they did in those forensic TV shows she loved to watch. And what about Allegra? No doubt she'd heard the news by now.

That was when she noticed Toni waiting for her, leaned up against the side of her police cruiser in the dark, and felt a pang of guilt. She was supposed to go to the station and make a statement, but it'd slipped her mind with everything else she had going on.

"I'm so sorry, sweetie. I forgot all about coming to see you," she said, climbing from the car as the garage door whirred open.

"You were busy, I'm sure." Toni pushed away from the car and gave Zoey a hug.

Zoey was grateful in that moment for her job making things more beautiful rather than dealing with death and destruction all day the way Toni did. But someone had to do it, and she was eminently proud of her friend for the way she managed it all, even if she didn't fully understand why.

With Toni, she always felt comfortable. Like they'd known each other forever. As if they were both cut from the same cloth, which they most definitely weren't. Zoey was born in Sydney to a wealthy family in the northern beaches, who were highly concerned about which private school someone had attended and whether or not they could afford a house in the right suburb. Whereas Toni had come from a working-class family in Newcastle, in which public school was the norm and houses were more often rented than purchased.

They were opposites in so many ways, and yet as Zoey grew older, she'd learned to let go of the expectations she had for other people and embrace them for who they were. It was one of the many things she'd learned while living in Kingscliff.

Kingscliff was a melting pot of upper class, working class, and everything in between. Hippies, academics, artists, surfers, business people, and farmers all came together in a village atmosphere where everyone was welcome, people not only knew each other's business but were usually all up in that business, and nothing remained a secret for long. And since there were no private schools nearby, the children all merged into one uniformed mass at the single small public school and then graduated into the public high school.

"I was busy, but it's no excuse. I'll come down tomorrow, I promise."

"Thank you," Toni said.

"How's the case going?"

"I came to give you an update," Toni replied. "We're investigating Mark's death as a homicide."

"Homicide? Someone killed him?" A shiver ran through Zoey. There'd been a murderer in her neighbour's yard, only metres from where she and her family slept.

"That's right, blunt force trauma to the head. We believe it was a potted plant that knocked him down. A heavy one. And then he landed on one of those sharp rocks edging the garden bed, which did the worst of the damage, I'm afraid."

Tears filled Zoey's eyes. She and Mark didn't always get along, but the thought of someone hitting him over the head and him dying alone like that, so close by, was overwhelming. If only she'd heard something. Maybe she could've called the police in time.

"Who would do that to him? Was it a burglary?"

Toni shrugged. "We don't have any suspects yet. We're still piecing everything together. Although nothing appears to be disturbed inside the house. From what we can tell, he was supposed to catch the plane to Cairns on Monday evening with his wife, but she ended up going ahead without him. She expected him the next morning, but when he didn't show up, she assumed he'd changed his mind."

"You've spoken to Allegra?"

"Yes, we talked on the phone. She's flying back Friday night. I'm meeting her at the airport."

"I bet she's devastated. I still can't believe it," Zoey replied with a shake of her head. "A murderer, loose in Kingscliff. In Pelican Grove of all places. It's a gated community, for heaven's sake."

Toni grunted. "Unfortunately gates can't stop anything bad from happening. Hey, can we talk about something else for a minute?"

"Everything all right?" Zoey asked as she walked to the front door with Toni in step beside her. Toni looked troubled, and Zoey switched into friend mode. "What is it? What's wrong?"

"Something's going on with Rodger."

"What do you mean? Is he okay?"

Toni rubbed both hands over her face and groaned. "I don't know. I'm probably being paranoid. He seems disinterested in me. Today he knew it was likely to rain, but he took the car anyway and left me to pedal to work."

"That's a little selfish but not exactly out of character for him."

Toni frowned.

"Whoops, I shouldn't have said that. It was blunt and rude. I'm sorry." She should filter her words more. That's what Dave always told her. *Use a filter, Zoey, people don't need to hear the truth in all its glory. A little sugarcoating never hurt anyone.*

"Do you think he's selfish?"

"Um..."

"He is, isn't he? How did I not see this before? It makes so much sense. He doesn't think of me or what I need at all. He went out with his mates the night before our wedding, and I didn't hear from him for forty-eight hours. He was supposed to pick Ryker up from Malcolm's and get his tuxedo, but he left the poor boy stranded there waiting. I had to go and get him myself. I wasn't even sure Rodger would show up at the church. At the time, I thought I was being too needy, but maybe I wasn't."

"It doesn't mean anything." Zoey backpedalled. The last thing she wanted to do was drive a wedge between Toni and Rodger. Toni was on her second marriage, and she'd been so miserable before she met Rodger. Her first marriage breakdown had been long and painful. Zoey had caught the tail end of it, and she didn't want to see her friend relive that nightmare.

It'd taken Toni a long time to recover, and she'd only been back at work about five years, married for two. She needed support and encouragement, not devastating, naked truth.

"It does mean something. He does this stuff all the time, and I'm only now realising it. When my mother died, he couldn't attend the funeral because he had already booked a weekend away with his mates for Blues Fest. I understood—at least, I told him so—but inside it broke my heart to have to deal with the funeral alone." She slumped onto the top step leading to the front door. "I'm so blind."

Zoey slid down beside her with a sigh. "You're right. Don't listen to me. I don't know what I'm talking about. I've had one of those days where I'm mad at the world. I'm completely irrational right now. Definitely not someone you'd listen to for advice or insight."

"No, I'm the one who's irrational. I didn't want to see it because I've already ruined a marriage, but this marriage isn't healthy. It's not working. And I don't know how to make it work."

Zoey rested an arm around Toni's shoulders. "I'm sorry, sweetie. I don't know what to say."

"Tell me I'm wrong."

"You're wrong."

"You don't sound like you believe that." Toni glared at her through reddened eyes.

"You're wroooong." Zoey lowered her voice and drawled the word, widening her eyes and waving both hands in the air as though hypnotising her friend.

Toni burst into laughter. "You're such an idiot."

"Thank you. I work hard at it." She hugged Toni to her side.

Toni wiped the tears from her eyes with the back of her hand. "In all seriousness, what should I do?"

With a sigh, Zoey shook her head. "Sweetie, I don't know. As I said, I'm not the best person for advice today."

Toni's face clouded over. "Then dig deep, Zoey. I need you right now to give me the gold. You've been married for twenty years. I know they haven't all been easy—I've been here with you for some of them. Pretend I'm not your friend. Pretend for a moment you're not terrified of ruining my life or hurting my feelings. What's your advice?"

Her words were like a knife slicing through Zoey's heart. She knew what she had to say, but Toni was right—she was afraid that if her friend took her advice and her marriage ended, she'd blame her forever. She couldn't bear the idea of Toni hating her or of her staying in a marriage that made her miserable because of something Zoey said.

"Okay, I love you. Here goes. My advice is this—you made a vow. He's your husband. Sometimes he's going to be a complete jackass. But you have to stick with him through those times. You need to communicate. Talk to him. Find out what's going on with him, and tell him how his actions affect you. If he's selfish, he probably doesn't realise it because that's the nature of being selfish. And it doesn't mean the marriage is over. There are plenty of people married to selfish spouses—it's something you have to work out. Together. But you can't do that if you don't talk about it." Her cheeks blazed with heat.

Toni leaned her head on Zoey's shoulder. "You're right. I have to fight for my marriage if I want it to work. So that's what I'm going to do."

Chapter Seven

When Rodger came in from band practice later that evening, Toni was not drunk. She'd only had one glass of wine. Granted, it was a large glass, but still only one. She was most decidedly not drunk, but regardless of that fact, the room swayed a little when he walked in and she jerked her head up from the Netflix show she'd been watching on her iPad. She needed to relax. Needed to stop being so tightly wound. Needed to be someone cool, calm, and fun.

"Hi, honey," she said, setting her iPad on the coffee table and going to meet him.

He dumped his bag on the kitchen bench and offered her a tight smile.

She leaned against the bench. "Did you have a good day?"

He shrugged. "Fine, I guess. How about you?"

"We caught a murder investigation."

"Oh, I'm sorry to hear that. Was it that fellow in Kingscliff? I saw it on the news."

"That's right," she said, wondering when he'd had a chance to watch the news and where. But she didn't want to start a fight. She wanted the opposite of that. They needed to talk, to connect, to find the strength to be vulnerable with one another, and opening with accusations wouldn't get them there. So she swallowed her questions. "Zoey's neighbour, Mark Cowderoy. She found him this morning."

"Wow, that's horrible," he said, eyes wide. "Is she okay?"

"She's fine. You know Zoey. Takes everything in stride." She attempted to calm her racing heart with a deep breath. She hated confrontations. She didn't want an argument, but Rodger had a tendency of making everything into a fight these days, no matter what she said.

"Are *you* okay?" he asked, studying her.

"Fine. I had a little too much wine. That's all." She set her empty glass on the bench and kissed his cheek.

He laughed. "That's not like you. Want another?"

"I might in a minute. I want to talk first."

His smile faded. "Okay..." The way he said it, she knew he didn't want to talk. Knew that it was the last thing on his mind. He was tired. There were dark smudges beneath his eyes. What he'd been up to, she had no idea, but she wasn't going to ask. Not tonight. Not until they'd had a chance to talk.

She led him to the couch, and they sat, awkwardly halfway facing each other.

"What do you want to talk about, honey? Because I've had a long day and all I want to do is watch a replay of Friday night's match and fall asleep on the couch."

"I know you're tired—it won't take long. I only wanted to ask how you're doing. You've been distracted lately, and I guess I'd like to discuss what's going on, to be open with each other."

He rubbed a hand over his five o'clock shadow. "Well, I've been busy with work, as you know. We're putting together a musical, and the kids are proving to be very difficult to wrangle."

"That's right. How's it going?"

"It's okay. We're rehearsing as much as we can, but because it's primary school, we don't get a lot of time to work on it. And then tonight I had band practice."

"What did you do before practice?" She couldn't help herself. There were always so many unanswered questions in their relationship, and curiosity was one of the reasons she was so good at her job.

"What is this, the Spanish Inquisition?"

"Of course not. I'm interested in your day. Nothing more."

"Okay, fine. We went to the pub for dinner."

"We?"

He groaned. "Do you have to know absolutely every detail of my life? Come on. This is starting to feel like a prison cell."

"A prison cell?"

He walked to the kitchen and poured a glass of water at the tap. "I didn't mean that the way it sounded."

"What did you mean?" She followed him into the kitchen, her hands on her hips.

He rolled his eyes. "I meant that you ask a lot of questions. Sometimes. Not always."

She swallowed back a retort. It wouldn't help to react in anger. She wanted them to connect, but it wasn't going the way she'd planned. He was angry, she was defensive—they'd never get to a point of vulnerability like this. But she didn't know how to get them there. She'd never managed to communicate well. Fighting was the only thing she knew how to do.

With a deep breath, she tried again. "I didn't mean to pry. I'm interested in your day and what you've done because I love you."

He eyed her as he downed the entire glass of water in three

gulps. Then he set it on the sink. "Well, it was a few of us from school. It's not a big deal."

"Great!" She feigned enthusiasm. "I'm glad you're making friends at school. It's always better when you enjoy the people you work with."

"Glad we got that cleared up. I'm going to grab a shower."

"I could come with?" she offered.

He waved her off. "No, I'm tired. I think I'm going to crash in bed early. We can talk more tomorrow. Okay? Love you."

He blew her a kiss as he ran for the bathroom. She blinked back tears watching him go. He couldn't wait to get away from her. What was wrong with her? Had she done something to upset him? She couldn't recall doing anything other than asking him questions, but they bickered all the time.

Maybe it was that—a conglomeration of all of the arguments they'd had recently. It had piled up until he wanted nothing more than to get away from her as quickly as possible when he came home from work, which was as late as he could manage. He finished work at three o'clock in the afternoon, so even with rehearsals, he should've made it home to eat dinner with her. Instead, she'd watched *The Bachelor* on the couch and eaten the chicken pie she'd made for him alone. He hadn't called, either.

She wasn't an expert on healthy marriages, but she assumed it was common to call your spouse if you weren't going to make it home for dinner. But perhaps she was expecting too much of him. It could be that he saw marriage differently and didn't realise that's what she expected of him. She'd heard once that anger resulted from unmet expectations, and maybe hers were too high. With a glance in the direction of the bathroom, she walked back to the kitchen to wash the dishes.

Chapter Eight

FRIDAY

21ST OCTOBER

When Toni got into work the next day, the first thing she did was drive to the crime scene. It'd rained again overnight. As she climbed out of the car, Callum met her in the driveway. He wore booties and gloves and strode to meet her.

"Good morning, boss."

"Morning. Any updates?"

"They've examined the footprint impressions at the scene and determined that one set of shoes belongs to the victim. There's another pair of shoe prints that appears to be a similar size, but with the rain and the muddy ground, it's hard to make out anything of substance."

"Similar size?"

"The forensic analyst said they're certain the footprints

belong to another adult. But other than that, they can't tell me anything definitive."

"Great, that's so helpful—our six-foot-tall adult male wasn't murdered by a child. I think we've cracked the case."

"We should head home then." Callum smirked.

"Anything else?"

"They're putting the pieces of the flowerpot back together and believe they've found all of it."

"That's positive. Maybe we'll get some fingerprints," Toni said, holding onto the bonnet of the car for balance as she slipped a bootie over one foot.

"We can live in hope. Also the wife is flying into town tonight."

"Let's meet her at the airport when she lands, see what she's like," Toni replied.

* * *

It was at the entrance to the Kingscliff State High School that Zoey first learned about the secret life of teenagers. That wasn't entirely true. She'd been a teenager herself once, but she seemed to have forgotten just how much she'd hidden from her parents by the time Isla had reached her teen years. After all, it'd been so long since she herself had gone through that stage of life that it wasn't much more than a blur of foggy rose-coloured memories.

She lingered at the gate, doing her best impression of a mother who was not hovering, so as not to be a complete and utter embarrassment to her fifteen-year-old daughter. She'd spent every day of the past decade dropping her child at school. With Isla in year nine, she didn't really have to take her. Isla could catch the bus or even ride or walk from where they lived. But Isla hadn't insisted on a change, and she didn't want Isla to go without her. Zoey hated the idea of sitting in the kitchen flipping through the morning news on her phone while Isla made her own way to high school. It seemed wrong somehow, after so many years of having to organise her entire schedule around her daughter's life.

And so she continued taking her whenever she was able, although Isla had banned her from actually coming onto the school grounds. Instead, she remained at the gate and watched her daughter climb the steps into the tall brick building. She wished she could say that her thoughts in those moments were of proud achievement or of stoic aspirations for the future. But that wasn't true. In those tender moments, watching her offspring walk away on long, gangly legs without so much as a backwards glance, she was thinking about all of the years ahead that she'd be living at home without her and with only Dave to keep her company, and she wanted to weep.

It wasn't that she didn't love Dave, she still enjoyed his company even after so many years. But Isla made the house loud and fun and full of life. She was the animated part of Zoey's day, and she dreaded her daughter leaving for good.

They should've had more kids. She'd told Dave that at the time. Why don't we have two or even three? But he hadn't gone for it. Said he couldn't possibly cope. What he had to cope with was a mystery to her, since she was the one who'd taken care of their daughter day after day. And what would she do with an empty house?

She'd asked Dave about that once. He'd looked at her over the top of his reading glasses with consternation. "Whatever we like, honey. That's the beauty of it."

But she didn't like it. Didn't see the beauty. She wouldn't have Isla there to make her laugh, couldn't see her daughter roll her eyes, or give Isla a hug that she would pretend to fight off in embarrassment. Whenever Zoey talked like this, Dave liked to remind her that Isla wasn't dying or mutating into a butterfly never to be seen again. She would simply grow up and start a family of her own, and then Zoey would have grandchildren. Didn't she want grandchildren?

As she was ruminating over all of this, one of the mothers she'd known since kindy days sidled up to her. Emily Lancaster was a gossip who always knew everything that was going on around town and in school. With her perfectly symmetrical brown bob and her stylish tailored slacks, she was always ready to share the knowledge she'd gleaned from Parent Teacher Association meetings, group projects, and her weekly volunteering at the high school tuck shop.

As much as Zoey couldn't in good conscience approve of spreading talk of people's private lives around town, she did find it useful under certain circumstances. She was a busy woman and didn't have time to stay on top of the day-to-day news, especially at Isla's school, so Emily served a purpose. She kept Zoey abreast of any developments that could impact her family in an abbreviated format that didn't interrupt her schedule in the slightest. There was a certain expediency in that.

"Did you hear about the drug bust?" Emily liked to open with the punchline. Her favourite pastime was to walk from mother to mother around the school's fence line, extracting looks of shock from every one.

"Drug bust?" Zoey asked, one eyebrow arched. She wanted to reply, *Did you hear about the murder?* And one-up Emily with a piece of gossip for the first time ever, but she still wasn't ready to talk about it.

As much as she hated to admit it, she'd been shaken by the whole thing. Images of Mark's body lying in the garden had flashed across her thoughts randomly, making her breath catch in her throat. Last night, she'd dreamed a zombie was chasing her along the beach and followed her into the waves. She'd woken terrified that she'd drown with a zombie clutching her heel. It'd taken her two hours and five different meditation apps to fall back to sleep again.

"Here at the school." Emily dropped her voice. "Some of the kids were dealing on school grounds. The police came and everything."

"Glad to know they're on top of it." It always amazed Zoey how many parents didn't keep track of what their children were doing. How they could be completely unaware that their children were using drugs, let alone selling those drugs to other children on school property, was beyond her. "Completely uninvolved parents, I'm guessing."

"Shameful," Emily said with a sniff. "If you aren't going to actually raise your children, why would you have them in the first place?"

"Exactly." Children committing crimes, parents who were out of touch with what was going on in their own families. It was atrocious, and something should be done about it. "Was that Kieran kid involved? The one whose mother drives the old VW van?"

"Not sure. I'm going to ask and see if I can find out who it was. But I wouldn't put it past him."

Zoey stepped away from the fence reluctantly. She'd love to stick around and hear more gossip, but she had a million things to do. "Well, I've got to get going. But keep me posted."

"Will do." Emily offered a mock salute.

* * *

School drop-off was one of the worst and best moments of Stella Thompson's day. On the one hand, she loved that she could leave Katie at the classroom door, kiss her little, round cheeks goodbye, then head off immediately on her daily run. Free at last. Her feet pounded the pavement, the music in her headphones lifted her spirits, and she didn't have to think or worry about anyone else other than herself for half an hour.

At five years of age, Katie still wasn't ready for the separation. It was something of an embarrassment as well as a guilt-inducing point of grief for Stella. Every single morning, without fail, they'd arrive at the school ready to go. Stella would plaster her patented *It's a beautiful day and everything is going to be a-okay!* smile to her face. Katie would pretend she was perfectly happy to attend school that day, unlike all those other days leading up to this moment. And they'd both fake it the same way until they reached the door to the kindergarten classroom.

Kindy was the first time Katie had ever spent five days a week away from Stella. When she'd attended preschool the previous year, it'd only been two days a week. But even then, the goodbyes had been a nightmare. Stella thought things would improve once Katie was old enough to attend what she called "big school". But it'd only gotten worse. She hated to ask, "How long can this go on for?" because she knew it wouldn't last forever and that these days when her daughter longed to spend as much time with her as possible would swiftly pass by. One day she'd recall their time together and wish they could go back to that moment. But today wasn't that day.

She hovered in the doorway to the kindergarten classroom, Katie's hand firmly gripping her own, and stared into the room with a longing expression. If only Katie could do what those other children were doing. They kissed their parents goodbye, smiled, then got on with the job of colouring or cutting out shapes at their little rectangular desks. Or sat in the reading corner and tugged books from the colourful bookshelf that made up the classroom's library.

But not Katie. Katie was unwilling to release Stella's hand and ready to scream the place down if her mother tried to make her. Her wispy blonde hair, freckled nose, and bright blue eyes were the perfect disguise for the rabid, hellish yowling that her tiny rosebud-lipped mouth could produce on a moment's notice.

Miss Galveston, Katie's kindergarten teacher who looked as though she'd stepped from a Disney princess movie and that tiny birds might appear at any moment to carry the hem of her dress around behind her, hurried to meet them at the door. She tucked a strand of brown hair behind one ear, her hazel eyes sparkling, and squatted at Katie's level.

"Good morning, Katie," she said. "Are you ready to have some fun today? We've got investigations. I know how much you love investigations. And I have a special role for you today. Something no one else gets to do. But you have to come inside and take a seat on the mat first. Okay?"

Katie looked wistfully over her teacher's shoulder at a mat in front of the smart board inside the classroom, then back at the place where the investigations were set up and ready to go. A structure that looked like a rainforest-covered cubby house stood beside the bag rack outside the classroom, then behind it was a colourful winding trail drawn in chalk on the pavement with something written beside it. Katie adored investigations. It was all she could talk about on the drive home from school. Stella watched her daughter's internal struggle play out across her freckled countenance.

"How are we today?"

Stella shrugged. "Good, I think. Right, Katie?"

Katie nodded, but there was a crease in her forehead, and she wasn't smiling.

"Ready for school," Stella added, wishing her words were true.

"Good to hear," Miss Galveston said in a lilting voice. There was a bang followed by a squeal in the back of the classroom, and she hurried off to find the source.

Stella sat cross-legged on the ground outside the classroom door. It was as close to the action as Katie would allow them to get before the hysteria kicked in. She smiled at her daughter, her heart pounding.

"Are you ready to go into class, chickadee?"

Katie shook her head but didn't say a word.

"Well, it's time for me to go. I've got to get to work."

"I know." Her voice was small.

"And you've got a fun day here with Miss Galveston."

A half nod.

"All right. I'll see you this afternoon, then." It was heartbreaking the way her daughter looked at her. As though she was betraying her by leaving her at the school. But what else could she do? She had a job, and it was the only income for their small family of two. They both had to eat, and they had rent to pay.

A year ago, she was still working from home as a virtual assistant, but the pay had been meagre and the hours unreliable. Back then, they'd lived in a friend's basement, which was cold, damp, and musty. Now they were by the beach, in a small, if somewhat dilapidated, flat overlooking the ocean.

It was a dream come true for them, but it relied heavily upon her bringing in a steady income from what was her dream job—working as an interior designer for Zoey Winton. She couldn't lose her job, couldn't mess things up. The basement they'd occupied had been sold along with the house above it, so there was nowhere for them to go if they were evicted from their flat. And if she couldn't get Katie to attend school, there was no way for her to go to client meetings or do her job effectively. It was a vicious circle of guilt, shame, and hunger that kept her world spinning, and she wasn't sure exactly how to manage it. All she knew was that she *had* to.

"Honey, you have to let go of my hand so I can leave."

Katie gripped her hand tighter. Behind her, parents filed

into the classroom and said their goodbyes, calling out greetings to Stella as they went. She waved and replied with quips about the weather and how it would be the weekend soon, then gave her attention to the small, determined girl in front of her.

Miss Galveston returned and offered Stella a look. She'd seen the look before. It meant, *The time is now*. She hated this part.

"Bye, chickadee," she said, giving Katie's cheek a kiss.

Katie's nose screwed up immediately, and tears flooded her eyes. "No!"

Miss Galveston promptly stepped between them as Stella extricated her hand from Katie's. As she ran down the footpath, all she could hear was Katie's screams, followed by the door slamming shut behind her. Stella ran and ran, out of the school, down the footpath, and along the side of the road. Tears blurred her vision, her feet pounding out a steady rhythm. She dashed at her eyes with the back of her hand as pain welled in her throat.

Perhaps she should've let Katie stay home for one more year. Surely next year she'd be better prepared for daily school. But if she'd done that, they'd be living who knew where, still breathing that musty air, and she'd spend her days juggling Katie's needs and the needs of her virtual clients. It wasn't something she wanted to do again. Not now, after all these years of struggle when she could finally see some light ahead.

She wished her parents were still around to ask for advice. They'd been older when they adopted her and had both died, one after the other, in the last few years before she'd moved to Kingscliff. She had no one. No wise maternal voice in her life who could tell her it was all going to be okay, that children weren't traumatised for life by being forced to attend kindergarten.

But it felt so wrong to leave Katie that way.

If only Katie's father had contributed to their life in some way. She'd never asked. Not in so many words. Hadn't given him the chance. It was only recently that she'd even told him about Katie. He hadn't taken it well, and she'd only seen him once since. She'd intended to ask for child support, but he'd been so angry with her for the secret she'd kept. He deserved to know he had a child, he'd shouted at her. And she agreed. After all this time, she'd almost forgotten her reasoning. Why had she kept it from him? Why hadn't she thought he'd like to know?

He'd said he wanted to meet Katie. It was a positive step forwards, in Stella's mind. It told her things could change. She'd hoped that was true. If only she'd done everything differently. The pain of her regrets built like a stone in her chest until she could hardly breathe.

Her tears dried as she ran, and she pushed herself harder, relishing the pain of it, the sharp pang in her side where a stitch formed, then dissipated as her steps lengthened. Running gave her the perspective she needed to see her life through a brighter lens. She stepped off the curb and headed into the park. The office was up ahead, then beyond it the beach and her flat. She'd finish up her run on the sand, then head home for a quick shower and change to get ready for a nine a.m. meeting. She loved meeting with clients, showing them her creativity, the things she imagined for their homes or businesses, and watching as excitement shone in their eyes. Just the thought of it lifted her spirits.

Chapter Nine

Crappola, Zoey thought as she put the car into drive. She looked over her shoulder to make sure there was no one coming before merging onto Beachside Drive.

Just as she'd feared, the bank hadn't approved their request for a loan. More like a line of credit, really, but either way, they'd said no. Said they didn't have enough incoming or assets to make the risk viable. But that made no sense, since she was clearly bringing in enough money to hire a full-time designer, Stella, and to pay herself. Well, she didn't pay herself much, or often, for that matter. There were always so many expenses. Running a small business wasn't for the faint of heart, as her accountant liked to point out whenever she grew irritable over a hovering tax bill or the constant stream of outgoings in one of their meetings.

She pulled over at a petrol station to fill up her tank. All the while, she thought about her business and whatever she could do to keep things going until her cash flow evened out. There was nothing for it but to talk to Dave. But what if he said no? Or worse, what if he didn't have any money to spare?

She had no idea what was going on with his business other than that it seemed to be doing well. He was always busy, and there were plenty of projects consistently occupying his time. Other than that, he didn't talk to her about money or the costs of doing business.

It hit her for the first time that he must know what she was going through. Ten years ago, he'd begun his business in Kingscliff, alone and without any local contacts. He must've gone through a similar cash crunch in the trajectory of his enterprise's success—after all, he'd since hired a dozen other engineers and several administrative staff, plus rented a set of offices in Coolangatta to house them all. He must've struggled to make ends meet, and yet she couldn't for the life of her recall him saying anything about it.

He'd made it look easy, but it couldn't have been. She wondered for the first time if there were other things in his life that her husband kept from her.

Maybe it'd been easier for him. Or perhaps it was simply that she was more dramatic and liked to talk openly about the things going on in her life. He certainly thought that of her—he'd told her often enough. Usually in a voice of utter exasperation, but sometimes with a smile and a kiss for the tip of her nose.

While she was paying for her petrol—the cost of it astounded her, and she couldn't help thinking that it'd been years since she'd even paid attention to such things, but now they seemed to jump out at her, leaving her gasping in disbelief—she noticed a few bunches of sad-looking flowers in black buckets close to the counter.

The flowers reminded her that yesterday was her anniversary, yet she'd failed to mention that fact to Dave, who had clearly forgotten about the event entirely. He hadn't even thought to buy her petrol station flowers at the last moment. Or a box of chocolates. When they were younger, he'd had Isla make her a card if he'd overlooked the celebration yet again. But now, he seemed to have given up entirely.

With a sigh, she reached for a bunch of flowers and paid for them along with her petrol. They dripped all the way to the car, and she wrapped the stems in a napkin from her glove box for the drive home. She glanced at them repeatedly along the way, sighing each time.

Was this what their marriage had come to? Her buying petrol station flowers for herself to celebrate their anniversary? It was pathetic, but what did she expect? She hadn't exactly set a precedent for lavish parties or getaways. For most of their married life, she'd selflessly and serenely given herself over to the task of being a wife and mother with enthusiasm. Perhaps a little too much at times. She'd neglected Dave—she knew that. It wasn't something she'd been willing to admit in the past, but now she could see the way he'd manoeuvred his life onto another course with its own trajectory.

He travelled along beside her, but they weren't on the same track. They were companions for as long as it made sense to be so. They loved each other, they had fun together, but when was the last time she'd really looked at him or talked to him about his dreams? They were travellers heading in the same direction. For now. But how long could they go on like this?

No wonder the anniversary had depressed her. She understood it all a little better. She missed the passionate love they used to have. The desperation of their young affair, the infatuation she'd felt when she watched him riding his skateboard or playing guitar at the local blues club. He no longer drove her to distraction—he drove her crazy instead, with all his little quirks. The way he snored all night long, only stopping to kick one of his legs and making the entire bed shake. The way he fell asleep every single night in front of the television. The way he never seemed to consider that she might like to choose what they watched in the evenings instead of him hogging the remote.

Who, among any of the rational, caring people she knew, wanted to watch a documentary about Bigfoot? Who? Or a reality show about a family building their house with uneven logs while they lived together in a small tent in Alaska? She knew how that story would end. Winter would come, and they'd *all die!* No one sensible wanted to watch it. That's who. He needed to unwind, to watch something that didn't require thought. That was his justification for his crazy television viewing habits. In the meantime, *The Bachelor* went on without her, handing out roses she never saw. And *Big Bang* reruns had everyone in the neighbourhood in stitches, except for her.

Those were *normal* shows, the kind of thing everyone else was watching. But not Dave. And the worst of it was, he fell asleep with the remote in his hand, and so she was doomed to watch his nutty shows alone or head off to bed. She'd given up viewing anything on her iPad or phone. Her eyes already ached from too many hours on the computer at night, and she was determined not to get reading glasses, even though Dave nagged her to. She'd had twenty-twenty vision her entire life, and she wasn't about to ruin her vision now by getting glasses and making her eyes too lazy to focus. Her optometrist assured her that wasn't how it worked, but she didn't intend to find out the hard way.

At home, she set the flowers in a vase and filled it with water, then washed the breakfast dishes.

"It's not fair that you won't let me ride home from school," Isla whined, striding into the kitchen and flinging herself onto the cushions in the breakfast nook.

"Good afternoon, sweetheart. Did you have a nice day?" Zoey walked over to kiss her daughter on the top of the head. She stroked her cheek. "You look tired. Is everything okay?"

Isla rolled her eyes. "Mum, you ignored what I said. I hate it when you do that."

"I don't want to fight," Zoey said, returning to the dishes. "Besides, why do you care about riding home from school?"

"You never let me do anything."

"Yes, I do. I told you that you could ride home from school if you fixed the flat tyre on your bike. But you didn't want to ride home from school then. You said it would mess up your hair."

Isla sputtered but couldn't seem to find words to respond. Zoey had rendered her daughter speechless. It was a rare moment, one she intended to enjoy. She grinned as she piled the last of the cutlery into the dishwasher.

"You don't trust me. You say you do, but you really don't."

"Where is this attitude coming from?" Zoey asked, setting down the kitchen spray and cloth to study her daughter. "I got home from work five minutes ago, I haven't seen you all day, and suddenly you're snapping at me—very aggressively, I might add. Could you at least engage in a little bit of pleasant small talk before you launch an all-out war? Hmm?"

"You never listen to me."

"Yes, I do. I think you could talk with some kindness or manners, and then perhaps I'd be able to take in what you're saying a little better."

Isla stormed from the kitchen and thumped up the stairs. The sound of her bedroom door slamming shut echoed throughout the house.

Zoey grimaced just as Dave walked into the kitchen.

"Oh, I didn't know you were home," she said, offering him a smile.

He stopped to smell the flowers. "Those are nice."

She bit back a retort. She'd be kind even if it killed her. An image of Mark lying prone in the dirt burned against her retinas. Dave driving away and leaving her to deal with Mark's cold body was hard to forgive. But at the same time, Mark's death reminded her life was short and she should do a better job of loving and appreciating her husband. Love was complicated.

"I'm about to start dinner. Any requests?"

He reached for a handful of grapes in the fruit bowl. "Whatever you want to make is fine. You're too hard on her, you know."

Zoey studied the contents of the freezer, considering whether to choose mince or if chicken would be better and wondering why she never remembered to get anything out to thaw before work, when her mind processed what he'd said.

She spun in place, still holding the door. "Huh? Too hard on her?"

He slid onto a bar stool, munching grapes one by one. "Yeah. She just wants you to hear what she's saying, and you're more concerned about how she's saying it."

"I'm attempting to teach our teenaged daughter some manners and how to communicate appropriately. And apparently I'm failing dismally." She reached for the mince. Spaghetti Bolognese would have to do. She wasn't inspired to try anything new.

He sniffed but didn't say anything.

"I've been meaning to talk to you." Zoey put the mince in the microwave and set it to defrost. It whirred to life, and she reached for her apron, tying it around her waist.

"Oh?" He chewed, popping grapes in the air and catching them in his mouth between bites.

"Can you stop that for a minute, please?"

He arched an eyebrow, setting the grapes on the bench. "Yes, ma'am. What is it?"

"As you know, my business has been growing..."

"I'm so happy for you," he interrupted. "You're doing a great job."

"Thank you," she murmured, resting her hands on the bench. "One of the issues is that we've run into something of a snafu with cash flow."

He nodded sagely. "Right, of course. It happens."

His words emboldened her. "Yes, absolutely. Apparently, everyone goes through it, but I didn't know anything about it until now. And we need money to get us to the next payday."

"You should see the bank about a line of credit. I'm sure they'll help you out," he offered, pushing a grape backwards and forwards with a fingertip.

"I tried that. They told me today that my business is too much of a risk for them. A risk they're not willing to take."

"Really? That doesn't seem right."

"That's what I think too. Glad we're on the same page. So, you don't think I'm too risky to invest into?"

He shook his head adamantly. "No, of course not. You're fantastic. The clients love you—I hear about it all the time through my contacts at work. You're the best at what you do, and people appreciate it. I don't think you'll run out of business anytime soon, especially if you expand into the northern end of the Gold Coast."

She grinned. "That's exactly what I plan to do. Which is why I was hoping you'd consider being my bank...or investor... if you prefer that term."

He hesitated, his eyes narrowing. "I see."

"As you know, I'm good for the money. I've got clients lined up—it's the bills that are killing me. That and the exorbitant taxes. The government is robbing people blind, and I can't believe I never realised that before now." She paused to draw breath, her heart hammering against her rib cage.

"I'll think about it." He popped another grape into his mouth.

"You'll think about it?"

He came to his feet. "Yep. Can't wait for dinner. I'm starved."

Had he said he'd think about it? She'd imagined how this conversation would go all day long, and that wasn't something she'd considered. In the role play she'd run through in her mind, he'd always said yes and given her a gigantic hug. Then he'd told her how proud he was, how grateful to be able to invest in their future. She knew him so well she'd believed wholeheartedly that she'd be able to predict his exact response to her request. Apparently, she didn't know him as well as she thought she did.

He walked to the door, then turned to look at her, a quizzical expression on his tanned face. "Aren't you supposed to be at the police station right about now?"

Shame washed over her. "Oh, crap!"

Chapter Ten

Toni stared at the murder board on the wall opposite her desk. So far, they had photographs of the footprints, the smashed flowerpot, the wife (Allegra Cowderoy), and Mark's boss at the bank where he worked. His boss was a little old man with white hair who was hard of hearing and walked with a stick, so Toni was fairly certain they could cross him off the list of suspects. But she'd asked him to look through Mark's clients to see if there was anyone there who might've held a grudge against him.

"Anything on the tapes so far?" Callum asked, rubbing tired eyes as he leaned against her desk.

Toni was in the process of running through the tapes they'd received from canvassing the neighbourhood for surveillance footage. She'd spent most of the day watching tapes made by helpful residents while uniforms questioned the neighbours about what they'd seen or heard.

"A very quiet neighbourhood," Toni said with a yawn.

"I haven't found anything either."

"The coroner confirmed it was blunt force trauma," Toni said.

Callum nodded. "That's what we thought."

"They're running a tox screen as well, just to make sure there wasn't anything else in his system."

"Do you think it was the wife?"

Toni smirked. "We haven't even spoken with her yet."

"Still, it's got to be her. She's conveniently out of town when someone hits her husband over the head? Classic move."

Her eyes narrowed. It wasn't like Callum to jump to conclusions. "You're already taking bets?"

He feigned shock. "No, of course not. That would be completely unprofessional."

"Don't let the Super catch you doing it," she said, smothering another yawn.

"Absolutely not."

* * *

FIVE YEARS EARLIER

The alarm clock beside the bed dragged Toni from a deep sleep. It chirruped "Here Comes Santa Claus" in an obnoxious, wheedling tone. Toni slammed her hand down on top of the clock, then immediately regretted the movement as pain sliced through her side.

She'd been shot.

The memory of the event flashed through her mind, drawing a grimace as she shifted into a sitting position. She'd been shot and she lived. Her colleagues called her lucky. She wasn't so sure it was luck. She had a good partner who'd saved her life. But why hadn't she moved in time? It'd been a week and she was recovering but she was lonely. No one had come to visit her in the hospital except her partner.

She shoved her feet into the reindeer slippers beside her bed. She hadn't bothered decorating the flat. What was the point? Malcolm and Ryker had moved to Kingscliff with Malcolm's new wife, Sandi. She owned a boutique shop on the esplanade, he'd told her. She couldn't move to Sydney—he'd had to go to her. He knew it was a large distance, but since Toni was single, it wouldn't take much effort for her to drive the twelve hours to see them. Would it?

She shook her head, pondering the discussion again as irritation buzzed around her body. Wouldn't take too much effort for a cop who worked shifts to drive twelve hours to see her son? Sure. Of course. Nothing to it. She could simply bob her head and blink.

Toni nodded her head and blinked. Grinning to herself, she muttered beneath her breath, "I'm losing my mind. But at least I find myself entertaining, even if no one else does."

She flicked on the television set and stood watching for a few minutes while she ate a bowl of cereal. It was Christmas morning, so every channel was flooded with Christmas church services, replays of carols from the previous night, or feel-good Christmas movies. She watched the news, crunching mouthfuls of muesli and fresh grapes. She barely took in the stories. Her mind was numb—probably the medication.

Finished with her cereal, she showered and changed. She had a flight to catch, and she was determined to see Ryker with a smile on her face despite the pain. She caught a taxi to the airport, expense be hanged. The idea of managing on the train with her luggage and the pain in her side was more than she was willing to face. Besides, she hadn't seen Ryker in six months, and she was beginning to get anxiety over the whole thing.

She found her seat on the plane and popped another pain pill, then rummaged in her carry-on to find the water bottle she'd purchased in the airport.

"Nervous?" asked a woman beside her.

"Huh?" The pill rattled around in her mouth, already

tasting rancid. She found the water and gulped it down. "Sorry. What was that?"

"Are you nervous about the trip? I noticed the pill, that's all. I get nervous, so I understand completely." The woman had long brown hair pulled halfway into a ponytail. Her makeup was flawless, as was her complexion. She wore a silky pantsuit and had one leg crossed over the other, with platform wedges and pink toenails.

Toni hated to think how she looked. She'd barely run a comb through her hair, had lost ten kilos in the weeks since the shooting, and hadn't donned a lick of makeup in months.

"Not really. A little bit, but not because of the flight. I'm going to see my son."

"Oh, that's nice, I'm headed home too. I should've been home two days ago, but my flight was delayed, then delayed again. Those massive thunderstorms..." Her voice trailed off as she peered out the plane window at the tarmac beyond. Baggage workers wandered up and down a ramp leading into the plane's belly. "I wish they'd hurry up."

"It must be hard to be away from home on Christmas morning," Toni said.

"Mmmm. Devastating. My kid is beside herself, so I bought extra-special gifts to make up for it. I shouldn't have taken the client meeting right before the holidays. My husband certainly doesn't understand it. I'm trying to start a new business, but so far...nada. It's hard to find interior design clients when you have no history in the business—no portfolio, no money, no rich friends, and you live in a beachside village." She laughed and ran fingers through her hair. It was silky smooth and cascaded over her shoulders.

Toni wished her curls would cascade. But they didn't do anything she wanted them to do. They sprang into tendrils, then frizzed at the slightest sign of humidity.

"I'm sure they'll forgive you."

The woman patted her hand. "Thank you. That's very kind. Where are you headed?"

"Kingscliff," Toni said.

"What? That's my hometown. I used to live in Sydney, but we've been in Kingscliff for about five years. I consider it home now."

"My husband moved there six months ago."

"Really? I wonder if I know him."

"Sorry, ex-husband. I don't know why I called him my husband. He's remarried, so he's definitely *not* my husband anymore. Much to his delight." Toni wanted to clap a hand over her mouth. Why was she unburdening her soul to a perfect stranger? She usually didn't show vulnerability to anyone.

"Your son's staying with him?"

"He lives there too." Toni wanted to burrow a hole directly into the earth at the look on the woman's face. Of course she was horrified. Most mothers were when she told them her situation. Who could allow their child to be taken so far away, to live with his father, and be okay with it?

"I'm sorry," the woman said, grasping Toni's hands between hers. "That's... I don't know what to say."

"I know."

"I'm Zoey, by the way."

"Pleased to meet you, Zoey. I'm Toni." Her heart hurt, her side ached. Everything was pain in this life she'd been forced to embrace. She had no choice. The psychologist at work had threatened that she'd have to leave the force if she didn't pull herself together, and so that's what she'd done. Pulled herself together. Piece by piece, bit by bit. She'd accepted her circumstances and chosen to live with them rather than fight. The fighting had cost her so much of her sanity, and she couldn't afford to lose more.

"Well, honey, you seem to me like the strongest, bravest

woman I've ever met. I have a feeling we're going to be friends because I love strong women." Zoey's words were tinged with warmth, and even though Toni usually didn't like it when strangers got up in her business like that, there was something about this woman that drew her in like she was sitting at the kitchen bench, legs swinging while drinking hot cocoa and eating laminations fresh from the oven the way she used to with her mother back when she was a kid, before everything went wrong.

"Thanks. I'm trying. It's hard sometimes."

"Of course it is. That's why you're strong. If everything was easy, you'd never have built those muscles the way you have."

"I guess that's something."

"Indeed. Now, when you arrive in Kingscliff, we've got to catch up. I know the best café where we can get a wonderful caramel slice. It's to die for."

"That sounds perfect."

Chapter Eleven

CURRENT DAY

Toni was thinking about the time she and Zoey first met five years earlier when she received a call from the front desk to tell her that her witness was there to give a statement about the homicide in Kingscliff.

She met Zoey in the reception area and took her back to a meeting room. Zoey spoke a mile a minute while they walked.

"I'm so sorry I was late. You know how it is. Disasters at work, disasters at home. It's never-ending."

"Don't worry about it. I don't have anywhere else to be, so it works out fine."

"What's that supposed to mean?" Zoey asked, her radar for inner turmoil clearly overriding her flustered state.

They sat at a table in the meeting room with the door shut before Toni continued. "It's Rodger. I did what you suggested —tried to talk to him about what's going on."

"And?" Zoey leaned forwards, hands clenched on the table before her.

"He basically brushed me off and acted like everything was fine."

"Noooo!" Zoey drew out the word, a look of horror on her pretty face. "I'm sorry. But I guess you'll have to work harder to get him to listen to you."

"Yeah, you're right." Toni shrugged. "I'm not very good at all this."

"All what?"

"You know—communication, intimacy, marriage. I made a complete wreck of the last marriage, and I've never really been able to hold down a long-term relationship. I don't know how to do it. And it seems like even when someone says they love me, it wears off after a while. I'm sure we'll end up divorced and I'll be single all over again. Why bother trying to live any other way?"

"That's not what's happening here," Zoey objected. "Don't talk like that. I love you, and that's never going to wear off. This friendship is for life, baby. And Rodger loves you too. It's *not* going to happen. He'll come around."

"I hope so."

"Definitely. But regardless, this is on him, not on you. You're doing your best to make it work. You bend over backwards for him all the time. I see you do it. You're a good wife. If he's a lousy husband, that's not your fault."

"So maybe I'm bad at picking people," Toni kidded with a sigh.

"I think that's probably true."

"What? Thanks for that."

"Well," Zoey continued, "I didn't want to say anything, but really, I think you could've done better."

Toni laughed out loud. "Now you tell me? You couldn't have brought that up two years ago before I walked down the aisle?"

Zoey leaned back in her chair and crossed her arms. "Oh, like you would've listened to me."

"Of course I would've."

"No, you wouldn't. You were in love. No one makes sensible decisions when they're in love. And they certainly don't listen to their friends who have qualms." Zoey rolled her eyes. "Please, you were done for. There was no turning back."

"Still... You could've said something."

"Next time, I will definitely say something."

"You're already planning my third divorce?"

"Of course. Gotta think ahead." Zoey tapped her temple with a grin. "So, what should we do about this statement I'm supposed to make? I've got to get home and finish cooking dinner for my family, seeing as how they're all so utterly hopeless without me."

Toni took down Zoey's statement. She had only a few extra questions to ask than she had done the other day. So far, the investigation hadn't turned up many leads, but Mark's wife, Allegra, was expected to arrive at the airport that night. She'd stated that she was in Cairns from Monday to Friday and that Mark had planned on following her up there on Tuesday morning, but when she went to the airport to get him, he hadn't disembarked from the plane as planned.

"One last thing. Was there anything about Mark and Allegra's life lately that had you asking questions? Anything different or strange? Anyone at the house you wouldn't normally see?"

Zoey chewed on a fingernail. "Hmmm... Not that I can think of. They're a pretty social couple. They don't have kids, and they often hold parties at their house."

"So, a lot of people around?"

"Yes, people come and go from there all the time. They sit on the front porch and turn their music up to full volume so it echoes all around the neighbourhood, and they sing."

"They sing?" Given the atmosphere in the upmarket Pelican Grove neighbourhood, Toni found it difficult to imagine their parties would be well received.

"Like it's a karaoke bar. And they *don't* have good taste in music. Usually Mark puts on something mournful, like one of those old country and western songs about the man whose dog got put down the same day his wife left him or something horribly sad like that. I mean, would it *kill* him to play an up-tempo, happy song occasionally?"

Toni arched an eyebrow.

"Whoops!" Zoey whispered with a grimace. "Sorry."

Chapter Twelve

"Last chance to get in on the action, boss," Callum said beside Toni. "We're at four-to-one odds—she did it. Do you want in?"

"Shut up, please. Some of us have to work." Toni crossed her arms over her chest.

Callum chuckled. "Yes, ma'am."

"Don't call me ma'am. And I've already said, you shouldn't be taking bets. At least not until we've interviewed her."

Callum whistled. "There she is."

A graceful woman with short blonde hair and a floral dress that blew about in the wind as she walked down the steps of the small plane headed their direction across the tarmac. She wore oversized sunglasses even though the sun had gone down an hour earlier and held her skirt with one hand to keep it from flying up. The other clutched an expensive purse to her side. Black clouds skidded across an angry sky overhead, and a flock of seagulls circled the airplane.

"Mrs Cowderoy?" Toni asked, stepping forwards to shake her hand.

"Yes, that's me. You must be Detective Kauffman. We spoke on the phone?"

"I'm so sorry for your loss," Toni said with a nod. "Please come with me. I've got a car waiting."

"Thank you." Allegra followed their lead and meekly climbed into the squad car waiting at the pickup area outside baggage claim. One of the uniformed officers they were travelling with shoved Allegra's luggage into the boot of the car, then climbed in beside her.

Callum pulled the car away from the curb while Toni swivelled in her seat to look at the woman. It was important to get a first impression. She wanted to observe the victim's wife as much as possible to see how she responded, to get a feel for her personality. There was a lot at stake in this case, pressure from on high to get it solved and fast. But she would take her time. She didn't want to miss anything and hadn't closed enough cases to be completely confident about the path she should take.

"I hope your flight was comfortable."

"Yes, thank you. It was fine." Allegra still wore her sunglasses and had her head angled so it seemed she was staring out the window. Her red lips were expressionless, and she appeared to be in mourning, as any wife would be.

"I understand you were expecting your husband to join you on Tuesday morning—three days ago. Is that correct?"

"Yes. As I said over the phone."

"Of course. I'm sorry, but we will have to go over your statement in more detail again at the station. After that, we'll let you go home. I'm sure you're keen to get some rest after your flight."

"Thank you. I appreciate it. It's all such a shock, and I have family coming into town next Saturday for the funeral, so I have a lot to do."

"Oh? I didn't realise they'd be done with the medical

examination by then." Toni was certain it wouldn't be complete within a week. It never was.

"My father called in a favour," Allegra explained. "He's a councillor."

Toni didn't respond. Instead, she sat in silence, digesting this latest piece of information. Allegra Cowderoy—clearly that was her married name—had friends in high places. Toni certainly wouldn't complain if the medical examiner sped things up. The faster, the better as far as she was concerned. As long as the integrity of the investigation was maintained.

At the station, Callum led Allegra to a meeting room. Toni took her time getting a cup of coffee and checking her email. She liked to make a witness wait for her. It gave her the upper hand in an interview, and she would take every advantage she could get.

Quite possibly, the wife was telling the truth and she'd been in Cairns when her husband was murdered. It should be easy enough to prove or disprove her alibi. But until then, she had some questions that needed answering. Namely, who wanted her husband dead? Because from what she'd gathered in her investigation so far, everyone loved the outgoing, friendly, and sports-obsessed Mark Cowderoy. He was a man of the people. A former surfing icon who'd married up. He was a town fixture, and one people were sad to see gone. But maybe his wife could shed some light on why he was killed and by who.

She carried her coffee into the meeting room and set it down on the table. Then she shuffled through her notes before finally making eye contact with Allegra. Without the black sunglasses obscuring her face, it was clear Mrs Cowderoy had been crying. Dark circles around her eyes spoke of a lack of sleep, even after she'd done her best to cover the evidence with makeup.

"Let's get started. We'll be recording this interview. I hope you don't mind."

Allegra dipped her head in agreement.

"You're a teacher at the local primary school. Is that correct?"

"Yes," she said.

"And Mark was in finance?"

"That's right. He worked at the Central Coast Bank."

"Do you know if his work put him at odds with anyone who might've wanted him dead?"

Allegra sniffed into a bunched-up tissue, then wiped her nose. "No, nothing like that. Everyone liked him. He was good at his job, but it was financial advice. Nothing sinister."

"And where were you on Monday night?"

"I flew to Cairns on the eight o'clock on Monday night, and after that, I was at my parents' house."

Toni noted the details, already forming the next question in her mind. "When was the last time you saw your husband?"

"He was at the house when I left for the airport around five thirty. It was peak hour, and I hate to be late for a flight. I was a little anxious, so I didn't say much to him. I called goodbye and headed out the door. He said he'd see me soon, and that was the last time I spoke to him." She dabbed at her reddened eyes.

"I know this must be hard for you. Can you tell me, is there anyone you can think of who might want your husband dead? Anyone he's argued with lately, or who might hold something against him?"

"Not that I can think of, no. He was a nice man—he was kind to people. Friendly, fun, outgoing. People liked him. I don't know anyone who didn't. And I can't imagine why someone would want him dead."

"Had you fought with your husband recently?" Toni asked.

There was a pause as Allegra twisted the tissue between her hands. "A few days before he died. It wasn't so much a fight as a disagreement."

"What was it about?"

"He said he'd been unfaithful to me. But he wouldn't tell me anything more than that."

"When was this argument?"

"Friday after school. He was supposed to come with me on Monday, but he said he had to meet with someone that night and would follow me up to Cairns on Tuesday morning. When I pushed him on it, he told me about the affair. But he wouldn't give details, as I said. We argued—I wanted to know more. He said we could talk in Cairns. But by then I was so disgusted I had to get away from him. I went to the beach and took a walk to clear my head."

"So that's why you didn't call him from Cairns on Monday night? The log here shows no phone calls from your phone to his after you landed, which is unusual, wouldn't you say?"

She sighed. "Yes. I was angry."

"But you don't know who he was sleeping with?"

She shook her head. "He said it was over. That he'd ended it a long time ago but there were some loose ends to tie up. He didn't want it to impact our marriage. He chose me over her."

"And how did you feel about his revelation?"

"Betrayed," she said. "But I loved him."

"Of course you did. I know this is hard for you."

"I didn't kill him, if that's what you're thinking. He was very much alive when I left the house. You can ask those kids next door."

"What kids?" Toni's brow furrowed as she scribbled frantically in her notepad.

"I don't know their names. There's a girl who lives next door."

"Do you mean the Wintons?"

"Yes, I saw her. She was with some boys. They were smoking pot in their yard, and they saw me leave. They would've seen Mark with the lights on inside the house, I'm sure of it. They can tell you."

Toni leaned back in her chair. Zoey wasn't going to like this.

Chapter Thirteen

"Time to do the dishes!" Zoey called down the hallway for the umpteenth time. "If you don't come down here right now, young lady, and do these dishes, I'm going to add a second chore."

She padded down the stairs and threw her hands in the air when Dave peered at her over his reading glasses.

"No luck?"

"She acts like she doesn't hear me."

"Maybe she has headphones on," he suggested, putting his book aside.

"I'm sure she does. I think I'm losing my voice shouting at her. Why is it so hard to parent teenagers?" She slumped onto the couch in front of him and tucked a leg up beneath her, lazing back against his chest. It was one of her favourite places, leaning against him. He wrapped his arms around her and kissed the top of her head. She could forget all the reasons she was mad at him when she was pressed to his warm, strong chest.

"Maybe you should yell less."

All the irritation returned in a single moment. She spun about and sent him daggers. "Thanks for the support."

He lifted his hands as if in surrender. "Don't shoot the messenger."

"Maybe *you* could try asking her to do the dishes instead of me. I think she tunes out my voice."

He chuckled. "Let's not get crazy now." He reached for his book.

"Are you going to read over my head?" she asked, snuggling again into his chest in an attempt to find that peaceful place.

"I'm going to try."

She rested for a while, listening to the beat of his heart through his shirt. He was warm and comfortable. She could easily fall asleep. It was as though all the anxiety of her day simply drifted away while she lay in his arms.

She realised it'd been far too long since she'd simply snuggled with her husband on the couch. They were both so busy these days; they didn't make time for each other. It wasn't entirely his fault—she was to blame as well. Before she began her business, she'd devoted all her time and energy to taking care of him and Isla. And he'd always been a bit of a workaholic. Besides, even when he was home, he was something of an introvert. It'd been her role to draw him out and initiate affection. She'd grown slack lately in that regard.

These days, she focused on her business more than her family, and she wasn't sure it was worth it. Unless he consented to bail her out, the entire thing could very well sink into oblivion, and what would she have to show for all her hard work then?

"Have you thought about my request?" she asked.

He grunted. "Which one, my love?"

"The money for my business."

He set his book back on the side table, reached around her, and squeezed. "Of course I'll help you. But with conditions."

She stiffened. "What conditions?"

"You have to slow down. We hardly see you, and when we do, you're a little more irritable than I know you mean to be. We miss you."

"Isla doesn't even notice," she objected.

"She does. We talked about it."

She spun on him. "You talked about me?"

"Yep. I asked her about life, how she's doing. I like to do that every now and then. See how she's tracking."

"And what did she say?"

"Not much."

She huffed. "It's like extracting teeth to get information out of her." Was Dave a better parent than her? She couldn't remember the last time she'd sat down with Isla specifically to ask her about her life outlook. She had no idea he could be so attentive. Maybe she'd underestimated him.

He chuckled. "Very true. But she did say she missed spending time with you. Not in so many words, of course, but I can read between the lines. And besides, I miss you as well."

"I'm here all the time," she argued. She heard what he was saying, but it seemed hypocritical after all the time he spent building his own business years ago when they hardly saw him other than at dinnertime and around the breakfast table.

"You're here, but you're not really here," he quipped. "And I know what you're thinking. I haven't exactly been the most present husband and father over the years. But I regret that. I missed out on so much, and I've finally understood, after all this time, that my career is satisfying, but it'll still be there when Isla leaves home. She's only living here for a few more years, and I don't want to miss that. I'm raising the issue now because we're finally at an age where things have a chance to slow down, and you seem to have taken it up a notch instead."

She drew a slow breath. "You're right. Of course. If you lend us the money, I will slow down. I won't have to work as hard because I won't have the stress of rent payments and stock purchases hanging over my head all the time." She felt low. Like the lowest of the low. All this time, she'd considered herself the good parent and Dave the one she had to fill in for. When had things gotten so turned around? She'd lost sight of what mattered.

"Good," he said, picking up his book again.

"But..." she continued.

He sighed and let the book fall back to the table. "But what?"

"I hear what you're saying. You think we should prioritise Isla."

"And each other," he added.

"I'm glad to hear it because I'm going to guess you completely forgot about our anniversary."

He grimaced. "Oh, wow. That was this week, wasn't it?"

She laughed. "Yep. Three days ago."

"I'm so sorry. That's terrible. It was a big one too, right?"

She lay back against the opposite end of the couch and studied him. He was still handsome even after all this time. He had a few flecks of grey in his hair, but he'd been an avid gym goer the entire time she'd known him, and he'd kept in good shape. "Twenty years," she said.

He slapped a hand to his forehead. "Yikes."

"Yikes indeed." She smiled. It was infinitely satisfying to be back on top.

* * *

When Toni called later, Zoey answered the phone with a rushed "Y-ello?" The phone was stuck between her shoulder and ear, her hands plunged in soapy dishwater. She shouldn't cover for Isla this way, doing the dishes for her when she'd been asked repeatedly to do them, but she felt bad about the whole *missing her* situation. Sometimes it was as though she could run around the house on fire and her daughter wouldn't notice—she was constantly nose-deep in whatever device or social media platform was most popular at the time. But apparently she wanted more time with Zoey, and the revelation melted her heart.

"I'm glad I caught you, Zoey," Toni said.

"Hi, sweetie. I'm doing the dishes. Why aren't you in bed yet? I thought you were the consummate early bird."

Toni grunted. "Still working, unfortunately. I might be here a while longer. That's why I'm calling. I wanted to ask you about Isla."

Zoey set down the scrubbing brush and dried her hands. "Okay. Shoot."

"I hate to even ask this, but do you know if she's involved in drugs?"

Zoey's heart skipped a beat. "What? No, of course not."

"I didn't think so, but I had to ask. One of the witnesses says she smelled pot in your yard and heard some kids over there. But she doesn't know which kids, so it could've been anyone."

Zoey sat at the kitchen table, her head spinning. "I guess so...but was it definitely our house? Maybe the witness is confused."

"No, it was your house. I confirmed."

"Huh."

"But you don't know anything about any drug usage or maybe friends who are into smoking pot?" Toni left the question hanging in the air between them.

Zoey racked her brain. "No, I can't think of anyone right now. But I'll ask Isla and get back to you if I discover anything. Is this witness helping you find out who killed Mark?"

"I can't talk about it, but keep me posted. Okay?"

She pondered Toni's question while she finished the dishes and wiped down the benchtops. Isla had always been a good child. She'd been shy when she was younger and had the tendency to please. As far as she knew, Isla wasn't into anything dangerous. She had friends, but not hordes of them. A few kids she was close to.

Lately, Zoey was fairly certain there was a boy involved in Isla's life, although their daughter hadn't specifically told them about him. After all, she was only fifteen. Zoey assumed that the two of them probably spoke occasionally at lunchtime and perhaps held hands. But she had noticed her daughter's wardrobe change considerably during the past year. She'd gone from plain shorts and T-shirts to wearing a lot of black, short skirts with colourful leggings underneath, and she'd even tried to bleach her hair blonde without Zoey's permission a few weeks earlier. Thankfully, it hadn't worked. Somehow the bleach didn't bleach, and her hair was like straw for a few days, but that was all.

Zoey wiped her hands on a towel and headed upstairs. Dave was in the shower, singing off pitch as she walked past their master suite. She knocked on Isla's door. Isla was still awake, seated at her desk doing what appeared to be homework.

Wonders never cease, Zoey thought to herself as she offered her daughter a conciliatory smile.

"I know, Mum. Dishes," Isla said, tugging headphones from her ears and setting them on the desk.

"I did the dishes for you," Zoey said, sitting on Isla's bed. Amazingly, her daughter's room was reasonably tidy. She'd spent years attempting to instil some pride into her child over the state of her bedroom. It'd only been in recent months that Isla had shown promise in that area.

"Okay, thanks."

"You're welcome. I want to talk to you about something."

Isla shut the lid of her laptop and crossed her legs in her chair. "What is it?"

Zoey intended to broach the subject of pot smoking but decided the opportunity to pry was too good to pass up. She could cover a few topics in one conversation. After all, Dave wasn't the only one who could have these handy little chats with their daughter.

"How's life?"

"Uh, okay, I guess."

"Anything new going on with you?"

"Not really. I'm studying the Russian Revolution in modern history, which is pretty cool. Did you know that the Bolsheviks killed all the good farmers? So, like, if you were a bad farmer, you were fine, but if you were good at it, game over." She grinned, running a finger over her throat dramatically.

Zoey studied her smiling daughter, a little concerned over her apparent delight at the Bolsheviks' violence, but that was a conversation for another day.

"Right, yes, of course. Bad, very bad. No one should be discriminated against that way. But actually, I thought I heard you talking to a boy the other day. So, I was wondering if perhaps you have a boy you're interested in or something like that?" Internally, Zoey cringed at how awkward she sounded. When had she become this parent? The one who couldn't manage to get the embarrassing words out? When she'd had the birds-and-bees conversation with her daughter, she'd been unflinchingly direct.

Isla's cheeks pinked. "Mum..."

"Come on—we can talk about anything. For instance, you

can tell me about this boy, and I could talk to you about *my* first boyfriend and what he was like. We can swap stories. It'll be great."

Isla studied her incredulously beneath a thick, blunt fringe. "Really?"

"Yes, absolutely... Are you...are you wearing eyeliner?"

Zoey brushed the hair from Isla's eyes, her shock growing with each passing moment. Eyeliner and possibly blush. Maybe even lipstick.

"Mum! So what? I'm not going anywhere. I'm sitting at my desk doing homework."

"If you're doing homework, why do you need to wear makeup?" Zoey followed her daughter around the room. Isla stayed out of reach, petulant and dismissive all at the same time.

"I don't *need* to wear it. I was trying out some things..."

"And where did you get it? Did you use *my* makeup?"

"Yes, but I didn't think you'd mind. You've always let me use your makeup."

"Not unsupervised. We did it together as a fun mother-daughter thing. I hope you didn't get makeup all over the bathroom. I remember one time, I came in and there was nail polish all down the front of the white cabinet door."

"Mum! I'm not three." Isla slumped onto the bed and tucked her legs up so her chin rested on her knees.

Zoey hesitated. "You're right, you're not three. But please ask before you use my makeup. And..." What else could she say? *Don't wear makeup, even in the house.* That sounded a bit pedantic and restrictive even to her ears. She wanted Isla to be able to experiment when she was safely ensconced at home, but watching her daughter grow into a young woman wasn't something she was ready to face yet.

Zoey sighed and sat in Isla's desk chair. "We're getting off track. About this boy..."

"I like him, that's all. It's not a big deal, Mum. Don't make it weird."

"Has he ever come to the house?"

Isla's gaze fell to the bed, and she was silent.

"Isla Rose!"

"No, of course not."

"I can't believe we're having this conversation when you're fifteen years old, but here are the rules of this house. No boys when your father and I aren't home. No boys in your room with the door shut. Understand?"

Isla rolled her eyes. "Yes, I know, Mum."

"And no drugs," Zoey continued, cognisant of the fact that this wasn't how she'd planned to tackle the subject. Isla was visibly shutting her out. She should've kept up the friendly, casual approach, but now that she was using her ranting voice, it was hard to walk it back. "What I mean is, I've heard that there are some drugs going around at school. We've talked about drugs before, and you know how much they can negatively impact your life. So I hope..."

"I'm not doing drugs, Mum," Isla said.

Zoey left the room satisfied. Her daughter was a sweet girl. She was experimenting with makeup around the house while doing her homework. She had her first boyfriend, and even though Zoey had forgotten to ask his name, she had a good feeling about him. After all, he must be a nice boy if Isla liked him. And Isla most definitely wasn't smoking pot. She really didn't even have to ask that question. She'd known the answer as soon as the words left Toni's mouth. She and Dave had always been very open with their daughter about the dangers of drugs. Zoey was a good mother. She knew everything her daughter was up to, and she'd taught her well. She was proud of the woman she was becoming. She went to bed with a smile on her face.

Chapter Fourteen

SATURDAY

29TH OCTOBER

Stella was having one of those days. Not a bad day, per se. But everything irritated her. Firstly, Katie had woken at five a.m., even though it was the weekend.

"Saturday morning!" Stella had groaned, shoving her head under the pillow. "Go back to sleep."

But Katie didn't go back to sleep. In fact, she objected strenuously to the suggestion and instead turned the television on with the volume up high, proceeded to lose the remote between two couch cushions, and poured her own cereal from the wrong end of the box. The cereal spilled all over the bench and floor, and milk went everywhere. And when Stella staggered from her room with wild hair blinding her, she'd crunched through the cereal and slipped on the milk. Now her neck was out, and every time she turned her head, a nerve pinched.

On top of that, the coffee at Singles had been cold by the time she got around to drinking it because she was busy on the phone with a supplier who hadn't considered the fact that she might not be working on a Saturday. When she drove to the shops to pick up her prescription, she'd received a parking ticket for parking halfway across a no standing zone, which had only happened because she was driving an old Pajero that she'd bought the previous week from the scrapyard and it was so big she could barely tell where it ended and the wide world began. But she'd got it for a steal so didn't think she could pass it up.

As she accelerated around a bend, clipping the curb on the roundabout, she recalled her recent conversation with Katie's biological father. She always referred to him as the biological father because he'd never been a father or a dad to Katie which wasn't his fault, since she hadn't told him about Katie's existence. It was merely a fact, an observation, not a judgement.

Her thoughts kept returning to the murder as well. When she'd moved to Kingscliff, she couldn't imagine a murderer lurking in the small beachside village. Ever since the murder happened, she'd been able to think of little else. When she took Katie for a walk, she wondered whether they were safe. When she ran alone along the beach, she often glanced over her shoulder. At night, she triple-checked every lock in the small apartment.

It was sad that a man had lost his life. But who could've done such a thing? And were they all in danger, or was it a crime of passion? She wished the police would hurry up and figure the whole thing out so that life could go back to normal. It seemed the whole town was tense. Only that morning, she'd witnessed a road rage incident at the roundabout. Road rage was an anomaly in a town with no traffic lights.

In the back of the Pajero, Katie sang along to the repetitive high-pitched song, "Baby Shark," as it blared from the vehicle's sound system. One day, these songs would drive Stella irrefutably mad, but in the meantime, she did her best to block them out. She'd think about other things, plan the next design project or the dinner menu for the week, or add things to her inner to-do list. Anything other than getting the latest kiddie pop hit stuck in her head for days on end.

A glance in the rearview mirror brought a smile to her face. Katie's head bopped from side to side as her cute little voice sang along. She held a Barbie in each hand, and the dolls danced to the music as well. Stella sometimes felt as though she might die from the intensity of the love she felt for her daughter. It was all-consuming and sometimes so overwhelming, she couldn't do anything but grin through tears and hope nothing ever changed. Every poignant second of Katie's childhood sifted through her hands like sand, no matter how hard she tried to hold on to them.

When she slowed for the next roundabout, she noticed something funny about the brakes. The pedal pushed all the way to the floor, and she didn't seem to be stopping. Panic gripped her for a single moment, but when she raised her foot and pushed down again, it worked. The vehicle slowed as if nothing was wrong. Did she imagine it? Was she losing her mind? Something was wrong with the brakes. Or was it?

She pumped them again, and again they worked fine. Perhaps it was the way this vehicle operated. She'd only driven it a few times, and then only around the small township. Maybe she simply wasn't accustomed to the way it worked. Everything about the Pajero felt different to the old Suzuki hatchback she'd driven previously, but unfortunately the head gasket had blown on it, whatever that meant, and she'd had to pick something out of what the wrecking yard had available. And this was the only vehicle that was drivable without expensive bodywork.

Now that she thought about it, it was disappointing that

Katie's father hadn't called her after their discussion. She'd laid everything out on the table and had expected that he'd want to talk more about it. But perhaps he needed more time. Heaven knew her life was complicated enough without having to include him in it. But if he wanted to spend time with Katie, she wouldn't stop him. Katie had started asking more and more about her father—who he was, where he lived, why she never saw him—ever since she began attending kindy the previous year and saw the other children's fathers dropping them off and picking them up, swinging them in the air and kissing their cheeks. She'd watched with avid curiosity, then turned on Stella with a hundred questions that left her heart aching.

"You wanna get some ice cream later?" she asked.

Katie stopped singing long enough to shout, "Yes! Gelato!"

Stella laughed. "You got it, chickadee."

"Mummy, is my daddy going to come and have ice cream with us? You said I might meet him soon."

Stella swallowed. She shouldn't have said anything, but Katie had been nagging her and she'd had a headache. She was trying to finish a design that was under a looming deadline, and Katie had a cold which meant she was home with her until she was well. Juggling working from home with caring for a five-year-old meant that sometimes things slipped through the cracks, or were forgotten, or words jumped from her mouth she never intended to let out.

"Well, that could be difficult to arrange."

"Call him and ask. Please."

Stella studied the road up ahead. There was some kind of commotion along the edge of the street. Cars parked on the curb, up on the verge. People walking alongside the parked vehicles or in the grass, all headed in the same direction.

"I don't think that's a great idea..."

"It *is* a great idea. I want to see him. Why won't you let me see my dad? You got to have a dad. It's not fair that I don't have one."

"I don't..." Stella couldn't focus on Katie's words with all the commotion around her.

It must be a funeral. There were dozens of people, all dressed up, many in black, walking on both sides of the street. And a hearse crept along the road ahead of her. It pulled into a driveway, then stopped, its back end still jutting out onto the road. "What on earth?"

She pumped the brakes, but nothing happened. "Oh, no. This can't be happening."

The Pajero barrelled along the road, narrowly missing a family that stepped in front of her. "Sorry!" she shouted, but they couldn't hear her since the windows were up and the speakers were blaring "baby shark doo doo doo doodoodoo" while Katie's sweet voice sang along.

"Get out of the way!" She waved her hand back and forth, hoping to catch someone's attention. But no one seemed to notice her. *Doo doo doo doo doo doo.*

Another pump on the brakes, but the vehicle didn't slow its pace. When internal lights began to flash and a beeping sound punctuated the deafening chorus about sharks, she didn't have time to look to see what the error message on the dashboard read. She was too focused on a game of *Dodge the Funeral Attendee.* The crowd thickened the closer she got to the driveway and the hearse that half blocked the road ahead of her. *Mummy shark...*

"Holy guacamole," she whispered beneath her breath, leaning forwards to pound the horn.

Everyone looked up then with confused or irritated expressions.

There was nothing for it. She'd have to mount the median

strip to get around the hearse. And why in the heck had it stopped in the middle of the road? *Doo doo doo...*

She was about to swing the wheel so the car would jump the median strip, even though at that speed, it would be a cringeworthy bump that might not only send them flying but might rip the front axle from the undercarriage. But as she poised, ready to make the turn, a teenaged girl with headphones stepped up onto it. The girl wasn't paying attention—she was looking down at her phone—and if Stella climbed the curb, she'd run directly over the girl. She had only a split second to make her choice.

"Hold on, chickadee. We're gonna hit..." she shouted, then grimaced as the Pajero slammed into the back of the hearse, knocking the rear door clean off at the hinges. The hearse scraped along the side of her vehicle, spinning to one side as it did. She held on tight to the steering wheel. People gaped in horror and ran in every direction to get out of her path, screaming and shouting for her to "Look out!" as if she'd simply fallen asleep at the wheel.

"Mummy!" Katie squealed.

"It's okay, chickadee. Hold on."

Then they were through the crowd and on the other side. The music continued blaring its obnoxious lyrics. She switched it off with one finger, then breathed a sigh of relief. From what she could tell, she hadn't hit anyone.

Katie started crying.

Stella glanced in the rearview mirror to see a long black casket fall from the back of the hearse onto the road. It landed with a cracking of timber and fell apart. She gasped, heart pounding. She turned at the next left where the road climbed a small hill, and the vehicle slowed its headlong pace. With shaking hands, she steered the Pajero slowly up onto the curb and applied the handbrake.

Stella spun in place to squeeze Katie's leg. "You okay?"

Katie nodded, sobbed.

"You stay here, chickadee. I have to check on something. Do. Not. Leave. The. Car. Got it?"

Katie nodded, wide eyed, and squeezed her Barbies to her chest.

"Good. I'll be back in a moment."

Stella locked the car behind her and ran back down the footpath, around the corner, and headed for the crowd. It seemed as though they'd been frozen in time. They were looking at the casket, or at her, or still gaping. Hardly anyone had moved.

"Is anyone hurt?" she shouted as she drew close.

No one answered, but they murmured together, moving away from the road.

She sprinted over to the casket, unsure what to do. One whole side had split open, and a body lay on its stomach on the hot bitumen. A man dressed in a black suit with a blue tie hovered beside the body, his complexion turning pale.

"I'm so sorry," she said, bending over the body. "What can I do? Should I help you get him back up?"

The man stared at her, gaping like a goldfish.

She knelt and pulled the casket towards her so it was flat on the ground. Then she reached for the body and tugged. He was heavy—she'd have a hard time moving him without help. She looked up at the man in black with a pleading expression. "Can you help? Again, so very sorry. I didn't mean to...but there was a girl with headphones. Stupid smartphones. They're gonna get us all killed. Am I right?"

She rubbed her sweaty palms down the front of her shorts.

He seemed to waken, then stooped to help her. Together they counted and heaved the man back into his casket. Then put the casket into the back of the hearse. Puffing, Stella took one look at the dead man's face, swallowed down a wave of panic, and sprinted away.

No, no, no. This couldn't be happening.

Katie had taken off her seatbelt and knelt on the back seat, looking out the window with one thumb stuck between her lips. It'd been a long time since Stella had helped her wean herself off thumb-sucking. Now it looked as though they were back to square one. That's what she thought as she slid into the front seat, sweat dripping down her temples. *Back to square one.*

Chapter Fifteen

The sight of Stella's vehicle barrelling through the funeral procession left Zoey completely stunned. Had Stella lost her mind? Was she on some kind of failed suicide mission? She hadn't even slowed her car before she collided with the hearse. And from what Zoey saw, it looked as though Katie was strapped into the back seat.

"Was that...?" Dave asked, standing beside her dressed in his best black suit.

"Stella? Yes, it was. But I have no idea what's going on. I'd better go check on her."

By the time Zoey made it to the footpath and the scene of the accident, Stella was running directly at the hearse in bare feet and a pair of short shorts with a mismatched singlet top.

"Stella, honey..." Zoey called, but Stella didn't seem to hear her.

Zoey strode towards her friend, concern making her heart race. That's when she saw that Mark Cowderoy's body had tumbled out of the broken casket onto the tarmac. She pressed a hand to her mouth. But when Stella and the funeral director heaved Mark back into the casket, Stella sprinted away, and Zoey was left standing on the side of the road in complete and utter confusion.

"What was that all about? And where's Stella?" Dave asked, glancing down the street.

She shrugged. "I have no idea."

That was when Allegra Cowderoy emerged from the funeral home, teetered down the driveway in her impossibly high black heels, and began to scream.

* * *

During her five years as a uniformed cop, Toni had seen some strange things. There was the time an old lady made her stomp around in the attic of her big, draughty old house to chase away the unicorns. Or the traffic stop that involved a dead octopus on the road in the middle of nowhere, hours from the ocean. But receiving the phone call from an irate widow that her husband had been knocked from his casket by Stella Thompson took the cake.

Toni hung up the phone and stared at it a moment before emitting a loud guffaw.

Callum sat on the desk beside her. He'd heard the entire conversation, which she'd taken on speakerphone.

"That's right. Get the laughing out now, Boss," he said, chuckling as well.

"I know it's not funny, but I can't help it. It's terrible. The poor man—someone killed him, and now he's..."

"Roadkill?" Callum suggested.

Toni slapped a hand over her mouth, the laughter bubbling up from within. "Stop it," she protested. "It isn't funny. Don't you dare make me laugh when we get there."

They headed for the door, each strapping on their holsters

as they walked. “So, what do you think is going on with Stella Thompson? You know her. Is she a bit nutty?”

Toni tried to picture what’d happened and couldn’t imagine it. “No, not at all. She’s sweet, kind, and very together. She’s a single mum who works for Zoey Winton as an interior decorator.”

“Well, Allegra Cowderoy is convinced Stella is the murderer, taking out some kind of vengeance on her dead husband’s corpse.”

“Highly unlikely. But we’ll look into it, of course.”

“Hey, Detective,” called out a uniformed officer at the reception counter as they pushed through the doorway from the office. “I was about to call you.” The man jogged over to meet them.

“Yes, Constable. How can I help?’

“I received a call a few minutes ago from a uniform—one of the officers who are questioning neighbours over the Mark Cowderoy murder.”

“We’re on our way out. Do they have something?”

“A Mrs Betty Smythe says that she was taking her dog out to do his business at ten o’clock before she retired for the evening when she saw someone leaving the Cowderoy house.”

“Did she say who it was?”

“She couldn’t see clearly, since it’s quite a distance and it was dark. But she said the person drove off in a white SUV around seven thirty or eight o'clock. It was hard to see in that light, so she might be mistaken. She thinks the driver was a young woman with a ponytail.”

“Thanks, Constable. That’s very helpful.”

She and Callum pushed through the front door and strode towards the cruiser.

“Stella Thompson drives a silver Pajero,” Callum said. “The neighbour could’ve gotten the colour wrong.”

"It certainly could've been her. But what was she doing visiting our victim? And why is she trying to run down his dead body in front of everyone who loved him?"

Callum shook his head as they climbed into the car. "I guess we're about to find out."

Chapter Sixteen

It'd taken fourteen missed calls and two frantic voicemails before Zoey finally reached Stella. Or more accurately, until Stella called her back. She'd fidgeted through the entire funeral, unable to concentrate on the grief she should be feeling over the loss of her young, handsome—if somewhat irritating—neighbour. It was a tragedy, a life cut short, and she felt the depth of it whenever she allowed herself to stop worrying about Stella for just a moment and take in the sombre proceedings going on around her. But mostly she couldn't stop thinking about her employee and friend.

She'd only known Stella a few short months, but in that time, they'd become close. Stella was like a sister to her already. She was easy to know and love, so thoughtful and authentic. A real friend for whom Zoey had thanked God more than once.

When she'd discovered Stella's history—a single mum with no close family—and saw her sketches of various decorating concepts, she knew she had to hire her. Stella hadn't had the chance to study design. She didn't have experience in the industry. She only had raw talent, but that was enough for Zoey. The rest could be taught, but an eye for design was something you were either born with or you weren't. It was very simple. And Stella Thompson was born with an aptitude for creating beautiful things or for making plain things infinitely more beautiful with a few simple changes.

Her involvement in Zoey's fledging design company was a gift. One she wasn't ready to part with. If Stella had gone loopy or was somehow involved in Mark's murder, which she didn't believe for one second, she might go to prison. And then what would happen to poor little Katie, not to mention Zoey's business? She didn't even want to think about it. It was too horrible to bear.

So the first chance she got after the funeral was over and she and Dave had done the rounds giving sympathies and kissing cheeks, she'd ducked out of the venue to call Stella.

When the phone rang and she saw Stella's name on the screen, she and Dave had been home for an hour, and she was about to jump in the car and go searching for her friend if she didn't respond soon.

"Stella, there you are!"

"Sorry, Zoey. My phone was dead."

Zoey didn't believe the excuse, but she wasn't about to start an argument over it. What mattered was that Stella sounded okay.

"Are you hurt? What about Katie?"

"We're fine—thanks for asking. I'm a little shaken, though."

"Of course you are. Where are you? I'm coming over."

"No need. I'm on my way to you now," Stella said.

When an old hatchback pulled up in front of Zoey and Dave's house a few minutes later, Zoey couldn't help thinking about what had happened to cause her friend to barrel into a hearse earlier in the day, but of course she couldn't ask such an impolite question. No doubt the police would be looking into why she absconded immediately from the accident, but for now, Zoey was glad Stella and Katie were okay and they'd come to her for help.

"I'm so glad you're home," Stella said. She looked as though she was about to burst into tears. Her lower lip quivered, and she tugged the corners of a cardigan around her thin frame as if to hug herself.

Zoey's maternal instinct kicked in. "Come inside. I'll make a pot of tea. And I baked some butterfly cupcakes yesterday that I think you might like, Katie. What do you say?"

"With buttercream?" Katie asked.

Zoey laughed. "My, aren't you the little connoisseur? Yes, with buttercream of course."

"Yay!" Katie sped into the house, her purple suede boots clip-clopping on the hardwood floors, followed at a more sedate pace by Zoey and Stella.

Isla helped by ushering Katie into the kitchen for cupcakes and a glass of milk while Zoey showed Stella into her home office. She offered her a seat, then sat behind her desk, linking her hands together in front of her.

"What a day," she said.

Stella drew a deep breath. Then her shoulders sagged and she started to cry. Zoey jumped to her feet and scurried around the table to embrace her friend. Stella shook silently, tears wetting her cheeks.

"I'm sorry," she said.

"Nothing to be sorry about." Zoey handed Stella a fistful of tissues from the box on her desk.

"The police called. They want me to come in for questioning. But I had to find someone who could look after Katie for me. I don't have anyone else..."

"You don't even have to ask. Of course we'll do it."

Her heart ached for Stella. She wanted desperately to pepper her with questions but held back, waiting for her friend to open up of her own accord.

"Thank you. I'm still in shock. The brakes on my Pajero failed. I only bought it last week..."

"I remember," Zoey said. "And that makes sense. I was worried."

Stella blew her nose. "You were worried about what?"

"I don't know... I thought maybe you were angry with Mark over something."

"You thought I did it intentionally?"

"I wasn't sure."

"Do you think the police see it that way? Because I'm about to go to the station... Maybe I should get a lawyer or something. I don't know any lawyers, though, and I'm sure they're expensive. Do you know a lawyer?"

Zoey patted her shoulder. "Oh, honey, I don't know about lawyers. If you think you should get one, then maybe you should. But if you explain about the brakes, I'm sure they'll understand that it was an accident. Still..."

"What?" Stella asked, wiping her nose.

"Why did you run away like that? You looked as though you saw a ghost, then dashed away down the street. It looks a bit...strange. That's all."

"I can't explain right now. I've got to go. They said I had until four p.m., and it's close to that now." Stella embraced Zoey. "Thank you. I appreciate you taking care of Katie. I don't know how long I'll be gone."

"Happy to help," Zoey said. "We can talk later. You know, I'm here for you."

"I know you are, and I'm so grateful." Stella squeezed Zoey's hand. "See you later."

Zoey watched her go, then surveyed the neighbourhood. To think this street was such a quiet place only a few days earlier. Nothing ever happened. Or so she'd believed.

Betty Smythe stared at her across the neatly trimmed yards between their houses, a pair of secateurs hanging loosely in one hand. Zoey waved to her, and the older woman waved back. Zoey walked inside and shut the door behind her. No doubt Betty noticed that Dave hadn't mowed the lawn in two weeks and was considering how to construct a strongly worded email to them about that fact.

She sighed, running her fingers through her hair. If only she'd had the strength of character to tell Betty how she felt about the neighbourhood association and their bylaws. Didn't she know there was a murderer loose in Pelican Grove? Who cared about the length of a lawn when Mark was dead and any one of them could be next?

It didn't seem as though Toni was any closer to solving the crime. Zoey couldn't imagine anyone she knew killing someone. So it must've been an outsider, someone breezing through town, who knew Mark through his work or something. It couldn't have been a local. But if it was a local, she wouldn't put it past Betty Smythe. That woman had the air of a psychopath about her.

Dave sat in his armchair, reading. He glanced up at her as she walked through the living room. "Everything okay?"

She nodded. "I've been thinking. Since you're bankrolling my company now..."

"I'm not sure I'd call it that," he objected.

"We should have a big launch party," she continued, as though he hadn't interrupted.

He leaned forwards, taking off his reading glasses and setting them on a side table. "But your company isn't new. You've been doing this for a while. Why would you launch it?"

"I know, but we've been operating as a small bootstraps business. I worked out of the house for a long time, and then we got our tiny little office space downtown. But we've never been able to take on the big clients because of the cash outlay upfront that I didn't have. Now we can rebrand ourselves and target the whales, thanks to your generous funding. An elegant launch party on the Gold Coast would give us some visibility and could potentially add to our client base. What do you think?"

He scratched his chin, studying her. "I suppose it makes sense. Although it sounds expensive."

She clapped her hands together. "A party! That's exactly what we need. It'll be good for the business, and after today, Stella is going to need something happy to look forward to."

His brow furrowed. "I'm not sure a big society party is going to help Stella..."

"Of course it will. Who doesn't love a chance to dress up and dance the night away?"

Dave shook his head, pushing his glasses back up the bridge of his nose. "Whatever you say, honey."

Chapter Seventeen

The one person Toni wanted to hear from most was Stella Thompson, and even though she'd promised over the phone that she'd be there as soon as she could manage, she still hadn't shown at the station. In the meantime, Toni and Callum had run through everyone who had attended the funeral and gotten no closer to the truth.

Apparently they all had differing stories about what'd transpired. It seemed impossible that there could be so much conflict surrounding an event that so many people had witnessed, and yet there was.

Finally, Stella breezed through the front door, her red hair hanging like a smooth, shiny curtain down her back. Her blue eyes sparkled, or perhaps those were unshed tears—it was hard to say.

Toni had always admired Stella. She and Zoey were close—she knew that much. They worked together and had become fast friends in recent months. But apart from the fact that Stella had a daughter, she didn't know much about her. She'd chatted with the younger woman at various functions and events, but all she knew of Stella was that she was the kind of woman who turned men's heads when she walked into a room, and she was polite and friendly, if somewhat taciturn. She smiled a lot but rarely laughed. It wasn't much to go on, and Toni had a lot of questions that needed answering.

Toni let Stella wait for a few minutes while she topped up her coffee, then joined her and Callum in the interview room. She set down her coffee cup and smiled at Stella. Callum sat beside her, leaned back in his chair, and flicked a pencil around in circles between his fingers. Toni shot him a frustrated look.

"Good evening, Stella, I hope you were able to find childcare for your daughter."

"Yes, thanks. Zoey's watching her."

"That's good to hear. We shouldn't be too long. I'm taking statements from everyone involved in the accident this afternoon."

Stella shifted in her seat. She seemed cool and calm, but Toni knew even the most confident person suffered from nerves in a police interview room.

"Can you tell me what happened?" Toni watched Stella's reaction, pen poised above a blank notebook.

"My brakes failed. I had it towed to the mechanic's directly after the accident. Apparently it was complete failure of the anti-lock brake system." She said the words in a staccato rhythm, as though reading them from an instruction manual.

"Wow. I've never heard of that."

She nodded emphatically. "Yep, it could've been a complete catastrophe."

"Could've?"

"I mean, worse than it was. Someone might've been hurt."

"Someone not already dead," Callum added before he resumed chewing on the end of his pencil.

"Thank you, Callum."

"No worries."

Toni tapped her pen on her notepad. "You said your

brakes failed, but why did you intentionally steer into the hearse? That's what some of the witnesses have told us." By some, she meant Allegra, though of course she couldn't say it.

"Oh, I didn't do it on purpose. A girl with headphones over her ears stepped onto the median strip, and I couldn't go around the hearse. I did the best I could, given how many people there were. I thought for sure I was going to hit someone. I'm so grateful I didn't. I don't think I could live with that."

"It is fortunate that no one was injured. How well did you know Mark Cowderoy?"

Stella paled. She crossed her arms over her stomach. "I didn't, really."

"You didn't know him?"

"Yes, I knew him, but not well." She fidgeted with the hem of her shirt. "I'd seen him around town."

"Do you ever wear your hair in a ponytail?" Toni asked.

"No." Stella self-consciously ran her hand over her sleek red hair.

"Have you visited the victim's house?"

"I've had no reason to do that."

"I think we have enough for now. I'll be speaking to the family later, and they may want to press charges, but I don't think there's enough here. We'll confirm your vehicle's brake system failure, though, of course."

"Absolutely," Stella said.

* * *

Toni finished the interview by cautioning Stella over leaving the scene of the accident, which she said she only did because her daughter was still in the car, and she had to call for a tow. Once they wrote down the details for the mechanic's so they could check her story, they released her.

"Sounds like the thing at the funeral was an accident after all," Callum said once Stella had left.

"So it seems."

"But she could be our killer."

"We'll need more proof than we have if we want a conviction. Have the autopsy results come in yet?"

Callum nodded, riffling through the files he carried everywhere with him on a clipboard. "Blunt force trauma. Time of death was approximately eight thirty p.m. to two thirty a.m. on Monday night. He had cannabis in his system. Also, the broken flowerpot found close to the body is the murder weapon, as suspected —had his blood and hair on it. He was hit on the head and fell, striking his head again on a series of rocks lining the edge of the garden bed. Nothing we didn't already suspect, apart from the cannabis." Callum let the papers fall back into place.

"So, she could've done it," Toni said.

"The timeline fits."

"And we may be able to place her at the scene, even though she denies it. Not to mention the accident today. Let's get a confirmation on the brake system failure and make sure she wasn't telling a porkie pie."

"You got it, Boss," Callum said, pushing to his feet and striding from the room.

Toni didn't like it, not one bit. But it was looking more and more as though Stella Thompson was the perp. One thing she knew for sure—this case was likely to tear their little community apart before it was all over.

Chapter Eighteen

SUNDAY

30TH OCTOBER

HEAVE.

Zoey tapped the word into her phone, then shook her fist in frustration. "Darn you, Wordle!" It was an obsession, and Zoey was nothing if not hip to the latest craze. She liked to keep up, to stay on top of what was going on in the world. She watched the news religiously, recycled everything (some things she shoved in the yellow bin she wasn't entirely sure she should be recycling but surely the more the merrier when it came to saving the planet?), she started her own TikTok account (then promptly forgot all about it and returned to Facebook), and she always changed her profile picture to whichever colour or platitude was fashionable in the moment. Wordle was one of the trends she'd embraced emphatically but not without some level of resentment, since she never seemed to be able to beat the scores of her online friends, which chafed her to no end.

Still, she found that the app allowed her to take out some of her frustration on something entirely meaningless, which was a kind of therapy, she supposed. And much cheaper than that bloke who charged them three hundred dollars an hour to talk about their marriage years ago when she'd been deep in a pit of postnatal depression without realising it.

When she'd finally understood what'd caused her slump, she'd said goodbye and walked out feeling much better about everything. Dave had apologised and hurried after her, telling her it was rude to walk out like that. But really, she hated therapy—all those questions and meaningful stares. It was too much for her to take. Wordle might be frustrating, but it helped alleviate her stress, and it was much more bearable.

"Mum!" Isla's voice came sailing down the stairs. "Something's wrong with the wi-fi."

"Don't shout, honey. Come here if you want to talk to me." Zoey set down her phone, crossed her legs on the amber-coloured leather recliner, and waited.

"What's wrong with the wi-fi? It's not working," Isla asked as she pounded down the staircase.

Her blunt fringe hung partway over her dark eyes, skinny legs protruded from a black and navy cross-hatched skirt, bony knees hidden under long black socks.

"There's nothing wrong with it. I changed the password."

Isla rolled her eyes. "Well, what's the password?"

"I'm not going to tell you until we've had a discussion."

Isla threw herself onto the couch. "A discussion about what?"

"You told me that boy you're seeing hasn't been to the house. But when I spoke to Dave a few minutes ago, he told me that you've definitely brought boys to the house. Boys.

Plural. Now I want to know who, and when, and what's been going on."

Zoey's voice quivered over the last sentence. She still couldn't quite believe that her darling little girl with the brown pigtails and the sweet gap-toothed smile was this moody, hormonal stranger who'd openly lied.

"I didn't lie to you," Isla whined, her nostrils flaring. "If you don't trust me, say so."

"Tell me who it was."

Isla huffed. "Fine, it was Ben. Are you happy?"

"Ben who?"

"Ben Sellers. He's in year ten, and he's really nice. He surfs, and he's in a band—plays the drums. You love the drums. And he's asked me to the formal. I want to go. I was going to talk to you about it at dinner when Dad's home. Can I go? Please? It's a really big deal that he asked an ninth grader to go with him." She put on her best big-eyed, sweet smile. But Zoey wasn't falling for it this time.

In fact, she was mortified. A tenth-grade boy who was in a band had been at her house, and she'd had no idea. Not only that, but Isla had lied about it. Who was this person standing so confidently in front of her, acting like nothing at all was wrong? "You can't go to the year ten formal. You're only in year nine."

"I don't mean the actual formal—I mean the afterparty. No one cares about the formal. He's taking some other girl to that, but he doesn't even like her. They're friends, that's all. He wishes he could take me, of course. But since he can't, he says we can hang out for the rest of the night. They're having a bonfire on the beach. Everyone's going to be there."

Zoey straightened her gym singlet. "There is no way, unless pigs fly over the frozen tundra of hell, that I would let you go to a bonfire on the beach after the formal to *hang out all night* with a drummer! Do you think I don't know what goes on at those parties?"

The internal door to the garage opened, and Dave walked in, his briefcase beneath one arm, an empty coffee mug in the other hand. He was about to greet them when Isla screamed as though she was being stabbed and stormed back up the stairs to her room, slamming the door behind her.

"Well, that sounds dramatic. You having a rough day, my love?"

Zoey slumped back into the armchair. "You have no idea."

Dave walked over to kiss her. She wrapped her arms around his neck and didn't let him go. "Can you deal with all that and I'll go to the spa for the day tomorrow?"

He laughed, extracting himself from her grasp. "Not a chance. I have clients all day, but nice try. What's going on?"

She followed him into the kitchen, where he filled a glass with water and gulped it down.

"Why did we have a child?"

"The circus wouldn't take us," he offered.

She grinned. "But you were so good on the trapeze."

"It really seems unfair. Discriminatory, in fact. We should sue."

"She's a little brat."

"Horrible. Let's give her up for adoption." His eyes sparkled as he refilled the glass. This was why she loved him. Sometimes she forgot.

"Yes, I don't think it's too late. Oh, but I'd miss her. I miss her already just thinking about it," she replied, poking out her bottom lip. "Do you think the adoptive parents would let us visit, and bring her gifts, and take her out to dinner?"

He laughed and wound his arms around her waist. "Perhaps we should keep her."

"That's probably for the best. But she really can be a brat sometimes."

"Definitely. It's those adoptive parents. They're a bad influence."

She laughed, then he kissed her.

Chapter Nineteen

FRIDAY

4TH NOVEMBER

Toni wanted to meet for a drink after dinner, and Zoey was in the mood to get out of the house after having to sit through the entire meal with Isla's brooding. Zoey and Dave swapped looks, and she wondered what her husband was thinking. Even after twenty years, she couldn't read him at times. It usually bothered her, but tonight they were allies on the same team, fighting the enemy of teen hormones and sulky outbursts about the wi-fi password.

Isla had been completely horrified when Dave had come up with the idea of confiscating her phone, rendering her completely without access to the internet or any way of contacting the outside world. She'd called him a prison warden and stormed back up the stairs, only emerging to carry a second helping of the chocolate pudding Zoey had whipped up for dessert back to her room with her.

Zoey collected the dirty dishes from the table with both hands and deposited them in the sink.

That was when Toni texted her about meeting for a night-cap. She'd grinned as she shoved the phone in her back pocket.

"I'm not doing the dishes tonight. You can work it out between the two of you because I'm going out with Toni for a drink. But this sink had better be empty when I get home."

Dave watched her leave. She blew him a kiss, and he pretended to catch it and throw it back at her. She laughed as she trotted up the stairs to get changed. A night out on the town—what a treat.

She may have overdressed for the outing, given the fact that Kingscliff's nightlife involved two restaurants and a pub, with around two dozen people at each of them, and she wore a sleeveless silk pantsuit with a string of pearls. There were twinkle lights outside the pub, and the only noise in the quiet village apart from laughter spilling from its doors was the sound of the waves crashing dark against the shoreline beyond the caravan park and the wind shushing along Main Street.

Toni waited at a small round table with tall bar stools on either side. She wore a simple buttoned shirt with a collar and a pair of black slacks. Her style always oscillated between waiter-chic and quirky hippy. She looked as though she was working at the venue rather than one of its guests. Completely oblivious, of course, to how attractive she was, in an athletic kind of way. Her long dark auburn hair was pulled back into a thick, wavy ponytail. She didn't wear a whiff of makeup. She'd bought drinks for them both, gin and tonic, and cradled one with her hand while staring into the distance.

"Penny for your thoughts," Zoey said, coming up behind her.

They embraced, and Zoey sat. "Thanks for the drink."

"I figured you might like to get right into it." Toni raised her glass. "Let's toast."

"What are we toasting?"

"To a night without husbands or children. Just girlfriends who always show up."

"To girlfriends." Zoey tapped her glass against Toni's. She sipped her drink, then set it down on the table again. "Everything okay with you? Have you spoken to Rodger?"

Toni shook her head. "No. I've barely seen him. I've been working this case night and day, and he's at rehearsals for a musical they're putting on at the primary school. He eats out with the other teachers most nights. Hey, you should come to the musical. It's next Friday."

"That sounds amazing. I'd love to. I miss the primary school musicals. They were one of the highlights of my year for a long time. It's hard to believe it now, but Isla was quite the actress back then. She's given it up, unfortunately. Too cool, I suppose. She used to play trombone in the band. She was terrible at it but awfully cute."

"Aww, fun."

"She still plays sometimes," Zoey said, spinning her glass slowly and staring at the clear liquid. "But it's not the same."

"I know what you mean. They all grow up."

"How's Ryker?" Zoey asked. "You don't talk much about him."

"He's fine. He's seventeen now, so he has his life and his friends, and even though I'm officially supposed to have him every other weekend, he's often working or out with his mates. That's how it goes for every parent, I guess."

"I know it's hard for you, though."

"I missed so much of his childhood. The time flew by while I was busy pulling myself back together, training for a new career, working, and fighting with his father. Now I'm ready to be there, to be his mother and to do all the things I couldn't for him before, and he's almost an adult and doesn't need me." She sighed. "It's hard not to feel like a complete failure sometimes. I wonder why I bother."

Zoey embraced her friend. "You bother because you're you. And he'll still need you, even if he's almost an adult. I've heard they need you for the rest of their lives. My parents live in Sydney, and until the last few years I still called every week and talk to Mum about everything that was going on in my life. I need to get back in the habit. I miss her."

"You really think he still needs me?"

"Absolutely."

"I think he's mixing with the wrong crowd at school."

"What makes you say that?" Zoey asked.

A trio of musicians piled into a corner on the other side of the pub and began tuning their instruments. Zoey wasn't surprised to hear that Ryker was up to no good. Whenever she'd met him, he rarely had a word to say. He grunted in response to every question he was asked. She overcompensated, of course, and tried to engage him in an insipid, smiling conversation about surfing, something she knew next to nothing about, or his job down at the local Woolworths. Even she felt nauseated by the way she fawned, but she couldn't help it.

She wasn't accustomed to people being openly dismissive of her. Perhaps he even disliked her, which was something she simply wasn't willing to accept. If he didn't like her, it was because he didn't know her. And she was darned if she wouldn't do everything she could to right that injustice.

"He comes home late, smelling of smoke. His attitude is horrible, he's rude to me all the time, and whenever I ask him about what he's been doing, he makes up a story that I know isn't true. I can generally tell when he's lying, or at least I used to be able to. I don't know what he's hiding. But between him and Rodger, I'm surrounded."

"You think Rodger is lying to you?"

Toni groaned. "I don't know. I don't want to believe he is, but there are so many little things that don't add up. Sometimes I wish I had a girl. Another female in the house to commiserate with. All these uncommunicative, grunting males with their secrets and manipulation of the truth."

"If only it worked that way!" Zoey commiserated. "I'm having the same issue with Isla."

The band broke out in a rendition of "Working Class Man," and Zoey had to raise her voice to be heard over the noise.

"What's going on with Isla?" Toni shouted.

"You know how I told you I asked her about the drugs and whether she had boys to the house?" Talking about it set her head buzzing with fury all over again.

Toni nodded and gulped a mouthful of her drink.

"And she said she hadn't done either. Well, apparently she's had several boys to the house. And when I confronted her about it, she said she's got a boyfriend called Ben who's in year ten and wants her to come to the formal afterparty with him."

Toni was leaning forwards so she could hear. Zoey felt as though she was shouting in her friend's ear.

Toni choked on her drink, coughing. "What? I hope you told her no. We have to break up those parties all the time, and there are so many things going on you don't want her to be part of. Trust me."

"I know, I know, and yes, I said there was no way I'd let her go. So she's not speaking to me anymore."

Toni patted Zoey's hand. "I know it's hard, but that's for the best. It's good parenting. Those kids are completely unsupervised at those parties. We've had to call the ambulance for alcohol poisoning so many times. Not to mention the sexual assaults."

Zoey shook her head in disbelief. "And they tell us to trust our teens to make their own decisions. Pffft."

"Do you think she lied about the pot as well, then?" Toni asked as she patted her chin dry with a napkin.

Zoey hadn't considered that. She'd pushed the thought out of her mind because she honestly couldn't picture Isla being involved in anything illegal. She was only fifteen, for heaven's sake. "I don't know. Maybe."

"Because if she lied about the one thing..."

"She could well have lied about the other, I know. Still, it doesn't seem like her. She's not that kind of kid."

"Until now," Toni said with a huff.

"Until now," Zoey admitted, her thoughts racing.

"Could you let me know if you find out, please? I'll have to bring her down to the station to get a statement. I was going to call you in the morning about it anyway. It's actually pretty important to the case. We need confirmation about something. I can't really talk about it, but it's imperative that she cooperates with us on this one."

Zoey's breath caught in her throat. "She's not in trouble, is she?" She could picture Isla being led off in handcuffs, Zoey's mascara running down her pale cheeks. Her heart skipped a beat.

"No, nothing like that. Don't worry—I'll tell you if there's anything you need to be concerned about."

She exhaled with relief. "Thank goodness for that. Since tomorrow is Saturday, she'll have to miss running club, but I'll bring her in first thing."

"Thank you," Toni replied. "Now, what are the chances I can get you out on the dance floor tonight? I think this song is calling our name."

Chapter Twenty

SATURDAY

5TH NOVEMBER

The loaner Stella got from the mechanic's shop was an old hatchback with one brake light not functioning and a funny, dank smell that could only be resolved by opening all the windows. The man at the garage only offered to lend her the car for ten days, then promptly informed her the repairs might take two to three weeks. When she asked him what she was supposed to do for transportation after ten days, the man had shrugged and said it wasn't his problem.

Thankfully, it was a warm November day, so they didn't mind having the windows down. But it threatened rain, and she'd kept Katie home from school with a fever. She didn't want to sit around the flat all day though, working. It was hard to focus with everything else that was going on. So when she'd finished responding to the onslaught of emails in her inbox, she'd grabbed their raincoats, slung her purse over her shoulder, and clapped her hands together. Using her most cheery voice, she'd roused Katie from where she lay sprawled on her favourite pink beanbag in front of an episode of *Bluey*.

"Hey, chickadee! Let's go out and get some chocolate milkshakes."

"Milkshakes?" Katie asked, sitting up slowly but not taking her little blue eyes off the screen.

"At a café. You love cafés, and you say we never go out for milkshakes. So, let's go crazy."

Katie tugged her attention away from the television screen and grinned. "Okay."

They drove around the corner at the end of the street, then down the steep hill to the main drag. Stella slowed to study the surf. It was wild, and the ocean a dark greyish-blue. White froth leapt from the shoreline, where the waves curled to the dark sand. Usually the beach glistened and glowed under the warm sunshine like so many jewels. But not today.

"I think we're gonna see a storm later," she murmured.

Katie was busy singing along to the music playing on the car's stereo system.

There were no parking spaces near the café, so they had to walk. By the time Stella had unbuckled Katie, whose teddy bear had gotten caught in her seat belt somehow (she claimed to have no idea how it could've happened, since she didn't touch the bear), fat raindrops had begun to patter on the car roof. Just before the seat belt finally loosened, Stella got her finger caught in it.

"We'll have to make a run for it," she said, studying the blood blister that'd formed on one side of her pointer finger.

"What's wrong, Mummy?"

"I pinched my finger. It'll be okay. Let's go."

They threw on their raincoats. Yellow for Katie, which Stella said reminded her of a daisy. And black for Stella because she preferred a classic look, although Katie complained that Stella wore far too much black and why didn't she wear pink occasionally, since pink is pretty and black isn't?

Stella couldn't help agreeing with her on that point and decided the next time she went clothes shopping, she'd look for bright colours to please her petite but demanding daughter.

With hands joined, they ran for the café. The closer they got to the single-story fibreboard building set next to the beach, the heavier the rain fell. It pounded against the foot-path around them, flicked up against Stella's ankles when they crossed the street, and ran down her face, no doubt taking the last remnants of her makeup with it.

On the other side of the street, they scuttled along the uneven brick path to the café's front door. She pushed it open and followed Katie inside. The noise of the rain was duller there, but they dripped all over the entry floor.

Stella sucked on her sore finger while she glanced around the café looking for somewhere to sit. She saw an empty booth and ushered Katie to it after helping her out of her raincoat.

They sat across from each other. Stella pretended to read the menu while she watched Katie with hers. She was still so little. Sometimes Stella forgot how small she was because she'd grown so much, but her blonde hair still had the toddler fluff with a few wispy tendrils curling around her round cheeks. Her hands were still a little chubby, and she'd only stopped taking midday naps last year when she didn't want to sleep at kindy.

It'd been a long five years. When Katie was a baby, Stella had never felt so alone in all her life. She'd taken her to the community health centre to get weighed and joined a parenting group where stay-at-home mums sat around in a circle, bouncing their babies on their knees, and talked about the hardships of lack of sleep and breastfeeding while all Stella could think about was how she was going to keep a roof over their heads or afford enough food to eat. She couldn't talk to them about the things she lay awake at night worrying about —couldn't talk to anyone about it. They didn't know what to say, and she hated the look of pity in their eyes. Besides, they couldn't help her. No one could. She didn't want their help. She could do it alone.

Her parents had left her a little bit of money when they died. Not much, since most of it had gone to their medical care in their final years. But five thousand dollars had given her the boost she needed to move to Kingscliff and put down a rental deposit on a flat by the beach.

They'd lived off whatever income she could earn since then. Whatever they did, they did it alone. The two of them against the world.

"Chocolate milkshake?" Stella asked.

Katie chewed on her lower lip, studying the menu items closely. "Yes, please. And a piece of pink cake."

"Red velvet cake."

"Right. Red velvet cake."

"I'm not sure if you'll like that cake because it's very rich. But we can share it if you like."

Katie smiled, setting down the menu. "Okay."

Asher Lee walked over to their table, smiling and wiping his hands on the apron tied around his trim waist. He met Stella's gaze, his eyes warm and welcoming.

"You're back," he said. "Hi, Katie. How are you today?"

"I'm well, thank you."

"That's good to hear. What can I get you ladies?"

Stella ordered their food, then watched as Asher went from table to table, chatting with the customers, laughing with them, and generally making sure everyone was taken care of. Coming to Singles was the only time someone took care of

Stella. Usually it was her taking care of everyone else—Katie, Zoey, their clients. Keeping other people content was her life.

"Ah, this is my happy place," she mused.

Katie had brought one of her Barbies with her into the café and was vigorously wiping her dry with a napkin. "What's a happy place?"

"A place that makes you happy. You know, like you are with the beach. You love the sand between your toes, making sandcastles and swimming in the ocean."

"Oh, yeah. It *is* my happy place. But I'm happy when I'm with you too."

Stella smiled, her eyes misting with tears. "I feel the same way, chickadee." She reached across the table to stroke the hair out of Katie's eyes.

The door to the café opened, and a group of women tramped inside, laughing and shaking raindrops from elegant umbrellas. One of the women was Allegra Cowderoy, and Stella made eye contact with her. She wore a bright blue halter top and denim skirt, with platform wedges and an expensive brand of sunglasses perched on top of her head, covered in raindrops. Stella dropped her gaze to the table and did her best to be invisible.

"Hey, sweetheart," Stella began. "Why don't you run to the bathroom before our food gets here? You probably need to go, and then you can wash your hands."

Katie set her Barbie on the table and wriggled down from the booth. "I'm busting."

"Off you go, then."

The bathroom was only a few metres away from Stella in the back of the café. Katie ran into the bathroom and locked the door behind her.

Stella held the menu up in front of her. She pretended to be absorbed by the list of toasties on offer. Ham and cheese, prosciutto and pineapple, pepperoni and mozzarella with a dash of oregano. When she snuck a look around the menu, she saw that Allegra and her friends had filled a booth at the other end of the restaurant. Either Allegra hadn't recognised her, or she was intentionally avoiding her. Either way, Stella was grateful. Her heart jittered as the adrenaline that'd pumped through her veins when Allegra first walked into the café faded from her system.

Katie emerged from the bathroom and climbed into her seat. "Where is my milkshake?"

Stella offered her daughter a smile, doing her best to regulate her breathing. Was this how it would be now living here? She'd forever be anxious about running into the widow of the man she'd had an affair with. Not to mention petrified of anyone finding out he was Katie's father. She'd managed to keep it to herself. And now that he was gone, she'd prefer it stayed her little secret.

It made no sense to disrupt everyone's lives, Katie's especially, now that there was no chance of her getting to know her father. Guilt swept through Stella, and she thought for a moment she might throw up. If only she'd brought Katie back to Kingscliff sooner and introduced her to Mark on their first meeting. She couldn't have known this would happen, but when Katie learned about it later in life, would she forgive Stella for her mistakes or hold them against her forever?

Stella thought about her birth parents a lot. Wondered who they were. Where they were. Last week, she'd written an email to the adoption agency that'd handled her adoption. She hadn't heard back yet, but the tension of the wait rested firmly between her shoulder blades.

She wasn't sure she wanted to know, and on the other hand, she desperately wanted to find out where she'd come from. But what if they didn't want to know her? They'd given her up—clearly they didn't have positive feelings about including her in their lives at the time, but maybe they'd changed. People did change—she was sure of it. She'd certainly changed since Katie was born. She was a different person from the carefree, impulsive young woman she'd been then.

Asher brought their milkshakes and the cake on a plate with two forks.

"There you go," he said, placing everything on the table.

"Thank you," Stella said.

He nodded. "No worries." There was a dish towel hung casually over his shoulder. He tugged it loose and pulled it back and forth between both hands.

Stella took a sip of coffee. Was he waiting for her to say something? "Everything okay?"

"It'll be okay, you know? I'm sure it seems bad right now, but it'll all die down and things will go back to normal before you know it. Don't let it upset you too much."

"You think people will forget?" Stella's eyes filled with tears. She blinked them away.

"Of course they will. It was an accident."

"I know that's not what people are saying."

"I'll set them straight. Anyone who knows you knows the truth. Now, enjoy your coffee and cake...oh, and your milkshake and cake." He beamed at Katie. "Let me know if you want some ice cream with it because I have a little left over from the milkshake and I don't know what to do with it."

Katie nodded vigorously. He left to get the ice cream while Stella did her best not to cry. She wasn't used to kindness. Not from someone she barely knew. She'd spent her life learning to be tough, not to show emotion, not to expect any help from anyone.

You have to look out for yourself. That's what Dad used to say. Even when he was driving, he'd shout that he didn't trust a single other driver on the road. *Keep your eyes open. Don't trust them. They're all looking out for number one. They won't be thinking of you.*

And so far in life, his words had mostly rung true. Until she met Zoey. She kept waiting for Zoey to walk into the office one day and tell her she'd made a mistake, Stella didn't belong there at all, and the job had been intended for someone else but she'd mixed up their phone numbers.

Please leave, Zoey would say, hands pressed to her hips, expression fierce. *You don't belong here.*

But it never happened. Zoey continued to go to work with a smile, to show Stella kindness, to praise her work and encourage her to keep going. She'd even suggested that Stella attend the local university to complete her degree in interior design. It'd take her about eight years at the rate she was going, but she'd started.

She never would've considered doing it if Zoey hadn't pushed her and agreed to pay the tuition. But now, with the accident and Mark's death, she could see it all beginning to unravel before her eyes. She'd be blamed for what'd happened, and the world she'd built for herself and Katie in Kingscliff would come crashing down around them both.

Chapter Twenty-One

MONDAY

7TH NOVEMBER

It wasn't snooping when it was in your own house. That's what Zoey told herself as she nosed through the bits and pieces that filled Isla's desk drawers. Why did a fifteen-year-old girl need to keep empty chip packets, torn pieces of paper, and half-finished sketches? It made absolutely no sense.

Would Zoey be sitting in a nursing home one day watching an episode of *Hoarders* only to see her own daughter featured on the show, blunt fringe tinged with grey? Or was it typical teen behaviour making it impossible for her to find anything she was looking for?

And what *was* she looking for, exactly? She shoved the drawer closed and leaned against it, puffing slightly from the exertion. Had she lost all trust in her daughter? She didn't object to searching Isla's room on principle. In fact, she believed every parent had a right to do just that. But she'd never felt the need before. Until a few years ago, she'd cleaned Isla's room for her once a week. She asked Isla to tidy up after herself each evening, and Zoey did a weekly deep clean that involved going through every drawer and cupboard. Still, she hadn't done that for about two years, ever since Isla had grown old enough to manage her own mess herself.

Zoey slid down onto her hands and knees and tugged on the drawers at the base of Isla's bed one by one. Each was stuffed full of clothing of every kind. Leggings, shorts, T-shirts, and jumpers were jammed in, scrunched up and spilling out all over the place. She pushed the clothing aside, searching in each corner, shaking out each item and folding it back neatly into place. But Isla would know as soon as she opened the drawers that Zoey had been through them if they were neatly folded, so she took them out again, messed them up, and returned them in the same roughshod manner they'd been packed into the drawers before.

She was on the third drawer when she found the pack of joints. There were a half dozen of them, hand rolled and sealed in a baggie. She stared at them in disbelief, then fell back onto her rear end and leaned against the wall, eyes glassy.

It'd been with so much confidence that she'd declared Isla's innocence. After all, she was the good girl. The one who acted in the school musicals, who came home with the outstanding report cards year after year. She didn't lie. Didn't bring boys home to the house. And she certainly wouldn't smoke pot. It was possible Zoey didn't know anything at all about her daughter.

* * *

"I've been too preoccupied with this business," she moaned to Dave later when they were getting ready for work.

Isla was downstairs eating breakfast. Zoey hadn't confronted her yet about what she'd found. They had all risen early—Mondays were a big day in their house. And since she'd made the excuse that she'd injured her ankle and couldn't possibly take Willow out that morning, Isla had done it for her. She might be a pothead, but she loved that dog even if she didn't feed or walk her most days.

Zoey slapped a palm to her forehead. "It's all my fault. None of this type of thing happened before I got back into designing. She had my full attention all day, every day. Now I'm busy racing around, looking after clients, fretting over rent and bills. And apparently, I have no idea what my child is up to."

Dave pulled on his socks. He sat on the blanket box at the foot of their bed, his expression grim. "Don't you think that perhaps you're overreacting a little bit?"

"No. You're under-reacting." She slumped onto the padded seat before her vintage dressing table with a grunt.

"You sound as though you're about to throw in the towel on the business you've spent years building. Please tell me that's not what you're doing now that I've agreed to invest."

She ran a brush through her hair as she regarded her reflection in the dressing table mirror. Her hair crackled and snapped with each violent stroke. "No, I'm not. Not really. Oh, I don't know what to think right now."

"We've put down a deposit on a very expensive venue for your posh soiree, and that caterer who you assured me was totally worth the exorbitant fee. Now you're telling me you might want to back out of the whole thing? And then what? What will you do?"

She set down the brush and flicked her hair over her shoulder. "I hadn't thought it through fully."

"Sweetheart, it's bad, I'll grant you that. But it's nothing we can't manage. She's been dishonest, she's interested in a boy, and she's experimenting. These are all things we can talk to her about and figure out together, as a family. I mean, we don't even know if the pot is hers. Maybe she's holding it for someone."

Zoey rolled her eyes. "Holding it for someone? You were the nerd in school, weren't you, honey? My poor naive husband."

He poked his chest out. "I might've been the nerd in school, but I'm the engineer now, aren't I?"

She laughed. "Yes, you are. But seriously, what are we going to do about this? And Toni wants me to bring Isla down to the police station this morning to make a statement. I don't even know what it's about. Do you think we need to call our solicitor?"

"He only does real estate contracts for us."

She chewed the end of a fingernail. "True, but maybe he'll know someone who can help."

"I don't know. I think you should go down there and cooperate. After all, our fifteen-year-old daughter might be capable of a lot of things we didn't think she was, but I don't think she's capable of killing a full-grown man with a flowerpot. Right?"

He had a point. If they were looking for someone with the upper body strength to cave in a man's skull with a terracotta pot, she doubted that their petite teen would be the one. "Besides," she continued his thought, "what possible motive could she have had?"

"Exactly."

"And Toni told me she'd be sure to advise if we had anything to be concerned about."

"So, let's not be concerned before we have to," he said. "We want the police to get to the bottom of this whole thing, so if there's anything we can do to help, we'll do it."

She nodded. "You're so right."

Chapter Twenty-Two

"Breakfast!" Toni called from the kitchen.

Ryker emerged, headphones in his ears, and slumped into a chair. She set a plate of eggs in front of him, then tapped her ear with a fingertip, and he peeled off his headphones so they hung around his neck. Then he reached for the salt.

"Big day ahead?" she asked.

He shrugged. "I guess. Exams begin next month, so we're revising. I've got a tonne of homework to do."

"Have you thought about the school dance yet?" she asked, pouring hot water over the instant coffee in her cup.

He looked glum. "Not really. I'm not going with anyone, if that's what you mean."

"Have you got someone in mind?" She sat across from him.

He wore his school uniform with the attitude of a disgruntled teen. His shorts were slung low around his narrow hips, and his hair was brushed to one side, partly obscuring his eyes. She noticed for the first time how much he looked like photographs of her father from when he was young. It brought a lump to her throat.

"Well, there is a girl...but she wouldn't go with me."

She reached for his hand. Miraculously, he didn't pull away. Sometimes he acted as though she was the enemy, but there were times like this when he was the small boy she remembered who needed her to tell him everything was going to be okay. He looked up at her, vulnerability in his brown eyes.

"Let me tell you a tip about girls, sweetheart. If you ask, they might say yes. But if you don't ask, they definitely won't."

He laughed. "That's not a tip."

"Yes, it is." She grinned. "I know it's scary to put yourself out there like that, but you can't look at it that way. You're a kind, handsome, fun boy. Any girl would be lucky to go to the dance with you. So, if she says no, you have to remember that she has a lot of other things going on in her life that you don't know about. And you can always go with a group."

He smiled and nodded. "Okay. Thanks, Mum." After a bite of eggs, he looked up at her. "What's going on with you and Rodger?"

"What do you mean?"

He shook his head. "Mum, I've been through this before. Remember? You and Dad..."

Was it happening all over again? Grief welled up in her throat, threatening to choke her. "I'm not sure." Her voice was small, broken.

"Are you getting a divorce?"

"No." She was adamant. "No, of course not. Sometimes married couples go through things. We've hit a rough patch, but we're going to work it out. We need some time, that's all."

He chewed on his toast, thoughtful. "So, you're going to talk about it?"

"Yes. I mean, I want to. It's hard to get a chance with Rodger at the moment. He's very busy."

"Hmmm," he replied, brows drawn low. "Maybe you should make time."

"You're right. We should. I'm going to."

"I want you to be happy, Mum."

She forced a smile. "I know. I'm happy-ish. Happy adjacent. Does that count?"

He laughed. "It's a start, I guess."

"You're a good boy," she said, reaching out to pat his arm. He wasn't five anymore. She should've come up with something better to say, but the words stuck in her swollen throat.

"You're kinda okay too."

Toni blinked back tears.

* * *

After Ryker left for school, Rodger came in. Sweat poured from his body, and he stopped at the sink to down a glass of water.

"Good run?" she asked, clearing the dirty dishes from the table.

He nodded and refilled the glass. "It's already a scorcher out there."

"Supposed to be hot for the rest of the week," she added.

He sipped this time, one hand pressed to his hip.

"I'm ready for work, which is basically a miracle." She laughed uncomfortably. "So, I thought maybe the two of us could stop at Singles for a coffee before work. We could pretend we're single all over again." The joke was lame and her delivery stilted. She wanted to roll her eyes at her own awkwardness, but instead she forced a smile.

He swallowed another gulp of water. "Sorry, can't. I'll be late if I do that."

She rinsed off the plates and loaded them into the dishwasher. "It's just that we haven't seen each other much lately, and I think we need to have a real conversation about what's going on."

"What's going on? What do you mean?"

"You know, between us."

"Everything's fine," he said. He had a way of making it seem as though she was comically overreacting to things. He'd play ignorant and give her a look that shouted, *You're being emotional and dramatic over nothing. Get a grip.* Only she wasn't. There was definitely something askew in their relationship. Nothing she could put her finger on. But there was a space between them that she'd filled for months with polite chitchat, that she'd ignored or pushed aside and tried to forget. But she couldn't anymore. They couldn't. She'd been here before and knew where it led, like Ryker said. If this marriage didn't work, she'd be the woman who was twice divorced.

With the first divorce, people could cluck their tongues and remark over how young they'd been and so different. That it wasn't surprising they couldn't make it work. After all, these things happened. But a second divorce—she knew how it'd go. People wouldn't excuse her the second time. They'd dip their heads and whisper together over finding the common denominator. Especially now that Malcolm had made it work with someone new. It'd be her fault, and no one would be able to convince them or her otherwise.

The fact was she didn't have the personality for marriage. Other people stayed married—their spouses loved them forever. But hers had an expiration date. There wasn't one particular thing she could point to as the reason for his love fading, but she knew it had. The same way Malcolm's had. And if the particulars were different, the common denominator was the same. It was her.

She steeled herself. "Everything isn't fine."

He huffed, set his glass in the dishwasher, and manoeuvred around her. "Don't be dramatic."

"I'm not being dramatic. You know I hate it when you say that. There's something wrong in our relationship, and if we don't talk about it, it'll only get worse. I want us to have good communication, to work on this relationship. We vowed to do that. Do you remember? I told you how hesitant I was to dive into another marriage, and you said, 'Don't worry—you and Malcolm didn't communicate enough, but we're going to make sure we talk about everything.' And when I replied, 'Everything?', you said, 'Absolutely everything.' Then you kissed me. We were standing on the steps leading down to Main Beach. I remember it like it was yesterday."

He crossed his arms. "I remember the conversation, but I don't know what you want me to say."

"Have coffee with me. We can talk like we used to. Spend some time together, laugh, have fun. We'll leave the serious conversation for later. I want to be with you."

He shook his head. "Not this morning. It's nothing to do with you—I have to get to school. I'm already running late because you've held me up. I don't have the kind of job where I can swan in at any time and sit down for a coffee at my desk while I scroll through Facebook. I'm a teacher, I'm busy, people rely on me to be where I say I'm going to be."

He spun on his heel, marched to the bathroom, and flipped on the shower.

She raced after him, her head light with fury. "I can't believe you said that."

He shrugged out of his clothes and stepped into the shower. "Sorry, can't talk. No time."

She stayed there a few moments longer, hands clenched into fists at her sides. How dare he suggest that she wasn't as committed to her job as him, or that her job was somehow easier because she didn't have to open the classroom at eight a.m. sharp.

"I didn't finish work until eleven last night!" she shouted in his direction, but he showed no sign that he'd heard her.

With a grunt of anger, she stormed out of the flat and down to the parking garage. Rodger's sports car sat in the space beside hers, fresh from the mechanics with new tyres, fancy hub cabs, a stereo she assumed would shake the foundations, and a glistening red paint job. She pressed the end of her key to his door for a moment, thought twice, then stepped away from the car. Her anger faded.

Had he already given up on them? She didn't recognise the person he'd become. He used to adore her. Was she so unlovable?

Chapter Twenty-Three

"Thank you for coming in, Isla. I really appreciate it. This shouldn't take long."

"Okay." Isla sat opposite Toni at the table, clenching her hands together. Her knuckles whitened, and her face was pale.

Zoey had brought Isla to the station to give her statement. These kinds of interviews always made Toni feel a little awkward. Isla was a child. She hated to pressure her into talking. But she was old enough that something she said might end up being invaluable to the case. Toni couldn't overlook that. So she straightened in her chair and cleared her throat.

"Can you tell me about the night Mark Cowderoy died? It could really help us out with the case. Did you see him that night?"

Isla swallowed. "Yes, I saw him."

Toni shifted her gaze to the sheet of notes on the table. She wanted Isla to feel comfortable, to talk openly. But she could see the girl was stressed. The question was—why? Was it normal nervousness over being in a police station, or was there more to it? Did she know something? “Do you have any idea who might’ve killed him?”

“I honestly have no idea who killed Mr Cowderoy,” Isla blurted, her cheeks reddening. “I promise, Auntie Toni. I was outside with Ben at around eight o’clock, smoking. At least I think it was eight o’clock. I’m not sure, though, since we didn’t keep track of the time. Mr Cowderoy came into the yard and took one of our joints and smoked with us for a few minutes.”

“So he was with the two of you?” Toni arched an eyebrow.

Isla nodded. “It was pretty awkward. I thought for sure he’d come over to confiscate the pot and call my mum. I don’t know why he didn’t. He seemed to want to hang for a little while, but he was fine when he left us. We didn’t stick around —as soon as he left, Ben rode his bike home, and I went inside and locked the door. I was scared he’d call Mum. But the next day, nothing happened. Well, nothing happened until Mum screamed.”

Chapter Twenty-Four

FRIDAY

11TH NOVEMBER

Going anywhere on a school night used to be a mission of epic proportions. Zoey remembered those days with a certain fondness mixed with an element of joy that they were behind her. These days she could go out, child-free, without having to give it much thought. She'd put the slow cooker on that morning with the ingredients for taco soup, and it'd simmered on the kitchen bench all day. The house was filled with the delectable scents of a Mexican restaurant.

She leaned through the doorway to Isla's bedroom. "I'm heading out. You're okay to serve the soup later? I'm not sure when Dad will be home, but you stay in the house, please. You're still grounded, and you have that assignment to finish. You have everything you need here, and I've got my phone."

Isla smiled and shifted her reading glasses to her forehead

as she spun in her seat to meet Zoey's gaze. "I'll take care of it, Mum. Don't worry. Soup, tortilla chips, and sour cream —right?"

"That's right. Thanks, honey. I won't be late. But please try to go to bed by nine if I'm not back yet."

"Okay." Isla waved goodbye.

Zoey kissed Isla, then skipped downstairs to the garage a free woman.

It was miraculous that she could simply drive away without a care. For so many years, she'd been chained to the house while her daughter slept. She recalled going outside one evening and staring up at the moon in wonder, realising it'd been years since she'd stopped to look at it since she never left the house after dark—or at least, it felt that way. When she did leave the house, it was generally with Isla and she was in a rush, or her daughter was hungry or tired, or they were on their way to the emergency room with a broken finger.

She sighed as she backed the car down the drive, took one last glance at the house, then accelerated along the road. She'd promised to pick up Stella and Katie on the way, since Stella's car still wasn't fixed and the loaner had to be returned.

A prick of guilt flitted through her thoughts. Given everything going on with Isla, perhaps she should've told Stella she'd take her and Katie to the school musical performance, but couldn't stay. She could still do it—head home and pull out a board game, perhaps Scotland Yard. It'd been a favourite of Isla's when she was younger. They could spend the evening playing, talking, and laughing together. How long had it been since they'd done that—just the two of them?

She had to make more of an effort to be an attentive, present parent. She vacillated between feelings of extreme shame and guilt over not spending enough time, sans screens, with her child. And defending herself with inward shouts of *I'm a good mother! I spend plenty of quality time with my child!* while huffing over the absolute hide of anyone who might suggest otherwise. The fact that no one *had* suggested otherwise wasn't the point. If they did, she could clearly show, line by line, all of the times she'd been there for her kid and how much time she'd given her over the years.

By the time she'd reached Stella's flat, she'd talked herself down off the ledge and regained a sense of peaceful calm over her mothering skills and the state of their family. Just because Isla had hidden things from her and Dave was no indictment of their parenting skills. They were very loving parents, but Isla was a strong-willed child, and a teenager, and there wasn't anything anyone else could've done differently.

"Heya," she said as Katie and Stella climbed into the vehicle.

Katie sat in the back seat, straight and small, with a pink giraffe stuffed beneath one arm. "Hi."

"Hey, Zoey. Thanks so much for doing this. You're a lifesaver. I truly didn't want to walk in this humidity. It's not too far, but we would've both been a sweaty mess by the time we got there."

"I'm glad to help. Nothing worse than when your car is out of commission. Are we going for prima donna status tonight, Katie? Standing ovation, here we come."

Katie blinked.

Zoey laughed. "No? Never mind—maybe next time. Everyone strapped in?"

Stella chuckled. "Let's see if we can get her to go on stage. That's all I ask." She handed Katie a pair of headphones, and the girl put them on.

"Some calming music," Stella explained.

"A bit nervous?" Zoey whispered as they drove.

Stella nodded. "She likes to be with me. Anything less is an utter disappointment in her eyes."

"Ahhh, I see. Well, it won't last forever."

"That's what they tell me." Stella smoothed her skirt over her long, lean legs.

"And don't let anyone bully you into believing you've got to fix it this instant. It's not something to be fixed. It's a normal part of being a five-year-old. She's still so little."

"I know," Stella replied. She seemed so together, always dressed perfectly, stylishly, but without any garish addictions like sequins or chunky jewellery. Classic beauty—that's how her mother would've put it. Stella was a classic beauty with her long, straight red hair, her porcelain skin, and her athletic physique. But there was a glimmer of tears in her eyes when Zoey glanced her way.

She patted Stella's leg. "They grow up so fast. I mean, look at me—I'm out on the town while Isla is at home doing her homework."

"On her own?" Stella asked.

"I'm not worried. It's one of the benefits of having a teenager. Before you know it, that'll be you and Katie. So don't let the small stuff bother you too much. You should take all the time you and Katie need for each stage."

"Thanks. I think I needed to hear that. All the other mums seem to have it totally figured out, and here I am, every morning at school, letting the teacher wrestle Katie from my arms while she clings to my neck screaming. It's hard..." Her voice broke. "I feel so guilty. All she wants is to be with me, and I want that too. But she has to go to school, and I've got to work. I don't know what else to do."

Zoey pulled into a parking space outside the school and set the car in park. They sat like that, in silence, for a few minutes with Katie humming out of tune to the music in her headphones.

"That's how parenting is," Zoey said suddenly, running her fingers through her hair in exasperation. "It's beautiful and messy and scary at times. It can leave you feeling spent, dizzy, and guilty, but then sometimes it brings so much unexpected joy that it bowls you over. None of us can escape the guilt or the sorrow, the pain or the frustration, as much as we might like to. It's all part of being a parent."

Stella sniffled.

Zoey searched the glove box for a packet of tissues and handed them to Stella.

"I wish we could check the box that says *only the good parts of parenting, please.*"

Zoey laughed. "Wouldn't that be great?"

"So, it's normal? Because it doesn't feel normal."

Zoey reached for Stella's hand and squeezed it. "It's completely normal. There's no right way to go about any of this. You and Katie have to figure it out for yourselves. But I will say it again—it doesn't last. None of it—the good or the bad. Everything changes."

"You seem like you've got it all together. Mum of the Year. The century." Stella blinked away the tears, smiling.

Zoey snorted. "Hardly. I don't even want to talk about it right now, but next time we grab some coffee, I'll fill you in."

Toni tapped on the car window, and Zoey opened it, squinting into the last rays of a purple sunset. "What are you doing here? I didn't know you were coming."

Toni shrugged. "Trying to be a supportive wife. Rodger's one of the teachers running the musical."

"He asked you to come? That sounds like progress."

"Nope. He didn't. I came anyway. I'm doing my best, but he's making it ridiculously hard."

"I'm sorry, honey. Oh, hey, you know Stella. Her daughter is in the show." She leaned back in her seat so Toni could see Stella.

Stella dabbed her eyes with a tissue. "Hi, Toni."

"Good to see you again, Stella." Toni arched an eyebrow at Zoey, who shrugged.

Whatever Toni was indicating, Zoey had no idea. She didn't understand her friend so much of the time, though, that she was used to it. Toni had her own way of viewing the world, and Zoey often felt as though they were communicating on entirely different planes.

"We're going to see if we can find Katie's class. I'll see you out there," Stella said.

She and Katie headed inside hand in hand. Zoey climbed out of the car and fluffed her hair in the side mirror.

"What was that about?" she asked.

Toni watched Stella and Katie making their way up the footpath towards the kindergarten classrooms. "She's a suspect in my investigation. It's a little awkward, that's all."

"Pffft," Zoey said with a wave of her hand. "Stella didn't do anything. She's the sweetest woman in the whole world."

"Regardless of her *sweet* factor, I'm still a police officer and have to investigate every lead."

Toni looked so unofficial dressed in her full, colourful skirt with a plain white singlet top, her long ponytail hanging over one shoulder. Zoey slung her handbag over her arm. "If you're going to avoid everyone who's a suspect in a town this size, you'll run out of friends very quickly."

Toni smirked.

"You do your investigation, but remember—you have to live in this town even after it's over, and since you and I are lifelong friends, it's very likely you and Stella will be as well."

They walked up the footpath towards the school hall, joining throngs of parents, all dressed up and all heading in the same direction with small children in tow. One boy, a toddler dressed in a Spider-Man suit, threw himself on the ground and let out an almighty scream, legs kicking. A father picked him up, flung him over his shoulder, and kept walking. The boy continued kicking and screaming. Toni and Zoey overtook the family, power walking to get ahead.

"Let's hurry so we can get the best seats," Zoey said, picking up her pace.

"I'm not sure it matters if we don't actually have children participating," Toni huffed along beside her. "Did you say life-long friends?" She grinned. "I thought I annoyed you no end."

Zoey pretended to ignore her. "So, do you know who did it yet?"

Toni's cheeks flamed. "A little louder, why don't you?"

"What? Everyone's wondering the same thing."

"That's why I think it's probably best if we don't discuss the case in public settings," Toni said as they found their way to a trio of empty seats in the fifth row.

The plastic chairs were pushed together until the metal legs touched. There was very little space in front and behind, and no space between them. They filled the hallway in long yellow rows, with parents squeezing themselves together as best they could.

"Oooffff." Zoey squashed past a man whose eyes were glued to his phone and sat next to Toni. She set her purse on the empty chair beside her.

"This is a little bit cosy," Toni said, glancing around.

A plump woman sat on the other side of Toni, her floral dress spilling over onto Toni's leg. Toni shifted in place to give her room until she was almost in Zoey's lap. Zoey glared at her and raised her hands in surrender. "Really? You should buy me dinner first."

Toni bit her lip to keep from laughing. "I can't help it. This woman is squashing me," she hissed.

Zoey leaned over to look, shook her head, and leaned back. "Don't you think whoever put out the chairs might've considered the fact that grown adults were going to be in the audience?"

"Let's not make a fuss. I don't want to upset Rodger," Toni said, shushing Zoey with a finger to her lips. Rodger reigned at the front of the room directing students to their places. He peered at them with a stern expression.

Zoey rolled her eyes. "Are they serving wine yet?" She wove about in her chair, scanning the perimeter of the hall.

"It's a primary school. I think you can manage without a glass of wine for a couple of hours."

Zoey arched an eyebrow. "A couple of hours? Is it that long? I'd forgotten what these things were like. But now it's all coming back to me in a rush of panic and sweaty armpits. Oh, wow—I can't believe I have to sit through two hours of other people's children singing off pitch without wine."

"I knew I shouldn't sit with you. It's like being friends with a very large, squirmy child. Please be an adult for two hours. I'm going to have to move if you can't shush."

"Nice," Zoey said before crossing her eyes and poking out her tongue.

Toni stifled a giggle. "I'm going to get in trouble with the teacher, and it's all your fault. It's like I'm back in primary school."

Stella showed up at the end of their aisle and shuffled her way through the narrow opening to her seat. Zoey removed her purse, and Stella sat with a grunt.

"How'd she go?" Zoey asked.

Stella sighed. "Don't ask. Did anyone bring a drink?"

"Oh, for heaven's sake." Toni threw her hands in the air. "Now I see why you two are friends. You're as bad as each other."

"What?" Stella questioned. "What did I say?"

Zoey burst into laughter, then covered her mouth with both hands to muffle the sound. She composed herself. "Stop it, or I'll pee my pants. I had a very big smoothie for dinner before I left the house. Both of you behave yourselves."

"Meal replacements again?" Stella asked with an arched

eyebrow. "You know those things aren't good for you. Full of processed junk."

"Leave me alone. It gives me the illusion that I'm doing something healthy, and I love my carefully constructed world of illusions. Besides, I've gained five kilos, if you can believe it."

"You shouldn't worry about weight. It's just a number. What's more important is how you feel, how much energy you have, how strong you are." Stella crossed one thin leg over the other as the lights were dimmed.

Zoey was about to reply with a smart comment about Stella's perfectly trim figure when someone opened the back doors to the hallway. It was dark inside, but outside the last remnants of the sunset illuminated the climbing equipment in the kindergarten playground. Leaned up against the edge of a blue plastic slide was her daughter. She stood with one foot cocked, hair flowing over her shoulders, with a boy's head blocking Zoey's view of her face. They were definitely kissing. Rage crawled up Zoey's spine.

"Don't wait for me. I've got to kill someone," she hissed, standing hunched over to creep past Toni and the woman in the floral dress.

"Please don't tell me your intentions before you commit a crime," Toni whispered after her.

Zoey waved but didn't respond. Her anger was focused on the back doors, which had swung shut. Isla had played innocent earlier, and Zoey had been so certain her daughter was pondering her mistakes and learning from them. But now, she was there, at the school, frolicking on the playground with her boyfriend. And where on earth was Dave in all this? Had she imagined the whole thing? It seemed more and more likely the closer she got to the exit that she'd misinterpreted what she saw. It didn't make sense that Isla and Ben were there. Isla knew she was at the musical—why would she risk being seen? It must've been someone else.

Chapter Twenty-Five

Zoey pushed through the back doors of the school hall, gathering steam as she went. The playground was empty. Long shadows drew cool shapes across the springy rubber underfoot. She stopped at the plastic slide and scanned the school grounds. Whoever it was she'd seen standing there couldn't have gotten far in that short amount of time.

There they were. Walking together on the other side of the road.

She half-walked, half-ran at them, nodding and smiling and slowing her pace whenever she passed a parent headed to the hall. When she reached them, she was puffing slightly but grateful for all the hours of kickboxing and Pilates sessions she'd done at the gym over the past few years. Five years ago, if she'd run even half as far, she'd have had to stand, bent over, blowing for a full minute before she could've spoken to anyone. Instead, she was ready to whisper-yell at her daughter the first moment she was close enough to be heard without making a public spectacle.

"Isla Rose Winton!" she hissed.

Isla stepped away from Ben and almost collided with the chain-link fence.

"What are you doing here?" Zoey stopped in front of her daughter and stabbed the air with a finger.

Isla pushed aside her panic with a look of innocence. "I wanted to see Ben."

"We had an agreement. You are grounded, and while I was out, you were meant to be doing your homework. Where does your father think you are?"

"I guess in my room."

"In your room." Zoey shook her head. These types of moments were the aspect of parenting she most dreaded. She hated having to confront her child. And even though she'd thought about what she'd do in this situation, and she'd considered consequences in advance and written out plans on a neat yellow notepad in her office about how she'd tackle teenaged insolence, she still had no idea what to say or do.

She always blustered her way through with a lot of stern looks and serious-voice monologues about trust. But in reality, she never knew quite what to say or do to sufficiently discipline her daughter without going over the top or breaking their relationship connection—something she'd learned about from Doctor Mariah in her parenting podcast. Apparently the relationship connection was the only thing keeping her daughter from a life of crime and she had to protect it at all costs. It was terrifying.

"The thing I don't understand is, if you're going to sneak out and expect not to be caught, why on earth would you come to the same place as me? You knew I was here." She shouldn't be giving her daughter advice on how to sneak out of the house, but she was flummoxed. Did Isla intend to be caught breaking her grounding? Or was she far more simple-minded than Zoey had ever realised? Either way, the ramifications were more far-reaching than this one interaction, and she wasn't entirely sure she wanted to know the answer. Was her daughter a possible sociopath with no apparent concern about parental discipline, or a few sandwiches short of a picnic basket?

Isla blushed. "Ben's brother is in the musical. He's supposed to be inside and couldn't get away for long. We haven't seen each other in ages."

"Apart from school, right?" Already Zoey's anger was fading. She did her best to buoy her outrage, but it was sinking like a popped balloon.

"Ben's going to a private school in Tweed Heads now. His parents found out about..."

"The pot," Zoey offered, one eyebrow arched.

"Yeah," Ben piped up, his hands pushed deep into his pockets. "Sorry, Mrs Winton."

Ben's blondish fringe swept across his forehead, obscuring two green eyes. Freckles were smattered over his nose. He was tall and skinny, and wore pants that looked as though they might've fallen to the ground if he wasn't holding them up by the pockets.

Zoey sighed. "So, you haven't seen each other at school, and you thought this was a good chance to catch up?"

Isla nodded. "Sorry, Mum."

"I wish you'd talked to me instead of sneaking out. I can't have you being dishonest. Especially after everything that's happened. You know that. How many times have I talked to you about having integrity?"

"A billion."

Zoey wanted to laugh, but she held it together. Her daughter was infuriating and beautiful and perfect and sneaky and so very stubborn. She was proud of her feisty spirit and worried about her falling into a life of crime all at the same time.

"So..."

"I get it. I won't do it again."

"And if you two want to see each other, you can talk to me about it after your grounding is over. I don't want any more of this dishonesty." She pointed her finger at them one at a time.

"Okay," Ben said.

"Fine," Isla added.

"Now, you're coming home with me, and I don't want to hear a word about it. Ben, it's nice to meet you."

Ben offered her a crooked smile.

"Actually, before we go, there's something I wanted to talk to you about." She explained to him about their neighbour's murder and how he and Isla might've been the last people to see him alive.

Ben's eyes widened. "I heard that a guy was killed, but I didn't realise it was him."

"It was, and I know the police are looking for anyone who might know something. Did you see him that night?"

He exchanged a look with Isla, who nodded. "She knows."

"Yes, I know that you were at my house."

"Okay... Well, yeah, we saw him. We were smoking..." Another look passed between the two of them. "Sorry, and well, he came looking for us. Said he smelled it through the fence and asked if we had one to spare. I figured he'd tell if we didn't share, so I gave him a joint."

Zoey was thrilled to hear that her murdered neighbour had shared a joint with her fifteen-year-old daughter and her secret boyfriend before he died. She couldn't wait to add the anecdote to her Christmas letter next month.

"Wonderful," she said. "And then?"

"He smoked with us. He was a funny guy. We chatted about hiking and camping—he seemed to like those things, and I was in Boy Scouts for years. It felt a bit strange to have him there at first, but he was cool."

Isla stared at the grass at her feet, not contributing anything to the conversation.

"Then what did he do?"

"Some guy called out, and I guess he went home. He stamped out his joint and left through the gate the way he'd come."

"A guy called him? Did you see who it was?"

"No, I think it was someone at his front door. He banged on the door a few times then shouted 'Allegra, Allegra, where are you?' He looked confused, but not worried or anything. Then he left."

"Did you see or hear anything after that?"

He shrugged. "Nope. Nothing. He said something to the guy, and they went inside. I don't know what he said. I couldn't hear it."

Zoey crossed her arms. "I think the police would like to talk to you about that. I'm sure it'll help them out. Do you think you could ask your parents to take you down to the station tomorrow? You should talk to Detective Antonia Kauffman."

He agreed. They said their goodbyes and headed back to where Zoey had parked the car.

"Do you think it'll help Auntie Toni?" Isla asked.

Zoey wrapped an arm around Isla's shoulders. "I have no idea. But it might."

"Are you going to watch the rest of the musical?"

"No, I think I'm going to take you home so I can see the expression on your father's face when he realises you haven't been in the house this whole time."

"Mum..." she complained. "Don't do that. He's going to freak."

"Oh, yes, he is," Zoey said with a grin. "Consequences, honey. Everything we do, good or bad, has consequences."

Chapter Twenty-Six

SUNDAY

13TH NOVEMBER

Frozen fish fingers and potato gems weren't much of a dinner. On the plate, beside the warmed-up peas and corn from the freezer, it looked downright pathetic. But it'd been one of Ryker's favourite meals when he was small. They used to eat it every Sunday night. He'd dip each fish finger carefully in tomato sauce and then take such big bites, she'd have to beg him not to choke. Every single time.

Now, he ate them like he was doing her a favour.

"You still like these, right?" she asked, setting down her fork.

He grunted. "Huh?"

"Fish fingers... Yes or no?"

He shrugged. "They're okay, I guess."

"Sorry, I should've made more of an effort."

"It's okay, Mum. I don't mind."

"Have you got everything packed to go back to Dad's?"

He smiled. There was a smear of tomato sauce on the corner of his mouth. "Yep. My bag's on my bed all ready to go. He should be here any minute."

"I'm going to miss you." She wiped the tomato sauce away with a napkin.

He pulled away. "I'll miss you too. But I'm ready to go home."

Home.

The word hit her like a mallet to the gut. She leaned back in her chair, heart heavy, and watched him eat. Her own appetite was gone.

"This is your home too, you know?"

His eyes betrayed the realisation of what he'd said. "Yeah, I know. I didn't mean it..."

"It's okay. You don't have to feel bad. Everything that's happened is my fault, not yours."

His shoulders sagged. "Don't say that, Mum."

She rested a hand on his. "I'm sorry. Is it so bad here?"

"It's not your fault. There's nothing wrong with being here. Only, I like being at Dad and Sandi's because you work so much, I hardly see you. Rodger's never here. And when I'm there, I'm not so alone. There's always noise and people about. Sandi stays at home with the little kids, so when I get home, she makes cupcakes or muffins, and she talks to me while I do my homework. Dad likes to watch football replays with me, and we work on setting up our fishing poles for the weekend. We listen to music and talk. Stuff like that."

He was right. Why would she expect him to feel any differently? Malcolm and Sandi had set up their home to be like a real-life version of the Brady Bunch. She lived in this sterile flat with a man who barely spoke to either of them. She worked long hours, and she left Ryker alone to do his homework. Whenever she offered to play a board game or asked him to go for a walk on the beach, he always turned her down. She wasn't sure what else to do, but clearly, she was doing it all wrong. "You're lonely here?" she asked.

He sighed. "Aren't you?"

While they finished eating, she thought about what he'd said. It broke her heart to imagine him sitting in the flat alone while she and Rodger were out working, meeting friends, or whatever else was going on in her husband's life. The musical was over—it'd gone well. She'd been proud of the effort he'd put into the show and the children. She'd told him so, and they'd celebrated with Ryker over dinner on Saturday night—fish and chips at the beach.

But it wasn't enough. None of it was enough to make up for all the things Ryker had missed out on because of her. She'd struggled for so long with depression and anxiety after Ryker was born, then again after her first marriage crumbled and Malcolm left her, that she didn't have enough of herself left to give to him. Depression was something she'd lived with since she was a teen, off and on. She'd easily climb back into it like a well-worn sleeping bag when things didn't go her way or life got too hard. When Malcolm had married Sandi and when Sandi had fallen pregnant the first time, it'd sent Toni spiralling yet again. But she'd pulled herself out of it and studied for the detective's examination. It was her work that gave her reason to get up every morning, that kept the darkness at bay.

After dinner, Ryker went to his room to finish his homework, and Toni sat outside on the porch with a glass of wine while she waited for Malcolm to come in his perfect car, from his perfect suburban home, where his perfect wife and two children were waiting for his return. He'd take her son back with him to that nirvana, and she'd be left here all alone wondering where her husband was.

The night was cool, with no humidity and a slight breeze

off the ocean. She could see the sparkle of the moon's rays against the surging sea in the distance between two tall conifers. The beach was a short walk from their flat, one of the main reasons she and Rodger had rented it. She'd always wanted to live by the beach. After Malcolm and Sandi moved to Kingscliff, she'd remained behind in Sydney for her job. But when the chance of a transfer came her way, she couldn't resist the offer to live close to Ryker. It'd been the best decision she'd ever made. She was stronger, healthier, wiser than before, and they'd rebuilt their relationship one brick at a time. But tonight, it felt as though he'd taken a hammer to those bricks. She felt them crumbling around her.

Malcolm's Volkswagen parked in front of the block of flats. He climbed out and waved to her before jogging to the door. She buzzed him in and set her empty wine glass on the sink.

"Your dad's here!" she called.

There was a knock at the door. She opened it with a forced smile. "Hi, Mal. Come on in. He'll be right out."

"Thanks," Malcolm said, stepping inside. "How did you go?"

"Fine. And you?"

"Good thanks. Did he get his history assignment done?"

"I believe he did."

"Glad to hear it. Hey, while we're waiting, there's something I wanted to tell you."

"Oh?" She sat on the arm of the couch, hands crossed in her lap.

"Sandi's pregnant," he said.

A stone wedged itself in her throat. "Wow. Congratulations, Mal."

"Thanks. It's amazing. A bit of a surprise, but we're over the moon. Three kids."

"Four," she corrected.

"Right, four total."

After they left, Toni went back out on the porch with the wine glass and the rest of the bottle. She propped her feet up on the railing, leaned back in the chair, and stared at the moon and stars overhead. She was a very small person in a very big universe.

After a few sips of wine, she went back inside to get the case file she'd brought home from the office. She flipped through it, running over the details in her mind. She'd tried in vain to get more resources assigned to the case. They didn't have the funds or the staff, she'd been told. So, she'd spent weeks now interviewing potential witnesses, watching hours and hours of security tape footage with Callum beside her. They'd eaten fast food, stayed up until all hours, and wasted time on leads that went nowhere.

A man across the street thought he heard a motorbike outside the victim's house at the time of the murder, but it turned out to be a teen with a beach buggy who'd stopped to check for a flat tyre. There were footprints in a nearby flowerbed, but they'd soon discovered the prints belonged to the homeowner who'd forgotten her key and climbed in a window instead. And after speaking to the airline, she'd discovered that Allegra Cowderoy had changed her flight to a later time on the Monday night. So her alibi no longer covered the time of her husband's murder.

Every day, her pool of suspects seemed to grow rather than shrink. She was missing something. There had to be a clue that was the key to unlocking the mystery of what happened that night. And she wouldn't give up until she found it.

Chapter Twenty-Seven

MONDAY

12TH NOVEMBER

"Haven't we watched this one already?" Callum asked with a yawn.

He balanced his chair on two legs, feet pressed to the edge of the table in the conference room.

"Nope. Not this one. It's the one from 22 Runham Place. You're thinking of 24 Runham."

"It looks exactly the same." He pushed a handful of popcorn into his mouth.

"It's almost exactly the same, but if there's something integral to the case on this video and we don't watch it, we're the ones who'll be in trouble. So stop your whining."

She kicked the legs of his chair, and he shouted as he plunged back to the ground. "And stop doing that. You'll end up hurting yourself."

"Sorry, Mum," he said with a grin.

She laughed. "Is this the last of the footage?"

He nodded. "I believe so. The uniforms gathered everything they could find in the neighbourhood."

"This one shows the front of the victim's house from a slightly different angle," she added. "Remember in the last one, we couldn't see that streetlamp because there was another house blocking it?"

"I remember it. Let's watch and see if there's anything new from this angle. Oh, by the way, Chelsea asked if we could go to the movies tonight after work."

"You should go. Although personally, I'll be staying away from screens for a while. I think the footage has burned itself into my retinas. I keep seeing blurred outlines of swaying trees and boring suburban houses every time I close my eyes."

Callum huffed. "I told her there was no way on God's green earth I wanted to watch a movie after this."

"So you're in trouble with the girlfriend, then?"

He laughed. "You know it. She's going out with the girls instead. Some chick flick she wants to see."

Toni rolled her eyes. "If you ever decide to get married, you're going to have to up your game."

"Isn't it the other way around?"

She slapped him on the arm. "Not if you want it to work."

"How about you? How's Rodger and Ryker?"

She pressed play on the video, then sat back with her elbows on the table to watch. "It's okay, I guess. Ryker basically told me last night that he prefers living with his stepmother than with me."

"Ouch."

"I know. I'm struggling with all of it today. I mean, I get it. Sandi's nice, as much as it kills me to admit that. And they have kids, so he's not alone. They're having another one, by the way."

"Wow, they don't waste any time." Callum offered her a sympathetic look. "I'm sorry, Boss."

She shrugged. "Whatcha gonna do?"

"That's hard, though."

"And he's not wrong—he said that Rodger and I are never home. Which is true these days. So when he's over, he spends a lot of time on his own."

"What does he do?"

"I'm not sure. I know he goes out with his skateboard a lot. There's a skate park down the road, and he's made some friends there."

"I know the place."

"Other than that, I guess he does homework and watches YouTube videos or something. But he said that at Sandi and Malcolm's house, she sits with him while he does homework and bakes him muffins."

"Wow. Kind of hard to compete with that, I guess."

"I don't know how to be that kind of mum. It's not me. Plus, I have a job. I can't be at home baking muffins while there's a murderer out there."

Callum rubbed a hand over his chin. "Not sure you can do much about that. Don't be so hard on yourself. I mean, it's good he has a nice family to go to—better than the alternative. Don't you think?"

"You're right. I'm only thinking of myself. I'm glad for him, that he has a family who loves him and he's happy there. If he left my place to go somewhere that made him miserable or with a mean stepmother, I don't know if I could handle that."

"He's a good kid, and some of that is what Malcolm and Sandi have done. It's hard, but maybe try to see them as part of your family too. You're all aiming for the same thing."

She nodded. "True. I should be grateful to them. Only, it's hard not to wish I had what they've got."

"But you'd go mad." Callum chuckled. "It's not exactly your personality to bake muffins and skip around the kitchen in an apron while the kid does homework. Is it?"

She grimaced. "Heck, no."

"So?"

"So, I should be myself instead."

"That's what I do." Callum grinned.

"You mean, a misogynist who serially dates the most beautiful women in town and then dumps them when things get serious?"

He raised his hands in mock surrender. "Come on. You make it sound so much worse than it is."

She laughed, fast-forwarding the tape. Something on the screen caught her eye. She stopped the tape and rolled it back, then played it again. "What's this?"

Callum squinted at the screen. "Is that a Pajero?"

"A silver one," Toni confirmed.

"I guess Betty got it wrong. She said it was a white SUV."

"We'll clean up the image and get a confirmation of the number plate. But I'd be willing to bet that's Stella Thompson's vehicle."

Callum clucked his tongue. "I clearly recall Miss Thompson telling us she'd never visited the victim."

"It wouldn't be the first time a suspect has lied to us in the interview room."

"I wonder what she was doing there," Callum murmured, leaning on the back of Toni's chair to stare at the still frame over her shoulder.

"Good question."

Callum picked up a handful of papers and flicked through them. He jabbed at one page with a fingertip. "Look, these are Allegra Cowderoy's mobile phone records. The victim's wife seems to have called Stella Thompson's phone number multiple times. But the calls are only a few seconds long each time."

"So Allegra hung up on her?"

"Or the other way around," Callum said.

"Kauffman!" Superintendent Evan Cowan barked. "My office."

"Yes, sir." She tucked her shirt into her pants.

"Wonder what that's about," Callum mused.

"Can only be one of three things—either we've run out of budget, he's firing me, or he wants me to put together this year's black and white ball."

Callum laughed. "Those are very specific."

"He's a specific kind of guy. I'll let you know how it goes tomorrow. Have a great night."

"You're sending me home early?"

She smiled. "We all deserve an early mark. Besides, we can deal with Stella tomorrow. She's not going anywhere. We've been working long hours, and I for one want to spend some time with my husband."

"You go, girl," Callum said, attempting to click his fingers as his hand zig-zagged across his torso. He was six feet tall and built like a tank. He looked utterly ridiculous and had the intended effect of making her laugh.

In Evan's office, she shut the door behind her and sat across the desk from him, waiting for him to speak. He finished typing something, then steepled his hands on the desk.

"How's the Cowderoy case? Any new leads?"

"Yes, sir. We're narrowing the field of suspects."

"To anyone in particular?"

"We've got some new evidence that implicates Allegra Cowderoy. Her alibi no longer holds water, and she lied to us about it. Plus, she's been calling Stella Thompson repeatedly and hanging up. Seems like there was something going on there."

"Good. That sounds promising."

"And we've also placed Stella Thompson, at his house around the time of the murder."

He rubbed his hands across his stubbled jaw and leaned back in his chair. "That complicates things."

"Yes, it does. But I'm confident we'll get the evidence we need, maybe even a confession. We need a motive, but it's only a matter of time until we uncover it."

"What about Stella Thompson? You know her personally, don't you?"

She wasn't aware the boss was aware of her personal connection to Stella. She'd have to tread carefully if she didn't want to be taken off the case.

"Yes, sir. I've met her around the community. We don't know each other well, but my impression so far is that she's not the type."

"Not the type to kill?" He grunted. "I think anyone's capable of that, given the right circumstances."

"Of course, sir."

"One other thing. Unless you're able to close this case by the end of next week, I'm going to have to bring in some help."

"What? No, you can't do that. This is my case."

"Sorry, Kauffman. I've given you plenty of time. The brass are breathing down my neck on this one. They didn't want me to give it to a local detective from the first day. The victim's wife has some connections that've caused me nothing but grief. So if you could get it sorted sooner rather than later, you'd be helping us all out."

She dipped her head. "You've got it, Boss. And when you say 'help,' you mean?"

"Brisbane Homicide Detectives."

She rolled her eyes. "Great. Just what we need—big-city coppers nosing around town and shutting everyone's mouths *tout suite.*"

He grinned. "I didn't know you spoke French, Kauffman."

"I'm a woman of mystery, sir."

His laughter followed her out the door. She strode through the office with a look of determination. Regardless of what he said or did, she'd be the one to solve this case. It was *her* case. She wasn't about to let some city cops horn in on her investigation right when things were starting to get interesting. The locals wouldn't speak to them, and they'd end up closing the investigation unresolved.

Chapter Twenty-Eight

TUESDAY

13TH NOVEMBER

The sun shone and it was a beautiful day. Not only because of the weather, but because there was something in the air. Stella felt it—things were about to change. Sure, they'd hit a rough patch with the whole car accident at a funeral thing, but it was a small rough patch.

She'd spoken with the police and hadn't heard from them again, so they must not be going to press charges. And she'd certainly been through much rougher patches than this one before—times where it felt as though she and Katie were sliding down sandpaper in their birthday suits. This one wasn't so bad, as far as dips in the road went. They were resilient—they'd get through it. In fact, one day they'd be able to look back on this period of their lives and it'd hardly rate as a blip on the timeline of their memories.

Stella picked her way through the grass beneath the

towering Norfolk pine tree. The steady shush of waves behind her soothed her gradually relaxing nerves. This was exactly what she needed to unwind. She had a picnic blanket folded up under one arm and her laptop under the other. She found a spot in the shade and was about to open the blanket and set it on the ground when she heard her name called.

She spun around to see Asher sitting behind the tree in the shade, a book in one hand. His back was leaned up against the tree trunk, his brown hair blowing gently in the wind.

"Hi," he said.

"Oh, hello. I thought I should come outside and enjoy this lovely weather. I see you've had the same idea." She set her things on the ground and tucked a strand of hair behind her ear. "You're not working at the café today?"

He smiled. "I am, but I'm on a break. You should come around to this side of the tree. The view of the beach is better. Plus, there's an anthill on that side."

She studied the ground and noticed the little creatures were already scampering over her sandals. "Yikes. Thanks for the heads-up." She flicked the shining black ants from her feet and joined Asher on his side of the tree. She set down her picnic blanket and sat on it, legs crossed.

Up close, his eyes were an amber colour with flecks of gold at the centre. He smiled, and his two front teeth overlapped a little bit.

"Do you live around here?" he asked.

"Over that hill," she said, pointing. "I walked here."

"Really? I live over there too. About a ten-minute walk."

"Five for me."

He nodded, grinning. "We're practically neighbours, then."

"I'll remember that when I need a cup of sugar," she quipped, opening her laptop and switching it on.

"Work?" he asked, dipping his head in the direction of her computer.

"I've got to get this presentation finished or Zoey will have my head."

He laughed. "She can be a little scary."

"Only when we're on a deadline. Otherwise, she's great. Oh, and she wants me to throw together an elegant Christmas bash as a kind of grand opening for the business. We're inviting everyone who's anyone."

"That sounds kind of fun."

"Yeah, except that the business has been operating for around five years. I've worked with her for almost an entire year."

"So, why the grand opening gala?" he asked.

"She wants us to take things to the next level, go after the big-dollar clients up on the northern end of the Gold Coast."

"I guess that makes sense," he said.

She flicked through her emails. "I'm sure it'll be a lot of fun, but I don't know how many new clients it will bring in, and we're spending a bomb on it."

Her phone dinged. It was Toni asking where she was. She replied, hit send, then returned her attention to her over-crowded inbox. When would she ever get to the point where it was under control? Sometimes she simply took everything from her inbox and dragged it into a folder, ignoring it all so she could have an empty inbox for a brief while. It was highly satisfying but not particularly professional, especially when some of the unanswered messages were from her boss.

"Where will you hold it?"

"The Grand Ballroom at the Palm Club." Stella had never been to the Palm Club. She couldn't afford it. Attached to a world-class golf course, only the very rich could afford a membership. Besides, there'd always been something about those kinds of places that she couldn't enjoy. All that affluence, the handshaking, and the endless posturing—it felt shallow and empty. She'd much rather sit at the pub looking out over the ocean, eating prawns with her fingers and drinking beer with her friends while a gritty band played cover songs in the corner.

"I've worked there. They sometimes call me in to wait tables for big functions. Maybe I'll get to work your party."

She hadn't realised how much she was dreading the event until he said those words and her heart leapt. "Do you think you might? Oh, please, see if you can. It would be such a relief to have a friendly face there. I know I'm supposed to network and make connections and be vibrant and full of festive cheer, but I don't like meeting strangers, and I'm no good at small talk."

"You do okay with small talk. And you were kind to me when I was a stranger."

"Was I?" she asked.

"It was about eight months ago. You were looking for something in your purse, and you stepped out onto the street. I was on my bike, heading to work—late as usual. And I swerved to miss you, a car clipped my pedal, and I went down. You sat with me, called the ambulance, and held my hand until they came. You told me stories about your childhood because you thought I was losing consciousness, but I wasn't. And when I asked for your name, you got all serious and said Stella Thompson."

"I can't believe I never realised that was you. All these months at Singles, and you didn't say anything and I didn't put it together."

He shrugged. "It was fine. I didn't expect you to remember me."

"I definitely remember, but you wore a helmet and sunglasses. I'm glad to know you're all right. I often wondered about what happened to that cyclist and whether he was okay."

"I was fine. I had some bruises and a bit of a headache for a few days, but otherwise I was in good shape. I thought a lot about the angel with the red hair who sat with me that day, but I didn't see you again for a couple of months. You came in with Zoey, and you ordered a chai latte with skim milk and a bliss ball. And I looked for a wedding ring but didn't see one."

She blushed. It wasn't that she was unaccustomed to the attention, but it was Asher. He'd never shown her the least bit of interest—well, no more so than what he showed any of the customers at the café. In fact, he generally gave Zoey more attention than he gave to her. But now, his earnest eyes focused on her, and the intensity of his words made her shiver. She wasn't sure yet whether that was good or bad.

She didn't like attention as a general principle in her life. She generally dressed down, wore simple and plain clothes. Classic style, as she liked to call it. The intention was to draw the least amount of attention she could, but men and women alike always noticed her anyway. And usually she didn't enjoy it, but today she wasn't sure exactly how to process Asher's words.

"Wow," she said. "You have an amazing memory."

"I like people," he said simply. "So, I pay attention."

That was it? He liked people. It wasn't that his attention was particularly focused on her and what type of snack she enjoyed. The realisation was a relief, but there was a tiny bit of disappointment mixed in with it. Still, he had wondered about whether she wore a wedding ring.

One of the emails in her inbox caught her attention. It was from the adoption agency. Her head felt light. With her finger hovering over the trackpad, she studied the subject line.

Re: Adoption

She swallowed, drew a deep breath, and clicked. The email opened, and she read it quickly before she lost the nerve.

> *Thank you for getting in touch. We have your adoption information in our archives and have located your birth mother. However, the instructions on the file are that she does not wish to reconnect. Those instructions were written thirty years ago on the day of your birth. We will contact her to see if this directive might change at this point in time since you are eager to meet her.*
>
> *The only information we are able to give you at this time is that your birth mother lives in Kingscliff, which is located in northern NSW.*
>
> *I will be in touch to let you know the outcome of our communications.*

Stella's breath caught in her throat, and she stared, frozen, at the email. Her mother lived in the same town as her. How was that possible? She remembered coming to the town every year for a holiday over the summer. Her adoptive parents had a beach house. They'd spent the entire school break living by the beach in the little hamlet. It's why she'd visited as an adult when she'd met Mark Cowderoy. It was a part of her childhood. The town held many of her happiest memories in its narrow, winding streets and on its long golden beaches.

She spent the next few minutes working on her presentation while Asher continued reading his book. While she clicked and typed, her thoughts were in an uproar. Her mother could be anyone. She might've already met her. How would she know? What if her mother decided that she never wanted to meet, and Stella knew her but didn't realise they were related? They'd live near each other but as strangers for the rest of her life. The thought made her stomach churn.

She couldn't think about it anymore. It was too much to

take in. And there wasn't anything more she could do. It was up to the adoption agency and her birth mother now. It was out of her hands. She had to focus on getting the presentation done, or Zoey would be even more stressed about the gala than she already was. She'd practically launched herself into the air when they'd had to change the venue on the day before they sent out the invitations because of a mould problem. Thankfully the Palm Club was available. Finding it had been a major victory for Stella.

The silence while she worked and Asher read was pleasant and only interrupted by a pair of seagulls fighting over scraps of chips in a box someone had placed halfway into the rubbish bin nearby. Wings beat and flapped as their squawking filled the air.

Watching them, Stella couldn't help noticing that one of the birds seemed to have some wire tangled around its leg. But it took off into the air, with a chip in its beak, before she could say anything to Asher about it. She watched it go, then spied a white police cruiser with blue lettering pulling into a parking space close by.

Toni and Callum climbed out of the car and ambled in her direction. Toni waved at her.

Her heart jumped into her throat.

"What are they doing here?" Asher asked, his brow furrowed.

"I think they might be here for me." A stone formed in Stella's gut.

Chapter Twenty-Nine

"We have evidence that you were at the victim's house the night of his murder," Toni said once they'd settled into the interview room at the station.

Stella stared at the cup of coffee Toni had made her. It was black and had an oily residue on top. Her stomach roiled.

"Yes, that's right."

"And you didn't think to tell us this before now?" Callum asked.

Of course she hadn't. They already blamed her for slamming her vehicle into Mark's hearse on the day of his funeral. She'd heard the rumours swirling around town—Allegra had called her a murderer and blamed her for Mark's death. If she went to prison, Katie would be an orphan with no one to raise her. She'd end up in the foster system. What if her foster parents were abusive? She might never see her daughter again. It would destroy their lives.

"I didn't want to say anything because I knew how it would look," she said.

Toni wrote in her notepad, her features expressionless.

"Well, you're right, it looks very bad. We have video footage of your vehicle parked outside Mark Cowderoy's house the night he was murdered at around the same time as he was killed."

Stella clenched her hands together. She wanted so badly to be anywhere else other than where she was. Even cold-calling potential clients to attend their Christmas gala was better than this, and she'd been avoiding doing that for days.

"I went to see him. I didn't want anyone else to know. But it was completely innocent." She knew how it sounded. It sounded like she'd gone there to kill him and had lied to cover up her crimes. Tears welled at the corners of her eyes. "I didn't kill him."

"It's our job to find out what happened to the victim, so we like to get a full picture of his final hours. Can you tell us why you went there?" Toni's eyes were warm and full of compassion.

Stella drew a calming breath. Her neck felt like it was on fire. It often broke out in red splotches when she was nervous. "Yes."

"What were you doing there?"

"I went to see Mark."

"I thought you didn't know him well."

"I didn't. I knew him years ago, but only briefly. Then we reconnected recently over the phone, and I went to see him," Stella said.

"Really? What did you two talk about?"

She swallowed hard. "Our daughter. He's Katie's father." She stared at the table. "I mean, her biological father. He never knew her. I went over there that night to talk to him about her. I'd called him a few months earlier, and that was when he found out she existed. On that Monday, I went there to talk to him about whether he'd like to be a part of her life."

"And what did he say to that?" Toni asked, jotting down notes.

"He was angry. He said I shouldn't spring it on him like that. It wasn't fair that I didn't tell him about her. That it could torpedo his marriage, and had I even thought about what it would do to his life? Things like that."

"So you fought. Were you angry with him?"

"I guess. But he was fine when I left. Upset, but fine." Stella played with her silver necklace that had a small horseshoe charm hanging from it.

"And why had you waited until now to tell him about Katie? How old is she?"

"She's five. Started kindergarten this year."

"So for more than five years you knew about her but didn't tell Mark? Why is that?"

Stella's shoulders slumped. "I don't know. I should've told him. I will regret it forever. Now Katie will never know her father, and it's all my fault. I suppose I didn't want to ruin his marriage, and I didn't know him, not really. We only dated for a short while, and when I found out he was married, I was completely ashamed, and I left town. I didn't come back again until two years ago when I decided that it was time to talk to him about Katie. She was starting to ask questions, and I didn't know what to tell her."

"You moved to Kingscliff so you could be near Mark?"

"Yes," she admitted.

"Why did Allegra Cowderoy call you?"

Stella frowned. "She didn't."

"Yes she did," Toni said. "She called you repeatedly. Each call only lasted a few seconds."

Stella's eyes widened. "Oh, she must've been the stalker."

"Stalker?" Callum asked.

"Not really a stalker exactly, but I kept getting these phone calls where the person would call and hang up. The phone number was blocked so I couldn't call them back. I started referring to them as my stalker."

"Why didn't you report it?"

Stella shrugged. "I don't know. It didn't seem like a big deal I suppose. And I have enough going on in my life."

"You didn't speak to her? Maybe threaten her or Mark?"

"Of course not," Stella said, her brow furrowed. "I didn't kill him, if that's what you're inferring. And I have no idea who did."

"Can anyone confirm that?" Callum asked.

Stella sighed. "I don't know. I don't think so, although if you have footage of me leaving his house, you can likely confirm that I left around seven thirty. He must've died after that because he was alive when I left. He shouted at me, in fact. So it's possible someone heard him and could confirm it."

"What did he shout?" Toni asked.

"'You're destroying my life...'" Stella admitted. "That was the last thing he said to me."

When Stella left, Toni leaned back in her chair and linked her hands behind her head.

Callum stood by the murder board, studying it. "If Stella Thompson didn't kill our victim, it has to be the wife. Right?"

"Looks like it," Toni replied. "She must've found out about the affair. She called Stella repeatedly and hung up on her. She potentially lied about her alibi, although we have to check with the limousine service she said drove her to the airport."

"I think we've found our perp." Callum grinned.

Chapter Thirty

SATURDAY

17TH NOVEMBER

When Toni's eyes blinked open, she found herself on the couch with the television blaring. The brilliant sunshine of the hot November day had been replaced by a cloying, humid twilight. Shafts of orange sunset filtered over the sky outside the sliding doors that led to their small veranda.

She sat up with a yawn, stretching her arms over her head. How long had she slept? She flicked off the television set and looked at her watch. Two hours. She'd had a two-hour-long nap, and her Saturday was nearly over. So much for spending time with her husband. So much for doing something enjoyable on her days off. She'd wasted the day away waiting for Rodger to come home, and it looked as though he still hadn't. Where was he? When she called him at lunchtime, he'd been shopping and said he was on his way home, that he'd see her soon. But she would've woken if he'd walked through the door.

The flat was dark, so she flicked on the kitchen light and set the kettle to boil. Her throat was dry, she had a headache, and her stomach growled. She'd hoped they might go out to dinner together tonight, just the two of them. To spend some time together as a couple. They didn't have to talk about anything, she'd told him. Just to be with one another. That's all she wanted.

He hadn't disagreed, but now that she thought about it, he hadn't agreed to her plan either. She'd simply assumed he would do it. Because what husband had secret plans that didn't include his wife on a Saturday night?

She couldn't think about it. It was too much.

She spent her days being suspicious of everyone she spoke to, questioning their motives, wondering if they were lying and why. It was happening in her personal life. She was too wary, too ready to believe the worst. Something had happened to hold him up—that's all it was.

The kettle boiled, and she poured steaming-hot water over a tea bag in her favourite cup—the one with the palm trees and a small desert island with a play on the words "sweet tea" and with a chip in the lip. Rodger had given it to her for Valentine's Day when they'd been dating about six months. It reminded her of those early days of heady romance and impulsive dates where they'd kiss for hours and talk until the sun came up. She missed those days.

She sat at the table with her cup of tea and a cheese and bacon roll that looked suspiciously like it might be past its use-by date and tucked her legs up against her body. Then she dialled Rodger's number, eating while it rang.

"Hello?"

"Hey, honey. It's me. Wondering where you are?"

He sighed. "Oh, sorry. I lost track of time. I'm still at the shops."

"It's been hours..."

"I know. I took in a movie, which only finished a few minutes ago. Then I realised I haven't found that fishing pole I've wanted forever, and I'm on my way to the fishing shop to see if they have it in stock. You don't mind if we have a quiet night tonight, do you? I'll probably be late."

A movie on a Saturday afternoon, alone? That made no sense. If he wanted to watch a movie, he could've done that with her. And now he had a fishing pole emergency? Anxiety tunnelled its way into her gut and combined with a salty rage.

"Do you have to do that now? I'd like to go out to eat."

"Another time, honey. Sorry—I'm not feeling up to it tonight."

When she hung up the phone, she sat and stared at it blankly for a full minute before moving. Her appetite gone, she chucked the rest of the stale bread roll in the rubbish bin, then ferreted around in the cupboard next to the sink for the bottle of gin she always kept on hand. She enjoyed the occasional martini but hardly ever remembered to mix one for herself. Tonight was going to be her night for learning how to mix the dirty gin martini she'd always wanted to perfect.

She poured gin into a shot glass, measuring it into a mixing cup over ice. It made absolutely no sense. None of it. This wasn't the man she'd married. He'd always been so happy to spend Saturdays with her. They'd go to the movies together, shop together, swim at the beach, or snorkel down by the pier. They'd watch whales from the pub, doing shots together every time they saw one blow spray into the air while they ate fresh oysters on the half shell. They had fun together.

He was one of the few people she'd ever met who drew that out in her. With most people, she was serious and shy, never knowing the right thing to say. In high school, she'd had the nickname "Buzzkill." "Oh, look who it is," they'd say. "Buzzkill is here." But not with Rodger—with him, she'd felt like the life of the party. He laughed at her jokes, listened to her stories as though he cared what she had to say. They had adventures together, and they never got bored. What had changed?

The first martini, she downed in a few big gulps. It made her cough, and her eyes watered. She filled the glass again, this time sipping more slowly.

It wasn't fair. This couldn't be happening again. Her first marriage had been a disaster from the beginning. They should never have gotten married because of a pregnancy. But it'd seemed like the right thing to do—he loved her, she loved him. It didn't matter that they were young—love would find a way. But it did matter because he changed the moment Ryker was born. He grew up overnight, and she fell into a deep depression that she didn't fully understand and that clearly scared her new husband. He spent nights at his parents' house with the baby while she sat on the floor of their musty little flat, her arms wrapped around her legs as she stared at the window and wondered what had happened to her life.

For years, she'd blamed herself. Their marriage failed because of her. Because she couldn't manage being a mum. She couldn't handle it. But now she knew it was postnatal depression and that it hadn't been her fault. Not only that, but she and Malcolm weren't suited to one another. It'd never have worked, even if she'd been emotionally and mentally able to cope with becoming a mother at such a young age.

And now it was happening again. But this time, she couldn't see why. Didn't understand what'd happened to drive her husband away. What had she done? She was in a good headspace. She'd spent years in therapy to learn to manage her emotions and keep them under control before they got to the point of plunging her into darkness. And she hadn't had a relapse. So, what was the problem?

A nagging thought in the back of her mind that she couldn't ignore kept pushing itself forwards. She shook it off, tried to avoid it as she sipped her martini, but couldn't manage to dislodge it entirely. It clawed its way into her brain and set up shop.

He didn't love her. Love didn't last. Not when it came to her. That's all there was to it.

She sobbed, and tears streaked down her cheeks as darkness crept over the ocean and into her heart. After two more martinis, she walked downstairs and stared out over the ocean. She stayed that way for a long time, arms folded, tears wetting her cheeks. It was dark and quiet outside. Most people were cosy in their living rooms watching television or eating together. She was the only one who was completely alone.

The cliff in front of her fell quickly to the dark, surging ocean below. Around her, fir trees increased the darkness of the small headland. She looked back over her shoulder towards the road and could only catch a glimpse of it through the trunks and branches. There was movement behind her. She wouldn't have noticed it if she hadn't looked back. She glanced around, wobbling on her feet. It was nothing. No one was there.

With her gaze back on the water ahead of her, she stepped forwards until her arms rested on the narrow railing that lined the lookout. She peered down into the blackness, watching the inky ocean smash against the black rocks below, sending a spray of white water skyward.

There were footsteps behind her. Someone running quietly through the trees. The sound stopped as quickly as it had begun. She walked through the gaps between the tall, thin tree trunks, her sandalled feet crushing pine needles and cones. A black shadow flashed away from a tree and behind another.

Her eyes narrowed as she focused through the darkness. Who was that? Was someone following her?

She'd gone several hundred metres into the thicket of fir trees before she realised it. She heard the footsteps again, and her heart leapt into her throat. What was going on? She shouldn't have come out here alone. She turned back and began to stumble through the trees. Her mind couldn't focus, and she found it hard to stay upright. She slammed into one tree trunk, then wrapped her arms around it to steady herself.

Behind her, the footsteps sped up, drew closer. Adrenaline burst into her brain, and she pushed away from the tree to run. It felt as though someone was right behind her. She could almost smell their breath, feel their heat. She ran faster and faster until she broke free of the forest of trees then fell headlong onto the footpath, grazing her hands and knees.

She brushed herself off. With a quick glance around, the light from the streetlamps making everything clearer, she saw that she was completely alone. There was no one chasing her. No one emerged from the tree line behind her. She shook her head and it spun. This was crazy. Now she was imagining things. She'd soon be back in the psychiatrist's chair if she wasn't more careful. With a sigh, she strode to the road and peered up at her dark, empty flat.

Then she called an Uber and directed the driver to take her to Malcolm and Sandi's house. She wanted to see Ryker, to ask him if he loved her or if his love had worn off like everyone else's seemed to.

He was the only constant in her life. Him and her work. Her work was always there. But she couldn't embrace work. Couldn't be wrapped in its arms and comforted when she was feeling low, or take it out to dinner to watch the sun set together. Policing wasn't enough for her. She needed more than that in her life.

She climbed out of the car, wobbling as she made her way up the path to the front door. It'd been ages since she was inside Malcolm and Sandi's house. She usually dropped Ryker at the curb or picked him up from the door. It was a nice house—a standard four-bedroom brick structure with a swimming pool in the backyard and a small garden out front. Malcolm had always wanted a suburban life with a wife and children—he'd told her as much after they were married and she'd said she didn't want any more babies. The look of pain in his eyes had only added to her despair—like she wasn't in control of her own life and that wanting to be, wanting to follow her own path, was selfish. She was a selfish person, and he deserved better.

With an open palm, she slapped the front door, then leaned against the frame, waiting. She could hear noise inside —happy chattering, the clatter of dishes, a television playing in the background.

The door swung open. It was Malcolm, his eyes wide. "Toni? I wasn't expecting you. Did you and Ryker have plans tonight?"

"No, I came over to see him," she slurred.

"Oh, okay. Um..." Malcolm studied her, clearly trying to think of something he could say to diffuse the situation. He was always trying to diffuse her. She'd been too much for him from day one—too much emotion, too much drama, too much pain, too much of everything.

"It's fine, Mal. I promise. I only want to talk."

"Well, come on in, then. I'll go find him. You can sit in the living room."

She staggered into the living room, realising for the first time how much she'd overindulged. It'd come on steadily over the course of the drive, and she regretted it immediately. She wanted to be clear in her words, but she couldn't get her thoughts straight.

With a grunt, she slumped onto the couch next to a little girl who was playing with a doll and her horse.

"Hi, Summer," Toni said.

Summer looked at her with big blue eyes. Her blonde hair was wispy, like spiderweb. It hung to her collar, but no further.

"Do you know how to ride horses?" she asked in a sweet voice.

Toni blinked. "No, not really. I've done it once or twice."

"Mummy says I'm too little, but I want my own horse. She could live in our backyard and drink from the swimming pool. Don't you think?"

Toni nodded. "That sounds like a solid plan."

"I think so too."

Ryker rushed into the living room, pulling up short when he saw her. "Mum? What are you doing here?"

He ushered Summer away like Toni was a drug-addicted felon on leave. Her brow furrowed. "We were only talking."

Ryker sat beside her on the couch. "You've been drinking. What's wrong, Mum? You never drink."

"Rodger..." she began. She couldn't finish the sentence. Already tears were welling in her eyes.

Ryker's face registered understanding. He sighed. "Right..."

Malcolm hovered behind Ryker, worry in his eyes.

Toni ignored him and cupped Ryker's cheek with one hand. Tears skidded down her cheeks. "You love me, don't you, kiddo?"

"Of course I do, Mum."

"That's not going to change, is it? Because it seems like everyone else gets tired of me after a while. And I don't think I could take it if you did too."

Ryker's eyes gleamed. "Mum...that's not going to happen. I don't like seeing you this way."

Behind him, Malcolm paced back and forth in the hallway,

pressing his hands to his mouth. He strode forwards. "Toni, don't go down this path again. You've been doing so well. You know that's not what happened with us—I didn't suddenly stop loving you. You've got to stop this."

She peered up at him through a blur of tears. "What was it, then?"

He sighed, crossed his arms. "We weren't right for each other. I don't know how else to put it. We were too young, and it was all too much for us both to cope with. I didn't stop loving you."

She sobbed, leaning her head against Ryker's shoulder. "I'm sorry. I'm so very sorry."

"It's okay, Mum," he comforted, stroking her head.

He got her a pillow and blanket and helped her lie on the couch. Then he squatted beside her and talked to her quietly until she fell to sleep. When she woke up, Rodger was there. He and Malcolm were in the entryway murmuring things to one another. Then he came to her, picked her up in his arms, and carried her and the blanket out to his waiting car.

Ryker ran after them and kissed her forehead. She told him goodbye. Rodger settled her in the passenger seat of their car, then hurried around to the driver's seat and climbed in. He drove home in silence, only glancing her way every now and then with a look of concern.

When they were home and he'd tucked her into bed, she asked him, "Where were you?"

"Let's not talk about it now," he said, stroking her hair away from her face. "It's all going to be okay. You should get some sleep."

She wanted to fight it, to fight him and get to the truth of everything. But she was sleepy, and her head was already starting to pound. So she let her eyes drift shut. She would deal with it all tomorrow. Ryker loved her, and that was enough for now.

Chapter Thirty-One

SUNDAY

18TH NOVEMBER

Grey-tinged clouds hovered on the horizon. Zoey tented a hand over her eyes and glared at them, willing them to go away. They were having a day at the beach, and there would *not* be rain. There simply would not. She could will it away if she wished to. It would not be fair if this perfect day was ruined by a little bit of rain.

She didn't mind a rain shower—it didn't bother her one bit—but she knew what would happen. Stella would say she had to get Katie home and would pack up and leave. Toni would glance up at the shower and use it as her excuse to be an introvert, especially since she seemed to be suffering from the worst hangover Zoey had ever seen her friend endure before.

Toni wasn't the type to drink a lot. Zoey always assumed it had something to do with her being a cop. But it could've also been the fact that she had a history of depression. Toni never said much about it, but she'd hinted at it once or twice when they'd been talking about friends who were pregnant or struggling with their newborns. And Zoey had befriended her when she was in recovery. She knew several women who'd gone through it. Postpartum depression. It was a real thing. She'd likely had a touch of it herself.

After Isla was born, she'd shouted at Dave so loudly, the neighbours had called the police on them and he'd had to assure them he wasn't being killed by his abusive wife and everything was perfectly fine. But she'd never forgiven the Cowderoys for it. Instead of compassion, maybe a casserole or an offer to babysit, they'd called the police. That wasn't how neighbours should treat one another. At least, not in Zoey Winton's world of manicured lawns and white picket fences.

That and the horrible karaoke parties they held on their front deck that'd kept her up until all hours of the night while she was breastfeeding and sleep-deprived. When they woke Isla after she'd spent four hours to get her to settle, she'd thought she might march over there and shoot them herself. But Dave had managed to talk her out of the confrontation—said it wouldn't achieve anything, and anyway, they didn't own a gun.

When she'd suggested a water pistol, he'd laughed. And they'd both ended up in a fit of giggles and had fallen into bed together. She remembered being happy to feel something, anything, other than a baby's spit-up on her skin or the smell of a dirty nappy in her nostrils. He always knew how to talk her down from the worst of it.

But Toni didn't have Dave—she had Rodger. And from what Zoey could tell of it, Rodger was no Dave. She wasn't sure how things were going between them, but from the things Toni had told her, Rodger seemed to keep a lot to himself. Blocking your wife out, not telling her everything, seemed like a heinous crime to Zoey. You didn't do that sort of thing. Not if you wanted your marriage to work.

At least he'd come to the beach with them and seemed to be having a nice time. He was particularly attentive to Toni today, so perhaps they'd turned a corner. She certainly hoped so.

"Mum, can you put on my sun cream, please?" Isla bounded over to her in a blue-and-white bikini that Zoey wasn't sure was entirely appropriate. But since she'd never been allowed to wear a bikini as a teenager and had learned to cover her body as much as she could, feeling nothing but embarrassed about her curves and wobbly bits over the years, she didn't want to dampen her daughter's obvious lack of shame. She wanted Isla to be confident and proud of her body. So, she pushed down the things she wanted to say about how much skin was appropriate and smiled instead.

"Sure, sweetheart."

She applied sunscreen to her daughter's very fair skin, then watched as she jogged off to play beach cricket with Ryker, Dave, and Rodger at the other end of the small beach.

Zoey lay back on her lounger chair and shielded her eyes from the sun with one forearm draped above her eyes. "This is the life."

Toni lay motionless on the lounger beside her. "Mmmm."

"You're very quiet today," Zoey teased.

"Shut up or I'll be sick directly into your purse."

Zoey laughed. "What did you get up to last night?"

"You couldn't come out with me, so I decided to drink alone instead."

Zoey sat up and regarded her friend with a worried expression. "Please tell me you're joking."

"Nope."

"This hangover is from drinking by yourself at home? Now that's depressing."

Toni swallowed. "It wasn't my finest moment."

"Oh, honey. I'm sorry. I should've been there for you."

"That's okay. It all worked out in the end. Ryker was very sweet, and Rodger rescued me."

Zoey lay back on her lounger again and tucked her kaftan around her body. "That's good to hear. I hate the way Rodger's been treating you. I hope he's learned his lesson."

Stella and Katie showed up then. Stella waved to them, and Zoey hurried over to greet her.

"You're here!" She kissed Stella's cheek with a sudden rush of maternal warmth for her friend. With everything that'd been going on in her life lately, she still made the time to come to the beach with them for an impromptu beach party. She was a good friend.

"Come and sit with me and Toni. You can tell us all about that mysteriously cute guy you alluded to yesterday."

Stella hesitated. "Is Toni here? I don't know..."

"What's wrong?"

"She almost arrested me the other day. Dragged me down to the station for questioning."

Zoey gasped. "What? I thought they'd sorted all of that out."

"Apparently not. I think she still sees me as a suspect in the murder." She whispered the last words, as if embarrassed that anyone might hear her.

This wouldn't do. Two of her best friends were at odds because one thought the other might be a murderer. It was utterly ridiculous anyway, since Zoey knew without a shadow of a doubt in her mind that Stella couldn't harm a fly. The woman was practically a saint, apart from the fact that she'd had a child with someone she wouldn't talk about and Zoey had never been able to get her to name. There were rumours, of course, but she didn't listen to idle gossip. It was virtually never correct.

"Come with me." She took Stella by the hand and pulled her across the sand. Stella didn't come willingly. She leaned back and away from Zoey, like a toddler who didn't want to go to bed. The sand was deep and dry and difficult to trudge through. Zoey was practically panting by the time they reached Toni.

Toni lay on her back, an enormous straw hat balanced over her face and a cotton coverup draped across her body.

"Toni, you don't mind if Stella sits with us, do you?"

Toni jerked into a sitting position. The hat fell into her hands. Sweat beaded across her forehead, which had a greenish hue.

"No, of course not. Come and join us, Stella."

"I thought..." Stella stammered.

"Never mind about work. We're not on the clock today. Are we?" Toni's voice was raspy and terse.

"Okay, great." Stella didn't look convinced but sank into one of the loungers that Dave had set up for them when they'd first arrived at the beach an hour earlier.

Zoey liked to get to events ahead of the crowd to make sure they had everything they needed. Dave reminded her that she wasn't actually hosting this event—it was a casual get-together at the beach. But she always felt as though she was the hostess, since most of her friends rarely pulled themselves together enough to manage their own families, let alone to consider what anyone else might need. It was a harsh reality, but it was the truth. And Zoey always liked to be truthful—at least to herself.

Zoey sat as well and tugged a bottle of sun cream out of her straw bag. She slathered it over her arms and legs while watching the others playing cricket. Isla was bowling, and Katie was on bat. Isla threw the ball as softly as she could manage, and when Katie tapped it with the bat, everyone jumped and cheered and patted her on the back. She grinned, gazing around in joy at them all.

"It's nice to see Katie enjoying herself," Zoey said.

Stella was sprawled on her lounger, perfectly accessorised with a red string bikini beneath a sheer black coverup and a wide-brimmed black straw hat with oversized sunglasses.

"She loves your kid. And Dave, too. I don't think she's met that other young man before, though."

"That's my Ryker," Toni murmured from beneath her hat, now perched lopsided on her head.

"Of course. How lovely he could join us all."

"He's known Zoey for years. She's like an aunt to him."

Zoey laughed. "I remember the first time I met him. He must've been seven years old. Those knobby little knees."

Toni grunted. "He was a cutie pie back then. It's hard to believe this lanky young man in front of us is the same person."

"And what about you?" Zoey continued. "You were so skinny, with that short hair and pale face. You looked like you'd stumbled out of a meth lab."

"Well, thanks a lot." Toni blew Zoey a kiss.

"You'd been through a lot, that's all I'm saying. And you're much better now."

"That's true. I came here looking for something, and I guess I found it. At least, I thought I had. Now I'm not so sure." She ran a hand over her eyes, then shoved a pair of sunglasses into place.

"Why did you move to Kingscliff?" Stella asked.

"For Ryker. He and his dad had moved up here, and I visited a few times. That's when I met Zoey. After a while, I decided to move because I couldn't bear being so far away. By then I'd already become a detective, so I transferred from Sydney."

"It seems like only yesterday we met on the plane," Zoey

mused. "But it was ten years ago, I suppose. Then later, you were here for a week, and you were staying in that little bed-and-breakfast down by the water."

"That's right," Toni said. "It's not there anymore. It's a Mexican restaurant now, I believe."

"Taquito's?" Stella asked. "I love that place."

"Yep, that's it. And I was struggling with Ryker's behaviour, if I remember correctly. I was at my wit's end. I wasn't used to taking care of him full-time, and I felt ashamed, like everyone could tell that I wasn't a good mother..."

"That's when I came along." Zoey laughed. "And when I saw Toni chasing Ryker down the street, I simply had to help."

"She caught him like a football," Toni added, chuckling. "He didn't know what to think about that. He went all quiet, staring up at her."

"With those big brown eyes of his," Zoey continued, grinning. "And I told him, 'It's too nice a day and you're too sweet a boy for a fuss like that,'"

"He wasn't too happy, but it helped change the mood," Toni said. "And I thanked you for rescuing me. I was so worried you were going to judge me. But you didn't... You said, 'Never mind all that. Wouldn't you kill for an iced coffee right now? Come on, let me buy you one.'"

Zoey reached out, took Toni's hand in hers, and squeezed it. "I could tell then that we were meant to be friends. I don't say that kind of thing to just anyone, you know."

"Ten years later and we're still in each other's lives. That's a record for me," Toni said.

"Couldn't do it without ya, hon." Zoey smiled.

Stella pushed her sunglasses aside and dabbed at her eyes with her fingertips. "That's a beautiful story. I've never had a friendship like that. Most of the friends I've had end up ghosting me at some point. And I have no idea why. I've basically decided that it's me and Katie, and if there are other people who share the journey with us temporarily, then that's fine. But when I hear a story like that..." She sighed.

"Well, you have us now," Zoey said. "And once we're in your lives, there's no getting rid of us."

Toni lay back on her lounger. "You can try. I've certainly shouted at Zoey enough times to scare off most people, but she doesn't take the hint."

Zoey playfully slapped her arm. "Oh, please. I've been a pain far more often than you have."

Toni smirked. "I won't disagree with that."

Chapter Thirty-Two

MONDAY

19TH NOVEMBER

Forty-seven years old today.

Toni lay back on the couch and stared up at the ceiling. It was unfair how quickly life passed by. She'd wasted so many years being depressed, angry, and shouting at the world. And now she was forty-seven. The number loomed in her thoughts like an expanding balloon.

Almost fifty. She was almost fifty. And everyone knew that fifty-year-olds were *old* people. They had retirement villages for people over fifty. Retirement villages! She wasn't ready to retire. She was still young, fit, and feisty. Well, feisty at the very least. Perhaps she should go for a run along the beach in the morning to test out the fitness claim. She hadn't done that in a while. But she used to do it all the time, so surely she wouldn't have lost all of her fitness so quickly. Although, climbing the stairs to her flat seemed to take it out of her. Yesterday when she was carrying up some groceries because the lift was full and she didn't feel like waiting for it to come all the way back down to the ground floor, she'd had to stop on the second level to catch her breath.

She would definitely go for that run.

She flicked on the television and leaned on one elbow to browse the channels. She stopped on a reality show. The menu declared it was called *Health Intervention*. There was a man dressed in a salmon-coloured T-shirt and jeans with a smug half-smile shouting at a trio of slightly chubby people who stepped up and down, up and down, on one of those aerobics steps she'd used at the gym a hundred times in a previous life.

"Stop!" he shouted. "Now, close your eyes and balance on one leg."

The trio did as they were told, puffing and sweating. One woman immediately over balanced. The other two wobbled precariously for several seconds before doing the same.

"If you're over fifty and you can't balance on one leg with your eyes closed for at least twenty seconds, I can tell you with complete confidence that you will not last beyond the next thirteen years."

The trio quickly shut their eyes to try again, buoyed by the new understanding that their lives depended entirely upon their ability to balance. One man's expression seemed to say, *I will not be beaten, I will balance*, as though achieving twenty seconds of balancing with his eyes closed would thwart the death sentence that hung over his head.

Toni switched off the television, a knot forming in her gut. She had no idea how long she could balance on one foot, but she was closing in on fifty. According to this man, she might not make it into her mid-sixties. Perhaps she should get back into Pilates as well. Strengthen up those core muscles. Aerobics wasn't the fashion any longer—it was all about Pilates now.

Rodger strode into the living room, running his fingers through freshly washed hair. "So, where are we going to celebrate this amazing achievement?"

"Achievement?" Toni asked.

"You're forty-seven. That's a big deal."

"It is?"

"Yep. Every year we're alive is a victory. So many people don't make it to our age."

She was becoming more and more like a decrepit old lady. This was how old people talked to one another.

"It's easy for you to say. You're still forty-five."

He laughed. "And don't you forget it. You're rounding up to fifty. I'm still mid-forties."

She groaned and held a cushion to her face. Her voice muffled by the cushion, she said, "Since I'm so over the hill, perhaps we could go to Sands for dinner."

"But they only serve fish," he complained, his hazel eyes screwing up.

"Seafood," she corrected, pulling the cushion free and sliding it beneath her head. "And we never eat there because you don't like it, but I love seafood. Besides, it's good for the old ticker. And apparently if I can't balance on one foot, I'm as good as dead."

"Huh? Well, since it is *your* birthday, I guess I can eat some prawns or something."

She bounded to her feet and threw her arms around him. He was warm and toned from all the running and cycling, and she breathed in his manly scent. The feel and smell of him filled her with so much happiness that she thought she might burst. They'd get through this. It was all going to be okay. He still loved her. It felt like old times again.

"Thank you! It's going to be great. You'll see. I've got to get dressed. I'll be quick. Stay right there."

* * *

Happy birthday, sweetheart!

A text from Zoey.

Toni smiled at it, then sent back a heart emoji.

Zoey texted back. *We'll celebrate together soon. Enjoy your date xo.*

Rodger was driving. Toni sat in the passenger seat in a slinky red dress with a sheer silver scarf hanging around her neck and earrings dangling to her collarbone.

"You look nice," Rodger said, glancing at her with a smile.

"Thanks. I thought I'd make a bit of an effort."

"I like it. You should do it more often."

She shrugged. "We should go out more often."

He tensed. She shouldn't have said that. She was blaming him—she knew that's how he'd take it. The only thing she wanted for the evening was for them to get through it without an argument. She'd have to be more careful about what she said.

She stared out the car window. Stars lit up the sky like a canopy of twinkle lights. The trees and bushes lining the road were black and haunting, throwing eerie shadows.

"How was your run earlier?" she asked.

"Fine. I think I have a blister, though." He grimaced. "My sock kept falling down."

"I hate it when that happens."

They found a parking space, and Rodger had called ahead to reserve a table, so they were able to go directly to their seat. It was as if they'd reverted to the way things used to be. Toni was so ashamed of her performance at Malcolm and Sandi's on Saturday night, but perhaps it was exactly what they needed for Rodger to pay attention to what was going on in their lives. He'd seemed determined to ignore the cracks in their relationship, but now he was being caring, attentive, and thoughtful. Hope raised her mood until she was her most outgoing, vivacious, and chatty self during the meal.

She ordered the barramundi and Rodger the garlic prawns. They talked about the past, all the things they'd done together. The holiday to Colorado when Rodger had broken his leg trying to impress Toni by jumping over a small rise on his skis. She'd had to drag him by the back of his jacket over to the main ski slope so she could flag down someone from the ski patrol. It'd made her giggle hysterically, and he'd been so angry with her, but still, she couldn't stop giggling.

"Stop it. I'm going to wet my pants," she'd hissed at him through a bout of silent but uncontrollable laughter when he'd shouted in pain going over a rocky bump on his rear end.

Perhaps that'd been the beginning of the end for them. He hadn't forgiven her for ages for it. She'd tried to explain to him that when she was in an awkward situation or had to do something that seemed impossible, like lug her six-foot-five husband across a mountain by the scruff of his neck, she always giggled uncontrollably. It was like a tic. She didn't do it intentionally. Eventually he'd gotten over it, and they'd put it behind them. Even now, reminiscing about it, he affected a pouting look and she had to stifle a giggle.

He reminded her of the time they climbed Mount Beerwah, a mountain that jutted directly from the earth up into the air with nothing but granite and a few hardy shrubs. It'd rained while they sat at the top eating their bananas and drinking from their enormous water bottles, and she'd had to scoot down the entire sheer rock face of that mountain on her rear end because she was afraid if she stood, she'd slip and then slide, tumble, and fall to her death.

"You laughed at *me* that time," she said. "See, we've both had a chuckle at each other's expense."

He grunted around a mouthful of rice. "I couldn't help it.

Your bum was so dirty, covered in brown mud. The jokes wrote themselves."

By the time they'd finished eating, Toni didn't want the night to end. So she asked the waiter to bring the dessert menu, and they both ordered something. Dessert was an indulgence, especially given the whole balance-or-die thing she'd learned earlier in the evening. But she decided it would be her last sweet treat for a while, just until she shifted the extra kilograms she'd gained in the past year. Apparently, her second marriage falling to pieces had increased her appetite. If only it worked the other way around.

"How's the case coming?" Rodger asked as he took a bite of crème brûlée.

"Fine," she mumbled, her mouth full. "I think we have a good handle on it now. It's taken us a while, but we're close to the end."

"You have a suspect?" He arched an eyebrow. "I didn't think you'd found him yet."

"Her," Toni corrected. "It looks like it was the wife. She doesn't have an alibi, lied about where she was, and she's been calling..." She stopped herself. She shouldn't said anything. She'd spoken to Rodger about her work in the past, and he knew the rules—the things she told him about her work were in confidence. Still, she didn't do it often. It was the fact that she wanted desperately for them to be close again, to put the crazy disconnectedness of the past year behind them.

"Sorry, I shouldn't be talking about this," she said, scooping up another bite of mud cake.

He leaned back in his chair. "Why not?"

"Because it's an ongoing case. You know I don't talk details when I'm in the middle of an investigation."

"You did with Malcolm. You said you talked to him about everything when the two of you were married."

"That's true, but we also had a very dysfunctional relationship, and I was in a bad place."

He shook his head and crossed his arms. Where was he going with this? He looked angry, but Toni wasn't even sure how they'd gotten onto the subject of her ex-husband. Was it because she went to his house that week, obviously drunk? Perhaps this was Rodger's way of having it out, although he could've waited until the next day to pick a fight.

"On that topic," she said in an attempt to lighten the mood. "Sandi's pregnant. Again." She laughed. "Can you believe it? You'd think they were trying to populate a new planet or something."

"Are you jealous?"

She set down her spoon. Her attempt to make him laugh clearly hadn't worked. There were bright red spots on his cheeks, and his eyes flashed.

"That's a bit harsh, honey. Jealous of who? Sandi?"

He nodded.

"No, of course not. Why would I be jealous of Sandi? You know I never wanted more children."

"Perhaps that was only with me. Maybe if Malcolm hadn't left, you'd have had more kids."

They'd been here before. Toni recognised the direction his argument was taking. It had been an ongoing discussion early in their relationship. She didn't want more children, and he wanted a bunch. She'd broken up with him over it at the six-months' mark when the subject had come up. But after endless conversations over the phone, tormented love letters from him, and his vow never to raise the subject again, that he loved her and didn't need anyone else but her, she'd taken him back. She should've known it would be a bitterness that would simmer below the surface. Something like that couldn't be ignored forever.

"Honey, let's not go back down this road. I thought we resolved it a long time ago."

He leaned forwards, eyes hard. "I thought we had too. But you went running off to Malcolm as soon as you were upset this week. Didn't you?"

"No, I didn't. I went to see Ryker."

"I can't believe I didn't see it before," he continued. "I'll never match up to your first love. You moved across the state to be close to him, and we've had to live in this tiny little town ever since so you can be near him."

"Near Ryker, not Malcolm."

"If you wanted to be with him so much, you shouldn't have divorced him."

Her jaw clenched. "He divorced *me*."

"And you've never gotten over it. Have you? I'm done. I'm leaving. I'll call an Uber, and you can take the car. Don't wait up for me."

He got up from the table and stormed out of the restaurant, leaving Toni sitting alone, gaping after him. What was that? Where did all that anger come from? She had no idea he'd been festering in so much bitterness for so long. It made absolutely no sense. She'd told him a hundred times how she and Malcolm had gotten married for Ryker's sake, how they didn't suit each other and had made each other miserable throughout the few short years of their marriage. Why would he think she still pined after her ex-husband?

It was true—she was often jealous of the life Malcolm had built for himself. And the fact that Ryker had lived with him for most of his childhood, and she'd been the one on the outside looking in. At least, that's how it'd felt. But she didn't pine after Malcolm. Even suggesting such a thing was insanity. Had Rodger lost his mind? Or did he really believe the things he'd said?

She paid the bill, her hand shaking as she gave her credit

card to the waiter. She strode to the car park, the cool air raising goose pimples on her bare arms. How could he leave her there alone on her birthday? They'd had such a nice time together at dinner. But even with the argument, they were married. What kind of husband left his wife at the restaurant because of an argument? And where was he going? Would he be back tonight?

She texted him the questions—*Where are you? When will you be back?*

When she climbed into the car, he still hadn't responded. She drove home in silence, her mind blank, her body shaking. This wasn't right. Everything he said was untrue, yet he didn't wait to hear her perspective. He simply judged her and left.

Tears slid down her cheeks as she parked the car and walked up the stairs to their flat. It was dark when she let herself in. She'd forgotten to leave a light on. She'd been floating on air before they left, so happy. Remembering it now made the tears fall faster still. There was something very wrong in her marriage. If only she knew what it was.

She collapsed onto the bed, still wearing her makeup and her dress, and curled onto her side. She stared at the wall for hours before she finally fell to sleep. And when she woke from a nightmare in the middle of the night, Rodger's side of the bed was still empty and cold. She felt the space where he slept with one hand, then rolled over and went back to sleep, her eyes swollen and her heart aching.

Chapter Thirty-Three

TUESDAY

20TH NOVEMBER

A clanging sound woke Toni from a very deep sleep. Or was it ringing? Her eyes blinked open, and she groaned. What was making that infernal noise? It wouldn't stop. Her phone. The realisation dawned, and she rolled over to pick it up off the bedside table.

What time was it?

She took in a lopsided view of the alarm clock through bleary eyes. Eight a.m.! She'd overslept. She was supposed to be at the office holding a briefing meeting for the entire team. She planned on telling them about the updates on the case and promising them they'd get to the bottom of the situation very soon. Oh, and the small fact that they'd have the case taken off them by Brisbane detectives if they didn't solve it by the end of the week. But no pressure, of course.

"Hello?"

"Boss, wondering if you're planning on joining us sometime today?" Callum's gravelly voice echoed in her ear.

She grimaced. "Sorry, Callum. I overslept. Can you take this one? You know the details. And I'll catch up with you all later."

He grunted. "No worries. I'll tell them you had an appointment."

"Perfect. I owe you one."

She hung up the phone and pressed it to her chin for a few minutes, staring out the window. Trees bent and shook with a northeasterly that blew in off the beach. Rain spattered the window. She hurried to shut it and noticed the carpet was wet. How long had it been raining? Usually the rain woke her, but not this time. She'd tossed and turned half the night, going over every word of the argument she'd had with Rodger the night before.

She'd decided not to tell Callum about the conversation she'd had with Cowan. If he told the team their commander planned on changing the group assigned to the case, she knew how they would take that. Not well. No one wanted to make way for out-of-town detectives, no matter what they said to the contrary. It made them look bad, and it didn't help solve the case any faster, at least in her experience. She'd tell them if it became a certainty. They didn't need to know yet.

The fact that her husband still hadn't come home didn't escape her attention. She casually scanned the entire flat to make sure he wasn't on the couch or in the office before stepping into the shower with a leaden heart. He hadn't come home. Hadn't called. Her phone had been on all night long, and she'd kept it next to the bed just in case. What was he thinking? And where was he? This was too much. They'd had fights before, but he'd never spent the night away from her because of it.

Was she holding on to something that was already over?

She couldn't believe that. They'd committed to spend their lives together. She'd had her doubts before the wedding. He'd had them too. He wanted things she couldn't give him. And she'd caught glimpses of a dramatic side to his personality that'd given her a fright. When she'd forgotten to confirm a booking they'd made for a trip to the ski slopes in Falls Creek, he'd shouted at her over it. Ranted and raved for a good hour about how he should've known better than to trust her to do it—should've done it himself. Now she'd ruined their entire holiday, and he'd been saving for it for months. That kind of thing. She'd apologised to him profusely, of course. But it hadn't made any difference.

Later he'd begged her forgiveness and said it wouldn't ever happen again. But it had, of course. Many times, and all for different reasons. He seemed to have a switch that flicked randomly and a rage he found impossible to control. But it didn't happen often, and he always promised he'd change. So, she'd taken him at his word, believing he meant what he said.

When they were married and she found he hadn't changed at all, and that in fact his temper was only worse now that they were tied together for life, she'd grown to accept it. His lack of emotional control was one of the things about him. It wasn't a part of him she liked, but then, she had plenty of flaws herself and she couldn't expect him to be perfect, especially when she was so very far from it. They were married, warts and all, so she accepted him and expected he'd accept her. She was happy. She thought they were both happy. And now she wasn't so sure.

Drying off, she studied her reflection in the mirror. Dark smudges beneath her eyes. Wrinkles across her forehead and bookending her smile. Her stomach had a small paunch now that she'd gained weight, but she still had good muscle structure from years of running, aerobics, and weight lifting. Activities she'd neglected lately. Her auburn hair hung to her waist now that it was free, although today it looked as though birds had spent the night nesting in it.

When the phone rang again, she was dressed. She answered with a toothbrush in her mouth.

"He-slurp-llo?"

"Hi, this is Vice Principal Woodrow from Kingscliff State High School. Is this Mrs Kauffman?"

Her heart stood still for a moment. "This is Toni Kauffman. Is everything okay, Mr Woodrow?"

"Ryker is fine. I wanted to talk to you about his grades. Is now a good time?"

She spit the toothpaste from her mouth, wiped her mouth, and sat down on the bed. "Now's perfect. I'm guessing since you're calling me that his grades are not going well."

"You're correct. As you know, Ryker has been a consistently good student. He generally receives Bs and Cs, and the occasional A. We've never had cause to be concerned about his academic progress at any time during the years he's been with us. But unfortunately, this year things have changed. And as you can imagine, his second-last year of school is the wrong time for him to be dropping the ball."

She pressed a hand to her forehead. "I didn't realise. How bad is it?"

"He can still salvage this. Exams are coming up this week. If he studies, he might be able to pass and lift his grades to the point that we'll let him continue on to year twelve."

She hung up the phone in shock. Her stomach clenched, and she thought for a moment she might throw up. How was this possible? Out of all the things that she'd spent hours of her time worrying about in recent months, Ryker's schooling wasn't one of them. He wanted to be a physiotherapist. He'd known for years what he wanted to do. If he failed, there was no way he'd get into the program at university. And then what would he do? She felt completely helpless. This wasn't something she could solve. And right now, she had to get to work before her big case was taken off her. Anxiety beat in her chest as she rushed out the door, letting it slam shut behind her.

* * *

Party of two, coming.
Party of one, not coming.
Party of four, maybe.

Stella flicked through the digital RSVP list, taking note of any changes that'd been made since she put together the guest list for Zoey. So far, they had sixty people confirmed and another fifty or so as maybes.

With a deep breath, she added some more names to the list in her laptop, which was pushed up against the steering wheel of her car. She was about to go into the venue to meet with the caterer but had arrived a little early to miss traffic. It seemed as though the traffic on the Gold Coast was getting worse with every day, quite possibly with every passing hour. She didn't know how people managed to live there with the constant stop and go, stop and go, the ever-present stench of petrol fumes. Give her a coastal village any day of the week. She loved that they could walk nearly everywhere and rarely needed to use the car if they didn't want to.

She'd finally gotten her Pajero back from the mechanic's. He'd promised her it was as good as new, although it still had the ding in the side. But the damage to the front of the vehicle was fixed, along with the anti-lock braking system, although she felt her heart rate accelerate whenever she pushed down on the brake pedal or came to a pedestrian crossing with people on it. What if it didn't stop? What if it happened again? She might run over the nice old man with the walker or the young woman in her yoga pants and fluorescent joggers pushing the expensive pram as she speed walked her way back to her pre-baby weight. And the thought of it sent her into a panic as she eased towards the crossing, one eye squeezed shut, the other wide with horror.

But the brakes had worked, and she hadn't run anyone down. Not yet, anyway.

She sent the newly revised guest list to Zoey. An email pinged into her inbox, and she glanced at it. Her breath caught in her throat. It was from the adoption agency. She wasn't sure she wanted to open it. If her mother still wanted nothing to do with her, that knowledge would hurt her heart in a way she wasn't ready for. She needed to steel herself, take some time to think about it, prepare her heart for the pain of it, build a wall around her heart to protect it. Something, anything other than more rejection from the woman who'd left her behind all those years ago.

She must've had a good reason. Stella liked to give people the benefit of the doubt. Whenever Katie came home and reported that one of the kids at school had been unkind, or called her a name, or pushed her down in the sandpit, Stella would commiserate and then say something along the lines of, "That's not acceptable behaviour and you don't deserve it. But we don't know what else is going on in her life." Katie would nod solemnly, soaking in that new piece of information as though it was a revelation.

"You're right, Mum. What if she's had a sad day?"

"Exactly," Stella would say with smug triumph. Her daughter was an emotional prodigy.

And she should give her birth mother the same consideration as Katie did the bullies at school. What if she'd had a hard day, week, or month? She didn't know what might make a woman give up her own baby for strangers to raise, but it'd have to be something bad. Something that seemed impossible to overcome. At least at the time. And if that something had changed, maybe she'd want to meet Stella.

Or maybe she was dead. Stella hadn't considered that possibility, but it flickered through her thoughts now. She might be dead. It'd been thirty years since she gave up her baby. If she'd been in her forties then, she could well have succumbed to some horrible illness since. The adoption agency might've been wrong about her, could've got the paperwork mixed up.

She shook her head. There was no way of discovering the truth without opening the email message. So she clicked on it, and it sprang open. Her eyes flicked back and forth across the letter, taking in the basic gist of it before she released a sigh of relief and went back to the beginning to digest it fully.

Her birth mother was happy to reconnect. They wanted to know if Stella would send her details to the agency and consent to her mother contacting her.

Stella lay back in the driver's seat, eyes closed as she breathed a deep, cleansing breath. Her mother wanted to reconnect. It was what Stella had longed to hear, and now that the possibility had become more than a mere idea, she wasn't certain it was for the best. Bringing a new grandmother into Katie's life could be fantastic. She could get all of the things she was missing out on by not having Stella's adoptive parents around any longer and never having met her father or his family. Katie often asked why they didn't have a big family like other people. This might be their chance.

On the other hand, what if the woman was a vagabond or drug addict? What if her only reason for getting in touch with them was to ask for money or to snatch Katie from her bed at night and make a run for it? The likelihood of that seemed improbable, but that was the thing—if Stella invited this stranger into their lives, she would have no control over who that person was or what she might do. It could be a complete and utter disaster.

She and Katie had built a nice life for themselves. Katie was finally beginning to settle into her classroom at school, they had a lovely little flat by the beach, they walked to Singles for breakfast on the weekends, and they spent their days off fishing, swimming, snorkelling, and riding bikes around the quaint seaside hamlet.

Was it sensible to invite an unknown into their neat and happy lives?

On the one hand, she desperately wanted to know her birth mother and to have a family again. And on the other hand, she was the one who was considered a suspect in a murder investigation and who'd run down a casket at a funeral, scattering the crowd and sending the deceased rolling across the tarmac. So perhaps her mother should be afraid to know her rather than the other way around.

She pressed a hand to her forehead and groaned. How had her life come to this?

But she'd wanted this for so long and hadn't been brave enough to take the first step until now.

She tapped out a response, including her contact details, and sent it back before she could rethink the whole thing. Then she climbed out of the car, slung her purse over her shoulder, and strode into the Palm Club.

The club was set on the edge of an immaculate golf course. Rolling hills of green, perfectly trimmed grass spotted with gum trees and short, squat bushes all carefully shaped. The woman at the reception desk took her back into the kitchen where staff busily sliced, fried, and steamed as they scurried around the expansive space.

A woman in a green suit approached, a pair of black-rimmed spectacles sitting comfortably on the bridge of her nose so she could see over the top. She peered over them at

Stella and set down a folder on the stainless-steel bench beside her.

"You're Stella Thompson?"

Stella smiled and held out a hand. "You must be Karen Little. Pleasure to meet you."

Karen ignored her outstretched hand, staring at it as though it carried some kind of infectious disease that might make her skin fall off.

Stella's smile faded, and she let her hand drop to her side. "I'm looking for Karen..."

"I'm Karen," the woman said abruptly. "I thought I'd be meeting with Zoey."

"She couldn't make it, so she sent me instead."

"Well, she should've made that clear."

"I'm sorry," Stella replied, confused. "I'm sure we can still manage to get through everything on our to-do list without Zoey here. If I need to, I can call her to confirm any changes."

The woman sniffed and set a hand on her hip. "I'm friends with Allegra Cowderoy. She and I go way back. And from what I understand, you're the prime suspect in her husband's murder investigation."

Stella took a step back. "Oh... I see."

"And I don't work with murderers. It's that simple. I'm the caterer, I get to choose who I do business with, and I'm not interested in working with a criminal who ruined my friend's life."

"I'm sorry you feel that way. I can assure you, I didn't have anything to do with..."

The woman raised a hand to stop her. "I don't want to hear your excuses or what you think I should know about the situation. I'm always going to be loyal to my friends. So, you can leave."

A lump formed in Stella's throat. She didn't want to cry in

front of this woman. So instead, she drew a deep, shaky breath. "What should I tell Zoey?"

"You can tell her to find another caterer," Karen said.

She stalked from the kitchen, the folder tucked beneath one arm. Stella watched her leave, her entire body quivering. This couldn't be happening. She'd never been attacked openly like that while doing her job. She wasn't sure how to respond or what to do next. She decided to call Zoey to update her. They'd have to find another caterer, and it would be difficult on such short notice.

The gala was coming up, and now they had no one to provide food. She couldn't think about the fact that Allegra was telling people Stella had killed her husband. She had to push those thoughts aside, or she would cry right there in the posh kitchen of an exclusive golf club. How many people were walking around out there under the impression that she was guilty?

She explained what'd happened to Zoey, who immediately jumped into protective, angry mode.

"How dare she? I should come down there right now and tell her what I think of her professionalism. That's a disgusting way to behave. What happened to innocent until proven guilty?"

Stella ducked her head and lowered her voice. The kitchen staff were sending furtive glances in her direction, no doubt wondering what she was still doing there and whether she was about to grab a cleaver and take them all out with it. After all, she was a murderer, according to the caterer. No doubt they'd heard all about her and were terrified to have her still standing in their kitchen.

As she walked outside and back to her car, she whispered into the phone, "You don't think I did it, do you?"

"What? Do I think you killed my neighbour? Pfffft—no, of course not. You don't have it in you."

"Thank you," she said, her lower lip trembling. "I hope other people can see that too. I can't bear the idea that they're all judging me for something I haven't done."

"This will blow over. I'm sure Toni will find the real killer, and everyone will forget you were even questioned."

Stella unlocked the car and climbed inside. "I hope so. But what are we going to do about the food?"

"I've got someone in mind. I'll give them a call and let you know what they say. Don't worry, it's going to be fine."

When she hung up the phone, Stella felt much better. Zoey was fantastic at coming to the rescue whenever she thought someone was in distress. All Stella had to do was show her vulnerable side, and Zoey would jump to fix whatever the problem was. Usually it irritated her—she didn't want saving. She was a fully capable adult who didn't appreciate being treated like a hopeless child. But today, it was exactly what she needed.

Once when Stella was still getting to know her boss and Katie was new to school, she'd mentioned her concerns that on the very first day of class, she'd noticed that some of the children could already read and write. It'd been something of a shock to her, given the fact that she'd mistakenly assumed they would learn to read and write while attending school.

It seemed to be the height of bad manners in Kingscliff to send your child off to school in need of schooling. Stella had muttered something to the effect that she hoped it wouldn't cause Katie any pain, knowing she was the only child in her class who didn't already have the alphabet and the array of first-level readers sitting on the timber bookshelf in the reading corner already memorised.

She'd forgotten all about their conversation and gone on with her workday. Zoey had disappeared right after their morning meeting only to reappear after lunch with an entire shopping bag full of alphabet flash cards, readers, chapter books, an alphabet poster, and a digital device that read along with Katie when she ran a laser pen over the words.

When Zoey handed her the bag, at first she'd been politely appreciative, but only because she was shocked into virtual silence. After she'd sat for a while, running over a design presentation but with her mind entirely taken up by the shopping bag on the floor beside her desk, she'd marched into Zoey's room to tell her that she'd had no intention of attempting to teach her daughter to read at home, since that's what her well-qualified teachers were for, and frankly, Zoey was stepping over a well-defined boundary about staying out of other people's parenting...but when she saw Zoey's eager, smiling face, she couldn't do it and instead asked if she would like a cup of coffee. Ever since, she'd accepted Zoey's well-meaning boundary crossing as a token of her friendship and learned to keep to herself the things she didn't want to share.

She started the car's engine with a flick of her wrist and performed a U-turn to head back to Kingscliff. Zoey would handle the caterer situation, and she could turn her attention back to the fact that her birth mother might want to talk to her. Excitement buzzed in her gut as a spike of adrenaline rose up her spine and fizzed in her head. This year certainly couldn't be accused of being boring. She'd had a few boring years in recent history and had caught herself on occasion wishing something exciting might happen to bring some spark back into her life. Perhaps she should've dreamed of a yachting holiday in the Whitsundays instead.

Chapter Thirty-Four

When Zoey walked into Singles café, she scanned the booths and the tables and spied Toni seated in a booth in the back of the room. She slouched in the darkest corner, shoulders hunched and shirt bunched around her neck. She wore sunglasses inside and was tearing a napkin apart, adding the tiny pieces to a pile of similar shapes on the table in front of her.

For a moment, Zoey considered walking right back out the door and calling Toni from outside to say that she couldn't make it. But only because she was so very tired, and everything had been going wrong all week long with the gala and with Isla, and she wasn't sure she could take any more pain or heartache.

With the way Toni looked, Zoey knew there was going to be another drama with Rodger. And as much as she loved Toni, sometimes she wanted to smack her over the head and tell her to get a backbone and leave the lout already. But she couldn't because that wasn't the kind of things friends said to one another. And so she'd have to pretend she didn't want to walk directly to the school and tackle Rodger in his classroom, then sit on him and make him promise to be nice to his wife.

Listening to her friends' woes about their husbands always made her ever more grateful for Dave. She took him for granted, she reminded herself. They'd been married twenty years, so she didn't know how good she had it. He was a catch. She should definitely bake him a cake when she got home, and maybe they could even go out on Friday night. Although that would mean leaving Isla home alone, and she wasn't sure she could ever do that again and trust her daughter to remain in the house without inviting anyone over.

All these years, she'd dreamed of the day that she and Dave could leave the house together in the evenings without Isla. *One day*, she'd think to herself as she rocked back and forth beside the window, bouncing a colicky baby on her shoulder. *One day we'll have our freedom back. This is simply a season.* And now the time had come. Their daughter was old enough that she and Dave could take the occasional date night alone, but conveniently Isla had decided to become a teenaged delinquent who couldn't be trusted. And the thought of that made her want to scream.

Toni's auburn curls were frizzier than usual, especially in the back. It looked as though she'd climbed right out of bed. Her clothes were mismatched, which wasn't unusual for Toni except that it looked as though she'd pulled them from the bottom of the ironing basket. And the buttons on her shirt were lopsided.

"Hello, honey," Zoey said, sliding into the booth across from Toni.

Toni nodded and smiled. "Hey, thanks for meeting me."

"You look awful," Zoey said, reaching out a hand to squeeze Toni's where it hung over the pile of tiny red napkin pieces.

"Gee, thanks."

"I mean it. What's going on with you? Have you even brushed your hair this morning?"

Toni patted around her head as though finding hair there was utterly unexpected. "Huh."

"Are you okay?"

Toni leaned forwards with a grunt. "How do you do it?"

"Do what? Brush my hair? It's easy, really. You stand in front of the bathroom mirror with a brush in your hand..."

"No." Toni waved her off. "I mean stay married. How do you stay married? Seriously, I want to know. Tell me the secret. Because there's got to be a secret. Right?"

Zoey smoothed her own hair back from her face. It was very clear that she had to choose her words carefully. She'd never seen Toni like this before, but it was obvious when someone was balancing on the edge. "There's no real secret to it. It's all about communication..."

"Communication! Blah!" Toni blurted.

Zoey startled. "Um, what?"

"That's what everyone says. Communication...blah, blah, blah. Why won't any of you smug married couples tell us the truth? Because I know it's not about talking—that's all Rodger and I seem to do. And the only thing it results in is us fighting and him storming off and leaving me alone at a restaurant in my best dress on my birthday." She sniffled and rubbed violently at her nose with the back of her hand.

"Oh, honey, I'm so sorry. Did he really do that?"

Toni nodded and sniffed again. Zoey dug around in her purse, pulled out a packet of tissues, and handed them to Toni. Toni blew her nose as Asher appeared at their booth.

"I hope you're not getting sick," he said, covering his mouth and nose with a chuckle. "I'll be forced to kick you out. I'm on a wellness streak. Haven't had a cold or flu or anything remotely like it for well over three years."

"Wow," Zoey said, putting on her best company voice.

"That's impressive. We promise not to get you sick. Don't we, Toni? Anyway, she's not unwell—just got a bit of a sniffle, that's all."

Underneath it, Zoey's throat ached, and her head pounded with the beginnings of a headache. She hated what Toni was going through, but the hardest part was that she couldn't do anything about it. She wasn't great at saying the right things or at being a listening ear—not naturally, anyway. She'd worked on improving herself in those areas with the help of a series of videos she'd found online once when scrolling through self-help topics like *Staying Fit over Forty*, and *Lose the Last Stubborn Pounds*, or *Build Better Boundaries: Learning How to Say NO!* But even when she didn't have the right words to say, she could jump to action and do something to help.

No lasagne or batch of biscuits would change anything. No night out with the girls or scrapbooking evening would repair their relationship.

Asher shot the silent Toni a sympathetic look as she wiped her nose with yet another tissue and set it on the pile of napkin pieces. Then he took their order and left.

"You chased him off with your gross little pile of snot rags," Zoey said.

Toni giggled. "Shut up, please."

"No, really, it's unhygienic. Look at it. There's a mountain of them on the table where we're going to put the *food*. Remember lunch? I'm starving, by the way. I hope you're hungry. I've ordered enough to feed an army. When I see tears, all I can think about is food."

Toni laughed, set her sunglasses on the table, and brushed the pile of tissues and napkins aside. "Forget about germs for a moment and focus, Zoey. My marriage is disintegrating, and I have no idea what to do about it."

Toni's eyes were bloodshot and completely free of

makeup. Her eyelashes were pale against her splotchy red cheeks. Her blue irises appeared translucent.

"How did you leave things between you?" Zoey asked, her voice softening.

"He never came home."

"When was this?"

"Last night," Toni replied. "I haven't seen him since, and he hasn't answered my calls. He texted to say he's fine and needs some time to process."

"Wow, okay."

"What does that mean—time to process? And where is he staying?" Tears rolled down Toni's cheeks, and she tugged another tissue from the packet to dab at them.

Zoey slid into the seat beside Toni and wrapped an arm around her shoulders. "I'm so sorry, honey."

She sobbed. "And now, I find out that Ryker is flunking year eleven. I had no idea he was struggling at all. He hasn't said anything, and he always seems to be doing homework. So I don't know what's going on with him either. Are all the men in my life lying to me every chance they get?"

"He's failing? Really? That's not like him. Maybe he and Isla are in cahoots. She's causing me heart palpitations at the moment."

Toni drew back and studied Zoey. "She is? Is this normal teen behaviour? Or something else?"

Zoey shrugged. "Who knows? This is my first teenager."

"Me too. Do you think it gets better again? It was so easy when they were little. They were hard work, but you always knew what was going on in their lives."

"We can only hope," Zoey said.

Asher returned with their lunch, and Zoey slid back onto her side of the booth and dipped a chip in tomato sauce. Isla had lied to her about so many things now, she wasn't sure what was true and what wasn't. But she honestly believed deep down that her daughter was a sweet and thoughtful child who was simply taking a moment to push against some boundaries. Things had to get better.

"How do you know you're doing the right thing as parents? That's the real question." She took a bite of her chip.

Toni dried her tears with yet another tissue and shook her head. "I always feel like I'm doing it wrong. But I don't know if that's only my insecurities after years of failure in that area, or if it's true."

"You're a good mum," Zoey said. "You love him, and he knows that."

"I love him more than anything. I think he knows it."

"He does," Zoey said with confidence. She'd seen the way Ryker was with Toni; she listened to him attentively and always spoke to him with patience and love. Over the years, she'd witnessed plenty of crises where Toni took care of her son, remaining calm and affectionate even when he lost his cool.

He was a mysterious kind of kid, always seemed to be holding back. She'd known him for years but didn't really feel as though she *knew* him. He was quiet but with an edge of insecurity that seemed to colour his interactions with the world.

"He's meeting me here after lunch," Toni said around a mouthful of hamburger.

"What are you going to say?"

"I don't know. I'm going to ask him what's going on in his life, I suppose. I don't want to condemn him without hearing him out."

"Smart. And how's work?" Zoey took a bite of her sandwich.

Toni swallowed. "It's the only thing in my life that's going well at the moment. We've had a bit of a breakthrough. I can't talk about it, but at our meeting this morning, there were a few things discussed that changed the trajectory of our investigation. You'll hear about it on the news, no doubt."

"The news? My best friend is leading the investigation."

Toni grinned. "But I can't be seen to be sharing that kind of information, now can I?"

"You have too much integrity," Zoey complained. "I hear all the time about these corrupt police officers—where are they?"

Toni feigned horror. "Hush your mouth. Not in my neighbourhood, they're not."

"Well, if you ever do decide to become corrupt, can you please do me a favour and arrest Betty Smythe for causing a public nuisance the next time she holds a neighbourhood meeting at her house? That woman is driving the whole neighbourhood batty with her grass height requirements and strict rules about no Christmas lights after the New Year."

Toni laughed.

Job well done, Zoey thought.

* * *

After Zoey left, Toni had to admit she felt much better. Her friend always had a way of lightening the mood and getting her to think about something other than whatever it was that was troubling her. She waited for Ryker outside the café while texting back and forth with Callum. She'd promised to drive him to the high school for his English examination and intended to have a little discussion with him about his grades on the way.

She'd done her best to smooth her bouffant in the café's bathroom mirror, but her hair was really beyond hope at this point. At least she didn't look like she'd simply rolled out of bed and walked out the door now. She'd noticed while staring mutely at her own reflection that her buttons were askew and fixed them as well.

However, the fact that she was wearing a paisley shirt that looked as though it'd come directly from the 1990s in a time machine and somehow found its way into her closet without her having any idea of how it got there, paired with some denim jeggings and mismatched Doc Martens, was something she would simply have to accept. How did she manage to put together a black shoe with a neon pink one without noticing? At least they were each on the right foot. She'd got that correct. But there was no time to go home and change. She'd already taken too long a break for lunch, and Callum was on her case about getting back to the office asap.

And besides, everyone at work was accustomed to her quirky style. Several of the admin staff had a running joke about her wardrobe choices and teased her lovingly whenever she tried a new outfit. But when she'd shown up to the morning meeting like this, with reddened eyes and a dazed expression, they'd all shot her strange looks. Still, no one had said a thing. Not until Zoey. She could always trust Zoey to snap her out of a fog.

While she waited, she ran through the positive affirmations her counsellor had taught her. She had no intention of letting the haze transform into a blue mood that could shift gradually and without her realising it into a deep and dark depression. Once she was down that hole, it was hard to pull herself back up out of it again. But it'd been years since it'd taken hold of her life. She knew how to keep it at bay now.

"Mum!" Ryker called. He jogged up behind her, a backpack slung over one shoulder.

"There you are," she said, kissing his cheek. "I was wondering."

"Sorry I'm late. I got caught up studying."

Did you just? she thought, scanning his expression for

some hint that he was intentionally misleading her, but he simply smiled in response and laid an arm around her shoulders. He'd overtaken her in height about two years earlier and ever since loved to rub in that fact by embracing her in a paternal way, towering over her with a glint of laughter in his eyes.

"Yes, I know you're tall," she often said when he did this.

He'd grin and kiss the top of her head. "You're a midget."

"I am not," she'd object. "I'm a perfectly normal height. You're clearly a giant."

She'd miss those familiar interactions when he went off to university. *If* he went off to university. All the things she'd understood to be true, all her expectations for him, were now in question. Who was this boy walking to the car beside her? He'd hidden so much of himself from her that she couldn't help wondering what else was going on in his head that she knew nothing about.

In the car, he turned up the radio. She listened to the music for a while, then turned it down.

"How's school going?" she asked.

He shifted in the passenger seat. "Fine."

"Nothing bothering you? Nothing you want to talk about?"

"Nope. All good."

"Are you sure?"

He sighed. "What is it, Mum?"

"I spoke to Mr Woodrow. He says you're struggling."

"I'm not struggling."

"Then what's going on?" Keep things light, draw him out, give him room to tell his side of the story. She should feel bad about using interview techniques she'd honed on criminals over the years on her son, but she needed to get to the bottom of things. And this was all she knew to do.

He hesitated. "I don't know. I'm bored, I guess."

"With school?"

"With everything. I can't picture what's coming."

She waited, gave him space.

"I'm supposed to finish school next year, but then what? What's after that? I don't see myself at uni."

She bit her lip, almost drawing blood as she did her best to stay quiet.

"That's it, I guess."

"Why don't you want to go to uni?"

"More study? I'm bored thinking about it. I want to *do* something with my life. I need an adventure or something to happen."

She understood that feeling. She'd felt that way herself many times over the years. It'd also gotten her into more trouble than she cared to admit. Especially when she let it build and fester over time and didn't do anything to satiate it.

"I get it. I do. Trust me, we're more alike than you realise."

He peered at her through narrowed eyes. "Really?"

"Of course. But the problem for me has always been that I shove the feeling down until I'm fairly bursting with it. Then, when I finally let it run free, it gets me into hot water."

"Like what?" he asked.

She grimaced. "Nice try. I'm not ready to talk to you about my teenaged transgressions. Not yet, anyway. Maybe when you're no longer a teen. You don't need me giving you ideas. But seriously, we should do something. We should have an adventure. I promise you, when the school year is finished, you and I can go and go on a trip together. We could go to New Zealand and hike the Milford Track. What do you think?"

He grinned. "Yeah. Okay."

"We all need adventure every now and then, honey. Some of us more than others. But don't let your drive for excitement push you into making bad choices for your life. You need to communicate with me and your dad. Let us know what's going on so we can do something to help. If we don't know how you're feeling, we can't help you. Got it?"

"Fair enough. I'll try harder at school."

"You've got exams all week. I'd like to see you studying. I don't think uni is boring at all—it's a chance for a whole lot of adventures. But if you don't study and do your best, you won't get into the course you want, and you'll probably struggle to enjoy it. How you face those hard things impacts everything about your life. It's not the grades so much as it is the attitude. I want to see you striving, doing your best. Enthusiasm for life is very important. Okay?"

"Okay, Mum."

She dropped him off at the high school, very satisfied with herself. He was a good kid. He needed some excitement in his life. Who didn't? This was something she knew how to deal with. Adventure was the thing that'd driven her forwards for so many years. It was what pushed her to become a police officer. It was the thing that'd made her impulsive so that she got pregnant without planning for it. She'd been such an enthusiastic kid, always looking for the truth, always imagining she was a hobbit on a quest or a girl riding a magical horse through Narnia. Books had given her the adventure she craved when she was young. But then life had beaten the enthusiasm right out of her and replaced it with a darkness she found hard to shake for many years. Maybe this was a wakeup call. She and Ryker could do this together—it might finally be something they could bond over. Something they could share, the two of them. And a flutter of something like hope passed through her.

Chapter Thirty-Five

Callum was waiting outside the police station when Toni pulled up. She climbed out, laptop bag slung over one shoulder, purse on the other shoulder, and a cardboard tray holding two enormous coffee cups balanced on one hand. She slammed the door shut behind her with the other hand and almost sent the coffee cups flying. With her tongue poking from one side of her mouth, she wobbled back and forth until the cups were righted again, then slammed an elbow into the car door. A slice of pain ran up her forearm from her funny bone, making her gasp.

"You right there, Boss?" He grinned. "Need some help?"

She handed him the tray of coffees. "Thanks."

Callum wore a pair of perfectly ironed slacks and a light-blue buttoned shirt that accentuated his muscular build. He clearly worked out and wanted people to know it by the way he dressed. Usually it didn't bother Toni, but today she was in such a state of disarray, it was as though he was showing off how much more together he was than her. She bit down on her tongue to stop herself from saying anything. Pain made her snappy.

"No worries. I've got an update for you."

"Go ahead." They marched towards the automatic glass doors.

"The limousine service finally got back to me. Wouldn't cooperate at all without a warrant, so it's taken a while."

"I'll say," she said, rolling her eyes.

"It seems Mrs Cowderoy didn't take a car to the airport at five p.m. like she told us. She called and changed the time to 8:30 p.m. There was a note on the file about it. Apparently, it's not unusual for her to make last-minute adjustments to her schedule."

They stepped through the glass doors and into the reception area. Toni waved at the receptionist and tapped her security pass against the inner door, then pushed against it with her shoulder. It was good to be back in the office again where things made sense.

Through all the tumultuous times in her life, work had been the one thing that'd kept her grounded, kept her going. There was always someone to help, a crime to solve, someone who needed rescuing. Every time she solved a case and put a perpetrator behind bars, she was saving someone in the community from being assaulted or murdered. It gave her a sense of purpose that distracted her from the conflicts and struggles in her life.

"So, Allegra was home during the time of death window?"

"Between eight p.m. and midnight? Yep. She could've done it. The kids saw Mark at around 8:30 p.m. in the garden, although they're not sure of the exact time it might've been earlier. No one saw him after that—not that we've spoken to, anyway. There was a vehicle parked outside the house, and its occupant drove off around ten p.m. But otherwise, we have no evidence of movement outside of that time frame. We didn't spot the limo in the security footage because the camera doesn't show the driveway, and apparently that's where the vehicle parked while waiting for Mrs Cowderoy."

Toni set her things down on her desk. Callum handed her the coffee cup. She sipped it thoughtfully, then settled into her chair. "The timeline fits. She had the opportunity."

"There's more. We got the DNA report back from the lab. They found two sets of DNA on the pot plant. One was Mark's, and the other was Allegra's."

"Makes sense, since they both lived there. They could've touched that pot at any time."

He grunted. "Yep."

"So that's not particularly helpful. Although there wasn't any other DNA, so that's something."

"The report stated that the likelihood of finding any DNA on the pot was minimal, given the makeup of the clay. They found a minuscule amount for each of the two matches, which could've been deposited by moving the pot around or basic gardening activities."

She switched on her computer. "Still, if we take all of that and combine it with the fact that Allegra called Stella repeatedly in the days leading up to the murder, it looks like we have opportunity and a motive."

"We should bring her in for questioning again," Callum suggested, swigging his coffee.

"I want an arrest warrant." Toni opened her email, and dozens of new messages pinged onto the screen.

Callum's eyes widened. "Isn't it a bit soon?"

"Look, we've got enough for a warrant. And she's clearly hiding something. If we arrest her, we have her on the back foot. Maybe she'll confess."

"And maybe she'll lawyer up," Callum added with a sniff.

"True. But we're under some time pressure here to get this thing solved. So let's see if we can turn up the heat and make her nervous today, give her some time to think, then we'll action the arrest warrant in the morning."

He grinned. "You got it."

Chapter Thirty-Six

FRIDAY

23RD NOVEMBER

Zoey had the ultimate suburban home, Stella decided. It was two stories of pure bliss. That had been Katie's description of the house when they'd first seen it. "Pure bliss" was her latest saying. She'd heard it on a commercial, something about a chocolate caramel swirl smoothie they were pushing at a local fast-food place.

With a taste that's pure bliss.

Katie had repeated the phrase everywhere they went for weeks. This hamburger is *pure bliss*. The sand between my toes is *pure bliss*. And the suburban mansion in the gated community of Pelican Grove, with its perfectly matched cream-and-tan decor and luxurious rectangular swimming pool surrounded by six-foot-high glass fencing, was *pure bliss*. It was easy to please a five-year-old generally, but Stella couldn't imagine ever being able to own something like the house looming behind her. Not as a single mother, and not on her salary.

Still, she couldn't complain. The two of them certainly didn't need anything this big. And the complex she and Katie lived in had a shared pool on the ground level. They were also within walking distance of the beach. So who needed a McMansion in a gated community? Not them, that was for sure. They had everything they needed. And they were friends with Zoey and Dave, which meant they could basically stop in for a swim anytime they liked. Which was even better than owning it herself because she could skip all of the maintenance and expense. The idea of taking care of a yard, let alone a big swimming pool as well, gave her a headache.

Katie ran down the side of the pool.

"No running!" Stella called.

Katie paid no attention. She was too absorbed in the game Isla had begun the moment Katie emerged shyly from the house in her brand-new pink bathing suit. Stella couldn't get over how well the teen got along with her five-year-old daughter.

"Aren't teenagers supposed to be sullen and have no time for little kids?" she asked, tenting her hand over her eyes to watch Isla blow a spurt of water into the air that sent Katie into a paroxysm of giggles.

Zoey was busily pouring her famous cocktail from a pitcher into a glass. The recipe was a secret, although Stella assumed from the flavour that it included rum, gin, vodka, and a dash of dreams come true. It was delicious and very strong, and she reminded herself to take it easy. The last time Zoey had served her signature drink, Stella and Katie had spent the night in Zoey's guest room since Stella couldn't summon the energy to stumble home.

Come to mention it, she wouldn't mind another stint in the guest room with its vanilla-scented towels, Egyptian cotton sheets, and the breakfast Zoey had served her on a tray in bed with fresh-cut flowers in a vase on the side. Stella didn't know how Zoey managed it all, but was secretly in awe of her somewhat over-the-top domestic skills.

Katie threw a pool noodle into the water, then leapt in the air with a squeal, tucking her knees up and bombing into the impossibly blue water. A wave slapped the side of the pool, sending up a spray that reached Isla's legs. She laughed and leapt into the water after Katie.

Stella leaned back on her lounger and lifted the fruity drink in the enormous wine glass to her lips. She took a sip. It was cold and refreshing with a hint of sweetness, and had already given her a nice, warm, heady feeling. It was a Friday afternoon, and she was lazing beside a pool sipping a cocktail. It was like being at a holiday resort, but without the hefty bill at the end of the visit.

"I'm going to have to order an Uber home if you keep serving me these," she said, lifting her cup in Zoey's direction.

Zoey said, "Ha!" and jumped onto the lounge chair beside her, holding her own orange-and-red concoction aloft.

"You're spoiling us. Katie's supposed to be doing homework while I cook dinner and wash the enormous pile of dirty dishes currently soaking in my kitchen sink."

"You need to be spoiled occasionally. You work far too hard."

"No, I don't."

"Well, you have to do it all yourself. And there's no one to tell you to take a break and put your feet up. So I'm doing that for you today."

Stella swallowed another mouthful of drink. "And I'm forever grateful to you."

"Besides, we have a few more things to talk about."

"The Christmas gala?" Stella offered.

"Yes. I found a new caterer, so that's all taken care of. I'll send you her contact information."

"Fantastic." Stella swallowed another mouthful of the fruity drink. It was delightful. Every mouthful was tastier than the last. "I thought we should do a steak option and a fish option. Does that sound okay?"

"Perfect. I'll leave the details to you to organise. If you can email the menu to me once you've confirmed it with the caterer, that would be great."

"Will do," Stella said.

The side gate opened, and Toni walked into the yard. She wore a strange outfit with mismatched shoes—one black and the other pink. Her shirt was patterned and hurt Stella's eyes.

She straightened in her seat. "I'm not being arrested, am I?"

Toni raised both hands, palms up. "Not today."

Zoey let out a high-pitched peal of laughter. "You two are hilarious." She kissed Toni's cheek. "What a pleasant surprise."

Toni sat on a lounge chair beside Zoey and rested her head in her hands. Her hair stuck out in a strange frizzy style all over her head. Usually it was somewhat tamed into curls, but today it looked as though Toni had rolled around and around on a carpet charged with static electricity.

"You okay, hon?" Zoey had hurried to fill another wine glass with her concoction.

"Fine, just need a drink."

"Well, lucky for you..." Zoey handed her the glass. "Bottom's up."

Toni lay back on the lounge chair and stared at the darkening sky. "Did I interrupt anything?"

Stella finished her drink and set the empty glass on a small plastic table. "We were talking about the Christmas gala. Sorry, boring work stuff."

"Don't let me stop you. I'm going to drink and stare at

those cute little fluffy clouds up there until my head stops pounding."

Zoey shot Stella a questioning look. Stella shrugged. "Okay, we were about to deal with the guest list. I sent you an updated version earlier. I think that's everyone now."

Zoey scrolled through the email on her phone, squinting and shielding the screen with one hand. "What about Allegra? I thought we spoke about adding her to the list. She's my neighbour, after all. I'm sure she'll decline, but it's a gesture, you know, after everything..."

Stella had intentionally left Allegra off the invitation list and hoped Zoey wouldn't notice. She couldn't have the woman who believed she'd murdered her husband at this event. It could cause trouble and would definitely distract Stella from what she was supposed to be doing—which was making sure everything went according to plan. How could she do that if she was constantly dodging Allegra Cowderoy?

Stella looked to Toni for help, but she was studiously ignoring their conversation and seemed to be tracing the outline of a cloud with her fingertip in the air. Stella's brow furrowed. Were they all losing their minds? Some kind of mass delusion. Everyone in town going crazy at the same time.

"Um... I thought we might leave her off the list. Given... you know?" She tipped her head in Toni's direction.

"Given what?" Zoey asked, topping up her glass.

"She means the murder," Toni piped up. "You can be a little bit oblivious sometimes, hon."

Zoey's eyes narrowed. "That's why I want to invite her. She's been through a lot. And besides that, she has a lot of rich friends. It'll be good for business."

She didn't want to upset Zoey, but inviting Allegra to their big party was inviting calamity. "There's something I have to tell you."

Toni didn't say a word and kept her gaze skyward.

Zoey sat back down on her lounge and rearranged the lace coverall over her bright blue bikini. "What is it?"

"Allegra thinks I killed Mark."

"But you explained that," Zoey said.

"Yes, I did. But she doesn't believe me...because I had an affair with Mark."

"You what?"

Toni sat up and shook her head. "I think I'm going to take a little walk inside. I need to use the loo. Be back in a jiffy."

Stella watched her go, her throat raw as tears threatened.

"What was all that about?" Zoey asked.

"I'm officially a suspect. I don't think she wants to taint her investigation or something. I don't know. Anyway, that's not the issue. The issue is I had an affair with Mark. It was a long time ago. Exactly six years ago, in fact." She watched Katie, who at that moment pushed off Isla's shoulders, flying into the air above her head and somersaulting into the water.

Zoey's eyes widened. "Katie?"

"He's her father."

"Does Allegra know?"

"I believe so. Anyway, she accused me of killing him. But of course, I didn't. Still, if she came to the gala, I think it might potentially cause some drama. What if she confronts me? And I'll spend the whole time stressed and trying to stay out of her way."

"Right, that makes sense. Scratch her off the invitation list. I'll do something else nice for her instead."

Toni returned then, her face freshly washed and her hair slightly tamer. "Safe to come back yet?"

Stella smiled. "Perfectly safe. Let's move on to a different subject."

"I can't believe it," Zoey murmured, staring at Katie who was slapping hands in a funny splashing game with Isla.

Stella didn't want to cry, and she was dangerously close to

it. She cleared her throat and in a too-high voice trilled, "New topic!"

"Yes, let's talk about something else." Zoey snapped back to attention. "Toni, how are you? What's going on in your life?"

"You mean besides the fact that my son is flunking high school and my husband is missing?"

Zoey slapped a hand over her mouth.

Stella startled. "What? Rodger is missing?"

Toni sighed. "I know where he is. He texted me this morning to say he'd be at home after school this evening. He said he's going to collect a few things, but he'll be back tomorrow and we can talk then. He still needs time to process. That's the word he used, 'process.' Apparently more time away from me to *process* his thoughts will solve all of the problems in our marriage. That's why I'm here. I'm avoiding seeing him and giving him space. Which means avoiding my own flat. I'm essentially homeless until he leaves."

Zoey squeezed her hand. "I'm so sorry, honey. That's hard."

"I think he's having an affair." Toni squeezed her eyes shut.

"Why do you say that?" Stella asked.

"He's been gone since Monday night. He won't tell me where he's staying. And he's picking silly fights with me and escalating them into utter dramas for no apparent reason. I've been killing myself trying to make sense of it all, but it doesn't make sense unless he's having an affair. Then it all makes *perfect* sense." She pressed both hands to her face with a groan.

Zoey sat beside her and embraced her. "Oh, honey."

"But you don't know for sure," Stella offered.

"No, I don't know for sure. That's true. Maybe I shouldn't get so worked up until I'm certain. I don't know.

My world has been pulled out from under my feet like an old rug."

Zoey clapped her hands together. "I know what you should do."

"What?" Toni wiped her eyes with a fingertip. There were red blotches all over her neck.

"You should follow him. We should all follow him. It'll be like we're spies. We can dress in black. I have the cutest little black scarf I bought the other day at David Jones, and I've been dying for a chance to wear it."

Stella stifled a giggle. "I'm not sure that's the priority here."

"Of course not, sorry. We'll follow him when he leaves the flat and see where he goes. That way, at least you'll know where he is."

Stella couldn't believe she was actually in agreement with Zoey's crazy plan. It was a ridiculous thing to do, but still. "It's the only way to know for sure."

Toni looked at Zoey, then at Stella, with an incredulous expression. "You're both serious?"

"Absolutely, you're a cop. Don't you do this kind of thing all the time?"

"With approval." Toni sat up straight. "I mean, it's against the law to stalk someone. Although he is my husband, so I'm not sure stalking applies."

"We're not stalking him—we're going in the same direction he is. That's all. And besides, what judge would ever convict you of following your own husband? If he's having an affair, you'll know and you can move on with your life. If he's holing up at some fleabag motel alone and crying into his pillow, pining after your life together, then you can breeze in and rescue him with a big, swoony kiss."

"Do you think he might be pining for me?" Toni asked, a hopeful expression on her splotchy cheeks.

"I don't know." Zoey patted her on the back. "I don't think he is, but it's always a possibility."

"Okay, I can't believe I'm saying this, but let's do it. Let's follow my husband and find out where on earth he's spending his nights."

"I don't have anything black with me..." Stella said. She should take Katie home and feed her dinner. Katie's bedtime was still six thirty. She knew it was babyish. In fact, Katie complained about it every now and then. But as soon as her little head hit the pillow, she fell right to sleep. She needed that much time to recover from her days at school.

"That's okay. I've got a stew in the slow cooker, and there's plenty for all of us. We'll eat, then Isla can put Katie to bed in the guest room. You can borrow some black clothes from my wardrobe. I have a tonne of them after I went through a phase where I wanted to be like Angelina Jolie and wore nothing else."

Toni chuckled. "I remember that. I called you Morticia."

"Not quite what I was going for." Zoey playfully slapped Toni's thigh. "Anyway, what do you think?"

"I'm in."

Chapter Thirty-Seven

"They're in here somewhere!" Zoey shouted as she rummaged through the storage room on the side of her garage.

"What are you looking for?" Stella poked her head through the doorway, then stepped inside and promptly sneezed.

"You're not allergic to anything, are you?" Zoey pushed aside a pink bicycle with streamers hanging from the handlebars and waded deeper into the room.

"Dust." Stella rubbed her nose. "Can you see anything? Should I switch this light on?"

"Yes, please," Zoey said. "The light from the roller door isn't cutting it."

The storage room had a roller door at one end, like a narrower version of a garage. It was raised, and a dull light emitted from the controller above Zoey's head.

Stella flicked on the fluorescent overhead, and it illuminated the entire space.

"Whoa!" Zoey shielded her eyes from the glare with a

raised forearm. Her eyes adjusted quickly, and she lowered her arm.

Toni joined them, cradling a glass in one hand. "Is there a reason you're fossicking through your storage room right now?"

Stella raised both hands in confusion. "We've discovered where all of Zoey's junk resides."

Zoey sniffed. "Everyone has a messy space. No one's perfect."

"I always thought you were perfect," Toni mused. "I take back everything I said about you."

Zoey's eyes narrowed. "What did you say about me?"

"All that's behind us now. Tell me why we're standing in your messy storage space inhaling dust and petrol fumes."

Zoey's features grew animated. "We have a mission, right? But we've been downing drinks for the past two hours. None of us is in any state to drive. Plus we can't ask an Uber driver to follow your husband, can we, Toni?"

Toni's cheeks flushed pink. "I'd rather not. I *am* a police officer, after all."

"Exactly, so we need an alternative form of transportation. Ah-ha! Here they are."

She wheeled a scooter into the centre of the room and proudly displayed it for the other two women to see.

"A scooter? You must be joking." Toni laughed and pressed one hand to her hip. "You want us to scooter across town in the dark, after...an unknown number of your ridiculously concentrated drinks? You do know I'm close to fifty..."

"Pfft. You're not almost fifty. And this isn't just a scooter. It's an e-scooter."

"Maybe I'm a little slow," Stella said. "But what's an e-scooter?"

"Does it browse the internet while you ride?" Toni burst

into a loud guffaw and slapped her thigh with her free hand, then gulped another mouthful of drink from her wine glass.

Zoey glared at her. "No, it doesn't browse the internet. It's electric—e for electric. And that's your last cocktail, Little Miss Comedian."

"Ah, that makes a lot more sense."

Toni poked out her bottom lip. "No more fruity drinks?"

"Can you help me with these, please?" Zoey grunted as she tried her best to pull another scooter free from the pile of bicycles and skateboards they'd accumulated over the years.

Toni set down her drink to help. "You have a lot of stuff."

"I know. Some of these bikes are from when Isla was little. The skateboards are hers too—apparently she desperately needs one of every type, although she hardly uses them anymore. I couldn't bear to part with any of them at first, and now I'd love to dump them all. But I don't have time to go through them." Zoey grimaced as a bike pedal rammed into her shinbone. "Ouch!"

All three of them worked together to pull two more e-scooters free and lined them up in the driveway. Zoey puffed lightly as she surveyed them. They were a little dusty but still seemed to be in good shape.

"Dave bought three of these for the family, plus one for a friend so we could go scootering together along the beach path and Isla could bring someone her age."

"The track at Coolangatta?" Stella asked.

Zoey nodded. "We love it. Plus, there's a nice, long path up around the bay past Brisbane."

"Do you ever use them?" Toni asked.

"We went scootering a few times, but now it's virtually impossible to get Isla to agree on an outing. She's either glued to her screens, or meeting friends, or too busy doing homework."

"Welcome to the teen years." Toni shook her head.

"I'd travel back in time to the primary school era in a heartbeat. Those were the golden years." Zoey brushed the dust off one of the scooters and switched it on. "Grab a helmet from the pile over there. We don't need any brain injuries tonight."

Everyone donned a helmet. Zoey had to stifle a giggle at the sight of Toni in her eccentric outfit, wearing Isla's bright green skate helmet, her frizzy hair poking out at odd angles. Stella, of course, looked elegant and stylish in Zoey's spare helmet—which was pink and streamlined. "So, are we ready to go?"

Stella hopped from one foot to the other. "I've got to pee."

"I do too," Toni said.

Zoey rolled her eyes. "Okay, ladies, before we go out into the night on our top-secret mission, let's all pee first. Meet back here in five."

* * *

With her eyes narrowed, Zoey leaned forwards on the scooter. The steady whir of the electric engine was punctuated by the sound of gravel beneath its wheels. They moved at a clipped pace, steadily making their way up and down the hills of Kingscliff towards the beach and Toni's flat. Back at the house, they'd left Isla singing nursery rhymes with sock puppets to Katie. The sight had moved Zoey to tears. She didn't often see that side of her daughter's personality. She had such a tender heart beneath the layers of teenaged angst.

Tears whipped away from her eyes in the wind, and she reached up a hand to swipe at them. The handlebars on the scooter wobbled, making the entire structure dip dangerously from side to side. She quickly grabbed hold of the handlebar again, her heart in her throat. She could easily wipe out on the road. She had to keep her attention focused on the task at hand.

"I can't see anything!" Toni shouted behind her.

"Oh, yuck, disgusting. A bug flew in my mouth, a big one!" Stella cried, followed by a lot of raspberry noises.

Whenever she had a task to do, Zoey had no trouble with focus. If there was a sacrifice to make, she'd make it. If there was pain involved, she'd grin and bear it. She didn't look back but simply called out over her shoulder.

"Come on, ladies, we have a job to do. Let's stay on task."

"Has anyone ever told you that you're a slave driver?" Toni asked.

Stella laughed out loud, then groaned and spat furiously. "Another bug! Is anyone else eating bugs like they're skittles? And can I remind you that there's a murderer loose in Kingscliff?" she added. "We probably should be more careful."

"I don't think the murderer is roaming around town looking for middle-aged women on e-scooters to take out," Toni replied.

Zoey laughed out loud. The handlebars wobbled, and she almost face-planted into a puddle on the side of the road. She dodged it at the last moment and got the wobble under control, her breathing ragged.

"Stop distracting me," she shouted back to the others. "I literally almost died right then."

Hysterical giggling erupted behind her.

"This is ridiculous," Toni said through bouts of laughter. "He'll be long gone by the time we get there. We're moving at the speed of a sloth on holiday."

"I don't want to go too fast. It's dangerous without headlights."

"No kidding," Stella said. "Why don't we have headlights?"

"We've never used the scooters at night before. I should've looked in the camping supplies before we left. I'm fairly certain Dave has headlamps, but I didn't think of it then, and now it's too late. We can't go back. So, we're going to have to suck it up."

Stella spat and blew raspberries again.

"I didn't mean literally." Zoey giggled.

Toni laughed, then coughed. "Ugh, bug!"

"Eyes open, mouths shut. I'll increase our speed a bit, and hopefully we'll make it to the other side of town..."

"Before dawn," Toni added helpfully.

Stella grunted. "Hopefully we make it alive."

"I'll second that," Zoey said.

The sky was alight with a silvery glow from an oversized moon that hung low in the sky. The ride gave Zoey time to think about what they were doing. She was starting to sober up and realise that the course of action she'd suggested might end in tears for Toni. What if their discovery was heart-breaking for her friend? But then again, what if it wasn't—it might be the very thing Rodger and Toni needed to get the conversation started on healing their relationship. If he was ending their marriage, it was better that Toni know it now rather than to keep on hoping for a reconciliation when none was coming.

Knowing was better than not knowing.

She wasn't sure she concurred with the sentiment, though. In principle, it made sense. But if Dave was having an affair or harbouring some horrifying secret, would she want to know about it? What if she could spend her whole life in blissful ignorance instead? Wouldn't that be better than uncovering a truth that tore her family apart and ripped the ground out from beneath her feet?

She couldn't decide. It was a difficult call to make. No, of course it wasn't difficult—she'd want to know. Unless...it was all about their daughter and what mattered to her. And she deserved stability and love. So did that mean Zoey would prefer to be blissfully ignorant? Not at all—she hated being kept in the dark. In fact, the times in her marriage when she'd been the angriest with Dave were after she'd discovered he'd kept something from her.

Usually it was something small, like a household bill that was higher than they'd budgeted for back in the days when those things could mean catastrophe for them. Or when he'd failed to tell her they were spending the holidays with his family in Melbourne, and she'd made plans with her own family in Sydney. She'd been furious with him then. He'd explained that he didn't like conflict, so he simply hadn't spoken up. But she'd railed on and on about how honesty was the most important thing in a marriage. So, clearly she'd want to know.

Toni and Rodger's situation was complicated. But Zoey was certain that in the end, she'd want the truth even if it hurt. And it seemed Toni was of the same mindset, since she'd concurred to the outing. And ultimately it was Toni's decision to make, not Zoey's. She set her face like flint and accelerated into the centre of Kingscliff, navigating the roundabout with knees bent, careful not to run into the tree with the twinkle lights. Toni and Stella followed close behind.

When they reached Toni's flat, they saw Rodger standing out in front of the building. Zoey pulled over to the side of the road and slowed to a halt in the shade of a giant Norfolk pine tree. It shielded her from the brilliant glow coming from the full moon that hung over the heaving ocean.

Toni stopped beside her. Stella slowed, but not soon enough, and rammed into the back of Toni's scooter. Toni's scooter jumped forwards, and her helmet fell over her eyes. She rubbed the back of her neck. "Ugh, look out! I think you gave me whiplash."

"Sorry," Stella whispered.

"There's Rodger," Zoey hissed, pointing. He hovered at

the curb behind a row of vehicles parked in front of their building.

They watched him in silence.

"What's he doing?" Toni asked.

"Are those suitcases by his feet?" Stella rose to her tiptoes and wove back and forth, her eyes squinting against the light from the streetlamp beside Rodger.

"Looks like it," Toni said sullenly. "That truck is in the way, though. I can't see properly."

"Waiting for someone?" Stella suggested.

"That's his sports car parked at the curb." As she spoke, he opened the boot of the car and placed the luggage into it. Then shut it again.

"He's definitely waiting for someone," Zoey said as he leaned against the car and crossed his arms.

"It looks like he's not planning on coming back anytime soon," Toni said.

"Or maybe he's donating some clothes to charity," Stella whispered.

"Maybe." Toni shrugged.

Birds squawked overhead. *Likely rainbow lorikeets*, Zoey thought, looking up. The rainbow-coloured parrots always returned to the same trees along the coastline to roost at night and made a racket when they settled down at dusk, but were generally quiet throughout the night unless disturbed. She couldn't see anything but heard them shuffling around in the branches overhead. They fell silent again within a few moments, but in that time, a dark-coloured car had pulled up to the curb in front of Rodger.

"Who's that?" Toni stood on tiptoe, her brow furrowed.

"I don't know, but it's a nice BMW," Zoey said with a sniff.

Rodger jogged around to the passenger door, then slid inside. He leaned over to the driver.

"Are they hugging?" Zoey asked, straining to see through the car's lightly tinted windows.

They all bent low in an attempt to peer into the vehicle.

"I didn't think to bring binoculars," Zoey muttered as she pushed her scooter forwards a few steps.

"That's one long hug," Toni quipped in a cheery whisper.

Then they all gasped in unison.

"That's not just a hug," Stella whispered.

The shadowy outline of two people kissing was etched on Zoey's retinas. She couldn't push it out of her mind now if she tried. It was impossible to mistake the clutching desperation of the couple's embrace for anything else.

"Nope, that's definitely a kiss. A long, passionate kiss." Toni's head dropped and her shoulders slumped.

"I'm sorry, honey." Zoey rested a hand on her arm.

Toni shook her head. "I knew something was wrong. I had my suspicions, but I hoped it was all in my head. I guess I was right. Why do I always have to be right?"

If only they hadn't come. If only Zoey hadn't suggested they ride through town like some kind of middle-aged *Mission: Impossible* crew on their way to save the world. It'd seemed like such an exciting adventure at the time.

As much as she adored everything about her family and their lives together, marriage and family had sucked every last drop of excitement from her life. Dave had often said that her enthusiasm for life was the thing he'd fallen in love with, the one thing about her that'd made her stand out. But was that enthusiasm gone? Or just dormant?

Deep down, something had prompted her to reclaim her past. Now, the look on Toni's face broke her heart, and it was all her fault.

Something landed on Zoey's helmet and dripped onto her cheek. It was warm and sticky. She glanced up in surprise.

Darkness shrouded the branches overhead. A few birds chattered, then fell quiet.

"What was that?" she asked, reaching a hand to touch the substance.

Stella shuffled forwards on her scooter and studied Zoey's helmet. "Bird poop."

"Poop?" Zoey shook her fist at the birds overhead. "Seriously? More poop! Everywhere I go..."

Stella stifled a grin. "What are you talking about?"

"I step in dog doo everywhere I go. And now apparently I can't even stand under a tree without a bird letting loose on my head!" Zoey hissed.

Stella clapped both hands over her mouth and shook soundlessly.

Toni shot them both a disparaging look. "Shhh. Can we please focus? Whose car is that? It looks vaguely familiar, but I can't place it. Surely there aren't very many people who drive a BMW in this town. Can you read the number plate from here? It's too dark, and they're turned on the wrong angle."

Zoey tugged her right sleeve down over her hand and used it to wipe her cheek. "Can you catch a disease from bird poop? I think a bit splashed in my mouth."

Stella burst out with a noise that sounded like she was choking, then shoved her head down and pressed her elbows to the handlebars to smother her laughter. As she did, her scooter lurched forwards directly onto Toni's foot.

"Hey! My foot! You're on my foot!" Toni slapped Stella on the back.

Stella set her feet on either side of the scooter and tugged it away.

Toni held her foot in one hand, massaging the top of it. "That hurt. What are you two doing over here? You're supposed to be helping me identify the woman kissing my husband."

"Sorry, Toni," Stella said, composing herself with deep, slow breaths.

Zoey glared at Stella, then smiled at Toni. "Sorry, Toni."

They focused their attention on the other side of the road, but the vehicle was no longer there. Rodger's sports car was gone too.

"They're gone," Toni groaned in dismay. She shimmied her scooter into the middle of the street and looked in each direction, desperately searching for the car. "No sign of them, and we didn't get a single digit from the plate." She threw her hands in the air.

Zoey shot Stella a worried look. She scooted out onto the road and stopped beside Toni. "I'm sorry, honey."

Toni glared at her. "All I needed was for you to focus for one minute, and you couldn't even do that. We could've run the numbers from the plate to find out who this woman is who's destroying my life." She accelerated away down the street in the direction of the beach.

Zoey and Stella followed her. Toni stopped in the car park looking out over the ocean, and they sailed quietly up beside her. The waves roared to shore. The moonlight glistened silver on the water's surface. The sand looked black with a pathway of silver that travelled to the moon.

"It's going to be okay," Stella said.

Toni huffed. She sniffled into her sleeve. "No, it's not."

"We'll find out who she is," Zoey said.

"It doesn't even matter. He's having an affair. Who cares about her? Does it really make any difference who she is?"

Zoey shrugged. "I suppose not."

"So, there you go."

"Do you want to come back with us for another drink?" Stella asked, her voice warm.

Toni sighed. "No, I'm going home. I'll get the scooter back to you soon, Zoey."

Zoey shook her head. "No hurry. We don't use them anyway."

They remained that way in silence, each looking out at the sighing ocean. The pain she imagined Toni must've felt ached deep in Zoey's soul. She wanted to comfort her friend, but there was nothing she could say to make it better. Toni had to go through it, had to experience the pain. Zoey couldn't take it from her, couldn't bear it for her.

This was part of what it meant to open yourself up to love —carrying the pain of love lost on your own when it was over. Risking losing the best of your heart for a few years of joy. Only Toni's heart could process the loss. Only she could choose healing again when enough time had passed that the ache of betrayal had waned. Zoey could do nothing but stand beside her.

"My marriage is over," Toni said suddenly.

"Are you going to confront him about it?" Stella asked.

"Yes, I will. At some point. I don't know when. I need some time to think."

"That makes sense."

Toni waved goodbye and scootered back up the hill to her flat. Zoey and Stella watched her go, then headed for home without a word. They rode back to Zoey's place in silence. Stella climbed the stairs to the guest bedroom and shut the door behind her and Katie. Zoey took a long hot shower, scrubbing her face clean with as much soap as she could take. If bird poop could cause illness, she was determined not to let it infect her. The soap got in her eyes, and she took a long time to wash it out again. Then she collapsed in bed beside Dave's snoring form, her eyes still stinging from the soap and filled with tears for her friend.

Chapter Thirty-Eight

SATURDAY

24TH NOVEMBER

Saturday morning dawned with a pattering rain. It was as though the whole world was crying with Toni, and she watched it trickle down the windowpane from where she lay in bed alone. Their bed. It wouldn't be theirs for much longer—only hers. It was clear her husband had fallen in love with someone else. He barely spoke to her anymore. He treated her with a kind of disdain—everything she did and said seemed to irritate him.

Her thoughts tumbled over one another as she felt the depth of intolerable emotions overwhelm her. Ryker had one year left in high school. After that, he'd head off into his adult life and forget to call other than when he needed something. And no doubt his needs would wane over time as he matured into adulthood. She'd be completely alone in the world, with no one to care about her. It wasn't fair. She'd done the best she could. She loved the people in her life the best she could, but it wasn't enough. They always left her, looking elsewhere for what she couldn't give.

She'd slept late. It wasn't like her. Usually she got up early on a Saturday morning to take a walk on the beach. She'd stop by Singles and buy coffee and muffins, or chocolate cream croissants if she was in a particularly luxurious mood, for her and Rodger to eat side by side out on the veranda while he browsed the morning news on his phone and she read another chapter in the latest thriller.

But not today. Today she'd stayed in bed, eyes shut, letting herself fall into and out of sleep over and over until her back ached so much from her old mattress that it was time to get up. She sat upright and stretched out her neck, tipping her head to one side and holding it there, then swapping to the other side. The tension slowly released from her muscles as she stretched her arms over her head.

A text message flashed on her phone screen, and she bent to read it.

It was from Callum.

Will pick you up at eleven. Arrest warrant in hand. See you then.

She messaged a response in the affirmative and glanced at the clock. She'd have to jump in the shower soon and wash off the stench of the previous day. Her reflection stared back at her from a mirror on the wall. Mascara ringed her eyes, giving her a tired look. Her hair was a frizzy kind of mane. And there were sheet wrinkles down one side of her countenance.

A yawn escaped her mouth, and she briefly considered how it didn't matter that her heart was broken—her body still did all the same things it always had. Her mouth yawned when she was tired, and her stomach grumbled over the lack of chocolate cream croissants she'd promised it through force of habit. Life went on, even though it should be over. She'd poured herself into this marriage. It may not have seemed like that to Rodger, who often complained that she was off with the fairies, but that was simply her way. She got lost in her head, pondered cases and thought about people from her past, wondered what Ryker was thinking, or chased thoughts down rabbit holes. It wasn't a lack of interest in life, as he'd accused.

But in the end, what she had to give wasn't enough for him. And maybe it never had been. She was only fooling herself to think it was.

The click of a key in the lock startled her to wakefulness, and she reached for her silk dressing gown, cinching it tight around her waist before hurrying out to the living room. She found Rodger searching beneath couch cushions, his hair neatly combed, his clothing stylish. He was put together while she had fallen apart. The incongruity of the situation momentarily silenced her.

He saw her standing there and stopped his frantic searching. "I need my laptop. Have you seen it?"

"Hi," she said.

He sighed. "Sorry, I should've said hello first. Hi."

"Your laptop?" she asked.

He nodded. "I've got end-of-year reports to work on this weekend."

"The work never ends," she said by rote.

He grinned. "True. Although it's the end of the school year for me. Thank goodness."

"You'll be happy, then."

His smile faded, and he shifted uncomfortably from one foot to the other. "Do you have plans for today?"

She shook her head. She had no desire to tell him the truth. "I'm having a lazy day."

"You should. You work too hard."

"So you always tell me." She offered him a wan smile. "Is that why you're leaving me?"

His breath seemed to catch in his throat. "Toni..."

"No, I want you to be honest with me. Tell me the truth. Stop stringing me along, Rodger."

He dipped his head. "Fair."

"I saw you last night. With her..."

His eyes widened, and a look of fear flashed across them. The emotion was gone as quickly. He hid it by rubbing his eyes with his fingertips. "I'm sorry you saw us. I didn't mean to tell you like that. I wanted us to have a chance to talk."

"So, talk," she said. She strode to the other end of the living room, her nerves tingling. This was happening. Whether she wanted it to or not made no difference. He'd set his mind on what he wanted, and he wasn't going to listen to anything she said. Better to get it over with, like removing a Band-Aid.

"I can't help who I love."

She rolled her eyes and made a sound like air rushing from a tyre.

"It's true—we fell in love. We didn't mean to, of course, but it happened. And I can't do anything to change that. I'm sorry."

Later she would keen and howl on her bed, alone, but now she would be neat, tidy with her emotions. She would hold them in and smile her way through the mess of their marriage until he told her the ending, like a sad story played out on the documentary channel. She would be regal, queen-like in her poise as he tore her world apart. She'd show him what grace looked like.

"You said you loved me too. Is that a temporary thing for you? Does it end when reality begins, or because it's me?"

He paced to the kitchen and filled a glass with water, downing it in two great gulps. "I can't say anything more than I'm sorry. It's got nothing to do with you or anything you did wrong. Although we haven't connected in a long time and I felt lonely in our relationship, so perhaps that contributed."

"That's not my fault," she raged, storming into the kitchen. So much for holding it all together like a regal queen. Her voice rasped with emotion. "You're never here. You're always at the school, doing rehearsals, playing basketball with your mates, out running or riding your bike. I've tried, I have. But I don't know how to make you happy."

"I like to stay fit," he said with a whiny tone. "You work long hours too."

"I'm not judging you for working hard, but it seems like you're judging me, so I'm defending myself. Am I allowed to do that?" She spat the words like they were hot water that had burned her tongue.

He stepped back, aghast. "I've never seen you like this."

"You've never stabbed me in the heart before, either. But you seem pretty good at it," she snapped, striding back across the living room to stare out the window. The wind had picked up and was peppering the window with fat drops of slanting rain. The trees across the road bent and swayed. She couldn't see the waves.

The weather looked the way she felt inside.

When she looked back at him, he seemed to have deflated like an old balloon. He picked up his laptop from the bench where it was charging, slid it into the case, and slung it over his shoulder.

"It's over, Toni," he muttered. "The sooner you come to terms with that, the better for all of us."

She gaped.

His face clouded over. "Goodbye, Toni."

Then he was gone, and the front door slammed shut behind him.

Chapter Thirty-Nine

When Callum picked her up an hour later, she was showered and dressed all in black, with her hair smoothed down into a long plait that hung over her shoulder. Callum opened the door from inside the cruiser and studied her for a moment without a word.

She shut the door, and they pulled away from the curb. They listened to rock music on the radio for a few minutes before she reached over to mute the volume.

"You okay, Boss?" He threw her a concerned look.

"Yep. Fine."

"Anything I should know about?"

She sighed. "Rodger left me."

He slammed a palm on the steering wheel. "That no-good..." He fell silent for a moment, then said, "I'm sorry to hear that. When?"

"This morning."

"Want me to take out a kneecap?" He arched an eyebrow.

She laughed. "I'll think about it."

"Ready to arrest a murderer?"

"Absolutely."

They pulled into Allegra Cowderoy's driveway with the lights flashing, but no siren. With the mood she was in, Toni was looking forward to this. She climbed out of the car and strode to the front door, leaving Callum in her wake. She pounded on the door and waited impatiently for it to open, her pulse throbbing in her ears.

"Hello, officers. I thought we covered everything we needed to cover when we spoke yesterday," Allegra said, her gaze darting from Toni to Callum and back again.

"Allegra Cowderoy, I'm placing you under arrest for the murder of Mark Cowderoy," Toni said, deep satisfaction surging through her veins at the look on Allegra's well-groomed, overly made-up features.

* * *

Two hours later, Toni sat at her desk after processing Allegra's arrest and flicked through pointless email messages, sending most to her recycling bin. It was over, they had the suspect in custody, and it looked as though all of the evidence was stacking up against her. She'd likely get out on bail, but they'd press charges, and Allegra Cowderoy would end up spending a good portion of her life behind bars for her husband's murder.

Cowan strode towards her through the office. Toni straightened in her seat.

"Job well done, Kauffman."

A thought struck her suddenly. "Thank you, sir. By the way, I'm changing my name back to Porter. Toni Porter."

His brow furrowed. "Okay." He looked like he wanted to say more but stopped himself. "That's fine, Porter. Just file the appropriate paperwork with HR."

"Yes, sir."

"And make sure we've got the right perp. I don't want to be embarrassed over this. You understand?"

"Of course, sir. We'll tie up every loose end before we press charges."

"Good to hear. Carry on, Porter." He dipped his head and marched away.

She leaned back in her chair and linked her fingers behind her head. It felt good to achieve something. On one of the worst days of her life, at least she could say that she'd put a murderer behind bars. And she'd cleared out her perpetually messy and bulging inbox. A productive day all around. End a marriage, arrest a murderer, tidy an inbox. So much done in the space of only a few short hours. She should celebrate.

An email blinked into her inbox, and she swore beneath her breath. An inbox was never clear for long—it was one of those things you couldn't check off your to-do list. A fact that bugged Toni no end. She liked to check items off her list. It meant something was under control even when everything else was spiralling.

The email was from a name she didn't recognise. She opened it and began to read. The blood drained from her features as she read.

It was from the adoption agency. She'd given up a baby thirty years ago, and they'd recently contacted her to ask if she was open to getting in touch with her now adult daughter. Thirty years had passed. She'd been a scared seventeen-year-old girl when she'd signed the papers to say no contact.

She'd thought her life would be over if she didn't sign it. And now, looking back, she'd have done everything differently. But was she ready to face the child she'd given away so long ago? She'd told them yes, that she was willing to call her daughter if they'd send the contact details through, and now that they'd arrived, she wasn't sure if she was brave enough to continue reading.

Her heart skipped a beat at the name written in italics in the centre of the message.

Stella Thompson.

That couldn't be right. They must've made some kind of mistake. Stella Thompson, her murder suspect? The one who'd run down the victim's casket in her Pajero. The new friend who'd helped stalk Toni's husband the previous night. Who had a full head of luscious red hair that fell straight, like a waterfall, to her waist, nothing like Toni's wild, brown mane. That Stella Thompson?

Stella was her daughter? The reality of that fact brought tears welling to her eyes. Stella was her daughter. The beautiful, confident, and talented young woman with the gorgeous little girl who seemed always to be quietly smiling. Stella was hers. She'd come back to Kingscliff after years away. Toni racked her brain to remember why—what was it that Stella had told her? It was to do with the victim—he was Katie's father. Her mind couldn't process the possibilities, the connections, the way it all came together. It was too much to take in all at once.

She ran to the bathroom, where she splashed water on her cheeks. Then she planted her hands on the sink and stared at her reflection in the mirror, searching for any sign that the two of them looked alike. Perhaps the shape of the eyes, but certainly not the hair, although Stella's father had very blond hair, indicating that there was possibly a link to red in his genetic makeup somewhere down the line. Regardless, none of that mattered because according to the adoption agency, Stella Thompson was her biological daughter, and she wanted to get in touch with Toni.

The only problem was they already were in touch. They were well on the way to becoming friends. And if the letter was right, Stella didn't know that Toni was her mother. This was going to be interesting. What would Stella say when Toni broke the news to her? Would she be glad, or would it be a major disappointment for her? Toni hated to think how it might go. And how awkward that conversation would be—"I know you think we're girlfriends, or at least we're headed in that direction, but here's a little spanner to throw into the mix. I'm your mother." She pressed both hands to her face, still wet, then grimaced at her reflection.

When she walked back into the office, she was smiling, but nerves were bursting into firework displays in her stomach. Callum stopped her in the hallway.

"Hey, Boss, we're heading out for a late lunch to celebrate. Wanna join us?"

"Sounds great, Callum. I'll switch off the computer first. Okay?"

He said he'd wait by the cruiser, so she trundled back to her desk in a daze. Putting one foot in front of the other was an effort. She couldn't focus on anything other than the email and what it meant for her and for Stella.

Her mind travelled back in time to when she was that petrified girl with the short, wild curls and the big eyes behind a pair of purple-rimmed glasses. She'd had an easy time of the labour, which the midwife told her was a good sign—she said her baby girl was going to have a sweet and easy disposition. Toni remembered believing every word the midwife said.

She clung to her promise like an oyster to a rock. A positive word, anything encouraging—she needed it desperately. Her own parents had said they'd disown her if she so much as thought about raising the baby herself without a husband. The boy she'd loved briefly with a passion they'd both thought would last forever had offered, but she'd turned him down. They were too young. What did she know about raising a child? She'd barely been raised herself.

And then she held Stella in her arms, although she'd had no name at the time. She'd studied her tiny fingers and counted her ten toes. She'd marvelled at the way her rosebud lips seemed to pucker and the tiny fluff of strawberry blonde hair at the top of her forehead.

When they took her away, Toni had cried for an entire week. Sore, engorged, and with a depth of pain in her soul she never knew possible, she'd moped around the house sniffling into a handful of tissues until her mother threatened her with boarding school if she didn't stop behaving that way. And so she'd stopped. She'd pulled her emotions into a neat bow and fixed it so that no one knew she was grieving. She carried a smile around on her pretty, young face. She went to the formal and graduated from high school, and still she gave a cardboard cutout of herself to the world every single day while the little girl inside withered and curled herself around the secret hidden in her heart.

When she'd met Malcolm, she'd fallen into him like a woman crawling through the desert who's finally found an oasis of sweet, clear water. She gave herself to him, body, mind, and soul, and he was flattered by her love enough to believe himself in love and ask her to marry him. But after the wedding, her pregnancy brought back all the memories—the pain, the grief, the despair.

Ryker was born a bouncing, healthy baby boy who should've snapped her out of her emotional spiral. Everyone expected it. They all told her so. They asked her what was wrong—why didn't she seem to be happy? Isn't this what she'd wanted all along? But she didn't know the answers to their questions. Didn't understand why looking at Ryker made her sad instead of happy. She'd longed for him, but when he arrived, she wasn't sure exactly what to do with him, and her uncertainty brought an abundance of shame that she couldn't seem to escape.

When she didn't return to the happy, bubbly woman Malcolm had fallen in love with, he was confused and did his best to stay out of reach of the poisonous barbs she flung his way. And when Ryker held her hand and blew bubbles from his perfect little mouth, the girl deep down inside who'd been hidden away for so long decided that it was finally time to let everyone know the depth of her sadness.

She swam to the surface of Toni's consciousness and breathed in the acrid air of her depression and let it wash over her until they were both mired in it like it was a stretch of deep, black mud from which there was no escape. It clutched at Toni's legs and bogged her down, sapping her strength and stealing her hope.

Toni recalled those times, and the deep pain that she'd never had permission to overcome that had brought so much destruction into her life. She sat down at her desk with rivers streaming down her cheeks as a wide smile broke like the sunrise on a brand-new day over her tear-soaked countenance.

Chapter Forty

Zoey pondered her annual holiday décor as she studied the half-built Christmas tree. Usually she decorated everything in red and gold, but this year she'd chosen aqua and silver. She wasn't sure the combination had quite the same level of holiday cheer as the more traditional colours. And since Christmas was her absolute favourite time of year, she felt it was important to get everything just right.

She held an aqua bauble aloft and studied it as it spun and reflected sharp points of light in every direction throughout the living room. "What do you think? Is it Christmas-y enough?"

Isla sat on the floor, legs jutting out at impossible angles beside her and a box of tangled twinkle lights in front of her. Her tongue poked out one corner of her mouth as she worked at untangling the mass of green plastic strings. She paused, looking up. "It's a beach theme. It looks great."

Zoey dipped her head in agreement. True, they lived in a beachside town, so it made sense to have a beach-themed Christmas. Especially since summer had begun and announced itself with a series of relentlessly hot and very humid days all in a row. It felt as though a storm was brewing, but there was hardly a cloud in the sky.

"You're right—it's perfect. I'm used to the red, that's all."

Isla seemed more and more disinterested in the celebration. It was something of a sore point for Zoey. She'd hoped to have a few more good years of Christmas excitement, but it seemed that she'd have to let go of those expectations well and truly.

"Do we really have to put all these up?" Isla asked as she tugged another ball of lights from the box. "Why can't Dad do it when he does the outside lights? I can't find the end of the string."

Zoey sighed. "Dad barely wants to do the jobs he's already got. And I have to pick my battles, honey, or I'll spend all my time fighting."

"You complain about me having too much time on my screen, but he's always on his phone. Why don't you say something?"

Zoey crossed her eyes at Isla. "Have I mentioned before how much I dislike fighting?"

"Ew...gross, Mum. Your eyes look crazy when you do that."

Zoey laughed. "You're so easy to disgust."

"Can I invite Ben to Christmas Eve?"

The sudden left turn gave Zoey whiplash. She hadn't been expecting that. She'd considered having the teen over for a family dinner one night to get to know him. He was spending a lot of time with her daughter, after all. And since Isla's grounding was officially over, she thought it might be nice to kick off her newly won freedom with some Ben time. But Christmas Eve was a time for family, not for scruffy teen boys who had a thing for her daughter.

She didn't even know what kind of thing it was. Were they dating? But how could it be called that when Isla was only fifteen and not allowed to go out on dates? Were they in love? They were too young to know what love was. It was a crush—a mutual one. Nothing more than that. And crushes didn't get invitations to the Winton family Christmas celebration. Dave would have a heart attack at the mere thought of it.

"Doesn't he want to spend that time with his own family, sweetheart?"

"No, he says he doesn't care. They don't do anything special for Christmas Eve. They sit around the pool while his parents get sloshed and listen to random pop music that has nothing to do with Christmas. So, I said he should come here. You make such a nice meal every year, and there's always far too much food."

Her daughter was very well practiced at the skill of using a compliment as a manipulation tactic. In fairness, she'd seen Zoey utilise that same technique on unsuspecting neighbours, teachers, and dance coaches over the years. She could hardly be angry with her—she'd clearly learned the lesson well.

Although she realised she probably should've taught her daughter other skills, like how to cook using the oven rather than the microwave, how to change a flat tyre on her bike (something Zoey was particularly good at when she was a teen, since it was her only form of transportation), or even how to be kind to frustrating people (a gift Zoey herself would benefit from, since she seemed to do nothing but frustrate her daughter on a daily basis).

"Thank you, sweetheart. That's very kind. Of course, I'll have to talk to your father about it."

Isla's sweet smile drooped. "No, you won't. You say that so you can get out of having a conversation with me about something. You never talk to Dad about it."

"That's not true. I'll talk to him about it, although I can't promise he'll be happy. He's not a big fan of your—what do we call him, honey? Your friend?"

"Boyfriend. He's my boyfriend." Isla pushed out her chin defiantly, but her cheeks burned red.

"Your boyfriend...okay. I'll talk to Dad about your boyfriend coming to Christmas Eve dinner." She hung a small angel on one side of the tree, then next to it a rocking horse. And through it all, she kept the same, composed smile. While inside, her heart was heavy and her thoughts in a jumble.

It wasn't that she objected specifically to Ben. She was sure he was a nice boy with very good hair. But what upset her was the way everything was changing. Isla was growing up. She didn't get excited about Christmas the way she used to when she was small.

Usually, she'd read Isla "The Night Before Christmas" after their Christmas Eve meal. Then together they'd lay out a plate of food for Santa and his reindeer—generally involving a ham sandwich, since their particular Santa wasn't a sweet tooth. Isla would go to bed all wide-eyed and heart thumping in her little chest as she wondered breathlessly what Santa would bring and whether she'd hear him arrive.

She'd inevitably wake up at four a.m. (if Zoey and Dave were lucky). Sometimes she'd get up while it was still dark and Zoey would shush her back off to bed, reminding her that if she got up in the middle of the night and interrupted Santa's visit, he might not leave any gifts. Then Zoey and Dave would roll out of bed and feel around on the kitchen bench for the coffee machine—an essential component of parenting small children during the holidays.

They'd complain in a whiny voice that it was far too early and they should all go right back to bed while Isla shrieked over her stocking and Santa's gifts. Then Zoey would sit on the couch, legs tucked up beneath her, and watch as Isla opened each gift. She'd sip her coffee and comment on everything her daughter showed her while she bounced with excitement. And her heart would be full. Secretly, she loved it all—

even the lack of sleep. It meant they were happy, and she'd do anything to accomplish that.

But now—there was no talk of Santa. She could barely get Isla interested in gift shopping. Dave was hidden in the garage somewhere looking for external lights. Isla was chattering on about how much Ben was looking forward to coming over for Christmas Eve dinner. And Zoey felt a looming sense of dread about the entire affair. Especially since this year none of the extended family could make it north for their annual celebration.

Instead, her mother had asked if they could fly down to Sydney after Christmas, and Zoey had consented, although she hadn't told Dave about it yet. He didn't like staying with her parents and would insist on getting a hotel, a completely unnecessary expense, which they'd fight over for days. She'd tell him, but she'd choose her moment. She'd had enough drama in the past week to fill a lifetime.

Perhaps next year they should skip all the drama and do something different. Maybe they could travel, go somewhere exotic or, better yet, educational. Paris. That's what they'd do —celebrate a cold (maybe even white) Christmas in Paris. They could learn about history, visit the Louvre, see the Eiffel Tower, and eat pastries while the snow fell. She shivered deliciously at the thought.

Isla was getting older, and things were bound to change. But perhaps instead of mooning over it and wishing she could turn back time, they could make new and exciting family traditions. Maybe there were still some things to look forward to after all.

Chapter Forty-One

SIX MONTHS EARLIER

The moon hid behind a menacing cloud and threw the entire world into shadow. Zoey tapped on the keyboard with a fury matched only by the gathering storm outside. She had to finish her invoicing, or they'd run out of money to buy the supplies they needed before too long. Invoicing was one of those things she put off until the last minute.

She wasn't a bookkeeper—she was a designer. Admin tasks were the last thing she wanted to spend her time doing, and they were usually done at home on a Sunday night so that she wouldn't have to tell Stella the next day in their regular Monday morning meeting that she'd forgotten...again.

This was no way to work, of course—she knew that. Only getting things done so that your employee didn't tsk-tsk at you wasn't a good plan. But it's how she operated, and until they were big enough to require a full-time administrative support person, it's how things would have to be. Still, maybe she should hire someone part-time. It would free her up to do the things she was good at. She couldn't help...gosh darn it. It was impossible to have a cogent thought with all that noise.

She slapped a hand, palm open, on the desk beside her, then rushed to the window and glared out at the neighbours' house. If looks could kill... She wanted to like her neighbours. She did. But they made it an ongoing struggle for her inner domestic goddess. Her goal was to be the woman everyone on the street came to when they needed something.

She was the resident person whose lawn was perfectly cut, whose garden bloomed in all the right ways, and whose carpets gave off a freshly laundered scent at all times. She was kind, thoughtful, and compassionate... And crap-a-duck, she didn't swear any longer either. But she wanted to, very much, at the cacophony that was once again blasting from Mark and Allegra's front porch.

Who held karaoke parties on their front deck, for goodness' sake? Pelican Grove was a gated community, a place people moved to when they needed to escape the bogan suburbs. But here they were, practically on her doorstep, singing drunkenly at the top of their lungs while their American country music blasted from loudspeakers across the neighbourhood. It was a travesty is what it was.

Something on their driveway caught her eye, and she focused her attention in that direction. It was Isla, out riding her skateboard on the half-pipe Dave had built for her birthday. Why was she practicing now and not during the daylight hours? Zoey couldn't help feeling a little irritated by it, but she supposed it wouldn't hurt.

The floodlights on the front of the garage roof were focused on the driveway, lighting Isla up like a Christmas tree. She was tick-tacking down the pavement, then whooshing up the pipe. She hadn't quite got the hang of it yet and tumbled down onto her rear, sliding the rest of the way until she reached the concrete. Then she picked herself up and tried all over again. Zoey couldn't help smiling at her daughter's efforts—she'd done her best as a mother to teach her resilience.

Every one of the child-rearing experts she followed on social media recommended resilience as an essential trait in the modern child. But once she did her due diligence, researching phrases like *how to teach my child to be resilient* and *building resilience into my life*, she'd realised with a startled rush of clarity that she'd never learned the skill herself and wasn't sure how on earth to impart such knowledge to a child.

She'd done her best and hoped it worked, and watching her daughter pick herself up, brush the dirt from her scraped knees, and climb back onto her skateboard warmed her heart even as it sent an anxious chill down her spine.

In the neighbours' yard, there was a clamour of raised voices. Then a car pulled out of their driveway and swung suddenly and inexplicably backwards over the grass towards Isla on her skateboard. Zoey slapped both palms to the window and cried out, but no one could hear her over that racket. Frantically, she slapped the window again and again as the car accelerated through their lawn, sending dirt and grass flying from its spinning wheels, headed for Isla, who was oblivious to its approach.

"Isla!" she shouted.

The girl continued tick-tacking along the driveway. As the car hurtled towards her, she finally looked up, and shock registered across her young, pale face. She grabbed the skateboard from beneath her feet and ran even as the car jammed its back fender into the half-pipe. It stopped suddenly then, and the driver climbed out to survey the damage.

Anger surged through Zoey's veins as she sprinted out of the office, down the stairs, and out the front door. She flew down the driveway and confronted the driver with an angry stabbing of fingers in his chest.

"How dare you! You nearly ran over my child."

He stumbled backwards, shock registering. "Sorry… I…"

Mark Cowderoy strode to meet her. "I'm sure he didn't see Isla there…"

"This is completely unacceptable, Mark," she began. "I've told you before— drunken karaoke is for bars. It isn't something civilised people do on their front lawns. None of us wants to hear you sing. It's bad enough to know this kind of talentless mediocrity exists in the world without being forced to witness it."

"Hey, hang on there," Mark continued, his face a dark shade of red. "There's no need to be nasty."

"Oh, there very much is a need. You and your wife are the wrong kind of people for this neighbourhood. There, I've said it. You don't belong here. And if you ever endanger my child again with your drunken friends, I will take you out into the bush and I will shoot you and no one will ever find the body. Do you understand?"

He stared at her, mouth opening and shutting like a stunned fish.

She stormed back to the house, ushering Isla along with her. Her head spun with rage—her skin fairly burned with it. Behind her, the party continued, but someone had turned down the music.

* * *

CURRENT DAY

Zoey woke in the middle of the night and couldn't breathe. Something was pressed down on her chest or maybe had covered her mouth. She wasn't sure—she sat bolt upright in bed, sweat streaming from her body. The dog rolled from her stomach and yawned.

"Willow," she hissed. "You're not supposed to sleep on top of me, you crazy dog."

She rubbed the place where the dog had laid and noticed the heat of it, again felt the pressure of her weight. That's why she'd felt she couldn't breathe—the dog was trying to suffocate her. She picked up the creature and set her on the floor. The animal trotted away, heading down the hall. She'd no doubt snuggle up beneath Isla's chin, which was where Zoey generally discovered her each morning. She didn't know how her daughter could sleep with a fully grown dog up against her chest.

It was so hot. Why was she under the covers? She threw them off and padded to the wall to switch on the overhead fan. That was better. Dave snored quietly on his side of the bed, completely unaware of the drama she'd relived. It'd been months since the altercation with Mark, and still the heat of it, the savagery of her own response, had it filling her dreams at least once per week these days. It was probably because he was gone. The way he'd died—violently—was something she couldn't put behind her. At least, not yet, anyway. Death had a way of changing perspectives, raising regrets, and stopping the crimes of the past from being forgotten.

Chapter Forty-Two

MONDAY

26TH NOVEMBER

The bars on the cell clanged with the sound of Toni's bracelet as she took hold of the door and flung it open. "Come on out, Allegra. We're going to have a chat."

Allegra's carefully groomed appearance was gone. She looked tired and defeated. She was in the perfect place for Toni to get some answers.

She led her to the small interview room on one side of the jail and sat behind the desk. Allegra sat across from her, arms neatly folded on the cold metal table.

"I want to talk to you again about what happened..."

"Did I tell you about my neighbour, Zoey Winton?" she interrupted.

Toni leaned back in her chair. "No, not really." She left space for Allegra to continue.

"She's the person you should be interviewing. She threatened Mark before he died."

"She threatened him?" This should be interesting. Toni couldn't imagine Zoey threatening a butterfly, let alone a grown man who lived in Pelican Grove. Her friend liked to boast about the neighbourhood's low crime rate and perfectly manicured gardens. She spent her free time crocheting cardigans for disadvantaged babies in far-off countries like Haiti and Uganda. Threatening people wasn't her style—unless, of course, they were seen wearing blue and green *without another colour between*. Toni laughed to herself, but coughed to cover it and pulled a notepad from her coat pocket. She clicked open her pen and wrote the date at the top of the page.

Allegra watched her, then finally spoke. "She said she'd take him out to the bush and shoot him and no one would ever find the body."

Toni arched an eyebrow. "Can you tell me why she said that?"

"Because she's a psychopath," Allegra suggested. "And because one of our guests drove their car across her lawn."

"I know Zoey is very attached to her lawn, but I'm not sure she'd kill someone over it."

Allegra's brow furrowed. Her eyes grew dark. "She hates us. We like to sing karaoke on the front porch with our friends—so sue us. It's a free country, and we can sing if we want to."

"Did she? Did she sue you?"

Allegra slumped back in her chair and studied her fingernails. "No, she didn't sue us. That's what I'm telling you. She killed Mark."

"A few days ago, you were adamant that it was Stella Thompson. Now you're suggesting it was Zoey Winton. It's hard to keep up with all your accusations, Allegra."

"All I'm saying is, you should question her. Instead, you're wasting your time arresting me for something I didn't do."

"That's yet to be determined. You lied to us. You told us you were on a plane to Cairns, when in fact we have evidence that proves you were still at home around the time of your husband's murder. We also found out that you called Stella Thompson and hung up on her repeatedly in the days leading up to your husband's death. Why is that? Did you perhaps discover your husband's little secret? An affair, a surprise baby—those are things worth killing for, not lawns and karaoke."

She sniffed. "So I knew about the affair. It doesn't mean anything."

"You should come clean," Toni said. "It's good for the soul."

Allegra glared at her. "I'm not saying another thing. I want to see my lawyer."

"No need—you made bail. Don't go anywhere, okay?"

Chapter Forty-Three

Katie waved goodbye at the door to her classroom, and Stella watched her step inside, smiling as she gazed up adoringly at her teacher. Tears pricked the corners of Stella's eyes, and she clasped both hands together in front of her chest. It was the first time Katie had walked into the classroom without her. The first time she'd gone happily to school without clinging to Stella's neck.

The victory filled her with joy, and she jumped around in a tiny circle, eyes squeezed shut, hands up over her head, palms raised. It was a good day.

Her run was invigorating, and she pushed herself harder than usual, enjoying the energy that came from knowing Katie was healthy and happy in her classroom at school. She jumped in the shower, already thinking about the workday ahead and all the tasks she had on her list of to-dos.

By the time she made it to the office with coffees from Singles in hand, she was pumped and ready to get started. Zoey was there, her laptop open and glasses perched on the bridge of her nose. She received a coffee with a grateful smile and took an enormous gulp of it before setting it on her desk.

Stella sat behind her own desk and flicked on her computer. "You look a little fatigued. Everything okay?"

"I didn't sleep well," Zoey said with a grimace. "Bad dreams."

"You should lay off the pizza before bed," Stella quipped. Zoey rarely ever ate pizza. She was obsessed with whole foods and organic everything.

"Hilarious." Zoey tapped away on her keyboard. "You're in a good mood."

"Katie didn't cry at drop-off, which is basically a minor miracle. Maybe this whole school thing is going to work out after all. I was worried for a while there."

Zoey shot her a grin. "Thank goodness for that."

"I thought I was going to have to grow my hair to my waist, buy a floral dress, and start homeschooling Katie on weekdays while selling organic hemp on the weekends to pay our way." She giggled.

"That was a *little* judgemental, but I'll let it slide since you're clearly having a moment." Zoey pretended to glare at Stella over the top of her glasses.

The phone rang, and Stella answered it with a laugh. "Hello, this is Stella Thompson."

"Miss Thompson, I'm calling from Kingscliff State School. It's about your daughter, Katie. There's been an incident."

* * *

Of course it would have to happen on the one day Katie was finally happy to go to school. Stella's heart raced as she hurried up the footpath to Katie's classroom, her flats slapping out a rhythm on the pavement. They still hadn't told her what the incident was, only that Katie was fine, but they needed her to come and pick her up immediately.

Great.

She'd planned on getting so much work done. It was going to be one of those days where she was efficient, smiling, and on top of everything. She was so happy that Katie was happy. It was as if their happiness was bound by an invisible golden cord. When her daughter was miserable, she couldn't help it—she felt the same way. Happiness was contagious, and she'd had such high hopes for her day. And now she was ditching work, again, to pick up her child from school, again. How had things gone so wrong, so quickly?

She knocked on the school principal's office door quietly and was led into the waiting room. She sat on a plastic chair, her feet tipped forwards, heels pressed to the legs of the chair. It was like she was back in primary school and waiting to be reprimanded. Nerves fluttered in the pit of her gut. Katie came rushing out of one of the rooms nearby and launched herself at Stella, who caught and embraced her. The scent of roses and vanilla from Katie's shampoo filled her nostrils.

"What's happened, chickadee?" she asked.

Katie sat on a chair beside her and pouted. "June was being mean to me, so I threw a rock at her."

Internally, Stella blanched, but she did her best to hide it. "You threw a rock? You know you're not supposed to do that."

"She threw one first," Katie objected with a sniffle. "It hit my leg and it hurt."

"She did?"

Katie nodded vigorously. "And she called me a *B* word."

There were any number of B words, but Stella decided this wasn't the time or place to figure out which one had been hurled at her five-year-old daughter on the playground, or why. Whichever it was, she was angry over it. Katie shouldn't have to put up with being called names or having rocks thrown at her while she was at school. What kind of child was this girl?

"You can go in now," said a woman with a dour face and oversized glasses. She raised a hand, pointing in the direction of an open timber door painted brown.

The principal's name was emblazoned on a gold badge. *Elrod Johnson.*

Stella told Katie to stay where she was and marched through the door, pulling it shut behind her. She sat across the desk from the principal, a balding man with a paunch that stuck out over his belt, obscuring it from view. He finished up a phone call in a hushed voice.

"Mrs Thompson. So good to meet you."

She nodded. "Miss Thompson, and it's nice to meet you too."

He dipped his head in understanding. "Fine, fine. Let's get right down to it, shall we? It seems Katie has thrown a rock at one of the other little girls in her class and hit her in the head. Unfortunately, the girl has had to go to the emergency room. There's a bit of blood, and they need to check her for any lasting impact, that sort of thing. As you can imagine, her parents are somewhat upset over the incident."

Stella swallowed hard. "Yes, of course. It's very upsetting. I hope she'll be okay."

"Let's all hope so. I've got no choice but to suspend Katie from school for three days. I'm sure you can see that I can't let an incident of this magnitude go unpunished. Children must learn that violence isn't tolerated at our school."

Stella hated him in that moment. It was irrational and ridiculous, and she was sure a qualified therapist would tell her that hate was a useless emotion or some other nonsense. But she did. She hated him. Him and everyone who would judge her daughter, who would make Katie's life that much harder than it already was. She would protect Katie from people like him if she could possibly manage it. She'd never let her be treated as less than the Junes of the world who had two parents to stand up for her. Stella would have to be mother and father for Katie right now.

"I have to stop you there, Mr Johnson. The facts as told to me by Katie are that June called her a name, a bad word beginning with B. She then threw a rock at Katie, hitting her in the leg. That's what provoked her. She was fighting back. And I personally don't see anything wrong with a little girl fighting back against a bully."

"Ahem. I see. Unfortunately, we don't approve of little girls defending themselves against other *equally* little girls with violence. Katie endangered a fellow pupil today. We will see you after three days." He signalled for Stella to leave his office.

She lifted her chin high and stalked out of the office. Katie looked up at her with a trembling lip. She caught Katie up in her arms, slung her backpack over her shoulder, and marched out of the school. She didn't slow down until she was off school property and her entire body began to shake. She set Katie down on the footpath and leaned against the chain-link fence, panting.

"I'm sorry, Mummy," Katie said with tears in her eyes.

"I know, chickadee. I know. Hey, I have an idea. Let's go and see Santa. We've been meaning to do it, but we haven't had time. What do you think?"

She'd talk to Katie later about the dangers of throwing hard objects. Their discussion would be calm and loving, and she'd hold Katie in her arms while she spoke of using words, not fists or rocks, to make her point. But for now, both of them needed a respite from the world's judgement. They needed a good dose of fun. It was often easy for Stella to forget, with her naturally serious personality, that fun should be an important element of their lives. Katie needed more of it, and Stella did too.

She took Katie by the hand, and they set off for home. They'd drive to the mall where they'd eat ice cream until they were sick. Katie could sit on Santa's knee and whisper into his ear about all the things she wanted from life. Stella would make sure to get a photograph because she knew Katie wouldn't pose for Santa photos for too much longer. Zoey had told her all about the year she'd discovered that Santa photos were behind her and had cried silently in the Target changing room while Isla tried on two-piece swimsuits instead.

Perhaps they'd even catch a movie. She'd get no work done today, but later tonight when Katie was safely tucked in bed with a freshly washed face to get rid of all the sugar stains, she'd pull out her laptop with a yawn and work until the work was done. That was the life of a single mother, and she wouldn't change it for anything.

Chapter Forty-Four

TUESDAY

4TH DECEMBER

"We're not staying home for the entire summer holidays because you have a boyfriend," Zoey stated in the calmest voice she could muster. She wasn't calm inside. She wanted to scream at her daughter for being so self-centred that she couldn't see how much the rest of the family needed to get away—she could only see what she wanted for herself.

Besides, Zoey was hoping the break away from Kingscliff would give Isla the separation from Ben that she needed to cool things off. No fifteen-year-old should spend so much time with her boyfriend. It would only get them both into trouble.

Zoey recalled being Isla's age as though it was another lifetime—some faded black-and-white film of a stranger's adolescence. But she did remember being as passionate about the boys she fell in love with. The only difference being that they never felt the same way and so she loved them with all her heart from a great distance and wrote their surnames after her own first name over and over in the front of her loose-leaf folder surrounded by hearts and rainbows.

This, however, was an entirely different situation. This was a real boy, with real feelings, for her very young daughter. And some time away might help the two of them forget the intensity of those emotions, at least a little bit. She could only hope.

"It's so unfair!" Isla shouted, stamping one of her Vans-covered feet in frustration. "You don't care about me. You want to take me away from Ben. He's the only person who sincerely loves me."

Zoey fought the urge to roll her eyes until they flew out of their sockets and bounced off the clouds over her head. She pegged one end of a white sheet onto the clothesline and then the other. She spun to face Isla, her frustration mounting.

"One day you will understand how much I love you. But until then, don't you dare say things like that to me. You will show me respect, even when you're angry." There were so many other things she wanted to say, but she would show Isla how to be an adult. How to manage her temper in the thick of emotion.

"I don't care what you do. I'm staying here!" Isla stamped back into the house.

"You will do what you're told, young lady!" Zoey cried after her retreating back as Isla slammed the door.

Raising teenagers wasn't for timid, she thought with another slow breath. There was a knock at the side gate, and Toni and Callum walked through, pulling it shut behind them.

Callum stepped immediately in a small pile of dog doo and swore beneath his breath.

"Sorry, they're everywhere. Like tiny little booby traps.

Dave is supposed to pick them up, but he never quite gets around to it."

Toni chuckled. "Don't you dare get that in my car."

Callum shot her a dirty look as he wiped his shoe clean on the grass.

Zoey pinned a shirt to the clothesline, dried her hands on her peg apron. "How nice to see you both. What can I do for you?"

Toni surveyed the backyard. "It's looking good back here. Did you change something?"

"I added climbing roses." Zoey waved her hand.

"Ah, yes, right. They look good."

"Thanks," she said with a confused expression. Why were they talking like strangers? And why was Callum at her house? Usually Toni came alone, so it must be an official visit. For the first time since they walked through the gate, she felt the tension of the moment in her shoulders.

"We came to talk about something Allegra Cowderoy reported to us."

"Oh?" Zoey pressed her hands to her hips.

"She said you threatened to kill Mark."

She'd had the dream again last night. Only this time, she'd run Mark and his friend over with the very same car that'd come close to hitting Isla. She'd woken with a shout and practically gave Dave a heart attack. He'd clapped his pillow over his head and called her a crazy person before falling promptly back to sleep. He was snoring before she could get out the words "I'm sorry."

"Ah, yes, that," she said. "It was nothing. Just a spat."

"A spat?" Callum's eyes widened. "Sounds more like a threat to me."

"But I didn't mean it. His friend nearly ran over my daughter. They used to have these drunken singing parties that woke the entire neighbourhood. It was unbearable. But I put up with it for years, even though it made us all loony. When I saw that car come so close to running down my daughter, I lost my mind for a few moments. It's what parents do. We'd do anything for our children. You know what it's like, Toni."

Toni eyed her with concern. "Someone tried to run over Isla? Why didn't you report this?"

Zoey huffed. "I wanted to call the police, but then I thought maybe you'd misunderstand the whole 'I'm going to shoot you and leave your body out in the bush for the birds' conversation."

Toni bit back a laugh. "Um, yes, well, it's entirely possible we might've been concerned about that."

"So, you explain it. You don't hide it. This looks bad, Zoey," Callum said, shaking his head.

"Surely you don't think... I mean, you know I'd never kill anyone."

"Where were you at the time of the murder?" Callum asked.

Zoey combed fingers through her hair. "I was at home with my family. We've been through all this before."

Callum sighed. "You'll need to come down to the station again. Put it all in writing."

"Fine," she said. "I know my way down there now. It's something of a second home. Perhaps we could put in a Jacuzzi."

Toni's phone rang, and she answered it with an abrupt "Porter."

Had she decided to change her name back to Porter already? She hadn't mentioned it to Zoey. That seemed as though it was a big step worth talking about.

"Did you say Ryker?" Toni's eyes widened. "No, that's fine. I understand. Thank you for calling to tell me first. Can we keep it between us for a little while longer? Okay, thanks again."

She hung up the phone and stared at the ground for a few moments.

"Uh, Toni? Is everything okay?" Zoey asked.

Toni startled. "Not really. Um... That was one of my team, calling to let me know they followed up on the drugs Isla and Ben were smoking the night Mark was killed. Apparently, they bought them from Ryker."

"Your Ryker?" Zoey asked incredulously.

Callum kicked the ground with his boot. He swore quietly.

"Yes, my Ryker. Look, we'll talk more about this later, but I've got to go. I've got a teenager to yell at."

Chapter Forty-Five

The drive back to the station was a quiet one. Callum drove. He switched the radio off and sat in silence, only glancing at Toni every now and then. She fumed in the passenger seat until finally resignation pushed her anger aside and she was swamped in sadness. It was all too much. How could this be happening? Ryker seemed okay. They'd talked about his schoolwork, and he hadn't mentioned anything else going on in his life. She was a police officer—he knew what she did for work and how hard drugs made things for people like her to do their jobs. He knew, after countless conversations over the years, how drugs impacted teenagers and how destructive they were to the community.

Yet he'd still done it. Their source was certain it was him. There was no way around it. It was being kept quiet, for now. But it wouldn't be forever, and he'd have to face the consequences of his actions. She couldn't protect him from that.

"It's gonna be okay," Callum said, rubbing his chin with one hand. "I'm sure it's not as bad as you're imagining in your head right now. So he experimented a little bit. It's not the end of the world. He's not a bad kid."

Her nostrils flared. "I can't believe it. After everything we've been through..."

"I'm going to let you talk to him alone," Callum said. He reached out to squeeze her shoulder. "Don't be too hard on him."

He pulled the car into the garage beneath the station and parked it, then climbed out. "I'll see you tomorrow, Boss."

She sat silently in place for several long minutes, then climbed over the handbrake into the driver's seat. By the time she reached Malcolm and Sandi's house, she was calm. Deeply sad, but without the swirling rage she'd felt when she received the phone call.

When she knocked on the door, she heard bedlam inside. Dogs barking madly, children squealing. Then Ryker tugged the door open with one hand while holding a dog by the collar in the other.

"Oh, Mum, it's you. Come in."

The dog sniffed her then trotted away. Ryker led her into the living room. "It's Mum!" he called in the direction of the kitchen.

A pregnant Sandi waddled into view.

"Wow, you look amazing," Toni said with a smile. "You've popped out."

Sandi held a spatula in the air. She grinned and rubbed her stomach. "You think so? I'm going to burst. It's so much more uncomfortable this time around. I'm making pikelets. Do you want some?"

Toni's stomach grumbled. She'd forgotten to eat lunch. "Yes, please. That sounds great."

Sandi left them to it, and Toni asked Ryker if he could call Malcolm. Her ex-husband worked from an office on the side of the house most days. Ryker ran down the hall to get him, soon returning with his father close behind. Malcolm had begun to lose his hair on top, and it looked as though he'd been running his fingers through it over and over. He tugged a pair of glasses off his nose and kissed Toni's cheek.

"Good to see you," he said. "Ryker told me you want to talk about something."

"I've heard from one of my colleagues that Ryker was seen selling pot to some of the kids at school."

Malcolm gaped. Ryker's face fell, and the smile was wiped away as though it'd never been there.

He snarled at her. "They're lying."

"No, they're not lying, Ryker. I know what you've done. And it's time for you to come clean with us both."

"This can't be real," Malcolm said, looking back and forth between Toni and Ryker. "Are you sure about this?"

"I'm sure." She sat slowly on the couch. Malcolm slid onto the cushion beside her.

Ryker paced across the room. "So what? So what if I made a few dollars with some weed I found?"

"You found?" she questioned.

"It's not a big deal, Mum. You know that."

She had to stay composed. All she wanted to do was curl into a ball on her bed and cry herself to sleep. Nothing was working out the way she'd planned. Her entire life was crumbling around her. But Ryker needed her to be strong. It was the only way he'd get through this.

"Honey, please sit," she said.

For once, he listened and did what she told him. His hands were trembling.

"This is a big deal. No amount of raging or ranting is going to get you out of this mess. You have to listen to me and do exactly what I tell you."

His gaze dropped to the floor, and he gave a barely perceptible nod.

"As you know, I'm in the middle of a murder investigation. My boss is under a lot of pressure to get this one solved, and I've arrested someone for it. But I need more information if I'm going to be able to help prosecute the case. If I can get you to cooperate and tell me everything you know about what happened the night Mark Cowderoy was killed, I might be able to get your charges dropped or at least reduced to community service. But you have to cooperate."

"Listen to your mother," Malcolm added, his features pale. "This could derail your whole life, son."

He looked at her with tears in his eyes. "Okay, Mum. But I don't know anything. So it won't work, will it?"

She sighed. "You were there that night, weren't you? You gave some joints to Ben and Isla to smoke." She wasn't certain he was there—she hoped she was right. It was his only chance at redemption. She held her breath while she waited for his response.

"Yeah, I was there. I drove over in Dad's car. He thought I was filling up at the petrol station for him."

Malcolm's lips tightened with anger.

"Sorry, Dad, but it's true. I sold them the joints and hung out for a while. Mark came over to smoke with us. I didn't know who he was, but he tried to be cool. Then I left and he was fine. He was still smoking with Ben and Isla. But I had to get back home."

Toni listened with gritted teeth. When all this was over, Ryker was going to wish he'd never even heard the word "joint" before in his life. She had so many chores lined up for him to do. He could volunteer at the local food pantry every weekend, he could wash her car and Malcolm's car for a year, and he was grounded for the rest of his childhood. But for now, her main concern was solving the murder and making sure her son didn't end up in juvenile detention over one mistake. That she was being a hypocrite didn't escape her notice, but he was her son.

"And that's it? You drove home? Can you remember anything else?"

He scratched his chin. "There's one other thing. I stopped on the way home to pick up a hitchhiker."

"You did what?" Malcolm shouted. He leapt to his feet and paced the room. "How many times have we told you...?"

"Let him finish," Toni said.

"I know, but I was high. Anyway, I stopped and he opened the door and climbed into the car. Well... It was Rodger."

"My husband?"

"Yep," Ryker said. "I didn't say anything about it because he called me out and said he'd tell you I was smoking pot if I said anything. So, I kept it to myself. I figured it didn't matter. I mean, it's Rodger. Something happened to his bike when he was out riding. I can't remember exactly what he said."

Toni kissed Ryker on the top of the head. "Thank you. And you're grounded forever, so you know."

Ryker gaped at Malcolm.

"So grounded," Malcolm confirmed.

"I'll call with updates," she said as she waved them goodbye. Then she walked out the door, her heart racing. What was Rodger doing near the victim's house on the night of the murder? And why hadn't he told her before now?

Chapter Forty-Six

FRIDAY

7TH DECEMBER

Zoey ran on tiptoe through the bathroom to the bedroom window and peered out the curtains, a mascara wand held high in one hand.

Bummer.

It was still pouring rain. Tonight was the gala, and it'd been raining nonstop for days. Big fat drops fell from the gutter overhead and sloshed to the sodden ground below. She hurried back to the bathroom and applied her mascara in furious strokes.

There was nothing to do but buy a tonne of umbrellas and hope for the best.

Behind her, Dave hovered. He'd helped all day to get the supplies they needed ferried to the club, but now, dressed in his tuxedo, he was without a task to occupy himself, and he always hovered when he didn't know what to do.

"Surely you're not wearing those shoes," he said, nodding his head in the direction of the six-inch-high silver stilettos she'd picked up weeks ago from her favourite designer shoe boutique in Broadbeach.

"Why not?"

"You need gumboots, not high heels." He chuckled.

She shot daggers from her eyes. "The last thing I need right now is your jokes. This is a disaster." Her voice became wheedling. "I've been planning this party for weeks—we've put a lot of money into it. Your money! Everyone is going to be there. I was so excited...and now look at it." She waved her hands wildly around her head. "We're all going to float away."

"I know. I'm sorry, honey."

"Stella's running around frantically buying every umbrella she can find, but she's had Katie home all day with the school suspension." She shook her head. "What a disaster. Who suspends a five-year-old for throwing a rock? Five-year-olds do things like that all the time. I hate to think how many times Isla would've ended up sitting on the couch at home if her principal had been so trigger happy. Poor child—she's going to get a complex. Thankfully, Stella's hired a babysitter for tonight. Katie shouldn't be out in this weather. None of us should."

She was chattering at such a high speed that her jaw actually ached. She wasn't sure she'd ever caused her own jaw to ache from talking before. She'd been on the phone all morning with the club, the caterer, Stella, and all of the guests who decided at the last moment to check that the event would still go ahead, because *you never know. Better to check with weather like this*. They were polite, and it made sense to be prepared, but she didn't have time for dozens of extra phone calls. Had no one heard of texting? Maybe she should've called it off after all. But she'd woken up to the sound of rain on the roof and thought, *It won't last all day.* But so far it had, and there was no sign of it waning. In fact, it seemed to be intensifying.

Dave massaged her shoulders until she relaxed against his touch. "You need to calm down a little bit. I know it's unrealistic to expect you to be completely at ease, but take it down a notch or two. I'm afraid you'll have a stroke or something. It's going to be okay. We'll all be a little bit damp, but we'll manage. And once everyone's inside the club, we won't notice what's going on outside. It'll be glamorous and elegant, and the food will be delicious. Focus on the positives."

She nodded, breathing in deeply. "You're right. It's happening whether I want it to or not. I can't change the weather, so I'll adapt. That's all."

"Good. I'm going to get the car warmed up. I'll see you down there."

She ran through the list of things they needed to be doing for the hundredth time that day, checking things off in her head as she went. By the time she was through the list, she'd finished applying her makeup. She looked at the stilettos, shook her head, and picked them up with one hand. Then she tugged on a pair of gumboots with the other hand. Dave might've been joking about the boots, but it was actually a good idea. She'd wear the stilettos once they were inside and the party was underway.

* * *

The steak was delicious, but Toni only moved pieces of it around with her fork. Her heart was in her throat, and she couldn't think about anything other than the fact that Stella was there, standing by the front door, looking over a run sheet with a woman Toni assumed was the club manager. The room was decorated all in blue and silver, with a gigantic Christmas tree in one corner and twinkle lights everywhere. Toni recognised some of the attendees, but most were definitely not from her social circle. There were more diamonds in the room than there were at the local jewellery store, and she'd never seen so many sequins in one place before.

She was a guest at Zoey's Christmas gala, and she had no intention of taking any of the attention away from her friend's big night, but all she wanted to do was to talk to Stella. To say "Hi, Stella, remember me? I'm your mother" or something to that effect. Something completely awkward and crazy, but that would change both of their lives forever.

She glanced around the room. Maybe now was a good time. She should walk right over there and say it. Get it out in the open. Having it hidden away inside her with no one to talk to about it was driving her crazy. She pushed out her chair and rose to her feet. She was immediately lightheaded and almost sat down again, but she steadied herself with one hand on the table.

It was now or never, and it was ridiculous to be so nervous about it. After all, it was only Stella. They'd spoken every few days in recent weeks. They were already becoming friends. The news would be a bit of a shock at first, but surely it wouldn't be horrifying.

As she shuffled out of her chair at the table, Stella strode across the room to Zoey. With a sigh, Toni inched back to her place and sat down again. She shoved a piece of steak into her mouth and chewed morosely. Maybe she should wait for another time. Stella was clearly run off her feet managing the event. It would be selfish of Toni to ignore that fact because she wanted to get this thing off her chest.

Her phone dinged, and she pulled it from the small blue clutch she'd purchased to match her brand-new cocktail dress. She'd never owned a dress like it before, but Zoey had insisted they go shopping together and had basically picked it out for her. It was strapless and had some kind of netting poking out all around the neckline, with a puffy skirt. She looked as though she'd stepped out of a nineteen eighties prom movie. Although Zoey had declared that she looked like a modern-day princess, so she'd figured she might as well make her friend happy and wear the thing.

The message was from Ryker.

On my way to your flat now. Still grounded for the weekend?

She typed back.

See you when I get home. Absolutely grounded forever.

Was that too harsh? Perhaps she should send him one of those laughing emojis to let him know she was partly joking. But he might think she was also laughing at him. It was ridiculous the way she second-guessed everything with him now—it was as if she didn't know him at all and was dancing around trying desperately not to step on his enormous, clodhopper-y toes.

She was his mother, for goodness' sake. If she had to be delicate around her own child, worrying constantly that he wouldn't like her anymore if she was too hard on him, she wasn't doing her job right. Why was it that the older she got, the less confident in herself she managed to become? Wasn't it supposed to work the other way around?

She chewed on a fingernail, waiting for him to respond, but the screen remained blank. He'd be in his room with the door shut when she got home, but probably not asleep. She could talk to him then. In the meantime, she was at a party. She should try to have some fun, maybe even meet some new people. It was time she moved on from all of the drama and sadness in her life. She should kick her shoes off (literally, because they were giving her blisters and she could barely walk in heels) and dance, and maybe even drink another martini before the night was over. But first, she'd sit in this comfortable, if somewhat wobbly, chair on her own and finish this delicious steak.

"Are you enjoying yourself?"

When Stella slumped into the chair beside her, Toni leapt out of her own.

She gasped and pressed a hand to her chest. "You scared the life out of me."

Stella looked gorgeous with her red hair gleaming beneath the soft lighting. It was long, straight, and smooth, and fell over one shoulder perfectly. She wore a green satin dress that fit like a sheath, and she'd shunned the high heels every other woman at the party wore—instead she wore a pair of gold gladiator sandals that made her look exotic, but Toni knew would be utterly cringe on herself.

"Sorry." Stella laughed. She stabbed a piece of steak with a fork from the next place setting and shoved it into her mouth. "I didn't get to finish my meal. I had to go and talk to the caterer, and one of the waiters took my plate. I'm starving."

Toni nodded and pushed her plate at Stella. "Go for it. I'm full."

"Are you sure?"

"Absolutely. How's it going—everything working out?"

"So far, it's perfect. The rain is a bit of an annoyance, but we managed with a lot of umbrellas and some towels at the entrance."

"Good work on that front. Everyone seems to be having a wonderful time."

"Why aren't you dancing?" Stella looked at her, eyes sparkling.

"I was about to, right after I finished this." She waved a hand at the plate of food.

"Sure you were. I tell you what. I've got a few things to do, but then the three of us should have a dance. What do you say?"

"Sounds perfect."

Her heart was doing the jittering thing again because this was another chance to talk to her daughter and she didn't want to miss the opportunity. It wasn't often that the two of them had a moment alone together, and she couldn't hold it in any longer.

Stella rose from her seat.

"Actually, can I have a minute?" Toni asked.

Stella sat down again. "Sure. What's up?"

Now that it was happening, the words flew out of her mind. She didn't know what to say. How should she put it? Half of Stella's attention was focused on the group of guests on the dance floor and half on Toni. She bopped along with the beat in her chair.

Toni swallowed. "Um, well, as you know, I have a son."

Stella nodded. "Right, Ryker. Seems like a nice kid."

"Eh." Toni dipped her head from side to side. "Yeah, we'll skip on by that conversation for now. But anyway, there's something you don't know about me. I also have a daughter."

"Oh, wow. How old is she? Where does she live?" Stella's full attention was on Toni now.

Toni wove her fingers together in an attempt to stop them from shaking. "Well, that's the interesting thing. I didn't know where she lived until recently. Until the adoption agency contacted me to let me know she was in Kingscliff, and she wanted to connect with me."

Stella froze. "What?"

"That's right," Toni continued. "Oh, and to answer your other question—she's thirty."

Stella steepled her hands on the table in front of her. "You're saying...it's me?"

"Surprise!" Toni murmured with a wobbly grin and both hands lifted like Stella had won a prize on a daytime talk show. *Congratulations! You're taking home a brand-new washing machine valued at over one thousand dollars!* Or in this case, taking home a brand-new mother with a history of deep depression, failed marriages, plus a broken family. Oh, and a drug-dealing half-brother. Ta-da!

Toni waited for Stella to say something.

Stella swivelled in her seat. She looked to the right and to the left. "I can't deal with this right now. I'm in the middle of a party. And I've got to talk to Zoey about the invoicing for the drinks... Someone's thrown up in the bathroom, and there's a mystery goop rubbed into the carpet in the corner."

"It's fine." Toni waved her away. "You go and deal with all of your mishaps. I'll still be here. Besides, I'm sure you need time to take it all in. It's a lot to. At least, it was for me."

Stella stood, then sat again. She took Toni by the hand, her eyes glistening. "I don't know what to say, but this is big. I don't want you to think I'm upset or angry or anything like that. I take time to process things, that's all. We'll talk...later. Okay? And I'm happy. Shocked, but happy."

"Would a hug be too much?" Toni asked as tears blurred her vision.

Abruptly, Stella wrapped her arms around Toni and hugged her tight. Then she leapt to her feet and hurried away. Toni watched her go through a veil of tears, then cleared her throat. Time for some dancing.

Chapter Forty-Seven

The gala was everything they'd planned, and Zoey couldn't have been more pleased with how the night played out. Most of the guests showed, although some of them didn't come and didn't let her know. But given the weather, she considered the evening a win.

The women wore elegant cocktail gowns, and the men looked handsome in tuxedos. Zoey smoothed the front of her navy-blue dress with both hands as her nerves faded. It was nearly over. They'd had appetisers and the main course. She'd addressed the group to talk about her business and where it was headed. She'd handed out dozens of business cards and had several wealthy attendees indicate they wanted to meet up and see some design concepts.

After the meal, the DJ managed to get most of the guests onto the dance floor. And dessert was on its way to people's tables while she watched from the back of the room. They'd gotten through most of the evening with very few mishaps, including when one of the ladies fell in the mud outside the entrance. Stella had given her a towel and helped her clean up, and the woman was currently in the centre of the dance floor, twisting in time to the music with a gigantic grin.

"We did it," Stella said, coming up beside her with arms crossed. Her cheeks were pale and she drummed her fingers in rapid succession on her forearm, but otherwise, she seemed happy.

"Well done. You worked really hard to pull this together, and I'm so pleased with the result. Have you seen Toni?"

"Thank you. It's a big relief to see it all work out. I think Toni already left. She snuck out earlier, with her shoes in her hand. Did you notice that Allegra came after all?"

"I said hello when she arrived, but I still don't know how that happened. I must've sent the wrong email list to the invitation place."

"It doesn't matter. She seems to be having a good time." Stella bopped in time to the music.

"You should go and dance," Zoey suggested.

"Do you want to?"

Zoey thought for a moment. She didn't have any other responsibilities for the evening other than seeing everyone off when they were leaving. "Sure, that'd be nice. I can finally relax. How's the weather going?"

"It's absolutely pouring still. Thank goodness there's valet parking. The valet staff will be soaked through, though. That reminds me—I should ask them to put dry towels on the car seats before they get in or else everyone will be driving home on wet upholstery."

"Good idea."

After Stella spoke with the parking attendants, they joined the rest of the group on the dance floor, and Zoey finally allowed herself to let loose and relax. Dave found her there and pressed a hand to his heart at the sight of her. It was silly and goofy, but it was so very Dave, and she found herself laughing at him before linking her arms around his neck to sway together in time to the music.

"Happy?" he shouted in her ear.

"Very," she shouted back.

Some of the dancers returned to their seats to eat dessert and drink the steaming coffee that the waiters were taking between tables in large silver jugs. The dance floor was clearing out, and Dave took it as an opportunity to go wild. He grabbed Zoey by the hand and spun her out and away from him, then tugged on her hand to pull her back. She landed breathlessly against his chest, and he kissed her softly on the lips before dipping her. The move just about threw her back out, and she was certain for one terrifying moment that she was going to land on her head with him on top of her. But he managed it somehow, and she was back on her feet, swaying and spinning along with him before she knew it.

She'd forgotten how much fun they had when they were out together, with no kid there to sit in the corner sucking up all their positive energy or shouting about how bored she was from the other side of the room. She'd forgotten how well he danced and how handsome he looked in a tuxedo. He was so cute, attempting the moonwalk to a modern pop song.

Twenty years of marriage. Twenty years with the same man. Twenty-three, really, when you considered their courtship. She'd loved him for twenty-three years. Longer than she'd lived without him. Her life could be divided into two distinct pieces—before she met Dave and after she met Dave.

They'd travelled together, had Bali Belly on the floor of a Balinese bathroom together, they'd surfed in Hawaii and trekked through India, they'd walked the El Camino in Spain and eaten gelato on the Spanish Steps of Rome. They'd moved away from their families and built a brand-new life together. They'd had a child and survived the terror of Isla's early childhood asthma attacks and regular trips to the emergency room while squeezing tight to each other's hands. They'd built two businesses and weathered the storms of economic downturns standing tall by each other's sides.

He was maddening and frustrating, and she hated the way he fell asleep every single night in his armchair. Then he came to bed late and woke her up with his snoring. She hated that he never picked up the dog poop when he said he would and that she had to find his socks for him every single day. He hated the way she made everything into "a federal case," whatever that meant. And that she always wanted to be part of every social activity no matter what it was, even if he was perfectly content to stay home in his armchair with the football game playing on the widescreen. But they loved each other, even with the irritation, the gradually expanding waistlines, and the troubling grey hairs she'd plucked from her eyebrows early that morning.

This was what it was like to grow old with someone, and she decided then and there that it was nothing to be depressed about. She linked her arms around his neck and rested her cheek on his firm, warm chest.

The sound of shouting brought her out of her blissful reverie. Was that Stella? What was going on? She straightened and spun about, looking for the source of the firestorm.

Allegra Cowderoy shone in a short azure strapless dress with legs firmly planted and arms crossed. She glowered at Stella, voice raised. "You killed him, I know you did. And somehow you've managed to convince the police it was me. I will *not* pay for your crimes, you fat, sleazy…!"

"How dare you!" Stella hissed, her voice quavering. "I had nothing to do with Mark's death. This is my workplace. If you have something to say to me, you can do so in private, not when I'm working. I think it's time for you to go home. I'll call you a cab."

Stella spun away from Allegra and headed for the glass sliding doors that exited to the valet parking area. When she was near the doorway, Allegra ran after her on impossibly wobbling heels. She reached Stella as she stepped through the open doors and pushed hard against her back. Stella stumbled forwards and fell to her knees.

Zoey gasped. She exchanged a look with Dave, and the two of them hurried after Stella and Allegra. The crowd followed.

"I'm not going to fight you, Allegra. You've had too much to drink." Stella attempted to brush the mud from her knees, but her hands were as dirty.

Allegra smirked. "You only like to fight people who aren't expecting it, I guess."

Stella's nostrils flared. "Stop it."

"Make me."

"How old are you? Five?" Stella cried. "My daughter is more mature."

"Ugh!" Allegra screamed, launching herself at Stella. She pummelled her with slaps and punches while Stella did her best to block the onslaught. "I've been trying to get pregnant for years, and you throw in my face that you have a child with *my* husband?"

Zoey wrung her hands and stepped back and forth, trying to figure out what to do. She had no idea Allegra wanted children—she always seemed so disgusted by everything Zoey's kid did. When Isla got a bad sunburn, Allegra's eyes had scrunched up and she'd waved her hands at Isla's back, saying, "That's horrifying. Put it away." Or when Isla had a runny nose, she'd acted as though she might throw up at the sight. Zoey had assumed children weren't part of the Cowderoy plan. But maybe she'd been wrong, and Allegra was compensating for her pain all these years.

"Dave, do something," she begged.

He shrugged. "Like what?"

"I don't know. Get between them."

Dave tipped his head to one side, then the other, studying the pair of spinning, slapping women. "How, exactly?"

The guests crowded around the women in a semi-circle. Some shouted at them to stop it. A few women were crying against their dates' chests. Some of the men wore half-grins and appeared to be passing five- and ten-dollar notes amongst themselves.

"Stop fighting!" Zoey shouted in her most authoritative voice. But it made no difference.

Suddenly, water dripped on her head. Not a small, singular drip, but a large droplet followed by several more in quick succession. She looked up, and a droplet fell directly into her eye.

"Dave!" she shouted, rubbing her stinging eye.

"What?"

"Look up."

He did. "Is that water damage?"

Once her vision was clear, she followed his gaze and saw a large jagged crack in the ceiling overhead. The crack was growing longer every second she stared at it.

"Everyone, look out!" Dave shouted, his arms flapping enthusiastically in all directions.

He grabbed Zoey by the shoulder, and the two of them took off at a run even as the ceiling gave a loud pop and crashed down all around them in a torrent of water and debris.

Alerted by Dave, the group of guests had begun to scatter and escaped most of the plaster and timber that fell to the ground. It missed Stella and Allegra by a metre, and both women stared up from their fight in horror, then dove for cover.

Zoey and Dave ended up on their stomachs on the Astroturf in the dark, with guests landing all around them. The ground squelched as Zoey pushed herself up into a seated position and surveyed the damage. The entire roof had come crashing down over the valet area and entrance to the club. The valet staff watched from a distance with shocked expressions. Zoey's guests lay or sat silently in the mud and grass all around the entrance. Some were struggling to their feet. Others gaped with hands pressed to their heads. Still others lay on their backs unmoving, staring up into the downpour. Every single partygoer was soaked to the bone, their elegant evening wear and perfectly coiffed hairstyles ruined.

With the rain pummelling her head, Zoey foisted herself to her feet. Her heels sank into the mud and she couldn't pull them out, so she tugged her feet free and padded barefoot to where the debris lay in piles. It didn't seem as though anyone was hurt, which was a small miracle given what'd happened. Dave's shout must've saved them in time. A lump lodged in her throat.

"Is everyone okay?" she called, and the sound of her voice surprised her with its strength.

There were murmurs of agreement as people lifted themselves out of the mud and looked around in astonishment. Some of the women hobbled inside for their purses and wraps. Then one by one, the guests mumbled their goodbyes and fished their keys from the hooks of the toppled valet box. They disappeared into the dark and rain.

"I think we can call it a night," Dave said softly beside her. "I'll grab your purse."

She told the manager they were leaving and to send her the invoice via email. The manager nodded in silence and waved her off, mouth agape at the damage. Then Dave took her hand, and together they walked through the rivers of water cascading across the darkened car park to their vehicle and climbed inside.

She couldn't cry. Couldn't talk. There was nothing more to say. Her beautiful, perfect, elegant party had been ruined.

And now no one would remember anything else about it. She curled into a ball in the passenger seat and stared out the window as Dave drove her home. And all she could think was that she should've packed towels since the leather seat would be ruined by her sodden, mud-covered dress.

Chapter Forty-Eight

SATURDAY

8TH DECEMBER

Another Saturday ruined. That's what Toni was thinking about as she drove Ryker home. They'd spent the morning fighting. She asked him again where he got the pot, he insisted he didn't know the person or how to contact them, and she didn't believe him. She'd nagged him about his homework, and he'd rebelled, openly playing video games with his bedroom door swung wide so that she could see inside.

Finally, she'd confronted him, and he'd asked to be taken home.

Home.

It was very clear he wanted her to know that he didn't consider her flat as his home, since he'd said it three times in one conversation. *Take me home. I hate it here.* Home was with Malcolm and Sandi, not with her.

She bit her tongue and led him down to the garage, where they climbed into opposite sides of the car. A metaphor for their style of communication—she never could understand him and what was going through his head. They were coming from opposing directions, and neither could comprehend the other's perspective. Now she was driving him home in silence, fuming all the way. Sometimes she didn't understand her son —she thought they'd talked everything through and things were good. And suddenly he was in a mood all over again, for no apparent reason. It was hard for her to keep up.

"It's a bit late to start being rebellious now," she said. "You've had years for this, but now that you're practically an adult, it's kind of stupid to suddenly begin rebelling against authority."

He sniffed, his elbow resting on the windowsill, his eyes trained on the passing scenery. It was still raining, but not as heavily as the previous day. Rivulets of water cascaded down the windscreen. Her wipers were on the highest setting, whooshing back and forth over the glass. She had the air-conditioning turned up high to keep the windows clear enough to see through. A car whizzed by on the other side of the road, sending a wave of water over the bonnet like the prow of a boat in a stormy ocean.

"Do you want to tell me what's going on with you? Or are you determined to ruin our last year living together?"

He laughed. "You're gonna blame me for this."

"These are your choices. I'm only watching from the sidelines."

He shook his head, his expression thunderous. "No, they're your choices."

"What is that supposed to mean?"

"I know about you, Mum. I know all about you and the kid you had before me."

She gaped. It was as though her heart had been laid bare

and he'd shoved a knife into it. The pain of the past was coming back to haunt her, and it tore at her well-built walls of protection with long, grasping claws.

"How do you know?" she whispered, staring straight ahead.

He sighed, lowering his voice. "Dad told me. He was angry with you about something at the beginning of the year. You'd had a fight, I can't remember what it was about. But he came inside fuming and sat down next to me. He said something about the baby. When I asked him what he was talking about, he said you'd given up a baby when you were a teenager and that you'd never really gotten over it. That no one could ever make up for the baby you gave away. There was some kind of hole in your heart that he'd tried to fix, but he couldn't. He started crying, and then he ran out of the room. We never talked about it again, but I couldn't stop thinking about it."

This wasn't how she wanted things to go. She'd always intended to tell Ryker about his half-sister, but it never seemed like the right time.

"I'm sorry. I should've told you," she mumbled.

"It all made sense, you know? Everything—the way you seemed to hate me, the depression, the distance."

"What? I've never hated you." Toni glanced at him. The car swerved into a long puddle on the side of the road, sending a wall of water skyward. She corrected, her eyes back on the road. "I don't hate you. I can't believe you'd say that."

"It felt like it sometimes. When you'd disappear into your room and shut the door. You lay on the bed for hours, Mum. I was small—I didn't understand. I thought you didn't want to be around me. Then Dad told me you were sick, so I did everything I could think of to help you get better, to make you smile. But it didn't work."

Her heart ached until she thought she couldn't take it anymore. "I'm sorry, honey."

"But when I heard about her, it all added up. She was the baby you wanted, and I wasn't. It was that simple. You lost her, and you didn't want me."

"No, that's not it," she shouted, tears pooling in her eyes. "Don't say that."

She pulled the car up in front of Malcolm and Sandi's house and switched off the engine. Ryker tore the door open and leapt out into the rain. He ran headlong down the street, away from the house. His lanky legs pumped, and his shoes slapped against the road, splashing dirty puddled water in every direction.

Toni shoved the door open and sprinted after him. Rain pelted against her face, her back, soaking her to the bone immediately. Her feet sloshed in her Doc Martens, aggravating the blisters on her heels from the previous night. He slowed his pace, and she caught up to him. They looked at each other, puffing.

"I tell you all the time how important it is to exercise," Toni said between gulps of air. "There's something very wrong if your forty-seven-year-old mother can keep up with you."

He shook his head. She couldn't tell if he was crying or if it was rain trickling down his cheeks. His dark brown hair was pasted to his head, and his grey shirt clung to his tall, thin frame.

"You didn't want to be a mother," he spat.

She shook her head. "I love being a mother. I'm not always very good at it."

"That's crap," he said. "It's an excuse."

"You're right," she admitted. "But it's also true. I'm going to try harder, I promise."

"It's not enough. All those years..."

"I know, honey. I'm glad you had your dad and Sandi to help you through it. I don't say that often enough, but I'm very grateful for them. Giving up my baby—it screwed me up.

I didn't know how much it would hurt at the time, and my parents didn't give me much of a choice. I realise now I should've taken her and run, that we could've made a life together. But I was *your* age, for heaven's sake. I didn't know anything, and I definitely didn't know what I was capable of."

He stared at her, hands balled at his sides. "You should've tried."

"I should've tried."

"I've hated that baby all year," he said, trembling.

Her heart felt like lead. "I'm sorry. But don't hate her. It's not her fault."

"You don't even know her and you're defending her."

She sighed. "I do know her."

"What?"

"Her name is Stella Thompson. You remember her from the beach that day? She's Auntie Zoey's friend, the one with the red hair."

"She's my half-sister?" He blinked, and raindrops dripped from his eyelashes.

Toni nodded. "I'd like the two of you to get to know each other. She has a little girl as well."

"I remember—Katie. She's cute." He smiled, hesitantly. "Wow."

"I only recently found out myself," Toni admitted. "So I'm still figuring it all out. But I want you to be part of the whole thing. We're family, all of us."

Chapter Forty-Nine

Driving home, Toni kept sniffling into a handful of tissues. Her eyes were red when she looked in the mirror behind the sun visor. She shoved it back into place and kept driving. The rain had slowed to a trickle, and there was a patch of sunshine on the horizon. Maybe it was a sign that things were about to get better for her. She certainly hoped so. She usually tried to keep her life drama free, but lately she'd been on an emotional roller-coaster ride that dipped and climbed and dipped again on a daily basis. She could do with a little bit of respite from all of the tears and angst. It was like being a teenager all over again.

She slowed as she approached Pelican Grove and decided to take a detour into the gated community. The code to the gate hadn't changed since their investigation into Mark Cowderoy's death, so she used it and the large, wrought-iron black gate swung open. She drove through and took a slow, steady tour of the neighbourhood.

With everything that'd been going on in her personal life, she hadn't given enough attention to finding the final pieces of the puzzle that would put Allegra Cowderoy away for her husband's murder. And she still hadn't asked Rodger why he'd caught a ride home with Ryker that night.

She'd seen Allegra at the party the night before but ducked out to head home while everyone was on the dance floor. When she'd called Zoey that morning, her friend hadn't answered the phone, so she assumed everything had gone well and she was sleeping late after an exhausting night. Toni had been anxious to get home to see Ryker, but he wasn't happy to see her anyway. She could've stayed and danced some more, although her feet were killing her as it was.

When she came close to Zoey's house, she slowed the car and looked at the large, three-story home with its fresh white trim and red-brick walls. The garage was shut, so there was no way of knowing if her friend was home, and as tempted as she was to stop in, she knew they'd need their rest today. She could talk to her tomorrow about everything that'd happened. There was so much she hadn't told Zoey yet, and she desperately needed her friend's listening ear. But not today.

As she passed Allegra Cowderoy's house, she was reminded yet again that there was more work to be done on the case. Allegra was out on bail, living her life as though she'd done nothing wrong. It was up to Toni to make sure she paid for her crimes, although with a little bit of space and perspective, she was beginning to wonder if she'd got it right. Was Allegra capable of killing her husband? She was out at a party having fun and dancing so soon after her husband's murder — it didn't look good, but it wasn't evidence of wrongdoing. An affair and a secret baby were a solid motive, but the only evidence they had was circumstantial—she didn't have an alibi, and her prints were on the murder weapon. But the weapon was a plant pot which Allegra had most likely handled countless times. It wouldn't hold up in court. She needed more for the prosecutor to build a solid case.

Near the exit, she noticed a sodden garage sale at one of the last houses on the street. She pulled up at the curb and wound down the passenger window to take a closer look. There were tables of china, bric-a-brac, and piles of baby toys all lined up or in neat stacks on the ground, and all soaked with rainwater. She grimaced—what a day for a garage sale. A bicycle leaned against the last table. It was a black road bike with an impressive set of gears and sturdy tyres. It dripped with rainwater. There was something familiar about the bike. She climbed out of the car and jogged over to it. A purple seat. The telltale word printed across the back of it. *Giant.*

She strode to the front door of the house, knocked on the solid timber door. It was painted grey, and a red-and-gold Christmas wreath encircled the brass knocker.

A man came to the door. He looked to be in his sixties and held an open book in one hand. His back was slouched over like he'd been sitting a long time.

"Can I help you?" he asked.

She flashed her badge. "Hi, Detective Sergeant Antonia Porter. I was wondering where you got the bike you're selling in your garage sale."

The man scratched at his balding pate. "Well now, that bike was in my garden. I kept waiting for someone to claim it. Even put up a sign on the noticeboard down at Coles. But no one came. Not sure how it got there, but I decided to sell it. I'm not going to ride it, so it doesn't make sense to leave it clogging up my garage."

She smiled. "Of course. I understand."

"Is there a problem, Officer?"

"No, not exactly. Do you remember what the date was? When did you discover the bike in your garden? And can you show me exactly where you found it?"

He set his book on a table in the entryway and stepped outside. He led her to the front of his house, where a hedgerow grew down to the road. "It was here," he said, pointing to the hedge. "Just under the hedge, like someone had shoved it in there. The back tyre was flat. And I believe it was..." He counted on his fingers and scratched his head again. "Oh, that's right. I believe it was on the eighteenth of October. I remember because that was the same week they found that poor fella up the road lying in his garden dead as a doornail. You know about him?"

All the heat drained from Toni's body. "Are you sure about that?"

"Absolutely certain. I brought the bike in, and I called my friend Harold to tell him about it. The report came on the radio while we were talking. I've got a police scanner in my living room. It's a hobby. I don't have much to do these days, I'm afraid. Model train building only takes up so much of a man's day, and he's got to have something else to do with his time." The man's cheeks reddened, and he cleared his throat, no doubt realising too late that his admission could get him in trouble.

But Toni had bigger issues on her mind than admonishing an elderly amateur sleuth.

"You don't have any idea who it belongs to?"

"Nope. No idea. But it's a nice one, so someone is missing it, I'm sure."

She waved him goodbye and got back into her car. Then she headed for the police station. She called Callum on the way and asked him to meet her there, then she pressed down hard on the accelerator. It was time to get to the truth of what happened, and it seemed she'd have to talk to her husband in order to do that. Clearly, he hadn't told her everything—he hadn't mentioned anything about being in Pelican Grove the night of the murder; he'd failed to mention that his bike was gone, whether lost or stolen; and he'd tried to blackmail her son into keeping quiet about giving him a ride back home. And one thing she'd learned in her years as a detective was that when people lied about innocuous things, they were generally hiding something much bigger.

Chapter Fifty

The police station was quieter than usual for a Saturday afternoon. Callum arrived soon after Toni, and they decided to set themselves up in one of the conference rooms so they could wheel in the evidence board and spread out all their paperwork and computers on the single, long table.

Toni held a whiteboard pen in her hand and paced from one end of the room to the other.

"What we know is that Rodger kept information from us, even though he seemingly has no reason to do so."

"It's strange but not definitive," Callum said as he sorted through paperwork.

"Don't make a huge mess," she complained.

He rolled his eyes. "Yes, ma'am."

"Do we have the printout of Allegra's phone records there somewhere?"

He shuffled through the paperwork and handed Toni a stack of papers stapled together in one corner. "Here you are. We haven't gone through them thoroughly yet—not enough funding. But I made a start on identifying some of the phone numbers. As I said earlier, she called Stella Thompson at least ten times in the two days before the murder."

Toni set the papers down on the table, bent over them, and trawled through them, using her finger to underline each number. She was looking for a pattern. And she found it on the third line. A single phone number, repeated over and over, at least once but usually two or three times every single day during the printout.

"What's this number?"

Callum shrugged. "Haven't found that one yet. It's unlisted. But I'm assuming a friend or relative, since it shows up so frequently. I was going to do some more digging on Monday. But apparently that's not soon enough for some people." He laughed.

She poked out her tongue. "Get over it. You weren't doing anything worthwhile anyway."

"I was about to go out on a date."

"She'll be devastated, I'm sure." Toni picked up her phone and sorted through the recent calls.

She found the number she was looking for immediately and held up the screen for Callum to see. "There it is."

"Whose number is that?"

"Rodger's. It's a new number so I hadn't memorised it yet."

His eyes widened. "Allegra Cowderoy has been calling your husband every day?"

She nodded. "He's having an affair, but I wasn't sure who with."

"Seems like Allegra is a fairly safe bet," he said with a growl. "What a jerk."

"Indeed."

Callum picked up another piece of paper.

Her eyes narrowed. "Where's that surveillance footage

from Mrs Smythe's camera? Let's look at the footage from an hour before Allegra left."

He opened his laptop and scrolled until he found it, then projected it to the large screen on the wall. They both found seats, and Callum crossed his legs on top of the table, leaning back to watch. They skipped ahead through segments of the video until they got to the time in question. Then Callum slowed it down for them to watch.

"There!" Toni shouted, pointing at the screen. There was something in the corner of the image. A movement, something blurred.

Callum rewound the video and played it back in slow motion. It was unmistakable once they knew where to look. In the very bottom corner of the screen, at approximately nine o'clock on the night of the murder, a man strode from the neighbour's yard to the Cowderoys' side gate and let himself in. A man wearing a bike helmet with tight-fitting Lycra bike shorts and a distinctive, lanky gait. It took only a couple of seconds and would've been easy to miss the first time they ran through the hours of footage. But the figure was recognisable, even when pixelated.

"Rodger," she whispered, her head growing light. She covered her mouth with both hands. "What kind of car does Allegra Cowderoy drive?"

Callum flicked through his files. "Um... Let's see. Oh, here it is. A navy-blue BMW."

Toni shook her head. "Now, that is interesting. Let's get a warrant."

* * *

On the drive to Allegra Cowderoy's house, Toni's mind kept sweeping back and forth over the details of the case, the things she'd known, the things she hadn't. She stared at the warrant in her hands. A warrant with her husband's name on it. How could she have missed this? She was the lead investigator on the case and her husband was having an affair with the victim's widow—surely that was something she should've picked up on before now. Had she seen the signs but ignored them? She didn't think so. Even Callum hadn't found anything pointing to Rodger.

"You okay, Boss?" he asked, one hand resting on the steering wheel, the other on the gear stick.

"Fine," she said in a small voice.

She wasn't fine, though. Not only was she losing a husband, but she might well lose her career over this. She had no idea how the commander would respond to her missing a key piece of evidence like the involvement of her own husband. If she'd told him about it before they left, he'd have yanked her off the case so fast, her head would spin. But she had to do this—had to confront Rodger herself and close the case.

Callum pulled into the Cowderoys' driveway and killed the engine. "How do you want to do this?"

"I'll take the front. You take the back. I'm guessing he's going to make a run for it."

"You know him," Callum said.

She did know him—at least, she'd thought she did. But everything happening now made absolutely no sense to her. "I guess."

"You don't have to do this, you know." Callum's eyes were dark with compassion.

"I do, though—he fooled me." She studied the front of the house. Three stories, like most in the street, brick veneer, painted grey. With a tile roof in slate. It was a perfect suburban home, in a perfect suburban community at the most beautiful beach in the world. And yet so much ugliness was hidden behind those walls.

The sun dipped beyond the horizon, throwing long shadows throughout the neighbourhood. The houses were bathed in a golden glow. Toni opened the car door and heard the quiet crash of waves curling to shore in the distance. The street was quiet apart from a dog barking a few houses down.

She gave Callum a nod, and he jogged around to the side gate and let himself through it. With a quick intake of breath, Toni climbed the steps to the front door and knocked. It was quiet inside. It seemed like no one was home. She skipped down the stairs and peered into the garage through a crack between the door and the wall. It was too small to see whether there was a car inside.

She thought she heard something come from upstairs. A muffled thud or a footstep. She couldn't say for certain. She hurried back to the front door and spun the knob. It opened. She stepped inside, all her senses on high alert. Tugging her firearm from its holster, she held it aloft as she scanned the empty living room. There was another sound from upstairs—a shuffle or a thump.

"Police!" she called. Her voice reverberated around the silent house, bouncing back at her. "Hello? Anybody home? Allegra?"

She crept into the dining room. A candelabra perched in the centre of a long oak table. Twelve neatly spaced chairs sat tucked beneath the edges of the table. A tasteful painting hung on the wall at the end of the room. Everything in the house looked as though it'd been carefully chosen by a team of interior decorators. Perhaps it was Zoey's handiwork. She did have impeccable taste.

There was no one in the lavish white kitchen, either. A damp cloth hung over the tap, the only sign that the house was lived in. There were no dirty dishes, was no clutter or mess. Everything was in its rightful place.

A voice behind her cried, "Allegra!"

Toni swung around, her finger on the trigger and heart pounding, to find a sheet-covered lump in the breakfast nook. She walked closer and pulled the sheet away from a tall, conical cage. A small yellow bird stared back at her. "Allegra! Beautiful!" it chirruped.

Stupid bird had scared the life out of her. "Shut up," she whispered, waving her gun at it. "I'm very busy and important. And you almost had your feathers blown off."

The bird tipped its head to one side and studied her through a single beady black eye.

She glanced out the window that led to the backyard and saw Callum doubled over in silent laughter. She glowered at him, eyes narrowed, and he waved at her, then wiped the tears from his eyes. Sometimes she missed working in Sydney. No one ever laughed at her in Sydney. At least, not to her face.

She covered the bird's cage again with the sheet and continued through the kitchen to the hallway that led to the stairs. She'd check upstairs first, since that was where the noise had come from. She tried to recall whether the initial report had mentioned any other pets. They didn't have a dog—at least, she didn't think so.

The stairs creaked loudly with every footstep she took, and she scowled at them in silence. *Really*? She was a petite person, but anyone would think an elephant was climbing the staircase with the amount of noise her footsteps generated. How was she supposed to sneak up on a suspect with stairs like these to climb?

The first room she found was the master suite. It was empty. The bed was neatly made with a pink floral doona. There was a giant photograph of Mark and Allegra from their wedding day hanging over the dark cedar king-sized bed. They'd changed in the years since their wedding—both looked so young and innocent, carefree and happy, in the photograph. They weren't the same faces Toni knew from the past few years of interacting with them at the various social functions around town. Something had hardened in their eyes, Mark's hairline had receded, Allegra's eyebrows had mysteriously lifted until she looked perpetually surprised, and her lips were decidedly puffier these days as well.

Toni searched the room, her gun held steady between both hands. There was no one in the massive en suite bathroom, either. The sound came again. A soft banging sound followed by a shuffle. Her breath caught in her throat. It was getting dark, harder to see the further into the house she went. The sun had completely disappeared beyond the horizon now, and the moon was nothing more than a sliver hung low in the sky. She used one hand to tug her torch from her belt and held it aloft beside her gun, flicking it on in one swift movement. The light from the torch blazed straight ahead but hid the rest of her surroundings in darkness.

Where had the noise come from?

She crept out of the master suite and along the landing by the stairs to the next room. It was a guest room, with a queen-sized bed and a widescreen television hung on the wall opposite. Her torch beam cut through the darkness, taking in the space one section at a time. The noise came again, a soft thud, a scratch. Was it coming from the closet?

She tiptoed to the closet and stared a moment at the closed door. She slid it open with a bang, pointing her gun into the space, back and forth, up and down. It was empty besides a few items of clothing in plastic bags hung at the end of the closet.

Her heart thundering against her rib cage, she walked to the window and peered outside. There was no sign of Callum from this side of the house. Lights had flickered on in neighbours' homes, and streetlamps lit up the road with circles of yellow light. Another thump, and her gaze caught movement outside the window. The top branch of a squat bush slapped and scraped against the side of the house, blown by the wind coming in off the ocean.

With a sigh of relief, she tucked her gun back into her belt and leaned against the wall. She was getting too jittery in her old age. Or maybe it was the fact that she hadn't had to pull her gun on anyone in months. Living in Kingscliff had softened all her previously sharp edges and dulled her instincts.

With a shake of her head and a brief smile at her own foolishness, she pushed away from the wall and followed the light from her torch out of the room and into the next. It was a study, with two desks on opposing walls. A quick scan of the room revealed nothing much of interest, although one of the desks was scattered with papers and the computer had a light glowing from its docking station. Had someone been here recently? Perhaps Allegra had been working on something earlier. Toni had come here looking for Rodger, but she had no way of knowing whether or not he'd be here. She'd never seen his car parked outside. If Zoey had noticed him in the area, she surely would've said something. Perhaps he wasn't staying here—it made sense he'd find somewhere else to hunker down, given everything that'd happened.

She turned to leave, and something crashed to the ground behind her. She spun around, reaching for her gun, but it was too late. A figure launched itself at her in the shadowy office, knocking her to the ground. She landed on her back with a huff, the air knocked from her lungs. The figure was dressed all in black, with a hood pulled up over his head. He clambered to his feet and took off running.

"Stop! Police!" she shouted, coughing and sputtering after him.

She scrambled onto her hands and knees, then pushed up to her feet to chase him. He leapt down the stairs, taking four or five at a time, then rounded into the kitchen and out the back door. There was an "oof" sound, followed by a grunt.

Toni shuffled, one hand across her gut, to the back door. Callum was there, holding onto a squirming Rodger, his hands behind his back.

"Great work there, Senior Constable."

Callum nodded, then clicked the handcuffs over Rodger's wrists. He stopped squirming. Callum tugged the hood from his head, and Rodger glared at her.

"What are you doing, running from the police?" Toni asked.

"I wasn't. Didn't realise it was you."

"I called out 'police' several times. And when you knocked me down, there's no way you couldn't recognise your own wife." Her voice was calm, but inside she was awash with rage.

He sighed, and his eyes grew glassy. "It was all a mistake. I didn't mean to do it. An accident—there are rules about accidents, aren't there, Toni?"

His gaze fixed on her. There was desperation in his eyes.

"Are you talking about the murder of Mark Cowderoy?" she asked, flicking on the recording device on her mobile phone and shoving it into her shirt pocket.

He sobbed. "It wasn't murder—that's what I'm saying. It was all an accident. A horrible accident."

Callum shook his head slowly, and his eyes found Toni's. She read his thoughts. It was time to take her husband in for an official statement. This was one thing she shouldn't be part of. And suddenly, all of the wind left her sails. She wanted so badly to go home, crawl into bed, and sleep for days.

Chapter Fifty-One

TWO MONTHS EARLIER

Mark Cowderoy was getting older, and he didn't like that, not one little bit. He preened in front of the bedroom mirror, the lights turned down low, studying his reflection. He leaned forwards until his nose was pressed up to the glass and plucked a grey hair from his part.

That's not good.

He studied the hair, then combed his fingers through his brown mane looking for more. The first grey hair. Soon there'd be more, and he'd become an old man. No children. A wife who despised him, and a career that was going nowhere.

No children wasn't quite accurate, though, was it? He corrected himself. He had a child. Well, if former lovers were to be believed. She'd come to see him right before Allegra left as if she'd been watching, waiting for her chance to ruin his marriage but thankfully Allegra was in the shower and didn't see her. Told him again that she had a daughter, that they shared a girl who was five years old. Five years—she'd never mentioned anything before. How could he believe her now?

She'd cried then, said she was sorry. She should've told him. But when she discovered he was married, she'd fled. Hadn't looked back.

So, it was his fault then? He'd raged at her over that. His fault that she hadn't told him he had a daughter. Years of marriage to Allegra, both of them trying so hard, longing for a child. And now to discover that he'd had one all this time and didn't know about her. That he'd missed out on all the best parts of fatherhood—first steps, first words, cute little toes, and butterfly kisses. It wasn't fair for her to steal those from him. She had blonde hair, Stella told him—like he'd had as a child.

She'd admitted her fault, and they'd left things open. She'd call him again soon, and they'd set up a date to meet. He wanted to know her.

Katie. That was her name, Katie. Another thing he hadn't had any say in. But he liked the name. Maybe it would work out—he wanted to be a father. His own father had been something of a disappointment. He never seemed to have anything positive to say. He was the reason Mark got into the world of finance—a career that sucked the life out of him every single day he was in it.

He'd never set out to be a banker, but at the age of thirty-five, it was all he had. He'd wanted to be a journalist, but his father had said, "There's no future in it, son. Better to work with money. People always need money." And that had been that.

He opened the bedroom window and leaned out, looking around the neighbourhood. It was a nice neighbourhood. He'd bought the house years earlier because Allegra fell in love with it. That brought a smile to his face—the house, she still loved. Him, not so much. It was a classy place to live, smelled of money. Well, almost.

In fact, it currently smelled of something even better than money. He hadn't inhaled a scent like that since his university days. And with the way he felt tonight, after the day he'd had, he could do with a little something to perk him up. He jogged down the stairs and pushed out through the back door, sniffed.

It was coming from next door. The Wintons had a teen daughter—likely it was her, although Zoey Winton always liked to act as though her child could do no wrong. She was a harpy who thought she was better than everyone else. She'd screamed at him in front of all his friends a few months earlier, threatened to kill him. She'd proved she was no better than anyone else that night—not some hoity-toity socialite at all, but another shrill housewife looking to yell at anyone having a bit of fun.

He walked to the fence and peered through the gaps between the slats. There they were. The girl from next door and two boys he'd never seen before. Never mind if it got him in trouble—he was reckless. Allegra was having an affair. He was certain of it. He'd suspected it for months but hadn't been able to prove anything. But he'd caught her earlier that day, texting her lover boy.

It was all he could do not to send her packing right then. They were supposed to be going on a trip to Cairns to spend time with family, but not anymore. He couldn't fly up there with her and pretend. They'd pretended to be a happy couple for long enough. But now he knew for certain that she'd found someone else, he couldn't do it any longer. She could go on her own and explain to her parents what was going on. He was done with it all, didn't care anymore.

When he'd asked her about the man she was sleeping with, she'd said they were in love.

In love.

It infuriated him. He wanted to fly into a rage, but he couldn't find the strength. The ache in his heart was too much, and that angered him even more. He wanted not to care, wanted to hate her for what she'd done. In the end, all he could do was tell her goodbye and not to come back, in a hollow voice. She'd left a few minutes earlier, and it might've been the last time he saw her. Even now, that thought brought a pain to his throat that he couldn't dislodge.

He coughed and heard whispering from the other side of the fence.

"Hey, it's only me, your friendly neighbour," he said through the fence. "Stay there. I'm coming around."

The night was dark. Only a few stars winked overhead; the rest were lost behind black, racing clouds. The wind was humid and whipped his hair into his eyes as he jogged out of the side gate and into the neighbours' yard. He was in bare feet and stepped on something wet and slimy. With a grimace, he raised a foot and heard the teens titter with laughter.

"Dog doo," said a girl's voice.

He nodded, irritation burning in his gut. "Great. That ends my day about the same way it started, then—in a pile of crap."

The teens laughed again, nervously. They were clearly worried about what he'd say next.

"Hey, can I have a hit?"

They looked at him, reddened eyes wide. A nearby security light gave him enough illumination to see their expressions and that they'd hidden the joints behind their backs.

"It's okay, I know what pot smells like. And I want some."

Reluctantly, one of the boys handed him a joint. The shorter one.

"Please don't tell my mum," the girl said.

He took a drag on the joint. "Of course not... What's your name again?"

She looked offended. "Isla. I've only been your neighbour for almost my entire life."

He chuckled as he blew out smoke. "Sorry, I'm not great with names. Especially kids' names. I tell you what—how about none of us says anything to anyone. It'll be our little secret."

They nodded vigorously in agreement.

He stayed with them a while, making small talk. The older boy said his goodbyes and left. Mark stayed a while longer until he finished the joint, then heard a noise in his garden next door. The gate on the side of the house clicked shut, and he froze, listening. That was strange. His wife had already left for the airport. He was the only one in the house. Who was in his garden?

Someone called out. It sounded like a man calling for Allegra. Anger began to climb up his spine, only heightened by the smoke clouding his thoughts. He jogged back to the gate and through into his own yard.

"Hello?" he said. "Can I help you? Who are you and what the hell are you doing in my yard?"

When he got closer to the shadowy figure standing by the back porch, he recognised one of the teachers from Allegra's school. Realisation dawned. It had to be him—he was the man she'd been texting, the one she'd fallen in love with.

"Sorry," Rodger Kauffman said. "I was looking for Allegra. We work together. Has she left already?"

Mark's eyes narrowed. "She has, but why don't you come inside and leave a note?"

Rodger smiled, his eyes glistening in the dull light from the porch. "Um, okay."

Inside the house, the kitchen light shone brightly, showing Rodger in his bike helmet and tight Lycra shorts. He was a wimp. A weedy-looking guy with hairless legs and a flat nose. What did she see in him, anyway?

"Here you go." He handed Rodger a pen and some paper.

Rodger set it on the kitchen table and jotted out a note. It was all a pretence. They both knew it. Rodger looked poised, as though waiting for something to happen.

"You could text her, you know," Mark said. "You've been texting her all day. Why stop now?"

Rodger straightened. "Sorry, what?"

"I know about the affair. Stop pretending. It's insulting."

Rodger raised his palms. "Let's not get overheated about this. We can talk about it, figure things out."

"Talk about you stealing my wife? I don't think so." Mark lunged at him, fist outstretched.

The problem was, he'd never thrown a punch before in his life. He wasn't the fighting type. He liked to work out at the gym and stare at himself in the mirror. He wore tight-fitting workout gear while he lifted weights and talked about reps and body fat percentages, but he'd never actually hit a man before. So when his half-shut fist connected with Rodger's cheekbone, it felt as though he'd broken the bones in his hand.

He grabbed his hand and held it tight to his body, yelping with pain. Rodger took the opportunity to pop him in the nose, but Mark managed to duck in time. Rodger's hand grazed his shoulder, leaving Rodger staggering and off balance. Mark spun on his heel and raced out the back door. He could go to the neighbours' for help. Call the police—there was a man in his house. The man had attacked him. They'd believe him. Rodger shouldn't be there. He was trespassing.

He ran through the yard and tripped on a plant. His bare foot smacked into the clay pot, and pain shot up his foot and into his leg as he fell headlong into the garden bed. He should get that motion detector fixed. It'd been on the blink for months now. One of the many things on his to-do list that Allegra nagged him over constantly.

Mark climbed to his feet when he heard footsteps behind him. Something hit him on the back of the head once, then twice. He fell into the garden bed. Dirt scattered around him like drops in a rain shower. Then the world faded to black.

Chapter Fifty-Two

TUESDAY

28TH JANUARY

The schoolyard teamed with children. Shouts of joy, freshly cut hair, gleaming black leather shoes. It was a new year, and school was starting all over again. The summer holidays were over, and not a moment too soon for Stella. She'd balanced having Katie home for six weeks with working on some of the biggest projects she'd ever managed for Zoey all at the same time. And it was a relief to finally have Katie back in school so she could focus on her work and maybe even have some time to herself.

With a sigh, she watched as Katie let go of her hand and raced to the playground to climb up the stairs and slide down the blue plastic slide, her dress flying up and revealing her little black bike shorts underneath.

"Well, thank heavens you thought to put her in bike shorts," Toni murmured beside her.

Stella chuckled. "It's not my first rodeo."

"I never had to worry about things like that with a boy. Although I did discover when he was about seven years old that he hadn't been wearing underwear to school all year and hadn't thought to mention it either to me or his father."

Stella laughed and shook her head. "Wow, that's... I don't know what to say."

"Being a mother to a boy is an entirely different experience. There's not much hand washing and a lot of pee to clean up."

"TMI." Stella crossed her arms. "How's he feel about starting year twelve today?"

She was getting used to the idea that she had a brother. She'd never had a sibling and always wanted one. A sullen teenager with pimples and gangly, hairy legs wasn't what she'd imagined when she pictured her dream brother, but it's what she had, and she was glad. He was fast becoming one of her favourite people. It felt good to be part of a family again.

"He seems ready. He's a lot more focused than he was last year. After our trip to New Zealand, we got him some tutoring over the break, so I suppose we'll see how things go. But he's definitely less angry. Talking has helped. Walking the Milford Track helped."

"That's good." Stella tented a hand over her eyes to cut the glare.

Katie was talking to a group of little girls. They all squealed in delight and raced to the monkey bars, then took turns swinging across.

"She looks like she's settling in well already," Toni said.

"The true test will be when it's time for me to leave," Stella murmured with a grimace. It was the part of the day she'd been dreading all week.

"She'll be fine," Toni assured. "Look at her. She's completely at ease."

"Hmmm..." Stella wasn't convinced. "How are you coping with the whole Rodger situation?"

"It's hard. He was denied bail, and the trial won't be for months yet. It's a wait-and-see game."

"But how do you *feel*?"

"I'm...angry, frustrated. I mean, why? It makes no sense. He's admitted everything—it didn't take much pressure. I wasn't in the room, of course. Callum took over the investigation as soon as we arrested Rodger. I had to withdraw."

"I'm sorry. I know you worked really hard on that."

"It's fine. I couldn't be part of it—the defence would have a field day with that." She chuckled. "And anyway, it's a bit too heartbreaking, honestly. But I'm okay—or I will be. I'm glad that the worst of it is over. And I have no intention of attending the trial. I'm leaving all of that to Callum to handle. I think I might even take a holiday."

"That's a great idea. I hear it's beautiful up in the Whitsundays."

"We should all go. We can make a family trip of it."

"We could snorkel," Stella added, her eyes shining. "I've always wanted to have a family holiday where we snorkel together. I know it seems oddly specific, but there was this girl at uni whose family used to do a big trip to Hamilton Island every year to snorkel on the reef. I was so jealous of her. My parents were too old, and I didn't have any siblings."

Toni grinned. "We'll do a family trip to the islands and all go snorkelling on the reef. It sounds like the perfect holiday."

The bell rang, its sound jangling throughout the playground and echoing around the school buildings. Katie grabbed her backpack, then took off, shouting, "Bye, Mum," over her shoulder.

Stella and Toni exchanged a surprised look. "Well, that was easy."

"I didn't even get a kiss." Stella's throat ached.

They watched as the teacher opened the door and let the kids inside. Stella wanted to cry.

Just then, Katie came barrelling back through the doorway with a big smile. She was missing a tooth. It'd come out one night the week before, and she'd solemnly placed it beneath her pillow for the "tooth fairy godmother" to take home with her. Stella had helped her write a letter for the fairy. It'd been cute and heartwarming, and she wished she could hold on to the moment forever, but she couldn't. It all passed by—every moment, every milestone, every heartbeat.

Katie rushed up to Stella. Stella bent to embrace her, and Katie kissed her cheek.

"See you later," she said, then she was gone again, back into her classroom.

Stella held the place on her cheek where the kiss had landed. A sweet, wet, hot kiss from her daughter.

"You okay?" Toni asked, winding an arm around her shoulders.

They walked together back the way they'd come. "Fine. I'm so happy. She's okay with me leaving. It's great."

"I know. It's wonderful and it's painful, all at the same time. Parenting, huh?"

Stella nodded through a blur of tears. "I'm going for a run. I'll see you later?"

"Lunch at Singles?" Toni asked.

"Perfect." Stella waved goodbye.

Chapter Fifty-Three

Toni drove to the police station and pulled into the garage. She called Zoey as she walked to the elevator.

Zoey answered with a rushed "Hello?"

"Sounds like you've had a busy morning. What are you doing?"

"It's unbelievable how much work it takes to get one almost-grown human out the door for the first day of school. And of course I had to take a hundred photographs to commemorate the moment."

"Of course." Toni grinned.

"I'm hanging out the laundry because I asked Isla to do it yesterday and surprise, surprise, she didn't. She kept saying 'I'm gonna do it, I'm gonna.' If I hear that phrase again, my head is going to explode."

"It's a classic."

"Oh no!"

"What's wrong?" Toni tapped the button for the lift, her brow furrowed.

"I stepped in crap again. I swear, my family is trying to give me a stroke. I don't understand why Dave can't pick it up and throw it in the bin. It's not so difficult. And now it's all over the bottom of my running shoe. Ugh."

Toni swallowed her laughter. "I'm sorry—that's horrible. Is everything else okay?"

"It's fine. I'm a little frustrated, and now I'm running late for work again. And I smell like a toilet."

"Is Isla happy to be back in school?" Toni was surprised how ready Ryker seemed. She'd thought for sure he'd be desperate to prolong the summer holidays and avoid facing his responsibilities, but he'd told her he was anxious to put the past behind him and do his best. She hoped he would.

"At first Isla said she was definitely *not* going to school, so I spent my morning convincing her that she had no other choice. She and Ben broke up while we were away on in Sydney."

"Ouch," Toni said as she pressed the button for the lift again. She'd never seen a lift that moved as slowly as the one at the station.

"Ouch is right. She doesn't want to go to school because everyone will ask her about Ben, and she'll have to talk about the breakup. It's unbelievable that these are the things that absorb her thoughts. I wish she was as obsessed with algebra as she is with boys. It's driving me crazy."

Toni laughed. "At least your husband isn't a murderer."

Zoey snorted. "And for that, I will be forever grateful."

"Husbands everywhere are rejoicing this very moment over how low my husband has set the bar for them. Every wife in Kingscliff is holding their husbands a little tighter now because of him. Really, it's heroic when you think about it. Marriages everywhere saved!"

Zoey sighed, emotion making her voice waver. "I'm sorry, honey. I know it must be hard for you."

Toni chuckled. "Well, if you can't laugh about it, you'll cry."

"For sure. Isn't there a saying about medicine and laughter...?"

Toni huffed. "It *is* kind of liberating to laugh at your worst points of pain."

"And you're nothing if not a liberated woman. I mean that—you are so strong. I'm really proud of you."

"Thanks, Zoey. You're a good friend. You have no idea how many people are avoiding talking to me right now."

"You're not getting rid of me that easily. Hey, let's catch up again soon."

"Definitely. Love ya guts."

"You too, honey."

Toni hung up the phone as the lift arrived on her floor and she stepped into the office. The noise and activity of the office always soothed her, although today she was particularly at ease. Her husband might be behind bars, but her son was healthy and happy again. He was at school, and he wasn't dealing drugs (as far as she was aware). She shivered at the prospect. But they'd spoken about it all at length, and he'd consented to attend counselling over the summer as part of the terms of his deal that her boss had signed off on.

Cowan had looked at her with pity in his eyes and said, "I think you've got enough to deal with, Porter. Let's give him some counselling and leave it off his record this time."

And that had been the end of it, much to her relief. It'd helped that he'd confirmed he would testify against Rodger at the trial, something that wouldn't be easy for him or any of them. Malcolm said he'd take Ryker, since Toni didn't want to be there. After he testified, perhaps Malcolm, Sandi, and the kids could join them in the Whitsunday Islands for some snorkelling on the reef, but that wouldn't be until next summer.

She stopped at the kitchen on her way through the office with a yawn. She hadn't slept well lately and was living off caffeine and adrenaline. She mixed several spoonfuls of sugar into coffee that looked as though it'd been scooped off the top of an oil spill rather than something intentionally brewed in the office coffeepot.

Callum stopped in the doorway and leaned against the doorframe. She grimaced at the coffee, picked up the sugar pot, and poured a stream into the thick black liquid.

"Hey, Boss," he said, crossing his arms. "Aiming for Type 2 diabetes all in one day?"

"What is this?" she asked, pushing the coffee cup at him. "Is this supposed to be coffee? Are they trying to kill us with this stuff?"

He grinned. "In a good mood, I see."

"Are you intentionally flexing your muscles right now? I can see right through that white T-shirt you're wearing. Has the brass finally approved your request to prance about in your undergarments at the office, or is it a special day today?"

Callum rolled his eyes. "It's always a special day when you're my partner."

She laughed. "Let's go, Fabio."

He screwed up his nose. "I don't know who that is."

"Come on, junior. Let me find you a pram to ride in. You're apparently too young to get my jokes."

He fell into step beside her. "You're obnoxious when you're happy. And we've got a case. So grab your notebook and meet me at the cruiser."

"I've got my notebook in my purse. Lead the way, Brad Pitt."

"Now *that* name I recognise." He grinned, opening the front door to let her walk through ahead of him. "My lady."

"What a gentleman." She flashed him a smile. "What's the case?"

"An apparent drug overdose. The super wants us to look into it, make sure everything's by the book."

They climbed into the cruiser. Callum spun the key in the ignition. The radio immediately burst to life, blasting rap music through the speakers. Toni grimaced and switched the channel to a classic rock station, then turned down the volume.

"Much better," she said, leaning back in her seat.

"Don't touch my radio," Callum sniffed, reaching for the dial.

She slapped his hand. "Not a chance, mate. I've had a good morning and don't want a throbbing headache, thank you."

"You never let me pick music I want to listen to," he said, backing the car out of the car park.

She smiled, crossing one leg over the other. "When you make detective, we'll talk, Fabio."

"Again with the weird name. Why won't you tell me who that is?"

She laughed. "Ah, I've missed you."

THE END

* * *

Want more?

Subscribe to Lilly Mirren's newsletter

And get a FREE book!

Plus you'll find out when the next book is released.

The Waratah Inn

The smash hit first book in the bestselling, heartwarming series. *Readers say*

"Wow, this series just gets better and better. I do not want to see it end. Looking forward to the next book."

You'll also get access to exclusive free gifts and giveaways.

SUBSCRIBE NOW

via the Lilly Mirren website.

Also by Lilly Mirren

HISTORICAL

Beyond the Crushing Waves

An emotional standalone historical saga. Two children plucked from poverty & forcibly deported from the UK to Australia. Inspired by true events. An unforgettable tale of loss, love, redemption & new beginnings.

Under a Sunburnt Sky

Inspired by a true story. Jan Kostanski is a normal Catholic boy in Warsaw when the nazis invade. He's separated from his neighbours, a Jewish family who he considers kin, by the ghetto wall. Jan and his mother decide that they will do whatever it takes to save their Jewish friends from certain death. The unforgettable tale of an everyday family's fight against evil, and the unbreakable bonds of their love.

THE WARATAH INN SERIES

The Waratah Inn

When Kate discovers her late grandmother's journals, she unearths information about a long-buried family mystery that leads her back to her grandmother's run-down inn, in Cabarita Beach. As she works to unravel the truth, can she find a path to healing along the way?

One Summer in Italy

Reeda leaves the Waratah Inn and returns to Sydney, her husband, and her thriving interior design business, only to find her marriage in tatters. She's lost sight of what she wants in life and can't recognise the person she's become.

The Summer Sisters

Set against the golden sands and crystal clear waters of Cabarita Beach three sisters inherit an inn and discover a mystery about their grandmother's past that changes everything they thought they knew about their family...

Christmas at The Waratah Inn

Liz Cranwell is divorced and alone at Christmas. When her friends convince her to holiday at The Waratah Inn, she's dreading her first Christmas on her own. Instead she discovers that strangers can be the balm to heal the wounds of a lonely heart in this heartwarming Christmas story.

EMERALD COVE SERIES

Cottage on Oceanview Lane

When a renowned book editor returns to her roots, she rediscovers her strength & her passion in this heartwarming novel.

Seaside Manor Bed & Breakfast

The Seaside Manor Bed and Breakfast has been an institution in Emerald Cove for as long as anyone can remember. But things are changing and Diana is nervous about what the future might hold for her and her husband, not to mention the historic business.

Bungalow on Pelican Way

Moving to the Cove gave Rebecca De Vries a place to hide from her abusive ex. Now that he's in jail, she can get back to living her life as a police officer in her adopted hometown working alongside her intractable but very attractive boss, Franklin.

Chalet on Cliffside Drive

At forty-four years of age, Ben Silver thought he'd never find love. When he moves to Emerald Cove, he does it to support his birth mother, Diana, after her husband's sudden death. But then he meets Vicky.

Christmas in Emerald Cove

The Flannigan family has been through a lot together. They've grown and changed over the years and now have a blended and extended family that doesn't always see eye to eye. But this Christmas they'll learn that love can overcome all of the pain and differences of the past in this inspiring Christmas tale.

HOME SWEET HOME SERIES

Home Sweet Home

Trina is starting over after a painful separation from her husband of almost twenty years. Grief and loss force her to return to her hometown where she has to deal with all of the things she left behind to rebuild her life, piece by piece; a hometown she hasn't visited since high school graduation.

No Place Like Home

Lisa never thought she'd leave her high-profile finance job in the city to work in a small-town bakery. She also never expected to still be single in her forties.

Glossary of Terms

Dear reader,

Since this book is set in Australia there may be some terms you're not familiar with. I've included them below to help you out! I hope they didn't trip you up too much.

Cheers, Lilly xo

* * *

Terms

Bonnet - Hood of car

Boot - Trunk of car

Carked it - died

Doona - comforter

Flat - apartment

Foodie - someone who understands and appreciates good food

Formal - like Prom, happens in year 10 and year 12

High school - grades seven to twelve

Kindergarten - the first year of school

Lift - elevator

Median strip - median (grassy separator between road lanes)

Mucking around - playing up or being silly

Nappy - diaper

Old ticker - heart

Petrol - gas

Pram - stroller

Torch - flashlight

Trike - tricycle (a child's three wheeled bike)

Tuck shop - School Cafeteria

Unit - apartment

Year nine - Ninth grade

Made in the USA
Las Vegas, NV
22 August 2022

53795188R00207